THE
IMPOSTER

OTHER TITLES BY MARIN MONTGOMERY

THE
IMPOSTER

MARIN MONTGOMERY

THOMAS & MERCER

Published by Thomas & Mercer, Seattle
www.apub.com

Amazon, the Amazon logo, and Thomas & Mercer are trademarks of Amazon.com, Inc., or its affiliates.

ISBN-13: 9781542022989
ISBN-10: 1542022983

Cover design by Anna Laytham

Printed in the United States of America

When I started writing this book, I never thought it would be from a mandated and not self-imposed quarantine or that we would witness a deadly virus straight out of a Stephen King novel, invading our lives and changing them in such fundamental ways. It has changed our routines and given most of us a "new normal."

I'd like to dedicate this book to all the essential and nonessential workers on the front lines who have risked their lives to provide those at home the opportunity to do just that—stay at home. I am one of the lucky ones who was sick but not to the extent I required hospitalization.

A special dedication goes to Dr. Li Wenliang, an ophthalmologist at Wuhan Central Hospital, who died February 7, 2020, at the age of thirty-three. Not only was he the first whistleblower to try to alert the public and his fellow doctors about the virus, but he also ultimately succumbed to it.

He was punished for his actions by his own government. He is survived by his wife, their young child, and, at the time of this writing, an unborn baby.

PROLOGUE
Deborah

Six Months Ago

Getting the mail should be an easy feat, except in this case, it's minus five degrees, and the blustery cold unavoidably renders Deborah's limbs numb.

She can't feel her face, even though it's mostly covered by a wool scarf, and her toes are frozen stiff as she trudges through the deep snow.

It doesn't help that the mailbox isn't twenty feet away but at the end of a long, winding gravel driveway, smack dab in the middle of a colorless sky, a subtle hint more snow is on the way.

Groaning, she curses the dreary landscape.

The mailbox is the only vibrant speck in the distance, a forest-green metal container with a neon-orange flag that sticks out like a sore thumb in the drabness.

Midwesterners do this every cold season once the promise of sunshine and bearable temperatures arrives. They swear it'll be their last, but the spring, summer, and fall make up for the bitter winter. By the time the last of the snow melts and the sunshine reappears, it's a fading memory—out of sight, out of mind.

Deborah angrily tosses her head, the blast of cold air penetrating the thick material of her down coat. Her rail-thin frame is made hulking by the layers of clothing—a turtleneck, a heavy sweater, and a wool coat. If anyone spotted her barely five-foot stature, they'd think she was a miniature version of an adult, playing dress-up in her mother's clothing.

Sticking her bulky glove inside the metal tin, she predicts bills and the hometown newspaper and, at her age, maybe an AARP magazine.

She's not wrong, but there's one more package—a manila envelope that takes up the width of the box but is thin, the edges creased to make room for it to fit.

She's unable to grasp the mail firmly in her bulky glove, and a gust of wind almost takes the contents from her clumsy grip. She yanks her glove off with her mouth, and it's mere seconds before her fingers succumb to the winter's version of a sunburn—windburn.

The handwriting's unrecognizable, though it appears feminine, due to the impeccable cursive spelling out of her address in broad swoops and curlicues.

No name is listed as the return sender, only a scribbled post office box.

Curious, but not enough to withstand any more blasts of wind, Deborah replaces her glove and lumbers back to the farmhouse, worn out and exhausted from her one errand of the day, the trek down the driveway exacerbating her depressing outlook on the unchanged scenery.

After cranking the thermostat to a temperature on par with a kiln, she curls up underneath an heirloom quilt from her deceased mother and sorts through the other mail before carefully opening the slim package.

Deborah gasps when a single picture falls into her lap.

Her hands shake as she scans the letter written on pale-yellow stationery.

No, this can't be.

This is too unbelievable.

Teetering between clutching it securely in her fist and gently examining it, she instead smooths the creases with her fingertips. The photograph's wrinkled, having been folded up and then flattened out. The lines draw a likeness to the worry etched on her face, all the years she can't erase of existing solely as a beating heart, thudding in her chest, on pace with her brain, ticking steadily, ready to detonate at any given moment.

Deborah wishes she could blot them out in one fluid ripple, all the hurt and sleepless nights, the impossible task of trying to move forward.

But more than that, *live*.

In those days, it was called a nervous breakdown; now it's referred to as an acute stress disorder, as if the change provides comfort to the sufferer. It makes no difference to her what you call it, what label you package it up with to sell to patients; the trauma is no less real.

A significant part of her died that day, and Deborah likens it to missing a limb. People might learn to live without it because they have to, but they never forget it's missing. Deborah knew she would never be whole again, but she took baby steps to move forward because it wasn't just her life she had to consider.

But here on her lap, the words jump off the page at her, and never in a million years did Deborah expect this would be in her mailbox.

Cautiously optimistic, she rereads the paragraph over and over, squinting at the out-of-focus words, until she remembers she needs her reading glasses.

Terrified to see the writing sharpened, she holds the paper in her trembling hand.

Dear Deborah,
(Or maybe I should call you Mother, but it sounds strange after all this time.)

I'm sure this picture brings up lots of questions—namely, what happened at the hospital all those years ago. You were led to believe it was a tragedy, and it was, but of a different proportion.

I have asked myself what I should do over the years, the voice inside my head telling me to let go of some of the hurt, anger, and blame. We all make choices that sometimes have unintended consequences. I tell myself you did what you had to do because you had no other alternative.

I don't want to punish you anymore with silence because it's only hurting me in the process. We both need to heal. It's time.

—S

Deborah must read it another hundred times before settling back to absorb the weight of the letter. She doesn't dare let the note leave her grasp, for as silly as it seems, she's worried it will float off into the air, a disappearing act.

Just like the letter writer.

Then, giddy with excitement, she gently lays the frail paper in her lap to clap her hands, but immediately, a wave of disappointment brings them to her gaping mouth, where she stuffs them.

What if it's a hoax?

Deborah stares at the envelope, and with no physical address, just a PO box, she wonders suspiciously if the writer is who they claim to be. It wouldn't be the first time someone's played an evil prank on her. Deborah trembles at the memory of the October the year after her husband's death.

Recalling the scarecrow in their cornfield, she remembers how she thought it was cute until she got closer. Those straw-like mannequins have been used for years to keep pesky birds from disturbing the crops, and she used to make one every fall until the accident.

Someone had placed one in their field, meant to resemble a decapitated body, a gory mess covered in red paint. The trespasser had used sticks as arms, giving it a Freddy Krueger feel that gave her the willies.

Scowling at the memory, she scolds herself. *Don't think that way, Deborah. Not everyone is out to get you. It just seems that way.*

Pacing the floor, she carefully considers what she wants her letter back to say, but then her pen wavers on the blank page. She starts and stops multiple letters, ripping the paper into tiny shreds and throwing them like loose confetti in the air.

Deborah then telephones the postmaster, whom she knows on a first-name basis after all these years, and he promises to research the identity of the box.

She impatiently waits for him to call her back, positive she's wearing a hole in the carpet with her constant pacing. The old rotary phone doesn't finish a full shrill before Deborah yanks it off the wall in apprehension.

With trembling fingers, she sinks into the nearest chair, and his answer shocks her. She hopes he doesn't pick up on her high-pitched squeak. The zip code associated with the post office box is in Florida, and it belongs to an S. Sawyer. Beyond that, he can't provide her any more details or a specific address tied to the box.

Deborah has so much to say, but it's impossible to write off the lost time in a matter of sentences. Lingering questions suppress her happiness. Should she express her long-buried feelings?

Her pain and anguish? Guilt?

To pour out her remorse after nothing but silence feels as disingenuous as her sham marriage was.

Deborah doesn't want to mess this up, and she wishes she had someone to confide in, her lips burning to talk. But practically a hermit, Deborah doesn't have close friends, only acquaintances, and she fears they would gossip behind her back and call her a lunatic. Her only interaction with other people is at church or when she volunteers at a nursing home.

Deborah gulps.

The last time she tried to ask someone for help, it ended up causing repercussions she had never considered and destroyed multiple families. She certainly doesn't need people to bring tired old speculations and theories to light when it comes to that fateful night. The only other person alive who witnessed what happened won't even speak to her.

And it's been sixteen years.

The cross pendant she permanently wears around her neck becomes a mass of knots, twisted by her troubled fingers. She remembers being a child in the front row for her daddy's sermons, hearing his stern baritone as he drove his point home about the day of reckoning.

After flipping the dog-eared pages of his hand-me-down Bible to 2 Timothy 4:16, Deborah reads out loud: "At my first defense, no one supported me, but all deserted me; may it not be counted against them."

The lesson is pounded into her brain like his fist into the pulpit. Everyone after death is called to account for their actions in life, and Deborah's no exception to the rule.

This thought makes her queasy.

She slams the Bible shut and puts her head in her hands, and with a deep sigh, Deborah is now well aware of what she must do. She must reach out to the only person who witnessed what happened that night.

PART ONE
DEBORAH

CHAPTER 1
Deborah

A few weeks later, Deborah's trying to enjoy her nighttime ritual of sipping a cup of chamomile tea before bed.

Though it usually comforts her, especially during wintertime, she's restless and fidgeting, kneading her fingers in her lap, where a second envelope that arrived today now rests innocently enough.

She gazes at the nightstand, where the sheet of pale yellow peeks out from the unsealed flap, the words committed to memory. Removing it would only risk tearing the flimsy paper. Eventually, other mail got piled on top of it, and indecisive, Deborah did nothing. It's not like she forgot what it contained—or her guilty conscience.

She slides on her reading glasses. This envelope also has no return address and is thicker, with more pages and further proof, enough details to dredge up the past and cause problems. *Stunning* details, full of particulars she thought were known only by a small group of people.

Most of whom are dead.

The scratches across the page appear rushed, as if the writer had limited time to collect their thoughts. Even though there are discrepancies between the shaky scribbles and Deborah's recollection, she doesn't need to memorize this letter because she was physically present, though mentally checked out.

Besides, the permanent imprint tattooed on her brain never fades.

Engrossed in forming a response, Deborah ignores a sharp scraping noise that pierces the silence until she's interrupted by a loud thump. Assuming it's an overgrown tree branch rasping the house, she doesn't bother to stand.

Out loud, she expresses her reply and continues to talk to herself. But Deborah halts midsentence when she hears the pitter-patter of footsteps moving across the wraparound porch.

She crawls out of bed and noiselessly tiptoes to the dark living room.

Startled by a melody, Deborah slams into the wall as the old grandfather clock chimes four times, signaling the top of the hour. Then, rubbing her sore elbow, she stands directly in front of the roman numerals, squinting at the glass-and-mahogany display.

It's far too late and cold for peddling beauty products or selling magazine subscriptions. Ever since they built a men's prison outside town, Deborah's not keen on unexpected visitors.

On edge, she moves into the kitchen to flick on the outside light.

The howling wind has a ferocious intensity, and Deborah narrows her eyes at the frost-covered gauge of the outside thermometer, which indicates it's a mere three degrees.

Her night vision has never been the best, and it's only gotten worse with age. Objects far away tend to blur and move in and out of focus, and she could swear a dark form jets across the snow-covered porch of the old farmhouse as she stares hard into the pitch black. Deborah hasn't been outside since earlier when she got the mail, and it's snowed at least five inches since then, which is why her heart thuds in her chest at the fresh tracks in the snowy ground.

Nervously, she jiggles the door handle to confirm it's locked.

Swallowing hard, she wonders why she's stayed out here, all alone, for all these years.

"I have protection," Deborah says out loud. "I have a gun."

Then, in the walk-in pantry, she bundles up in a scarf and coat and quickly laces up her snow boots. Groaning at the weight of the old Winchester rifle locked in the gun closet, she realizes she's forgotten how heavy it is against her tiny stature.

Cautiously, she unlocks both the dead bolt and the damaged screen door, the netting frayed and torn. Her teeth chatter as soon as the icy blast hits her face. With the heavy and unyielding gun slung haphazardly over her shoulder, Deborah steps outside into the cold temperatures.

The wind makes it impossible to catch her breath, and Deborah gasps for air. She inhales a lungful of arctic chill, and as it slides down her throat, it's as if she's swallowed a block of ice.

As she walks the perimeter of the porch, an explosion in the direction of the barn jolts her.

After slipping on the ice-covered snow, Deborah tries to steady herself by grabbing a corner piece of siding, except the board is loose, and a single yank pulls it directly off the house. A wind gust picks up at the same time, and without anything to latch on to, Deborah's thrust forward and drops the board.

Deborah's shrieks are carried away in the draft as she meets the slippery ice head on. The rifle escapes from her clutch and tumbles to the ground. Luckily, the snow pads her fall, but only enough to act as an ice pack against her immediately bruised face and knees.

Mumbling "Ouch," Deborah notices dark-red blood seeping from her knuckles.

Dazed, she clenches the powdery substance in her hands until a black figure appears out of the shadows.

Assuming it's Esmeralda, Deborah calls out to her, expecting paw prints to dart across the porch, light and effortless, accompanied by a purring sound. But the footfalls coming closer are weighty and forceful, like a person's.

"Esmeralda," she moans, staring at her outstretched arms. Then she watches in horror as the snow-covered feet stop in front of her motionless body.

Frantic, she glances over her shoulder for the rifle, her eyes darting uselessly across the whiteout conditions.

Resignedly, Deborah levels her gaze with dark pants, then moves her eyes toward the torso, also clothed in black. When she reaches the stranger's face, Deborah lifts her chin in defiance, but she's disappointed to see a mask covering their features, the only exception the narrow slit in the front for the nose and eyes.

She tries to make eye contact, but just as abruptly, the heavy boots step forward and crush her fingers underneath what are surely steel-encased toes.

Before she can scream, a swift kick lands on her forehead, and she tastes blood as it slides from above her left eye, down her nose, and into her mouth.

The assailant steps around her, and before Deborah can try for another shriek, she's being dragged down the porch steps by her feet, each clunk the sound of her head hitting the concrete.

Usually, the stars give her comfort, but tonight they seem to be frozen stiff in the sky, as if they are too cold and numb to twinkle. Her body mimics this behavior, and she shuts her eyes against the blustery wind, her scarf like a noose as it gets tangled in frozen pieces of grass and gravel as Deborah's hauled across the stretch of property.

Her hands clench at the ground, but it's futile; the solid clumps of snow are unforgiving against her swollen hands.

A sorry excuse for a scream catches on her chapped lips, emerging as nothing more than a pleading whisper.

Deborah silently begs for it to be over, but she can't form a coherent thought, with shock settling in every fiber of her being. It's not until something hard jabs into her skull that she realizes too late the rifle is in the hands of the intruder. Deborah doesn't remember much of what happens next or how long she's beaten against the ice-covered ground. She does know that if it weren't for the weather and the lingering smell of manure and hay, she probably wouldn't have woken up and crawled into the ramshackle barn for cover.

Later, baffled to wake up in a hospital bed, Deborah stares in loathing at the uniform four walls. They're a dizzying reminder of the life-changing news delivered to her in the same medicinal environment. Even with the decades gone past, she gets goose bumps at the similarities when she's face to face with a doctor.

This time when the white coat rests a hand on her shoulder, she flinches. His hands are smooth and less calloused than before. Back then, the doctor's rough hands felt gritty like sandpaper when they inspected between her legs, poking and prodding during the examination.

Before, when she wanted to interrogate the doctor and ask him questions, he refused to meet her eyes. His stare was fixated on the ugly watercolor painting behind her.

Deborah still recalls how her husband, Jonathan, was seated beside her, clawing her wrist with his bear-size hands. Both he and the doctor couldn't refrain from digging their fingers into her skin. Staring down at her lap, she clutched the thin cotton hospital blanket wrapped around her protruding abdomen.

"I'm afraid I have some news to share," the doctor told her. He stumbled over the "news" part, as if he couldn't decide if that was the right word to use.

"News?"

"I'm sorry, Deborah. It's unfortunate what happened to her."

But this isn't thirty-four years ago, and presently the man in the white lab coat speaks to her with compassion and makes eye contact, explaining it's a good thing she made it into the dilapidated structure because she was this close to dying of hypothermia.

He warmly tells her, "You must have a guardian angel watching over you."

Puzzled, she asks, "What do you mean?"

"If the police chief hadn't stopped by after the department received a call about a potential UFO sighting in the sky, you'd be a frozen carcass, found in the spring when the ground thawed."

Deborah does remember hearing a blast, but she figured she imagined it, and she says so. Her brain feels like mush, all the events a jumbled blur.

"Nope," the doctor says. "It was some dumb kid trying to set off fireworks."

"In the middle of winter?"

"Yep. In the middle of winter." He rolls his eyes. "Stupid kid. But it got the police out to investigate."

Reaching a hand to her forehead, Deborah touches an elastic bandage. "It feels like someone lit them inside my brain," Deborah moans.

"That's not surprising, considering you have some circular lesions from the butt of the rifle, called friction blisters. We're going to keep you under observation for a few days." The doctor looks jubilant. "But I must say, you have a thick skull, Mrs. Sawyer."

"I've had to have one," she mumbles, more to herself.

"You have some surface lacerations from being dragged, but you're fortunate to be alive. We did a CT scan, an x-ray, but we're going to do an MRI today for a more comprehensive view, make sure there isn't abnormal brain activity like a concussion. My concern was an intracerebral hemorrhage, a brain bleed, but there's no evidence of that."

"That's comforting." Deborah sighs with relief. "What about the farm? Is it still standing? Did they take anything from the house?"

The doctor shrugs. "The police didn't say anything about a robbery."

Deborah's asking out of concern for her safety. It's not like she has anything to confiscate. Deborah's lucky she wasn't shot with the old rifle for having nothing of value but a few old antiques. Her intention has never been to draw attention to herself. Any person with a lick of common sense knows that people get caught by being too flashy or materialistic. When you give someone a reason to pay attention, that's when the spotlight shines brighter on you.

But why now? she wonders.

And did the letters have anything to do with this unplanned visit?

If Deborah had perished, she could picture the people in town clucking their tongues, shrugging their shoulders in mock grief, and speaking about the irony. She was found mere feet away from where Jonathan had tragically died.

And most would have said she got what she deserved—karma at its finest. The religious zealots would claim God had a hand; others might say the ghost of Cindy had a hand, that it should've been Deborah, not Cindy, who died all those years ago, as she was an innocent bystander in the whole sordid tale.

As if I asked Cindy to involve herself, Deborah thinks bitterly.

CHAPTER 2
Deborah

When Deborah goes home from the hospital, she's still wearing a bandage wrapped around her head and some adhesive strips on the less severe abrasions.

Though she's starting to recuperate from the superficial wounds, Deborah freezes in nervous anticipation when she hears a knock at the front door, expecting the worst.

By far, the psychological damage from the trauma is going to surpass the visible imprints.

Tempted to ignore the unwanted visitor, Deborah halfheartedly drags her feet to peek out the picture windows facing the highway.

Spotting the neighbor's old truck, she lets out a sigh of relief.

When she opens the door slowly, she's face to face with him. Even in her fragile state of mind, he's a sight for sore eyes, even tired ones.

Robert lives on a neighboring farm and is a widower. They lost their respective spouses around the same time, and their families used to be close until tragedy struck.

Holding up a grocery bag as a peace offering, Robert tells Deborah he came to check on her. He mentions the prayer circle at church and says the congregation has added Deborah to their prayer chain.

Flustered at this thought, she assumes Robert feels pity for her. Even though Deborah sits in the same pew at church every Sunday, their interactions have been cordial but distant for years.

Suddenly self-conscious of her appearance and used to having a spotless house, Deborah becomes embarrassed because she has a few dishes in the sink and hasn't dusted since before the "incident."

She didn't plan to invite him in, but after they stand awkwardly at the door for a few minutes, she feels like she has no choice.

After she motions Robert to sit at the table, they stare at the empty chair between them in an unbearably long silence fraught with tension. Unpleasant memories belong to this chair and the owner. It was once Jonathan's, and his cigarette burns are stubbed into the fabric, the pockmarks a permanent reminder of his bad habits. It's apparent they both feel the ghost of him sitting in their midst. The blame game is as prevalent now as it was back then. Neither of them needs to say out loud that they think the other bears a majority of the responsibility for Jonathan's death, because neither would be wrong. No one can deny mistakes were made—some well intended, a few reckless, others vengeful.

But guilt, that's a dangerous thing. That'll eat your insides alive, as Deborah is well aware due to the acidity in her stomach lining.

"If people in town had minded their own business"—she runs her hand through her hair, unsettling a few sparse grays—"we wouldn't be sitting here like complete strangers."

"I know," Robert admits in a clipped tone. "But there was *truth* to some of it. We had to be careful."

After she offers a cup of coffee, black with no cream or sugar, the way he used to take it, they finally start to talk like old times. Slowly she loosens up, and laughter creeps upon Deborah; smile lines finally appear on her wrinkled face. She's forgotten how good it feels to have a conversation where there's actual dialogue. The farm cats aren't so adept at answering back.

When Robert leaves, he promises to come back and install an outdoor security camera and some floodlights. The seventy-acre farm has far too much land to have eyes on all of it, but she's grateful the house will be protected. Deborah tries not to read into this renewed friendship, telling herself it was born out of neighborly obligation and nothing more.

But she is pleasantly surprised when he calls the next day to invite her over for a friendly card game. Deborah cautiously accepts. Like a true gentleman, he picks her up, and they sit in front of his fireplace to play gin rummy and hearts.

Deborah returns the favor a few days later by inviting him over to watch television.

Then he cooks dinner for her, and they sit at his dining room table and trade stories.

After a few weeks she suggests they have their own book club, which might seem silly with only two people, but they agree on an author to read.

Sometimes Robert will sit in the recliner and nod off when it gets late, and Deborah then feels relieved not everything has changed with time. He'll fall asleep with his head at a painful-looking angle, his snores loud enough to rouse an army. Deborah giggles at the memory of him doing this during church sermons. His wife would give him an elbow in the ribs or loudly whisper for him to wake up. Deborah would snicker at her outbursts, since they drew more attention than his inconvenient naps because of the echo in the high-ceilinged chapel.

When his eyelids finally flip open, he wears a sheepish expression on his face. Slapping his knees, he slowly pulls himself out of the chair. He doesn't ask to stay the night, and she never offers, their companionable silence enjoyable for the two of them up until a point.

One warm afternoon when the snow has melted, hopefully for the last time, they go down to the pond on the edge of Deborah's property to fish, a perfect, cloudless April day upon them.

They don't need much in the way of conversation, both able to enjoy each other's company, but Deborah is abnormally quiet, a lot weighing on her mind as of late.

She had struck the letters from her memory, but now, after a long dry spell, another one has arrived. She's dying to tell someone, and Robert's the closest she has to a confidant. Pacing the grass, she makes the decision to tell him.

With a glance over his shoulder, he shoots her a questioning glance before he throws out his fishing line.

The last thing she wants to do is alienate him, and suddenly shy, Deborah second-guesses if she should share the secret. Maybe she should wait. It might spark old memories that they've both tried to bury.

"What is it, honey?" Robert reaches out his arm to grab hers in an attempt to stop her aimless wandering. "What's wrong? You're lucky that patch of grass is still dead because you've trampled it repeatedly."

Deborah can't help but grin at the term of endearment, often said by her husband but not meant. It was a force of habit and now sounds different coming from Robert.

Natural, even.

She blushes like a teenager, beaming with pride. "I've really been enjoying my time with you."

He squeezes her arm. "I feel the same." He's quiet for a moment, and then he says, "I know that's not all."

"No. It's not." She shrugs. "You can read me like a book."

"Always have." He guffaws.

Looking down at the brown grass, she murmurs, "I have something to tell you." She hurriedly adds, "I got a couple letters in the mail. Three now, actually."

Deborah tells Robert about the letters while his fishing pole bobs up and down, the rippling water movement the only sound. She can tell he's unnerved by the red flush that spreads from his face and down his neck, disappearing into the collar of his shirt.

He finally responds, "Did you write back?"

"No." She bites her lip. "I'm not sure what to say."

"Do you think there's an ulterior motive for reaching out?"

"Yes." She rests a frustrated hand on her hip. "Money."

"After all these years . . ." There's a sharp exhale on his end.

"I thought it was just us there that night."

"It was," Robert promises.

"The letter mentions the gun . . ."

"What about it?"

"They claim to know what happened to it."

"I dumped it in the pond, Debbie." He shields his face from the sunlight. "It's someone messing with you." He reaches a hand out to hold hers. "Everything's going to be fine, honey. I'm here with you now."

"Do you ever think about that night?"

"No." But his abrupt release of her hand tells her he's being untruthful.

"I hear his shrieks sometimes in the night."

"Deborah . . ."

She chokes on a sob. "I wish my actions hadn't hurt so many people."

"Stop," Robert demands. "This doesn't help us, getting all emotional. No one was there but us."

Deborah inhales a ragged breath, reminding herself all she can do is breathe. *Just breathe, Deborah.*

"I don't know what to do," she whimpers. "I'm worried this can only mean trouble."

"Not on my watch." His voice sharpens. "Give me some time. I take it you kept the letters?"

"Yes." Her voice quivers.

"Give them to me. I'll think of something." He nudges her arm gently. "You'll let me know if another letter comes?"

"Of course, but there's more." She hesitates. "The letters are sent from a PO box that supposedly belongs to her."

Robert grimaces. "After all this time?"

Not trusting herself to speak, Deborah stares down at the hole she's dug in the barren grass. Before Robert can respond, she watches his hand tremble, the line bobbing up and down. "I think I got something."

Watching in amazement, Deborah's impressed at how Robert expertly holds the line almost taut. "Did you get a hit?"

Nodding, he keeps his hand underneath the reel while his index finger and forefinger skillfully press down on the line.

"Nibble or a bite?"

"They might've just taken the bait." Glimpsing tiny swells in the water, Robert lifts the rod up at a ninety-degree angle to reel it in. They both chuckle when they realize the lure is gone, but no fish is attached to the hook.

As they enjoy the solitude, Robert moves closer to her as she snuggles into his side. When he brushes a large hand through her windswept hair, Deborah winces. Nothing seems to get past him, and looking concerned, he tenderly touches a swollen lump on her head.

Sounding alarmed, he asks, "What happened to your head?"

"It was a fall, nothing serious." Yet Deborah can't meet his eyes.

"Looks pretty serious to me." Robert motions to her leg. "You also weren't limping a couple of days ago."

Her mouth puckers like she's tasted something sour. "This getting old is not for the weak of heart."

He sighs. "How did you fall?"

"Trying to carry a laundry basket down those dreadful stairs."

"Those stairs are a death trap. How is it that no one's fallen down them before this?"

Deborah's mouth drops open and she stammers, then thinks better of it and shakes her head. Robert waits for her to continue, but she stares distractedly out at the water. She's not sure she wants to tell him what prompted her to lose her balance. She knows he's already worried about her mental state. Depressed and weepy, Deborah's unable to sleep, night terrors a constant invasion.

"Debbie." He softens his voice. "What don't you want to tell me?"

If anyone else called her Debbie instead of Deborah, she'd automatically correct them. But she finds she doesn't mind at all when he says it.

Finally, she relents. "Do you believe in ghosts?"

"I know I've heard enough ghost stories to last a lifetime, yet every one ends with more questions than answers."

"Well, the farmhouse is over a hundred and fifty years old." She takes a deep breath before she lays it on him. "A lot of people have lived and died on this land."

"What do you mean?"

"I don't think my fall was accidental." Deborah shrugs out of his grasp. "Someone shoved me down the stairs."

He looks incredulous. "You were *pushed* down the stairs?"

Her face burns crimson.

Robert's eyes convey the dread that Deborah feels. "By whom?"

"I don't know." She sighs. "But I felt a hand grip my shoulder."

"Whose hand?" His eyes drill into hers.

"It felt cold . . . too cold, like it didn't belong in this world."

"You think a ghost made you lose your balance?" He snorts. "Come on, Debbie, you can't honestly expect me to believe some evil spirit pushed you down the stairs."

Deborah silently counts to ten, trying to maintain her composure. She knows how this must sound.

"Maybe it was the ghost of Jonathan," he adds disdainfully. "Or Edward?"

Ignoring his scorn, she hurries on before she loses her courage. "It didn't feel as heavy as a man's touch. More delicate, like a female."

"A dead woman pushed you down the stairs?"

"Maybe Cindy," she muses.

"Don't bring *her* into this." His eyes narrow in annoyance.

Defensive, Deborah says, "I think someone wants to hurt me." Tears start to cloud her eyes, and seemingly taken aback by her emotion, Robert shifts uncomfortably on his feet.

"I know since they built that prison, this place hasn't felt safe," Robert says empathetically. "And I'm sure that random act of violence didn't help matters."

"How can you be so sure it was a random act?"

"I think they thought you'd have cash or jewelry, a robbery gone bad. One of our other neighbors got their place cased for the very same reason."

She says, brooding, "Do you think I'll ever know who wanted to hurt me?"

"Doubtful." He sighs. "If they stole something, there would be serial numbers to trace or something to find."

Rankled, Deborah stares off into the distance at nothing but fields and an endless highway. She wishes she could go back in time, before she knew of anyone named Jonathan or Robert, before she had to carry the weight of the world on her shoulders.

"Maybe you'll remember specific details along the way," he offers. "Has your memory been jogged since you came home from the hospital?"

Unsure if she should admit this, Deborah says quickly, spitting the words out in a jumble, "I swear they had blond hair."

"Because of what?"

"They had light-colored eyebrows. That's about all I could see in the eye slits."

"What about their eye color?"

"Unnaturally dark, like charcoal." She automatically tenses up. "I could only see for a moment on the porch."

"You think it was a guy with blond hair and dark eyes?"

"I don't know," she admits. "But it definitely was a man."

Deborah thinks about this as they pack up their fishing gear. If it was a chance encounter with a stranger, then why does she have an unsettled feeling of being watched?

Shuddering at this idea, she doesn't hear what Robert says until he lightly taps her on the shoulder. Deborah leaps backward before she realizes he's asking her a question. "Are you okay?" He frowns.

"Yeah, I, uh, I just was thinking about all of this." She waves a hand around. "It's a lot."

"I know," he agrees. "That's why I just asked if you had given any more thought to my suggestion."

After the assault, Robert asked if she'd consider seeing a psychologist, psychiatrist, or hypnotist. Sensitive about her past and feeling harped on, she told him to drop it.

"Look," Robert says, "you told me you can't sleep since the . . . since the incident. You're sleep deprived, and I'm sure it's not helping you function. I mean, you're skin and bones, and you didn't have the weight to lose to begin with."

Without looking at him, she stares straight ahead. "You think a shrink can fix me because I'm crazy?"

"Yes. I mean, no." Robert clears his throat. "That's not what I mean. I'm worried about you." She stiffens when Robert lays a hand on her arm. "What happened to you was disgusting and senseless. Random or not, it doesn't matter. There's no way to escape unscathed from something that awful. You're a strong woman, but dammit, there are limits, Debbie."

"I know," she murmurs.

He hunches his shoulders. "I'm just scared, is all. I don't want to lose you."

Flippant, she asks, "Are you afraid I'll lose my mind again or that someone will finish the job?"

"Both." He shakes his head sadly. "Both, Deborah." It's not the answer she wants, but it's the truth.

"I don't want you to be worried for me." She threads her small fingers through his large ones as they walk back toward the house.

Deborah can't help but notice his troubled expression at the sight of the thin gold wedding band she has on. "How could you still wear that?"

"It comforts me."

"That ring isn't symbolic of peace. A lot of lives got ruined." His tone is harsh. "I'd hardly call that reassuring."

"It reminds me of how relieved I felt when that night was over," she explains. "It was like a resurrection of sorts." Deborah could breathe again, and it was as if she had risen from her own grave, even if it meant putting Jonathan in his.

And it felt good.

Wholesome, even.

She can tell by Robert's clenched jaw he disagrees. "That might be why you feel Jonathan's presence. Maybe it's time to think about a change."

Not wanting to rock the boat, she tugs on his fingers. "Do you really think trying to talk to a professional again will help?"

"It couldn't hurt," he chides her. "We need a fresh start, Debbie."

"I've been burned before," she divulges. "I don't want to be taken away and force-fed pills."

"I wouldn't let that happen to you."

Inside, she screams, *You let it happen before,* but she knows that's not fair. It was a different time, and there were others to consider. It was selfish to ask him to put her needs above everything else.

"Being assaulted had to be traumatic for you." He tightens his grip on her hand. "I hate that it happened and I wasn't around to protect you. But if it hadn't . . ." His voice trails off.

"What?"

"I doubt we'd be standing here right now." His sorrowful eyes peer deeply at Deborah, the mood becoming somber. "It's a terrible thing to say. I just . . . I'm glad we reconnected."

His old pickup truck is pulled around the garage, hidden in the brush, just in case his kids or their neighbors drive by. They both agreed they aren't ready for tongues to start a-waggin' again, at least not this soon.

After setting his fishing pole and tackle box in the bed of the truck, he slides his hands gently around her waist to give Deborah a warm embrace.

After they separate, Robert gives her a kiss and climbs up into the driver's seat. "Wait." He opens the middle console, rummaging through the contents until he finds what he's looking for. "Ah, here it is." Pressing a business card into her hand, he seems ambivalent. "A friend gave me this card a while back, you know, when I was dealing with my wife's death . . . or I should say, when I hadn't dealt with her death." He takes a deep breath. "This doctor comes highly recommended."

Unsure of how to respond and on rocky footing with the topic of his wife's death, she closes her palm around the heavy cardstock. "Thank you."

"I won't bring it up again," he promises. "I just want you to feel better. PTSD is a real thing."

Though her external injuries have healed, her renewed terror at living on the farm alone hasn't. After every sunset, at the first trace of dusk, her insides clench in apprehension as Deborah imagines a stranger waiting in the gloomy night, ready to pounce and finish the job.

"I know." She nods her head. "But even with seeing someone, I don't know if I'll ever feel safe again."

"It might be time for a change." Robert is grim.

Before he drives off, he gives her hand one final squeeze, and Deborah can't imagine giving him up for anything. If Robert thinks she should seek help, then maybe she should. It might even make him more inclined to want a relationship with her, especially since he witnessed the fallout from before. She doesn't want him to think she's unstable. Or deranged.

That's all in the past, isn't it?

But in this moment, Deborah is suddenly unsure.

CHAPTER 3
Deborah

Sitting in her vehicle until 8:00 a.m. on the dot, Deborah clasps the now-tattered business card in her hand. She arrived early for the appointment, but her nerves got the best of her. Distrustful that this quack doctor would be any different or wiser, she circled the block, then opted for a parking spot behind the building, instead of in plain sight. She's had enough curious and threatening stares over the years in this tiny town.

Robert recommended this woman, she reminds herself, and he's not like Jonathan; he's better. Kind. His concern is from a place of caring, not selfishness.

With this in mind, Deborah hesitantly enters the office from the back door instead of the front entrance. After shutting it softly behind herself, she's tempted to open it and run back to the safety of her automobile.

The shades are drawn in the waiting room, if you can call the small area that, but Deborah doesn't spot a receptionist, which is a relief. In fact, there's no check-in desk or bell, and there's *always* a bell to ring for service.

When she announces her presence aloud, it's garbled, and even her name sounds foreign to her ears.

She starts to pace the small room, and fighting the instinct to run, she forces herself to take a seat in a plush chair in the corner. Then, unable to relax in the elegant chair, Deborah fiddles with the strap of her purse.

Staring at the pale-blue walls, she's reminded of an article she read in one of her home-improvement magazines, or maybe it was *O*, Oprah's magazine. It said the walls of doctors' offices are painted soft colors like this shade of blue or light green because the colors have been shown to be soothing.

Though she despises bright, vibrant colors and loud wallpaper, the pastel tone isn't warming her up to this visit. Deborah agreed to come only to show Robert she was serious about starting the healing process and merging their lives.

Suddenly, as if Deborah had snapped her fingers, a woman in her midforties appears. Too much of her face is covered by thick black glasses, a contrast to the platinum hair. The picture Robert showed her on the website when she scheduled an appointment online matches the woman perfectly, minus the white lab coat and black dress with *Dr. Alacoy, Clinical Psychiatrist* on it. Today she's more casual, wearing linen pants and a flowered tunic.

At first glance, she appears harsh—cold, even, not a strand out of place in her stern updo—but when Dr. Alacoy opens her mouth, the crinkles at the corners express her desire to smile, and it transforms her demeanor instantaneously.

Deborah feels an immediate warmth and familiarity with this woman. Maybe it's because they've bumped into each other around town, but she feels like a kindred spirit.

"Deborah Sawyer." The doctor not only shakes her hand but allows her soft one to linger over Deborah's trembling one. "I'm Alice Alacoy, and I'm so glad you could make it."

"You came highly recommended."

"That's sweet of you to say." She lets out a slight chuckle. "I'll ignore the fact this town has limited options, and there aren't many choices."

This is true, as Deborah's previous doctor has retired.

Unsure what to say, she simply stands to follow the tall woman into an adjoining room, an exact replica of the one she just came from. Painted the same color, it has coordinating furniture. The only difference is the large, polished mahogany desk sitting astutely in the middle. It's uncluttered and empty, save for a laptop and printer.

Dr. Alacoy points to the sitting area on the left, where an overstuffed chair and a small leather couch beckon them. A little side table rests between the two pieces of furniture. "Take your pick."

"Where will you be sitting?"

"On whichever one you don't choose. That is, if you're comfortable with it." She motions to the desk. "Or if you prefer, I can sit here and take notes. It's just not as easy to hear you across the room."

Hesitating for a moment, Deborah chews her lip before deciding on the couch.

"Great!" Dr. Alacoy claps her hands. "Before we get started, is there anything I can get for you? Maybe some coffee or tea?"

Deborah rests her purse next to her, though for some reason, keeping the strap around her fingers feels oddly therapeutic, so she keeps the leather loose around her knuckles. Deborah winces as she has a flashback to them bloodied and bruised from the steel-toed boots that stepped on them.

Dr. Alacoy offers to light a candle. "I've got either vanilla or a lavender one."

Deborah read in the same magazine that mentioned relaxing paint colors that flowering plants could alleviate anxiety. Maybe a scent could calm her nerves. "How about lavender?"

"Perfect." Dr. Alacoy scans the room and locates the candle on the window ledge. After setting it on a mosaic glass platter, she pulls a lighter from her pocket. "Did you know they used to use lavender to help purify mummies?"

"No, I did not."

Dr. Alacoy sniffs the air. "The camphor is subtle, yet distinct."

Deborah inhales a deep breath.

Dr. Alacoy smiles at her. "Lavender has been an essential oil since practically the beginning of time, used to soften the skin and cover up odors back then but also as part of the embalming process."

"I like that it's not an overpowering smell."

"Absolutely. That's the draw of it. The way it sucks you in without being overly potent." With the candle between them on the side table, Dr. Alacoy casually steps out of her clogs and tucks her bare feet up underneath her, as if they're old friends catching up and need to be as comfortable as possible.

"First"—she reaches for Deborah's hand and gives it a gentle squeeze before she lets it go—"I'd like you to call me Alice. No 'Dr. This' or 'Dr. That.' I'm here to act as a guide in your journey to self-enlightenment and healing. I'll know I've done my job if you feel better than you do at this moment."

Alice fixes her with a caring smile. "This is a judgment-free zone, and it only works if we have open communication lines and trust. I realize this isn't easy—I'm a stranger, and telling someone your innermost thoughts or feelings can be hard, especially with a *shrink*. By the way," Alice mutters, "I hate that word. *But*"—she gives Deborah's knee a quick tap—"if I can listen and advise you on the best course of treatment, then we will make progress. But it's not just up to me; it's up to you."

Deborah slowly nods, unclear what Dr. Alacoy is implying.

"You'll have to do the work, put in the time." Alice peers at her through the massive lenses of her glasses. "I take it you're open to whatever type of therapy or recommendation I make?"

Deborah feels her face redden, as if Alice can detect her reservations.

"You're here because you want to feel better?"

"Yes."

"You seem unsure," Alice points out gently. "I just want to make sure you're on board. Many people are coerced into seeking help, and the success rate is minimal if it's not what you want."

"Of course I want to feel better," Deborah snaps.

Alice sits back as if she's been slapped but quickly recovers.

"Sorry, it's just"—Deborah takes a deep breath—"I've had some bad experiences with therapy. To be honest, I've seen a psychiatrist before, and I have mixed feelings."

"Don't apologize," Alice murmurs. "It's quite all right. You're not offending me." They consider each other for a moment while Alice rests a finger on her chin. "Was it because of the doctor or the treatment?"

"Both." She sniffs. "I didn't like the outcome."

Alice opens her mouth to speak, but Deborah isn't ready to address her comment.

"I value my privacy." Deborah twists the thin gold band around her finger. "Nothing stays quiet in a town this size; everyone knows everyone's business, regardless if they should."

"Are you alluding to something public or a breach of confidentiality?" Alice must notice Deborah's pained expression and adds, "Your concerns are valid. Our conversations and sessions are strictly between you and me, unless, of course, someday you want or need a medical release for other treatment. Also, to be clear, even though you were referred to me by a mutual friend, he isn't privy to our sessions unless you want him to be."

Deborah stares down at her lap, silently processing this. Trust is a hard thing to come by, especially now.

Alice's blue eyes flash with worry. "I want to hear about what brings you here today and delve into the past, but first, let's start with your medical history so I have the full picture." She reaches forward and pulls out a notepad from the small drawer in the side table. "Do you mind if I take some notes? This way, I can go back for clarity if I need to."

"Uh . . ." Deborah twists uncomfortably on the couch. "I guess not."

Alice starts off with simple yes-or-no questions, as if earnestly preparing Deborah for the easy parts of an exam until she can interrogate her on the harder subjects. And finally, Alice does just that, making a smooth transition by asking Deborah about the "incident" that prompted this visit. Tapping her pen against her cheek, Alice says, "Let's talk about what happened."

"Okay." Deborah anxiously tugs at her cross necklace. "About three months ago, in January, I was inside my home when I heard a noise outside."

She tightens her grip on the thin chain. "It scared me since I'm on a farm in the middle of nowhere. Besides that, it was nighttime and the middle of winter. I thought I saw something outside, but I told myself it was my mind playing tricks, especially since my night vision isn't the best."

Alice is fixated squarely on her, her pen poised, unmoving.

"When I went outside to check it out, I managed to slip and fall on a patch of ice." With a quivering voice, Deborah falters. "I was right; someone was there, and that person hit me repeatedly with my own rifle, kicked me, and left me for dead."

The color drains from Alice's fair skin. "Before we talk about the aftereffects, I have to ask: Is there a police report?" The creases in Alice's forehead deepen. "Do they have any suspects?"

"Yes." Deborah sighs. "There's a police report, but they haven't mentioned anyone. Ever since they built that men's prison outside of town, we've had an influx of crime." Deborah shudders. "Escaped convicts using the farms as their hideout."

"I'd like to think they are still investigating this closely." Alice shakes her head. "How awful."

"It definitely has been a test of my faith."

"Were you wearing that necklace?" Alice nods at the cross tangled in Deborah's fingers.

"I was." Deborah gives her a small smile. "It belonged to my mother. My father was a preacher."

"It might've saved your life."

"I thought psychiatrists didn't believe in the power of prayer and God?"

"I wouldn't say that. To each their own." Alice shrugs. "And this is about your beliefs, not anyone else's."

"Speaking of saved lives, I'm lucky I was found and didn't freeze to death." Deborah groans. "I spent three days in the hospital while they did some tests."

"I'm guessing you had some injuries from this?" Alice asks. "Maybe even concussive symptoms or a hematoma as a result of the fall?"

"Yes, I had a concussion." Deborah focuses upward on the ceiling so she doesn't burst into tears. "As a result, I'm experiencing a lot of headaches. Migraines, actually. I'm dizzy as soon as I wake up, and my ears ring at times."

"Did they do a brain scan?"

"Yes. Both a CT and MRI."

Alice stares at her notes, tapping her pen in thought. "First, I'd like to request those medical records so I can review both scans. I'm guessing your brain activity didn't show signs of tumors or torn tissue?"

"Correct."

"Anything else you've noticed since then?" Alice points to Deborah's leg. "Any issues with your motor skills? I noticed you had a slight limp. Did they do a neurological exam to check your coordination and balance?"

"That's from another accident," Deborah stammers. "I fell down the stairs a week ago." Ignoring the surprise behind the large spectacles Alice is wearing, Deborah continues, "I live in an old farmhouse, and the steps are wooden and pretty steep. I sprained my wrist and hurt my leg."

"How did you fall?"

"I tripped."

"Did anything cause you to trip?"

"My own klutziness," Deborah says with a nervous laugh.

"Any hallucinations? Visual or auditory?"

"No," Deborah lies. It's more than the attack that has Deborah concerned. Lately, her brain has seemed muddled, as if she's taken a handful of hallucinogenic drugs, like the time in high school when she mistakenly ate some shrooms and objects appeared to take on their own ominous shapes.

A couple of days ago, Deborah was driving at nighttime when she swerved to avoid a collision with what she thought was a deer, but in reality, it was a telephone pole.

Embarrassingly enough, she was pulled over as a possible intoxicated driver. The police officer cautioned her about driving in her lethargic state, said being unalert was as dangerous as driving drunk. She couldn't tell him the wooden posts reminded her of moving animals, the electrical wires impersonating outstretched limbs.

But she doesn't feel like confiding in Alice about what happened. If Deborah said it out loud, even to her own ears, it would sound bonkers. She doubts Alice will be able to cover up a judgmental reaction. She'll probably suggest she be thrown in the loony bin for good.

Alice tilts her head, as if suspecting her of dishonesty. "Another reason for the neurological exam is to check your vision. You'd be surprised how your body works in conjunction, or against, other muscles, organs, and tissue. Speaking of, when was the last time you had an eye exam?"

"Hmm . . ." Deborah tries to remember. "I believe it was last year."

"I'd suggest both visiting your optometrist and scheduling another neurological exam, since the fall was recent."

"Okay," Deborah consents. "I can do that."

"Has a doctor prescribed any meds?"

"Pain pills—Oxycontin. For sleeping, trazodone."

"Wait, Deb . . ." Alice writes something on her pad.

"Deborah," she corrects. "I go by Deborah."

"Of course, *Deborah*," Alice repeats. "Deborah. Got it. Since you were prescribed sleeping pills, can you talk to me about your issues with sleeping?"

"I didn't sleep well to begin with, and it's even worse now. It's hard to feel like I get a good night's rest."

"What happens when you go to bed?"

"Nightmares," Deborah stammers. "About the stranger coming back to finish me off."

"Do you know if you talk in your sleep?"

"Uh, no, I don't."

Alice points at Deborah's wedding band. "I noticed the ring, and if it's one thing I know, your spouse will tell you when they don't get rest because of you. My husband woke the whole household up, including the farm animals, much to our detriment." Stopping suddenly, Alice shakes her head. "But I'm digressing. My point is they'll typically mention if you talk in your sleep, flail—heck, even kick or punch."

Deborah raises her eyebrow at this. "People punch in their sleep?"

"Some people have very vivid reactions." Alice shrugs. "Especially to dreams. Have you ever had a dream that seemed so real you woke up and were mad about it?"

"Now that I think about it, yes," Deborah says. "But I live alone, so I couldn't tell you about my sleep patterns."

Alice looks at her with curiosity.

Deborah explains, "I was married, but I've been widowed for a long, long time, and my boyfriend . . ." The word *boyfriend* sounds so juvenile coming out of her mouth, so Deborah rephrases. "Robert and I tend to sleep at our own houses."

Alice claps her hands. "I didn't know Robert was dating anyone, but I'm glad to hear it."

In her head, Deborah mutters a curse word. She wasn't supposed to tell anyone they were dating; it was what they both agreed to.

"Do you mind if we keep that private?" Deborah's face burns with embarrassment. "We . . . we wanted to keep it between us for now. We connected after my attack, and we're moving slow."

"Certainly." Alice shrugs. "Our sessions are strictly between us. I know you mentioned being a widow, which has to be difficult." Alice leans forward. "What was your husband's name? I want to be sure I know who you're referencing when we talk."

"Jonathan."

"How long has Jonathan been gone?"

"About sixteen years."

"What was his cause of death?"

"It's complicated." Deborah presses a hand to her forehead, suddenly feverish.

Alice stares at her in puzzlement. "He's deceased, though?"

"Yes. My . . . my husband . . ." Deborah's heart starts to pound, and she's sure Alice can hear it. "Would you mind . . ." She clears her throat, unable to catch her breath. With a racing heart, she whispers, "Could I please have a glass of water?"

Alice presses gently on Deborah's shoulder. "Absolutely. I'll be right back."

Deborah's mind is reeling while she waits for Alice to exit the room. Her footsteps echo across the hardwood when she returns with the water.

After thrusting the cold glass into Deborah's palm, Alice hands her a couple of pills. "These are just regular old Tylenol."

"Thank you," Deborah murmurs. "I've got the worst headache."

"I figured." Alice motions to the couch. "I could tell by the grimace on your face." Leaning forward to move a decorative pillow, Alice offers, "Go ahead and lie down if you'd like."

"I'm sorry," Deborah apologizes, moving her purse to the floor so she can lie down. "I'm not feeling so hot right now."

"Nothing to be sorry for." Alice gently helps Deborah reposition herself on the couch, settling the pillow underneath her head.

"Do you mind if we stop for a minute?" Deborah shuts her eyes.

"Of course!" Alice shoves her feet back in her shoes and perches on the chair. "We are in no rush. I'm on your timetable."

Feeling dizzy, Deborah is relieved Alice doesn't continue to pepper her with questions but is content to sit there in silence or at least accept the lull in the conversation.

Though she means to ask Alice a burning question, she quickly forgets what she wants to know, the pounding in her head taking precedence.

Half-asleep, Deborah feels a cold compress on her forehead and a hand resting on her shoulder.

Just as suddenly, the warm touch disappears, but the washcloth stays in place.

A moment later, she hears the door rattle open and shut with a soft thud. Deborah can listen to Alice talking to whoever is presumably the next client, but the voice has a familiar lilt to it.

She groans; the last thing Deborah needs is someone local thinking she needs to be shipped off to a mental ward again. Even though that would be the pot calling the kettle black, she's used to the hypocrisy.

Deborah's grateful when she overhears Alice say, "My office is currently occupied, so let's do our session out here today."

She doesn't realize she's fallen asleep until Alice gently tugs on her shoulder. Timidly, Deborah sits up and runs a hand through her tousled hair. Thanking Alice for respecting her privacy, she feels less stressed and more relaxed after her nap.

"Of course." Alice ushers her out to the main room. "I can tell we're going to be in it for the long haul. We're going to work through this together, all right?"

Deborah gives her a noncommittal smile.

"I'll see you in a week, and we'll go from there."

Hurrying out to her vehicle, Deborah breathes a sigh of relief.

CHAPTER 4
Deborah

The following Wednesday, Deborah shows up at Dr. Alacoy's office, prompt but nervous. She's wearing dark sunglasses, her old fears causing anxiety about being spotted in the back lot.

When she walks inside the building, she's grateful the shades on the windows are still drawn.

"Hi, Deborah!" Alice greets her cheerfully and summons her to the back, where she motions for her to pick either the chair or couch again.

Today Dr. Alacoy is wearing a crisp white blouse tucked into dark jeans with a brightly colored scarf wound around her neck. Her hair is still in a severe bun, and her earrings are simple gold studs.

Deborah sinks into the soft, buttery leather couch as Alice settles into the chair with her notepad, this time keeping her feet on the floor.

They make small talk before they dive in. Deborah notices that Alice likes to slide her diamond wedding band up and down her ring finger.

"So," Alice asks, "how're you doing this week?"

"I'm okay."

"Your limp doesn't seem as pronounced. Are you getting along any better?"

"They gave me a cane in case I need it, but I do okay without it." Deborah fails to mention she's able to cope because of the pain pills she's taking quite frequently. She doesn't want to rouse concern in Alice that she's painless only when medicated.

"How're the nightmares?"

"The same."

"I want to circle back to your sleep patterns, if that's all right." Alice waits for Deborah to nod her head. "Before the nightmares started, did it just take you a long time to fall asleep, but once there, you'd stay asleep, or has falling asleep and waking up in the middle of the night been problematic?"

Deborah clenches the leather strap of her purse again for emotional support. "I could fall asleep, but I'd wake up a lot, and sometimes I don't know where I am."

"Can you elaborate on that?"

"I'll find myself wandering in another room of the house. I've fallen out of bed in the middle of the night and woken up on the floor."

"Last time we discussed an updated visual and neurological exam." Alice pushes her glasses up the bridge of her nose. "To rule out issues with your coordination and vision. Have you made an appointment with either doctor?"

"I made an appointment with a neurologist and my eye doctor. My vision's been a tad blurry," Deborah says. "And sometimes objects seem to take on other shapes or get twisted."

"Do you drink alcohol?"

"No." Deborah makes a face. "I don't even keep liquor in my house."

"Have you ever heard the term 'REM sleep behavior disorder'?" Alice asks. "Also known as 'rapid eye movement behavior disorder'?"

"I haven't." Deborah shakes her head.

"Are you familiar with the typical sleep pattern?"

"I know there are sleep stages."

"Yes, correct. There are two, actually. One is called nonrapid eye movement, and the other is rapid eye movement. In someone with a sleep disorder like the one I mentioned, the REM is either lacking or absent, causing someone to act out their dreams. This can force a person to jump out of bed or take part in behaviors they normally wouldn't."

Deborah tilts her head, unsure of what to say. The room suddenly feels stuffy, and Deborah unbuttons her light jacket. "Maybe I'm getting a hot flash." She waves a hand toward her forehead in a cooling motion.

"I can check the temperature and turn on the fan," Alice offers. "I want you to be comfy."

"I'll survive." Deborah gives her a weak smile. "I'm starting to fall apart in my old age."

"You're hardly old." Alice chuckles. "I can't even believe you have a daughter old enough to be out of the house."

"A daughter?"

"Yes." Alice gives her an inquisitive stare. "You mentioned her last time."

"I didn't." Deborah frowns.

"Yes." Alice scans the notepad with wire-rimmed glasses that are better suited for her face and not so colossal.

"No." Deborah licks her lips. "I wouldn't have a reason to mention her."

"Oh Lord." Alice taps a hand to her forehead. "Please forgive me."

Deborah stares her down, swallowing a biting comment.

"How unprofessional of me!" Alice shakes her head in annoyance. "But Robert mentioned your daughter in passing. He gave you a compliment." She rushes to add, "This was before you and I had even met."

"Why would the two of you be discussing me?"

"I thanked him for the referral after you made an appointment." Alice gives her a wink. "He mentioned he knew you from way back because his son and your daughter went to high school together."

"And our farms aren't too far from each other." Deborah shrugs. "And we go to the same church."

"I know his kids are grown." Alice grins. "And you certainly don't look old enough to have one that age, so you better let me in on your secrets."

"My advice is to get knocked up at nineteen," Deborah says calmly but seriously. Deborah's mother warned her it was easy to get pregnant at that age, and a giggle escapes her lips when she thinks back to her warning. It went unheeded since her mother's advice wasn't always reliable. A lot of the time, it was passed down like an old wives' tale.

Alice gives her a peculiar look. "What's so funny?"

"Something my mother told me as a teenager."

"Let's hear it," Alice says. "I need a laugh."

"She told me how easy it was to get pregnant. She said just looking at a man would do the trick, and for some reason, remembering her saying it all those years ago and how I didn't take her seriously made me chuckle."

Jonathan's idea of intercourse was equivalent to that of a farm animal. He'd shove his sweaty body into hers in a frenzy, releasing his aggression after a couple of thrusts and grunts.

She wasn't sure they could conceive because it was over so fast, and he never asked if she got any pleasure from it. In her mind, it wasn't lovemaking, so it didn't equate to making a baby like in the romance novels she would devour.

"Tell me about your parents. Are they alive?" Alice asks. "I know you mentioned your father was a man of God."

"My father was a preacher, and he died when I was in my early twenties. Heart attack," Deborah says. "My mother died a few years later, an accidental overdose. I miss my mother the most," she muses. "She was strong and scrappy."

Deborah's mother wasn't an affectionate woman; she doled out love sparingly, but when she did indulge her child, she gave the warmest hugs, which made Deborah feel wholly and completely loved. Deborah had promised herself that when she became a mother, she wouldn't withhold affection or love, and there would be an abundance of it.

Her thoughts drift from her deceased mother to her estranged daughter. Though the estrangement was entirely unexpected, it shouldn't have been. She made a solemn vow to be the best possible mother. Yet she feels like a failure.

Alice's voice cuts into her thoughts. "Did your mother hate being a preacher's wife?"

"You mean because that's what she was known as, with no identity of her own?"

"Yeah," Alice says. "It would be hard to have the expectations for you to be perfect all the time. No one can stand on a pedestal and never fall."

"She had her moments. But she prized the role, and she knew how to bring out the best in my father. No one could've brought out his personality more than her. And he could be difficult." She gasps involuntarily. "And cunning." Deborah no longer wishes to talk about her parents, so, deciding on a subject change, she murmurs, "That reminds me, Alice. Speaking of our families, why don't I know any other Alacoys? Did you not grow up around here?"

"I didn't." She offers a small smile. "Weird, right? I grew up in Ohio."

"What brought you here?"

"Marriage." Alice shrugs. "And even now, I live twenty-five miles away."

"And this is where you wanted to open up a practice?"

"Not necessarily. I have office space countywide. It's an easy drive, all highway." Alice glances at her notes, back to business. "I know you live on a farm. And I'd like to know how you feel living out there, considering the circumstances. Can you elaborate on your mindset since the accident?"

"I have a security system now," Deborah mentions. "And the police on speed dial."

"Do you ever see yourself moving into town or closer to . . . ?"

"Civilization?" Deborah chortles. "I know the land is invaluable, especially to certain individuals who want to rezone it for something else." Deborah sighs. "Unfortunately, everyone has always wanted the farm for their own intentions. I realized too late my husband married me for the stretch of property my folks passed down to us after we got married."

"Speaking of your husband. I think you said his name was Jonathan," Alice murmurs. "Last time before you left, the loss of him was mentioned." Alice crosses her legs. "Please correct me if I'm wrong, but it seemed to trigger a negative response along the lines of a panic attack. Is this something you want to talk about?"

"Not particularly."

"I'm guessing he had to have been very young when he died," Alice says gently. "If it was sixteen years ago?"

"Yes," is all Deborah feels like responding with.

"Then let me ask you this." Alice taps her fingernails on the arm of the chair. "Will talking about it help with unresolved issues from the past?"

Deborah doesn't answer, focusing on the polished hardwood floor. Her eyes drift to the empty desk, devoid of photographs or wall hangings near it.

Maybe because Alice isn't here every day, she doesn't bother to decorate.

Or maybe she doesn't want her clients to have a peek into her homelife. All it takes is one psychopath to threaten your family. Alice probably prefers to keep her personal life private. It's not going to keep Deborah from asking, though.

"Do you have children, Alice?"

"I do," she says hesitantly. "I have a son and a daughter."

44

"How old?"

"My son is seventeen. My daughter is in her twenties."

"Are you married?"

"Yes," Alice says coyly. "Why do you ask?"

"Because I made a lot of decisions based on keeping my family together, right or wrong."

"I can understand that." Alice abruptly stands. "If you're not ready to talk about your late husband, we can save that for our next session." Touching the knotted scarf at her throat, Alice says, "In the meantime, we can look at something to help with your other ailments. Besides what you mentioned last time, are you taking any over-the-counter meds or other prescriptions?"

"No."

"Antidepressants?"

"Nope."

Alice moves to the laptop at her desk. "I want to prescribe something different as a sleep aid and a medication for your migraines. Let's try these and find out if there are side effects and go from there." Clicking her nails on the keyboard, Alice confirms, "You said you don't drink or keep alcohol in the house?"

"I do not drink."

"Good to know, because you shouldn't drink on these meds," Alice warns. "Where do you want me to send them?"

Deborah prefers to handle most of her business in the next town over. Her prescriptions are filled at the small pharmacy there, and it gives her an air of anonymity. Deborah's relieved Alice doesn't ask her about using a different zip code.

After tapping a few more keys, Alice gives her a smile. "Okay, I submitted the scripts. You should be able to pick up today."

"Thank you."

"I'd like to see you in a few weeks, if that's all right with you." Alice scans her computer screen. "To see how you're adjusting and to talk about whatever you're comfortable with."

"That works."

Alice hands Deborah an appointment card, which is nothing more than a circled date and time. As she's exiting the office, Deborah makes a quick stop. Twisting around, she turns to consider Alice. "Dr. Alacoy?"

Barely glancing up from her laptop, she murmurs, "Uh-huh?"

"What was the compliment, then?"

Alice peers at her from over the screen. "Beg your pardon?"

"You said Robert paid me a compliment."

"That he did." Alice grins. "He said you made the best pies in the county."

Deborah shrugs. "I did win a blue ribbon at the state fair."

"Where I come from, the state fair doesn't compare to the one here. Maybe I'll be lucky enough to try one sometime."

Giving her a thumbs-up, Deborah pauses at the door to retrieve her sunglasses. Sliding them back on, she smiles to herself, thinking of Robert.

With a glance in both directions, she heads to her car, a noticeable bounce in her step that's still with her when she gets home. Then, with more energy than she has had in a long time, Deborah goes on a cleaning spree, wiping fingerprints and dirt from the windows, dusting the furniture, and sweeping the kitchen floor. Running the vacuum over the carpet, she maneuvers it through the downstairs rooms until her hip starts to throb. *It's not like I'm going to venture upstairs anyway,* she consoles herself. *It's too spooky up there.*

Robert's coming over for dinner later, and she smiles, remembering the compliment he paid her to Alice. Scouring the cupboards and the walk-in pantry, Deborah checks to see if she has all the ingredients to bake an apple pie.

By the time it's in the oven, Deborah has flour smudged on her cheeks and discarded apple cores on the countertop and floor.

With an hour timer set and feeling sudden fatigue, she crashes in her usual chair, watching mindless television while rocking back and forth, as if she can lull herself to sleep. The constant motion prevents Deborah from thinking about the strange man seated next to her in Jonathan's recliner. She asks herself why she hasn't gotten rid of the battered chair, but she doesn't have a good answer. Mainly because after Jonathan died, she didn't want her daughter to ask questions or take offense. Deborah supposes she's had sixteen years to make a change and hasn't. The man in the usually empty spot seems disturbed, his face covered in bits of toilet paper and shaving cream, as if he didn't bother to consult a mirror while shaving his stubble.

Peering at him with concern, Deborah notices a rough patch of skin that looks like a scar, as if something as sharp as a razor is jutting across his face. Perhaps a knife?

When he notices her looking, he moves his head toward her, as if wanting to engage her in conversation. Trying not to flinch at the sight of his half-closed eyelid, Deborah drops her gaze to her hands clenched on the armrest. She doesn't want to be rude, but his lid reminds her of something absentmindedly stitched up by a needle and thread.

His lips move, but she can't make out the words. Deborah is annoyed by this; she's always hated when people try to talk over the television. Jonathan used to do that, and she'd eventually get huffy and walk out of the room. Though now that she thinks about it, that was smart of him. It ensured he got the remote and television all to himself, and with only one TV in the house, it was calculated, like everything else he did.

Though she wants to focus on the chatter of the infomercial, Deborah cocks her head to the side, straining to hear what he keeps repeating beside her. She doesn't want to look at him, but it's no use.

"You owe me money," he says testily. "You wanna keep the farm, don't ya?"

Surprised at this pronouncement, Deborah shushes him.

"I mean it. Pay up."

Trying to keep him out of her line of sight, she goes so far as to pick up the remote and turn the volume louder, a universal signal to be quiet.

"I'm not leaving until we're square."

"Would you just shut up?" Deborah's lip quivers. "Please! For five seconds."

"And then what?"

"Then I'll deal with you."

But it's no use; his incessant demands don't cease, and frustrated, Deborah explodes out of her chair. Tossing the remote into Jonathan's recliner, she angrily strides into the kitchen. When the timer beeps to signal the pie is done, she can still hear him chanting from the other room.

Frustrated, Deborah watches the glass pie tin rattle after she sets it down harder than she intends to. Avoiding the living room and the man's raised voice, she walks the long way around to enter her bedroom. When she's safe inside the master bedroom, she locks herself in the bathroom.

After reaching into the medicine cabinet, Deborah fumbles with the bottle. She cups her hands in place of using an actual water glass, tips her head back, and swallows the pills down quickly, imagining them slowing down the rampant thoughts running through her mind. Her brain needs a break from the uncontrollable mania.

She slowly sinks to her knees and crawls to the corner of the bathroom, resting her back against the wall. With no recollection of nodding off, she wakes to find spittle pooling in the creases of her mouth. After she swipes her hand over her eyes, her vision appears blurred, as if due to a smudged contact lens.

Wondering why the television is blaring, Deborah drags herself from the bathroom into the living room. At first, she thinks Robert must've let himself in somehow, but she enters an empty room. The television's on a talk show channel Deborah dislikes; wrinkling her nose in annoyance, she searches for the remote.

Frustrated it's not in its usual spot, she starts to lower herself to the floor, wondering if it fell underneath the couch or one of the chairs. That's when she glances at Jonathan's empty recliner, where it rests innocently enough.

Odd.

"What's it doing in his chair?" she mutters, staring at it in confusion. Scratching her head for a moment, Deborah suddenly remembers the loud stranger demanding payment.

But for what, she hasn't a clue.

Deborah rocks herself slowly back and forth, an unsuccessful attempt to self-soothe. She keeps envisioning the man as she stares out the picture window. Her diminished recollection tells her the memory was real, down to his contorted face.

But she's doubtful about their interaction. Involved in an internal battle with herself about what she saw, she's relieved to hear the wheezing of Robert's beat-up truck coming up the drive, the exhaust pipe sounding like a smoker's cough.

She prefers his presence so she doesn't have to be alone with her memories. Lately, they've been nothing if not frightening.

CHAPTER 5
Deborah

The grocery store is a good twenty miles away, and Deborah waits until she dodges the pothole to call Robert.

Deborah has learned from experience that half a mile after you bounce over it, cell service becomes available. It's the reason for many flat tires, yet the city refuses to fix the soon-to-be sinkhole, made worse every year by the snowplows and farm equipment that bump over it. The county says it's not within their jurisdiction, so she's left veering off to the side to avoid the natural crater's jarring consequence.

"We need to talk," Deborah says as soon as he answers. "I keep getting all these weird crank calls and hang-ups."

"Where are you?"

"I'm headed to the grocery store."

"Okay. I'll come to meet you. I'm about to take a lunch break."

"Except . . ." When Deborah admits she's in a neighboring town, he chuckles at her but agrees to drive that way, with a gentle reminder he won't be able to stay long.

They agree to meet in the produce aisle, as clichéd as it sounds, before they disconnect.

Deborah's wrapping a sprig of rosemary in a plastic bag when he appears by her side. He greets her warmly, his smile making her giddy inside, even though she's filled with dread.

"I got another letter from the Department of Transportation." Deborah tosses a bag of organic carrots next to the herbs.

"About what?"

"They want my land to build a road for nothing more than convenience. Can you believe that?" She frowns. "It's not for sale, but they're claiming eminent domain."

"I heard they wanted to expand, connect the county route to the expressway." His fingers clasp the metal of the cart.

"My father would be rolling over in his grave," Deborah mutters. "And so would his ancestors. Why would I care about accessibility? I live out here for a reason," she says bitterly. "No one bothers me, and I don't bother them." Her shoulders droop. "Or at least, no one used to."

"I bet they'll eventually come for my land." He sighs. "The economic development they claim will result isn't as necessary as they want us to believe. Though," he ponders, "maybe it's not such a bad thing."

"How can you say that?"

"Because maybe it's time for a change." He cocks an eye at her. "I was hoping someday soon we could talk about our future."

Deborah holds her breath. "What do you mean?"

He leans down to whisper in her ear. "Maybe us starting a life together, if you'll have me."

"Like moving in together?"

"That." He guffaws. "Among other things. Potentially moving somewhere else. Somewhere warm."

"I didn't take you as the kind that would want to leave your roots."

"I know it's a lot to consider since my kids are here, but it might be a good change for us." He squints at her. "You ready to battle another winter?"

"No," she concedes. "But the kids don't know about me; won't it be a pretty sudden bomb to drop on them?"

"Yes. Which is why I'm not trying to rush us into making an impulsive decision. I just want us to consider our options. I will tell them soon about us," he promises. "I'm just waiting for the right time." She wants to protest he's been saying this for months, but it's a useless argument. It's a sensitive topic. She knows his kids have had a hard go of it, considering they lost their mother.

Watching Robert walk ahead and grab a carton of milk in the dairy aisle, she's aware of how time has aged him. His shoulders aren't as straight as they used to be; now he has a slight stoop from not only time but stress and heartbreak.

Both of them have shouldered a lot in the preceding years.

Deborah maneuvers the cart, absentmindedly tossing items in until the cart groans as one of the wheels catches on an endcap display, upsetting the cereal boxes. An overworked and underpaid grocery clerk stops stocking a shelf to gawk at the commotion. Deborah hurriedly fixes the capsized cardboard and keeps moving.

His voice appears back beside her, a calming presence. "It'll all be okay."

"I don't know." Deborah sniffs. "Can we make this work?"

"Of course."

"I need you now more than ever." She gently strokes his thumb.

"I'm here for you, Debbie."

After deciding to make a stew later, Deborah adds beef bouillon cubes and chuck steak to the cart's contents. Then, realizing she didn't grab all the ingredients on her initial walk through the produce aisle, she glances up at the fluorescent lighting and scans the colorful array of fruits and vegetables. She likes to watch the misters, the whoosh of the jets as they spray the produce at different times, the cleanness and freshness of this area in particular.

The sudden thud startles her as a plastic bag with a white onion lands in the cart.

"You read my mind." Deborah smiles at Robert.

"I know exactly what you need." Robert gives her hand a squeeze before glancing at his watch. "Unfortunately, I've gotta get back to work. Talk to you later?"

Nodding as Robert disappears from sight, she's amazed at the way he vanishes like a long-ago memory, without a lingering whiff of spicy cologne in his wake.

It's better than the alternative, the smell of whiskey and sweat she swore her husband couldn't scrub off his skin, no matter how hard he tried.

After moving aimlessly through the aisles, she heads to the conveyor belt to check out.

As she's loading her groceries into the back seat of the ancient Ford, Deborah is at first giddy, thinking of having Robert all to herself.

When she finishes stacking the last of her reusable tote bags, she slams the door. Trying to be a good citizen of the world, she goes to return her cart to the designated corral.

Her hands pause on the warm metal as goose bumps rise on the back of her neck, signaling that someone is watching.

Deborah can feel eyes on her.

Trying to be subtle, she pretends to search for a place to return the cart so she can find out who's watching her. Using her hand to shield against the direct sunlight, she's able to slide her gaze across the parking lot.

Sure enough, a man's intently staring at her from the comfort of his vehicle. She tries to place where she might know him from, whether it be at church or around town, but there's nothing memorable about his burgundy truck or his license plate. The plate belongs to a different county, and though she knows most of the people here from the neighboring towns, he doesn't strike her as a familiar face.

His hairy arm lazily hangs out the window, and she notices a snake tattoo wrapped around his bicep.

Anxious about walking her cart to the stall since it means passing him, she shifts from foot to foot, hesitating. *It's not illegal for people to sit at the grocery store,* she berates herself. *Or look out the window.*

Walking as briskly as she can with a limp, she passes him, noticing the red bandana wrapped around his scalp. She wonders if he has a shaved head or is going bald underneath the faded fabric, or maybe another tattoo is stretched over his skull.

She shoots him a dirty look, just in case, just so he doesn't get any ideas.

His voice carries out of his open window, but Deborah doesn't bother to stop, sure he's hollering at someone else in the lot. Maybe his buddy or wife is in the store shopping for groceries, and he's their ride.

As she darts her eyes toward him, he yells something, but Deborah's not close enough to hear, nor does she want to backtrack and lessen their distance. Something about him makes her nervous.

A loud honk startles her, and tripping over her clogs, she stumbles on the pavement and goes down hard. The same aggressive driver gives another sharp beep as the woman driving swerves around her.

Sighing, Deborah wipes her hands, dirty and indented from the pebbled ground, on her pants. By now, her cart has drifted into the center of the lot. Deborah mutters something unsavory, forgetting about the man suspiciously watching her for a second.

It's not for long, since a powerful thud draws her attention from her skinned knee to over her shoulder.

His burly figure has exited his truck, and his vast body barrels toward her. If he wasn't a wrestler in his formative years, she'd be surprised.

When she landed on the ground, her purse spilled some of the contents and loose change, and breath mints are rolling on the cement, glinting in the sunlight.

The runaway cart has now settled against a parked car.

"Ma'am?" The mustached stranger squats down to Deborah's eye level.

Clenching her hands, she whispers, "What do you want?"

He reaches a hand down for the strap of her handbag and swoops it up. "Just helping you with this."

"Not today, you aren't." Deborah screams, frantically waving her hands at a couple walking by, "Help! Someone, please help me!"

The thirtysomething man runs over to her side, concern etched on his face. "Is there a problem?" His female companion has already yanked out her phone, ready to place an emergency call if needed.

"This man"—Deborah points at the apelike man—"tried to mug me."

"What in the hell?" The mustache jumps up. "That's not true."

Confusion is on all three faces as each one peers at the others. The female bystander stares at all of them in morbid curiosity.

"You have my purse." Deborah motions to his hands.

He's taken aback, because indeed, he's grasping her purse; the beefy man knows what this looks like to the couple. They exchange a smirk as his jaw hangs in bewildered silence. "I was just doing you a favor, trying to help you."

"Would you please hand her back her purse," the hero asks politely.

"This is a misunderstanding, is all," the man blathers. "She fell. I was only offering her some assistance."

Deborah shifts impatiently, waiting until he hands, no, shoves the handbag into her arms.

"Looks like you lost a few things." The woman motions to the ground. "Let me get that." The young lady leans over and picks up the mints and change, returning them to Deborah.

"Thank you." Deborah smiles at the couple. "I appreciate your help."

Avoiding the pointed stare of the incredulous stranger, she spins around and hurries toward her car. She can feel his eyes drilling into her back as she puts distance between them, but she doesn't dare glance over her shoulder to confirm this suspicion.

With a slam of the car door, she fumbles with the lock. Careful to check her mirrors to make sure he's not in pursuit of her, she guns the engine too fast, and the vehicle shoots forward like a rocket.

Deborah's eyes dart back and forth between her side mirror and the windshield as she exits the parking lot, her mind a disorganized mess, more chaotic with each passing mile. Focused on what's behind her in the rearview mirror, she isn't paying attention to the road and the bulky object bolting across the center strip. Swerving too late to avoid what she suspects is wildlife, she braces for impact. Her body jerks forward as she stomps on the brakes, and relieved she wore her seat belt, Deborah waits for the deafening sound of scraping metal and the thud of a carcass.

The car grinds to a screeching halt, the smell of burnt rubber causing her to cough. It takes her a second to realize it's from the friction and heat of the tread on the road as she ground to a stop.

Dazed, she rubs her neck and peers out the window, expecting to see a wounded animal that's now roadkill. But there's no lifeless body splattered across the concrete.

She removes her seat belt and shakily steps out of the car, suspecting the animal ran into the fields. When she walks back toward what she assumes is the scene of the crime, there's no telltale sign of blood or matted fur, only tire marks.

Swallowing hard, Deborah slowly turns in a full circle, carefully considering her surroundings and the absence of wild animals and traffic. A feeling of defeat is tugging at her consciousness.

"I know I saw something," she mutters.

Even though she's relieved her vehicle and the suspected animal went unharmed, Deborah is apprehensive as she repositions herself in the driver's seat, telling herself she's being paranoid because of the incident at the grocery store. She might not be able to trust others easily, but she can trust herself, right? She knows what she saw, and that's all that matters. Her hands tremble on the wheel as she drives under the speed limit the rest of the way home, her eyes wildly squinting from side to side at the open road, sure another object is going to lurch across her path.

PART TWO
SIBLEY

CHAPTER 6
Sibley

It's barely 6:00 a.m. on a Friday, but I'm already frazzled, juggling multiple items in my arms. Wishing I had an extra set of hands that could follow me around and hold a catcher's mitt underneath my struggling grasp, I sigh.

The struggle is real as I focus on staying upright without spilling my iced coffee or tripping over my own feet.

Unfortunately, my twentysomething paralegal and right-hand woman, Leslie, isn't due in for another hour.

My rigid grip on the plastic tumbler keeps my drink at arm's length from my black-and-white pin-striped blouse, lest it dribble down the front and necessitate an outfit change before my first meeting of the day. Believe me when I say this has happened more than once; a change of clothes is now stowed in my office closet.

Some call me clumsy, others headstrong, depending on if they're my friends or the opposing counsel.

In my other hand, I'm carrying a laptop case and a half-zipped gym bag, having just finished a workout in our office's downstairs exercise facility. One tennis shoe rests on the carpet while I shove my foot into a stiletto heel.

I wince as my poor pinkie toe swipes the uncomfortable edge of the navy suede, another blister earned from taking the stairs up to the sixteenth floor instead of using the elevator. I'm a glutton for punishment, I guess, or maybe it's an accurate reflection of my life, the constant maneuvering and balancing act I have to do to keep up a well-heeled and well-manicured facade as the only female divorce attorney in my office.

I fumble with the lock on my door, and using my weight, I jam my side into the wood, creating a broad enough passage to let the bulk of my body and bags in.

The refillable cup starts to tip, and muttering a curse word, I hurriedly cross the office to set it upright on my solid glass desk, just in time.

Then, after shoving a coaster that resembles a brass-plated white agate underneath the Colombian roast, I settle into my plush leather chair to finish the task of changing out of my other shoe. I don't think a stiletto on the right and a running shoe on the left would be a convincing fashion statement, but maybe I can defer to Yeezy on that.

After gently tugging my hair out from the ponytail holder, I shake out my strawberry-blonde locks and use my hands and some dry shampoo to add body, my day-old blowout still holding its end of the bargain.

At least something is. I smirk, thinking about my marriage.

Holden and I have been together since our early twenties, and a decade later, we've hit a rough patch.

A few months ago, he got tenure at his university, and I was ecstatic for him. He'd been working toward this for years, and it was the career trajectory he wanted.

Me, not so much, and my stance is admittedly selfish.

I was used to his career taking a back seat to mine. It was the argument I always had in my back pocket. Being the breadwinner, I could toss that in the ring when it came to chores or as justification for how I spent our money, my needs always at the top. And now that the tables have turned, I've become the resentful and nagging wife. After his promotion, the little time we have together has been sucked up not only by teaching but by his research and mixers, and our relationship is no longer a priority.

Worse yet, Holden no longer seems to need or want my opinion or validation.

I draw in a depressed breath, staring at the three-foot swordlike plant sitting on the ledge underneath the window. Called a snake plant, it adds coziness to my midcentury office, the furniture and decor reminiscent of an era gone by but not forgotten. I'm not a fan of the scaly reptiles, but the snake plant was a gift from a client.

I gulp, not sure *client* is the right word.

I touch a finger to my lips.

Friend, maybe.

Ever since that night a couple weeks ago, my husband might beg to differ on this point.

So we skidded from one rough patch into another onerous stretch.

Outside, a shrill blare from city traffic interrupts my thoughts. I'm about to glance out the window when a buzzing in my purse distracts me.

I ransack the contents of my catchall handbag and dig my phone out on the last ring.

"Speak of the devil," I mutter.

Before I can say hello, my husband says coldly, "We need to talk." I'm startled at his tone. He adds, "It's urgent."

I hastily reach forward for my coffee, instead catching the cup with my elbow. It topples over, the dark liquid pooling over the transparent glass, its movement swift as it spreads over the length of my desk.

"Shit," I murmur.

"So," the voice accuses, "you know what it's about?"

"No," I sigh. "I just spilled my coffee."

Frantically, I open the frosted-glass desk drawers in search of a leftover napkin. My hands shake as I fumble with a couple of airplane bottles of vodka, both empty. They roll around in the drawer, loose and free, rattling underneath a pile of papers.

I rummage around for anything I can use to wipe the desk off, then push them aside, unable to find anything useful.

Glancing at my watch, I ask, "When do you want to talk? Tonight work?"

"How about now?"

My eyes home in on a tissue box on the middle table that separates the two chairs across from my desk.

Jackpot.

"Give me a minute," I offer. "Let me check my calendar."

I tap the mute button and set the phone down before rushing to clean up the mess I've made. The liquid has taken over the desktop, and I catch droplets about to plunge onto the plush navy carpeting in my office.

An aggravated scowl appears on my face, and I'm annoyed I didn't ask for tile flooring.

After sopping up what's left of my morning drink, I toss the tissues in my wastebasket and settle back in my chair.

"Sibley?" Annoyance penetrates the silence. "You there?"

Taking the phone off mute, I respond, "Uh-huh. I can spare a few minutes now. My next meeting's in a half hour."

"You do that," he hisses. "I'm glad you can spare some billable hours. If we need more time, should I make an appointment with Leslie?"

"Whoa!" I snap. "What's wrong?"

"You clearly know."

"Obviously, I don't." I reach for a pen cap to chew on, something to refocus my mind as the usual craving hits. I need to focus on this conversation when what I really want is a drink. I lick my lips, thinking about the bottle stashed in my closet, underneath my change of clothes and a raincoat for the few days a year a monsoon or thunderstorm unleashes a torrent of rain.

I'm better than this, I tell myself, but it doesn't ease the longing.

Exasperated, he asks, "Do you have something to tell me?"

"You know I don't like these games." I chomp down hard on the plastic. "I'm trying to be available, but I don't have much time, so what gives?"

"Fine, then. I'll cut to the chase." Holden lets a pregnant pause linger. His flair for the dramatic is giving me an ulcer. "Why am I looking at a dating profile for you?"

This is not what I expected to hear out of his mouth. I thought he was referencing something else entirely.

The stash of empty bottles I've hidden all over the house.

Our joint checking account, which I've depleted.

I'm baffled. "A dating profile . . . for me?"

"Repeating what I say only buys you time and further implicates your guilt, Sibley."

"I'm processing the words you just said," I say. "You're staring at a dating profile of me?"

"Yes."

"Care to share it?"

"You wrote it, so you should know. And I quote, 'Just looking to see what my options are. To be up front and scare you away, I'm still married, still unclear on what I want from this, but easily available if I think we'll have some fun. Are you still reading? You are, aren't you?'"

Speechless, I open my mouth and then close it.

"Oh, and then you added a devil emoji. I must say these pictures are very flattering. Going risqué on a public site is ballsy for you, and with your career, it seems a bit over the top, but lately, you have been reckless."

Even with the air-conditioning blasting through the vents, a bead of cold perspiration trickles down my lower back and into the black pencil skirt I'm wearing. The chilliness of my office doesn't make up for the dread dripping into my waistband.

The phone chimes in my ear, signaling a text. I glance down to see a screenshot of my supposed dating profile.

It's certainly me; there's no denying that. My stomach drops three more times as the accompanying pictures come through.

The first is my professional headshot. I'm buttoned up in a suit jacket with a camisole underneath, my hair and makeup expertly applied, the smattering of freckles across the bridge of my nose absent. This one is used on the firm's website and in marketing materials. Hell, it's on various billboards throughout the valley. I used to take a different route to avoid it on my way to work.

Gaping at the other three photos, I'm confused. These aren't for public consumption. In one, I'm scantily clad in a bikini, holding a piña colada while relaxing on a white-sand beach. It was taken a little over a year ago in Key West on a much-needed vacation, and if you look closely, Holden's tan shoulder is next to my freckled one.

The next is a seductive pose, my blonde sex kitten hair big and tangled, a come-hither look in my green eyes. I'm wearing lingerie, a black corset and thong, the result of a night when I had too many glasses of merlot and a pang of deep sadness I couldn't shake unless it was with an AmEx card. The $700 price tag I could stomach more easily than the empty pit in my gut. The need to feel sexy was worth the high price, except he didn't appreciate it one bit.

My jaw clenches at this memory.

In the final pic, I flash a coquettish smile at the camera, one of my hands tucked into the front of my white lace panties, leaving little to the imagination. I'm engaged in an intimate moment touching myself and enjoying it, taunting the photographer.

A flush rapidly spreads down my neck. The last two photos were supposed to be private. He promised me only I'd see them, and I've never shown them to anyone. I saved them in the cloud. Could someone have hacked them?

But why?

Because they're borderline pornographic, I chide myself.

"Are you there?"

"Yes," I manage to whisper.

"You don't seem to have much to say."

Biting my nail, I struggle to think of anything else to add in my defense. I must be a shitty attorney if I can't make a solid case on my own behalf. "I bought that lingerie a couple of months ago." I shrug. "You had no interest."

"Hmm . . ." His voice rasps. "Looks like you showed it to someone."

"No." I stare closely at the last picture, at my painted red lips and kitten eyeliner.

His voice rises an octave. The tone is less controlled and hysterical— a perfect match for the unsettled thoughts in my mind. "I don't believe you."

I keep my chin up, glad he can't see it quivering. "We can talk about this tonight."

"Is there anything to talk about?"

"I didn't—" I start to say, but just as quickly, I close my mouth.

"First, your birthday, and now online dating? You're *fucking* unbelievable."

Pressing my eyes shut, I try to remember, but it's all a haze—a loop. I heard about different dating apps from friends who rejoined the dating pool after messy divorces or because they hadn't met anyone the organic way, whatever that is anymore.

A few nights ago, when I was out, or maybe it was last week, I went to a happy hour with a group of women for networking opportunities. We all work in different industries, and usually, there is an eclectic mix. It's once a month, and it's great because there are always new people who join.

A topic of conversation that came up was how vastly different dating is in this day and age, compared to the experiences of those of us who have been married a long time, which is a decade in my case. This prompted a couple of the women to show the different types of apps they were on, which then brought out a comical array of stories from everyone, mostly about first dates. I could hardly take a sip of my wine, I was laughing so hard.

I was curious at the types of profiles some of the women described, and a few offered to show me. One newbie to the group showed me how a couple of the apps worked. All she had to do was swipe left or right. She talked about the "thrill" of swiping, how it was like a fun game.

I toyed with the idea of setting up a profile just for curiosity's sake. *But I didn't, did I?*

Or did I?

Holden interrupts my thoughts. "You didn't what?"

"Huh?" I rub my temples. "Nothing."

My hands start to shake, and when I rub them together, they are ice cold. The chills racing up and down my body cause me to wonder if I should be home in bed. Maybe I'm coming down with something.

Or maybe it's guilt.

It could even be my own lack of awareness, a missing memory I can't seem to retrieve.

I wouldn't have used those pictures to set up a dating profile.

I couldn't have.

I rest my head in my hands. But what if . . .

No, Sib, don't go there . . .

What if I was a couple of bottles deep?

You're a lot of things, but you're not your father, I warn. *Stop transferring his bad behavior onto yourself.* As much as I loved my father, I don't want to end up like him. I didn't see his anger so much as I saw him feebly controlling it. He'd be most accurately described as a bitter alcoholic.

No. *No way.* I'd never embarrass Holden or myself like that. We have our share of problems, but not to the extent I'd advertise my rocky relationship status on a dating site with provocative photographs he didn't know about just to get back at him.

Our careers are important to us, and with them, our privacy. I know what it's like to grow up in a family under constant scrutiny, plagued by rumors and innuendos. Holden and I both understand how critical it is to keep our personal issues to ourselves. It works for our public persona, yet it's crippling to the sustainability of our marriage to shove down unresolved issues like a college frat boy guzzling shots.

Except, the annoying voice of reason in my head chirps, *you do stupid shit when you've been drinking.*

I groan.

"Sibley, are you even listening?"

"Of course." I panic, worried I've missed something he's said. "Where are you?"

"Home for the moment. I'm about to leave for class."

"I thought you didn't have class until one?"

"I have a meeting at ten. It's on the shared calendar." His smug voice makes me want to smack him. "You know, the Google Calendar you insisted we start using?"

Refusing to engage in this battle, I ignore the snarky comment. "Tonight, then."

The door barrels open, and startled, I frown at the intrusion, the phone glued to my ear. The only person who doesn't knock consistently is my redheaded Amazon woman of a paralegal, Leslie.

Still, even she knows to announce herself before strolling in first thing in the morning.

Except it's not her but my wrinkled seventy-two-year-old boss, Roger Felderman, one of three managing partners of the firm.

His office is one above, but it might as well be on a different planet.

Only the three of them—Roger, Paul, and John—have luxurious suites on the seventeenth floor, their offices inaccessible to the rest of the building. Primarily I see them in monthly meetings or at company galas. They only come down to our level, literally and figuratively, when someone deserves a promotion or royally fucks up.

I think about all the cases I've won and how dedicated I am to my clients here. I've always wanted to be made partner, but it seems like it will be another five years before that will be possible. Maybe the latest case has shown them how much they need me in this corner office and on a fast track to becoming the first woman partner in the firm.

Maybe it's time, I think excitedly.

"Roger," I say out loud, automatically disconnecting and turning the ringer off.

Hurriedly, I scan my blouse and skirt for coffee stains. As always, Roger looks immaculate in his suit and polished shoes, his white hair still thick, his back straight as a steel rod.

I realize too late the empty vodka bottles are lined up on my desk next to my now-empty iced coffee.

"Sibley." He acknowledges me with a curt nod. "Mind if I come in for a minute?" It seems a silly question since he's already invaded my territory.

"Depends"—I offer him a big smile—"if it's good news or not."

He doesn't return my smile, which automatically worries me.

"You may certainly come in." I stand and cross the room, relieved I've changed into my heels so my five-six height doesn't diminish against his imposing figure. "You're always welcome to visit. I don't see you enough."

He doesn't acknowledge this comment; his troubled eyes simply scan the contents of the desk, narrowing in on the liquor bottles.

Shit. I wipe my sweaty palms on my skirt.

It's too late. I can't swoop them into the trash, since they've already been spotted.

"Mimosas for breakfast?"

"No." I titter nervously. "I found those in my drawer from our last company mixer."

In college, I was required to attend sobriety classes as punishment for a public-intoxication ticket. A man there taught me an invaluable trick. As the CEO of a large organization, he spent most of his time with stakeholders and clients, which meant lots of drinks, dinners, boozing, and schmoozing. He recommended I order a club soda and Sprite to keep in hand so that I wasn't pestered continuously to have another and so I could control my sobriety in a room full of avid drinkers.

This method means I have total control.

Until lately, that is.

Roger motions toward the door. "I didn't see Leslie at her desk, so I thought it would be a good time to catch you."

"She's in at eight."

"Any potential new cases?"

"I have one in about fifteen minutes."

"No problem. This won't take long." He motions to the other chair. "Why don't you have a seat?"

This can't be good, a managing partner asking me to sit in my own office.

"Fine." My legs would have given out if not for the chair, so I gratefully settle into the leather. I picked out these chairs because they're luxurious enough to relax in, and though they mold to fit you like a glove, they have enough support, so you don't sink into them.

Believe it or not, I learned a lot about furniture and easing clients into tense, lengthy conversations by testing out different seating arrangements. I just didn't think I'd be on the receiving end. I physically shove my hand under my thigh to keep from bringing it to my mouth, one of my bad habits Roger doesn't need to see.

"Sibley." His vibrant blue eyes are fixated on mine. "You've been a great addition to the team for the eight years you've been part of this firm. You're a remarkable lawyer with an uncanny ability to get to the crux of the matter, and that's what I'm going to do right now—just rip the Band-Aid off and get to the heart of it."

I slowly nod.

"Paul and John and I, we've never questioned your judgment." There's a slight pause. "Or integrity. Or I should say, we haven't had to until recently." His eye contact never wavers. "We take our responsibilities in this field and client relationships very seriously here."

"Yes, we do."

"That's why this is so disappointing to our group."

I stare at him blankly.

"We received a complaint."

Spit it out! my brain screams. "Stemming from what?"

"It's unethical to sleep with a client, Sibley. I don't need to tell you the legal ramifications or the risk you're putting yourself at—and the firm." His hand gingerly touches his impeccable hair. "Not to mention the other questions your lack of judgment raises."

Stuttering, "I don't understand."

"You're married. At least, you were." He shakes his head. "Maybe not after this."

"Who am I . . . what are you talking about?"

"You know I would approach you first about any concern regarding inappropriate behavior. I'm not one to mince words, but this came to Paul's attention, and we discussed it privately. We've kept an eye on the situation, and it's unfortunate." Glumly, he stares at me. "Hell, maybe we should have acted right away and not waited. I don't think any of us wanted to believe it."

"I'm not sure what you're talking about." I wipe my clammy palms on the chair.

"We have photos."

Mortified, I ask, "From a dating profile?"

He tilts his head. "I beg your pardon?"

"Nothing."

"Even though your client interaction happened after you left the building, we were still notified. It doesn't change the impropriety of it."

"With all due respect, Roger, can you please tell me who this involves?" I'm louder than I intend, and the voice in my head commands my composure. It is, after all, a sign of a seasoned attorney, the ability to remain calm under pressure. The partners don't do well with feminine wails, from what I've seen with the staff.

"You should know who you're sleeping with," he spits out. "I shouldn't have to tell you. Mr. Marcona."

"Nico?" I gasp. "You think I'm sleeping with Nico Marcona?" There is such a thing as a dumb question, and I have my answer. His mouth is a flat line. "We only went out one time," I hurriedly add. "For drinks. To discuss his case. Nothing happened."

Nico's divorce required a lot of time, and it's true I didn't mind his presence. We spent a lot of time discussing his case and how to proceed, and in the beginning, we had clear boundaries. He would come to the office during regular business hours, and someone would always be around, other attorneys or Leslie.

But as we got more comfortable with each other, I did a poor job of keeping my personal and professional lives separate, and I made a rookie mistake: I confided too much in him about my own problems.

The lines became distinctly blurred.

And then the night of my birthday happened.

"Sibley, do me a favor. Don't look me in the eye and lie to me. You're better than that. You've put your career at risk, and your future with the firm." He eyes me sadly. "I know temptation runs rampant in life and especially with this type of clientele." He sighs. "We've had eight years together. I don't want to think even worse of the situation . . ."

"And me," I finish.

He nods.

"I'm . . ."

He holds up a hand. "I'm going to have Tim come in and pack up your office."

CHAPTER 7
Sibley

"What?" I shake my head incredulously. "You're firing me?"

"This is a serious breach of trust, not to mention an ethical dilemma, considering a bar complaint could be filed. Piss off the wrong person, and this could become a serious transgression. It is, don't get me wrong, but we are going to deal with it internally." Roger slaps his knee. "We have to take the best course of action for the firm in case this blows up in our face."

"And in this case, you're terminating me?"

"Not exactly."

"What does that mean?"

"We want you to get help."

"With what?" I slump in my chair. "I'm not a sex addict. What is this even about?"

"Not that type of addiction," he says uncomfortably. "Unless that's an issue too."

"*Who* wants me to get help?"

"The partners. Paul. John. Myself." He waves his hand helplessly. "Even Dr. Bradford."

Wait, Holden's been involved in this decision? Son of a bitch. I clasp my hands together so he doesn't see them shaking.

Roger continues. "We do care about you, Sibley. That's why we want to approach this with some sensitivity." He clears his throat. "Your husband mentioned you'd had a rough childhood, compounded by mental illness in your mother and the tragic death of your father."

Wait, Holden mentioned my *upbringing* to my bosses? When?

I grit my teeth. Roger waits for me to respond, but I'm focused on Holden and the final nail he's pounded in the coffin of our marriage. All bets are now off when it comes to my husband.

As he waves his hand toward my desk and the offending bottles, there's an awkward pause. "That's why we want to see if we can remedy this among ourselves."

"It's not what you think . . ."

"Paul used to struggle with alcohol addiction, and he's been sober now for ten years."

"I don't have a drinking problem," I say quietly. "And I have a meeting in five."

"You're missing the point, my dear. My secretary already spoke to Leslie. Your next appointment is no longer your concern; it's been reassigned."

"I'm not . . ."

"There's nothing more to say, Sibley. Do what we ask, and let's hope we can move forward. We're suspending you without pay in the hopes you will focus on recovery."

I think about the savings account I drained. Someone might as well put me out of my misery now. "What, exactly, are you asking me to do?"

"Tim has the packet. It outlines the requirements for us to reinstate you." He winces. "I'm afraid it's not going to be easy to earn our trust back, if that's even what you want."

"I want to keep my job," I say shakily. "Keep being the best at what I do."

With a glance at my ring finger, he says, "If you do decide to pursue this thing with Mr. Marcona, be warned, it will result in your immediate dismissal."

My jaw drops. I count to ten in my head to save myself from saying something I'll regret later on.

Roger rises slowly, but with the confidence of a distinguished attorney who's been practicing for the length of time I've been alive. He can't be rushed, even after having a difficult conversation.

"The plant," I say. "Can you make sure the plant is watered?"

He gives me an odd stare.

"It releases oxygen during the day instead of at night," I lamely add.

Raising a bushy brow, he says, "Your office will still be taken care of."

Tim appears in the doorway as suddenly as Roger disappears, an empty cardboard box in hand. "Sibley Bradford." He shakes his head; pity laces his voice. "Today is not your day."

I raise my chin at him haughtily. "Depends on who you ask."

"What do you need?" He waves his arm around the office. "I'll pack it up and walk you out."

"My purse, laptop . . ."

He holds a hand up to interrupt.

"Items out of the closet," I finish.

"The laptop is company issued. You can't take it with you."

"But it has all of my case files."

"Orders from Roger." He throws his hands in the air. "Don't shoot the messenger."

I brush a strand of hair behind my ear in frustration as Tim follows me around the office like I'm on an invisible leash, scanning the items I grab, tossing them in the box.

Without asking and despite my protests, he starts to rifle through my gym bag and laptop case before proudly removing a computer charger, as if feeling self-important at this discovery. "This has to stay."

I roll my eyes.

"Anything else?" he asks innocently.

I motion to the closet. "I have a small plastic container in there, filled with some personal effects." Mostly sentimental: it contains some old photos and accolades I've received over the years, including a box of stationery that belonged to my mother. I've written a few personal letters on the pale-yellow paper, and each time, I catch a lingering whiff of the floral scent of her patchouli.

As Tim reaches onto the top shelf and pulls out the bin, I stand close enough to steal a glance over his shoulder, studying the contents of the closet for my stash of vodka.

"Anything else?" Giving me a side-eye, he notices my stumped gaze on the shelf. "If you're looking for the bottles, they've all been removed."

"What do you mean, 'all'?" I murmur.

"There were multiple."

"One." I shake my head. "Maybe two."

"Six."

"We have a lot of clients that like to drink," I say defensively.

He shrugs. "Doesn't matter to me, Mrs. Bradford."

"When were they taken?" It sounds as if we're talking about a person, a child, being removed from its custodial parents.

"Last night."

"Well, you did a poor job. You missed all the airplane bottles," I say sourly.

"No, I didn't. They were all empty."

My face reddens. "Do you know why I'm being asked to take a leave of absence?"

"The bottles gave me a hint." Tim frowns and quickly pats me on the arm. "My brother had a wicked drinking problem."

"What happened to him?"

"Well," Tim says sadly, "he died."

"Of cirrhosis or another type of liver disease?"

"No." Tim motions me out the door. "He hit and killed a pedestrian."

"On second thought, wait!" I quickly retrieve the snake plant, grunting at its heaviness. Tim gives me a confused look, and I snap, "It was a gift, and it's mine."

I'm standing numbly as Tim locks up my door when my colleague and friend Tanner Ellis comes around the corner. I hadn't thought far enough to consider the humiliation of being walked out in front of my cronies.

As particles of soil spill out of the top of the terra-cotta pot balanced precariously in my arms, I question why I bothered with the damn plant, but it doesn't take Freud to know why. It was a gift from Nico, and it's not like I was the one keeping it alive. Our night cleaning crew watered and tended to it like it was their own.

It thrived, unlike our professional relationship, which is now wilted and dead.

My face burns at the sight of Tanner gaping when he notices the box of my belongings cradled in Tim's arms.

Shock and confusion are apparent in our wordless but powerful eye contact.

"Take the stairs," Tanner says with finality. "Brett and Connor are on their way up."

I nod my thanks as Tim glances at my stilettos and then my face. With confidence I don't feel, I march to the stairs and yank the heavy door open, the metal staircase uninviting, on par with my blatant dismissal.

Tim takes the descent of sixteen floors without missing a beat. He goes into morbid details with painstaking clarity about his brother's suicide after he accidentally killed someone.

When we reach the bottom, I can only offer him a sympathetic whisper.

My Tesla sits in its covered parking spot, the block lettering on the sign announcing it's reserved for Buckley, Felderman, Shackler & Associates.

I pop the trunk as he settles the box in the back. The hefty manila packet that Roger sent home catches my eye, but not before a loose bottle of vodka captures Tim's.

Once rolled up tightly in a towel, the bottle has unwound itself and is now noticeable. Our expressions freeze, and I watch him watch me. His brown eyes meet mine, and I see him for the first time not as our security guard but as a person who has suffered an enormous loss. There's a heavy sorrow behind his gaze.

"Please come back," he says. And I wonder if it's as much about the job as it is about the implications if I don't. Because if I don't return, it'll mean my own demise, and I might have a tragic tale on par with his late brother's.

Before I can shut the lid of the trunk, his hand snatches the bottle out.

I stare after Tim as he walks away, whistling a song I've heard but can't place. The lyrics are forgotten, but the melody is haunting.

CHAPTER 8
Sibley

Safe from the outside world for the moment, I lean against the headrest, listlessly closing my eyes to the morning sounds of birds and chatter as the world moves on around me. My fingers hang on to the steering wheel like mere threads that, if plucked, will cause me to lose my last remaining grip on reality.

As much as I fight it, I don't have the power to push away the memories, at least not today. A wise person once said a single deviation from a plan can change the trajectory, good or bad, and four months ago, my course was interrupted in one fell swoop.

On that fateful day, I was prepping to meet with my next client when Leslie walked in with a man. It turned out to be him, and I felt his presence long before I looked up from my computer.

As soon as he walked into the room, he commanded it.

Demanded it, even.

It wasn't because he was tall or movie-star handsome or because he spoke in sharp staccato taps, enunciating every word.

I would learn it was because he knew how to work a room in a tailored suit molded to his body, complete with a three-day scruff of beard that had more gray than black.

His eyes were not green or hazel but an olive color that would change based on his moods. Darkening when he was pensive, subdued when he was carefree, which was rare.

At six feet, Leslie, standing taller than this man, seemed bowled over by him, his existence enough to overcome her height. "Sibley, this is Mr. Nico Marcona."

I stood, wobbly in my nude pumps, my insides twisting, though I was unclear from what at the time—desire, intrigue, maybe a combination of both.

"Hi, Mr. Marcona." I stepped around my desk to shake his hand. My handshake is firm, reliable. Just like my reputation. "Sibley Bradford. Pleased to meet you."

"Likewise."

Our hands stayed entwined, pumping in the air.

"Mr. Mar—"

"Please! It's Nico."

"Nico, then. Please have a seat." I gave Leslie a megawatt smile. "Thanks, Leslie."

Taking a seat behind my desk, I watched while Nico sank down in one of my two chestnut-colored Italian leather chairs.

Leslie mouthed something totally unprofessional over Nico's head at me. Out loud, she said, "Do you need me to stay and take notes?"

I didn't blame her; she was dying for a chance to breathe the same air as this man. He was a magnet.

"Actually . . ." He twisted his body to consider Leslie. "I'd prefer it was just her and me." The way he delivered the news wasn't condescending but rather apologetic.

"Of course." She gave him a pleasant smile and nodded to me. "I'll be at my desk if you need anything."

While she was exiting, he rested his palms on the smooth leather armrests. "These are really something. Let me guess, Restoration Hardware?"

"Close, but no."

"I'm guessing not a secondhand store."

"I cannot give Goodwill credit."

"Custom?"

"If you must know"—I laughed—"yes."

"Don't worry, I'm not complaining about the exorbitant fees you charge to have this kind of furniture."

"If you were concerned with my retainer, you wouldn't be here." I narrowed my eyes at him. "Then it would be about cost, not outcome." I considered the notepad on my desk. "Plus, it looks like you are a referral. Bill McElroy."

"Your name wasn't just on the tip of his tongue. I've had a couple friends refer you. Say you're one hell of a bulldog."

"I like that, as long as they didn't tell you I resemble one."

"No. They said you were pretty." Nico pauses. "But that word seems paltry, doesn't do you justice."

With a reserved smile, I didn't respond to his compliment. I wanted Mr. Marcona to hire me for my intelligence.

For my ability to win. My record.

I could give him the best possible outcome for his contentious divorce.

"Let's begin," I offered. "I'll take notes the good old-fashioned way." Moving my Montblanc to my notepad, I wrote the date, and when I glanced up, his eyes were locked on my left hand. Specifically, my ring finger.

"Wow." He whistled. "A divorce attorney still married?"

"I'd be more concerned if I were divorced. Meant I hadn't learned my lesson."

"Which is?" He raised a brow at me.

"It's cheaper to stay together." I smirked. "And I kind of like him still."

"How long?"

"Married for over ten."

"No seven-year itch?"

I met his eyes head on; a storm was brewing behind them. "I don't believe in that sentiment."

Nico responded with how I must have been different from most people or had married someone I was better suited to.

Clients tell divorce attorneys every infraction their spouse has committed over the last decade, including burning dinner or leaving dirty dishes in the sink, like those are worthy of the death penalty.

When Nico went into a diatribe explaining how his wife, Christine, didn't want a divorce, I cut him off. "Everyone wants a therapist. I can only offer my services as they pertain to the law," I said. "Vent to girls you meet on dating apps. Or your family and friends."

His jaw hit the floor like a caricature, and a tense silence lingered between us.

As he crossed his arms over his chest, I could tell by Nico's surly demeanor he was shocked at my interruption. People didn't typically barge into his speech. It probably reminded him of Catholic school, and I was the nun chastising him with a ruler across his knuckles.

His hand tugged on his ear, which I would learn was a nervous habit.

"Nico"—he went to protest, but I held up a hand—"I'm going to represent your best interests. I can be your sounding board, but as you pointed out, we're on an expensive clock."

He was taken aback, his eyes becoming putrid green slits as he decided if I was a pretentious bitch or a cutthroat attorney.

I could be both.

If a man said this, he'd be thrilled. They love dick-measuring contests.

But I had tits—great tits, but tits nonetheless.

And Mr. Marcona hadn't bought into my legacy quite yet.

"I can refer you to a great therapist, but all I want are facts about your divorce. Not any marital-dissatisfaction-survey answers."

Those eyes fixed me with a steely gaze. I didn't think it was possible, but they flickered a shade darker as they pinned me to my chair. "Fair enough."

"Let's talk about the law. Assets. Division of both. The nitty gritty."

"Okay." When he steepled his fingers, his jacket sleeve revealed his expensive watch. "I'll let you dominate the conversation."

"Thank you." I tried for stoic.

He must have been placated, because his eyes started to soften, returning to jade green.

"For me to offer the best defense, I need to know everything, and I mean *everything*, as it pertains to finances. Divorces are expensive, but so are fuckups." I never broke eye contact. "Your friends and family have surely offered all sorts of advice. Some of it warranted, mostly frivolous. I need to know about any offshore bank or dummy accounts where you're hiding money you don't want your ex-wife to find. This way"—I leaned forward, his eyes smoldering into mine—"I can either advise you against it or turn a blind eye."

Lifting his hand to signal a question, Nico threw me for a loop. I presumed it would be about money. I was wrong. "What about cheating?"

"I don't care who you are fucking. Neither does the court."

"Not me." His voice soured. "My wife."

"It doesn't matter, since we're a no-fault state." I kept my tone neutral. "Emotions have to be kept in check. Are we clear?"

"Yes, ma'am." He saluted me. "By the way, you'd make one hell of a dominatrix."

"How do you know I don't moonlight as one after work?"

A small chuckle escaped his lips, and I liked the sound of it. Even better, Nico was relaxing in his chair, leaning back into the leather, becoming less rigid.

We were making progress.

"Be glad we aren't in New Mexico, where you can sue the lover of your spouse if they're withholding affection." I raised a brow. "Or in Mississippi, where a reasonable cause for divorce is being an 'idiot.'"

"I wonder what baseline they use," he joked, "to determine if you're an idiot or a *stupid* idiot."

"And worse yet"—I laid a finger against my cheek—"in Tennessee, it takes your spouse poisoning you before you have grounds for a fault divorce."

"So moral of the story, be glad this is a no-fault state?"

"Exactly." I gave him a smug look. "However, it *is* a community property one, which gets everyone twisted up inside. But consider this from both angles. Any children?"

"Three."

"Did your wife give up a lot to raise the kids so you could advance your career?"

"No. She has a nanny and spends her time shopping and cheating."

"Duly noted."

"Also, be forewarned, Mrs. Bradford." Nico frowned. "I'm not out to play dirty, and though you don't want to hear the sordid details, you might want to hear at least one part."

"Which is?"

"Her lover is trying to blackmail me."

And that was the beginning of my introduction to Nico Marcona, who is no longer in need of my services.

Dammit, Nico. I punch the steering wheel angrily with shaking hands. Was it him who ran to the partners and tattled about our evening together?

As I watch my hands tremble, it's as if a 6.9-magnitude earthquake is flowing through my veins, making me convulse in agony.

In the rearview, I see a stiff-lipped and staunch attorney, Jeff Carsten, passing behind me, his voice growing audibly louder. Assuming he's talking to me, I sink down deeper in the leather, fearful I've been spotted.

A sigh of relief escapes my lips as I realize his earbuds are in, his gesticulating arms almost laughable as he talks to someone on the other end.

He'll be unhinged at my abrupt dismissal, I think sourly.

I try to call Leslie, but it goes directly to voice mail. I'm indecisive about whether I should wait for her to arrive so we can have a private conversation or hide my tail between my legs and call her later. Eventually I choose the latter.

Forcing myself to drive, I head toward the busy freeway. It's still early morning and a peak time for rush hour traffic.

Upset and humiliated, I'm in the mood to speed, but it's impossible in the dense morning commute. All I can do is maneuver through the traffic to the far left side, reserved for motorcyclists and high-occupancy or electric vehicles. Then an incoming call flashes on the large screen.

I know the number by heart, yet I've never saved his name in my phone. We don't bother with a greeting since he despises those. It took him a long time to break me of that, a midwestern habit of asking a few generic questions before getting to the "meat on the bone" or the "heart of the matter" ingrained in me.

So I begin with, "Find Christine yet?"

"Looks like she's headed to a loft on Seventh."

"Really?" I tap a finger to set the car on autopilot. "That's too predictable."

"Does it matter where she's headed?" He never usually asks, but this time, he does. "What's it to you who Nico's soon-to-be ex-wife bangs?"

"She has something up her sleeve," I protest. "And it's affecting my client."

"If you say so." I hear him spit. "But it's a community property state, so why do you care?"

"It's personal," I say bluntly.

"My point: it shouldn't be."

Tapping my finger to keep the self-driving feature on, I think of my options. Not ready to confide in Chuck all my suspicions, especially since he knows those involved, I stay silent.

We are longtime acquaintances, and we both know that "friends" would be too far of a stretch. He doesn't make friends with his clients, nor should he. That's why Chuck's excellent in his line of work. As a retired former detective and now a private investigator, he typically researches fraud cases, which prompted his services in the first place. Even with his standoffish demeanor, he's been a mentor and guide since day one.

"We'll just call it your fiduciary duty." He grunts. "By the way, I hear you're on a required sabbatical."

"Already?" I groan. "That was lightning speed." I tense up. "Let me guess, one of the attorneys called you?"

"No shit! You would've made a good Sherlock. Maybe even Nancy Drew. Real insightful. Tanner got to me first."

Opening my mouth to offer a sarcastic retort, I hear him mutter "Fuck" under his breath, then again, with added emphasis.

"Chuck—"

"It's not a loft. It's a house. Gated."

"So?"

"I'm watching her speed through the front gate."

"Congratulations." I'm snarky in my reply. "That's typically what people have to do to enter . . . go through them."

"Yeah. No shit, except it's Seventh and Campbell."

"Wait," I plead. "Tell me Seventh Avenue, not Street."

"Then I'd be lying, just like the woman barreling through the gate." Another curse word follows.

When he repeats the full address, I offer, "Maybe they know each other from a previous life?"

"Sure." He adds disparagingly, "Except in our current reality, she's at his house at eight in the morning."

"What the hell is she doing there?" I seethe. There has to be a reasonable explanation, except none comes to mind.

"I've done work for your firm for years. I told you I'd never get involved in a dispute between the two of you." He pauses for a beat. "But this is fucked."

"I can't deal with this right now," I mutter under my breath. "But I'm on my way over there."

"Sib." He begs me to go home and take care of my own shit, but I respond by disconnecting. When he calls again, I decline, my focus on the next exit, where I get off and speed in the direction I've just come from.

Chuck sends me a text telling me not to bother; the gate is locked, so I can't see anything, and he's already got pictures of Christine Marcona heading in. I wish it were enough, but coupled with my job instability and the recent turn of events, I need an outlet for my frustration and anger.

Stopping at a gas station, I grab a bottle of Tito's Vodka and then make my way to the address that Chuck just left, careful not to stop and draw attention to my movements, a camera peering intently from the iron gate.

I'm familiar with the compound, a large main house built next to a smaller guest one, a circular driveway wrapping around and between the two properties. A relatively empty parking lot is across the street in front of a flower shop and café, so I take my chances and idle, determined to wait until the woman leaves.

I have all day, literally, to sit here, and I must follow this through to the end.

Yanking the Tito's from the paper bag, I unscrew the red cap and start taking small sips. It isn't long before they become longer swallows, and the metal fortress blurs before my eyes.

An incoming call interrupts my pity party, and my colleague Tanner starts rambling before I can even say hello.

Picturing his dark, slicked-back hair, the result of expensive pomade, and the equally exorbitant Italian loafers perched on his desk, I'm anesthetized to his seemingly innocent reaction. "I'm just *sick* about what happened." Glibly, he says, "I never would've agreed to that type of a deal."

"What deal?"

"Come on, Sib. Cut the shit."

"Roger told you guys already?" I act surprised. "And here I signed an NDA."

"I ran into Leslie in the hallway after I passed you." He sighs. "This is just a sorry excuse for them to push you out."

I don't point out Leslie wasn't in the office before I left.

"I'll do my penance," I say. "Maybe it'll be a good disconnect from the world."

"If you say so, but I don't think you've done anything wrong," he says nimbly. "As long as we've been friends, I'd tell you the truth."

"Thanks for suggesting I take the stairs today."

"No problem, Sib." He softens his tone. "It wasn't fair for you to run into the other attorneys like that."

We end our call, and between the sun and the liquor, I end up shutting my eyes, forgetting about my mission. A full-on throttle startles me from my hours-long nap, and I see five missed calls from Chuck. The roaring engine is a dead giveaway for the homeowner's Porsche 911 Turbo. I would know, considering I've been in that very vehicle more times than I can count.

With mounting apprehension, I watch as the gate slowly opens, and the sports car is carefully finessed up the small incline to avoid a collision with the concrete underneath the low chassis.

Hurt by his actions and feeling careless, I try the alleyway, thinking I might get a different vantage point of the two of them. I'm fuming and want nothing more than to catch them in the act.

It's a tight fit, and when I make it through the narrow entrance, a block wall prevents me from viewing anything on the premises, him or her. It's pointless to climb the concrete, since it's so smooth I wouldn't be able to find a foothold.

Disappointed, I gun the engine, and in my haste, I take the corner too fast. Instead of making a smooth entrance onto the road, I end up on the sidewalk, clipping a bright-yellow fire hydrant. As I swerve to avoid more damage, the nose of my Tesla slams into a retaining wall behind it. The hood crumples instantly, and smoke fills the air as the sound of metal scrapes into the unforgiving cement.

Startled by both the impact and my airbag deploying, I manage to toss the bottle in the back seat before I lose consciousness.

CHAPTER 9
Sibley

When my eyes flicker open, it takes a moment to convince myself there's not a football helmet situated on my head. An excruciating pain squeezes like a tight fist around my skull. My hand moves to my forehead, where I connect with gauze instead of my skin.

My throat is parched, as if coated in a solid layer of cotton.

Troubled, I stare down at the watercolor-print duvet covering me. "How did I wind up in my bed?" I murmur, bewildered at the pain that radiates from my clavicle. It feels like I sat in the sun for too long and burned one particular area of my body to a crisp.

Coughing, I struggle to sit up and adjust my position comfortably—it's made difficult by the razor-sharp pain searing from my left side when I twist toward the bottled water on the nightstand.

What in the world happened to me?

"Holden," I call out hoarsely, my voice barely making a dent in the cavernous master.

My eyes dart around the room for my purse, but I don't see the tan leather in its usual spot on the dresser.

"Holden," I try with more emphasis, wanting my phone.

I hear a door slam downstairs and sudden heavy footsteps on the stairs. The door whips open, but instead of Holden, it's Chuck. His longish graying hair is in a ponytail, and his shirt is covered in red splotches.

Puzzled, I ask, "What're you doing here?"

He fixes me with a peculiar gaze.

"And you've got Kool-Aid or something on your shirt."

"You had an accident." He leans against the wall with his arms crossed. "This is your blood."

"An accident?"

"You totaled your car."

"That's impossible." I squint my eyes at him. "What day is it?"

He appears unfazed.

"I was at work," I say stubbornly.

"Except you weren't. You were spying on—"

Before he can finish, Holden stalks into the room, and his blue eyes, his best feature, widen as they spot me seated upright against the headboard, multiple pillows behind my back.

"Thank God." He hurries to my side, his tall frame leaning down as he kisses my cheek gently. "You scared the hell out of me." His soft beard rubs against my skin, annoying me. It's a source of contention between us. I keep asking him to shave the damn thing; he keeps resisting.

Groaning at the pain, I admit, "I'm still not sure what happened."

"You hit a fire hydrant," Chuck offers from across the room. "Followed by a concrete wall."

Holden's relief is short lived after hearing this, his mouth twisting into a frown. He steps back from my side to sag onto the mattress near the foot of the bed.

"Your colleague here"—Holden waves toward Chuck and directs an accusatory glance at me—"whom I've never met, brought you home."

I concentrate on the mirrored dresser behind his head, incapable of returning his silent but deadly stare. He removes his glasses and cleans the lenses on his T-shirt, a habit that buys him time to calm down.

Chuck cuts in. "Your wife and I have done work together for the past five or six years. She hired me for a case, and I was in the neighborhood."

"You just happened to be in the 'neighborhood' where Sib was when she had a car accident?" Replacing his glasses on his face, Holden looks incredulous. "What exactly were you two doing?"

"You can't accuse me of sleeping with everyone," I snap.

Holden glowers at me, again removing his glasses for a second cleaning.

"I'm not sure what's going on, Holden," I say weakly. "But from your tone, I can tell you're upset. Is this about my car?"

His voice is laced with contempt. "Do you remember what happened today, Sibley?"

I close my eyes against the pounding in my head that strikes me like a hammer, blow by blow. "I'm in a lot of pain. Can I please have something?"

"With your history," Holden says briskly, "there's no way I'm giving you any type of opioid."

"Then maybe I need to go to the hospital and have a real doctor check me out."

"A doctor already did that as a favor to me," Chuck snaps. To Holden, he grunts, "He left something comparable for her to take. I'll go get it."

"Who left what?" I screech. "Can I have some water, please?"

Neither one acknowledges my questions, and when I hear Chuck's footsteps pounding down the stairs, I'm forced to open my eyes.

The bed squeaks underneath Holden's weight as he shifts to hand me the bottle. A coolness hits my palm when he thrusts it into my hand.

"Thank you," I murmur. After unscrewing the cap, I tilt my head back and take a couple of long swigs. "I feel like I was in a car accident."

"Well, you look like it. You gave me quite the scare." Holden's warm hand settles on my shoulder. "I heard a knock on the door, and then

Chuck was carrying you in the house. I had no idea who he was and thought he had hurt you and was trying to extort us or something."

"Extort us?" I moan. "For what?"

"I don't know. I hadn't thought it through." He sighs. "You were bruised and bleeding, and it's the first thing that came to mind. And then I thought about the conversation earlier. Between your pictures and the dating profile, it became an amalgam of uncertainty."

"What pictures?"

He squints at me. "Don't you remember talking to me this morning?"

I stutter, "I know I got up this morning and went to the gym . . ." A block of time has been erased, as if the day's been split into two parts. "You were still in bed when I left this morning." Then, accidentally moving my body too fast, I grimace.

"We talked this morning, fought, actually, about you dating other people."

My eyes widen. "What're you talking about?"

"You don't recall your dating profile? The provocative photos I saw?"

I want to furiously shake my head, but slowly is all I can manage, the throbbing making my movements jerky and sluggish.

"Never mind." He squeezes my hand in his. "It's not important right now."

"What happened to me?" My free hand drifts over my throat and collarbone area.

"The airbag deployed, thank God, especially since you weren't wearing your seat belt. You've got some burns and lacerations from the airbag and shattered glass."

"Where was I?"

"Chuck said near your office." His voice is resigned. "You're lucky you weren't arrested and charged with multiple infractions."

"What do you mean?"

"You were drunk."

"No way."

"Yes way."

"Holden," I protest. "I was at work."

"Until you lost your job."

My mind spins out of control when he says this. Suddenly, tears burn my eyelids. "What happened to my job?"

"Answer me this." Holden curls his hands into fists. "Why were you over by his place?"

"Whose place?"

"Sib . . ."

"I don't know what's going on right now."

"How convenient."

I withdraw into the sheets. "What happened at the firm? What happened to my job?"

"They asked you to take a leave of absence."

Suspicious, I ask, "How do you know?"

As much as I hate lying to Holden about what I remember, I have to play dumb. I might not remember the accident, but I do remember everything before the crash. Unable to fold my cards yet, I find it easier to claim temporary amnesia at this point.

"Because they told me they were going to," he confesses. "They asked my opinion first. We discussed an intervention. Luckily, Chuck brought the envelope with him from your vehicle that contains the disciplinary measures taken against you, which frankly couldn't have come at a better time."

Curious, I ask, "And you think they're fair?"

"I think asking you to go to rehab is more than reasonable." He huffs. "They could've just as easily fired you."

"Rehab!" I yell in outrage. "Come on, Holden, you're crazy." I expect him to crack a smile and tell me he's joking, but his mouth remains in a tight line. "You have to be kidding me."

"My wife is all banged up, lucky she didn't kill herself or someone else in a drunk driving accident, and this is what you want to say to me?"

"Holden," I plead, "I'll quit drinking. But rehab? That's ludicrous."

"You've said that before."

"But I mean it this time."

"Sibley . . ."

"This is a wake-up call."

"It should be, but I fear it's not." He throws his hands in the air. "We're out of options."

I don't know what to say, so I stare down at my hands, observing small cuts on both knuckles. Before I can think of an answer, a loud tap on the doorframe causes me to look past Holden at Chuck's sun-wrinkled face.

His loud baritone carries across the room. "You don't have a choice in the matter, Sibley."

"What're you talking about, Chuck?"

Without breaking eye contact, he crosses the room and hands me a pill. "Here's something for the pain."

I put it on the tip of my tongue and swallow it with the rest of the water.

"What don't I have a choice about?" I finish.

"I'll make you a deal."

"Charles," I sigh, using his real name. The name he hates to be called.

"It's straightforward. You should've been arrested and charged with a DUI."

I give him my best, albeit pained, smile. "You called your cop buddies, and I appreciate the favor; I really do . . ."

"And took you to my doctor friend. And got your car towed to the junkyard. And brought you home." His brief glance nails me to the headboard. "Let me be clear. There is no second chance. Or fourth.

Or seventh. You have a drinking problem, Sibley. Your work has asked you—no, instructed you—to go to a clinic. If I tell them what happened or breathe a word of this to them, they'll fire you in a heartbeat, whether you're charged with driving under the influence or not."

"Why would you do that?" I grit my teeth. "Are you threatening me?"

"No." His voice softens. "You remind me of my own children, and I'm not going to let you just trash your life. You've worked hard, and I know you've had a hard go of it, losing your father, having an absentee mother . . ."

Taking a quick peek at Holden, I can tell he's hurt this strange man he's never met knows about my past when it's hard for us to discuss.

"How did you know about . . ." I hold up a hand. "Who told you?"

"I'm a PI. You don't think I investigate colleagues I work with too?"

"Don't you dare bring my parents into this," I say, but without conviction.

Chuck points at Holden. "Your husband loves and cares about you. The firm cares about you. We want you to get better. We're rooting for you. All of us. But we can't do the work for you; you got to take ownership of that part."

I sniffle loudly. "You would never do this to your own kid."

"I absolutely would, and I did. My son, Joseph." He motions for Holden to switch spots with him. As he settles next to me on the bed, his eyes drill into my tearful ones. "Joe got in trouble for theft and drugs and was going down a nasty path. I put him behind bars when I was an officer. Hardest damn arrest I've ever made."

"You put your own son in jail?"

He nods. "And I don't regret it one bit. He needed that to straighten out. And now I'm going to serve you up some tough love as well." His hand swipes a tear from my cheek. "You could have been killed today."

"But I was just trying to help," I whisper.

"I told you nothing good would come of it."

Since I don't remember, I don't bother to argue, but that doesn't mean I can't search my memory for a reason I would go against Chuck's advice.

"Sib." Chuck cuts into my pensive thoughts. "I've known you for a long time. Go to rehab. Get your head right. I'm going to keep after the other case we were working on, but I'm calling a time-out on the Marconas."

"But what about . . ."

"No rebuttals."

Glancing between Holden and me, he adds, "I have a letter from my cop friend. Your license is automatically suspended for ninety days, but if you go to rehab and complete the program successfully, you won't be charged with driving under the influence."

"I don't think that's legal."

"Sibley." Holden stomps his foot. "You will sign off on this, or we will have other matters to discuss."

Chuck shakes his head at him, as if in warning. "You don't have anything to discuss right now except Sibley's health and mental wellness."

"Oh, really?" I challenge Holden. "Like what?"

Blushing crimson, Holden doesn't engage, likely realizing he's about to unleash our own marital problems on someone he doesn't know. "The firm was making you sign off on rehab, anyway," Holden says pointedly. "To keep your job."

Chuck's eyes look troubled at this declaration, but he says nothing. Instead, he leans forward and grips my hand in his large one. "I'll talk to you soon, okay? Papers are downstairs." Chuck nods at Holden. "You have my cell, right?"

"I do now."

I motion to where my handbag usually rests on the dresser. "Speaking of that, I need mine. Did you happen to bring my purse home?"

"I did." Chuck beckons to Holden. "I gave it to your husband."

"Good. Call me if you need anything."

"Let me walk you out," Holden offers, following him out of the room.

"Bye, Chuck," I sputter, scared I'm going to drown in a puddle of tears.

I hear the two of them talking downstairs, but I can't make out the words. I wait for my husband to come back and unleash a violent maelstrom of words on me, but the controlled disappointment in his voice is worse.

"We leave next week for the . . ." His voice cracks. "For the facility. That'll give you some time to rest and heal."

I stare at the ceiling, unable to meet the aqua pools of chagrin in his eyes. After a light stroke to my wrist, he disappears from the room.

Smashing the pillows beneath my head, I restlessly wait for sleep to come. Since I can't move to my usual side position, I lie still on my back, my groggy eyes flickering open and shut as the whir of the fan lures me to sleep.

CHAPTER 10
Sibley

Dreading rehab, I alternate between sleep, depression, and frazzled nerves. Recovering from a car accident is one goal. Surviving the shadow of my husband is another. Holden's been overbearing, leaving the house only for work and the gym.

Before Holden goes to the university to teach his night class, my best friend from college shows up wearing a guilty smile, as if hiding a secret from me.

I know Holden asked Adrienne to keep an eye on me. They've become friends over the years, so he implicitly trusts her. It helps she's a counselor at a high school and can put anyone at ease with her warmth and snorting laughter. She's a lot more soft spoken than I am, but she strengthens her tone when she needs to get her point across. It can be razor sharp and deadly when she's pissed. I've always told her she'd make a good trial lawyer.

Adrienne and I bonded in undergrad over family tragedies and our love of *Sex and the City*. Looks-wise, we're complete opposites. Adrienne's curvy, long legged, and tall; I'm thin and of average height. I'm blonde, blue eyed, and fair skinned. She's African American and has the most incredible, one-of-a-kind brown eyes with gold flecks in them.

Because of my soreness, we embrace in an awkward hug before I lead her to the living room to watch—what else?—reruns of *Sex and the City*. Making small talk, we settle in on the couch, half watching the show.

"I have to show you something." She yanks her laptop out of her purse, which might as well be a suitcase, since I swear I've seen her remove a four-course dinner from there.

"What's that for?" I ask curiously.

She scoots closer to me, pointing at the list of approved items on the rehabilitation center's website. After reading out loud an underlined sentence about the type of clothing allowed—only comfortable garments such as sweatpants, athleisure, or lounge wear, nothing provocative—she shrieks in amusement. "Can you believe this?"

"Hmm . . ." I raise a brow. "Is this an instance where my clothing will cause me unwanted attention, and it's my fault if I'm hit on or assaulted?"

"Clearly, they don't want you to get the other clientele riled up." She shrugs. "Or maybe the staff. After all, you are in the middle of nowhere."

"Ugh." I motion to the rest of the list. "It might as well be a prison. Especially with no cell phones or laptops, no keys, and no snacks."

"Seriously, aren't you scared shitless?" she asks. "I'm worried about your health. You do drink like a fish. You can drink me under the table!"

"Adrienne, *anyone* can drink you under the table." I roll my eyes. "Two drinks are all it takes."

We both giggle at this. Adrienne isn't a big drinker. We both had an alcoholic parent. But where she hardly touches alcohol, I go through binges. If I'm honest, it was shortly after I met Nico Marcona for the first time that I started slipping again, but not because of him. I'd put more blame on my marriage.

"Addiction doesn't just pop up one day, Sib." She squeezes my fingers before letting them go. "Your dad was an alcoholic."

I stare down at my wineglass, which is filled with water, a change from the Riesling I usually sip while relaxing on the couch, though this is hardly a time to unwind. "Unfortunately, that excuse doesn't work." I raise my glass. "But I do blame my husband."

"Spoken like a true addict," she chides. "When you're an alcoholic, you blame others for your judgment."

"I'm not trying to justify my behavior." I'm noncommittal. "It is what it is."

"I'm just wondering if you've dealt with your past."

"In terms of?"

"It holding you back," Adrienne remarks. "You told me before that you just took off on a whim for the desert after you graduated high school."

"Yeah. A lot of kids leave home to go find themselves," I add. "Or go to college out of state, like I did."

"But you didn't have a plan. You just packed your car and left."

"It seemed like the right kind of weather." I turn the volume down on the television. "And I met Holden and you and built a life out here. Not a bad choice—at least, not until recently."

"But what about your mom? You said she's never remarried."

"No. She hasn't. My mom has a lot of issues stemming from my dad's death."

"Like health?"

"Mental." I stare down at my lap, twisting my hands anxiously. "She had a nervous breakdown after I left."

"I can only imagine," she murmurs. "Your dad died unexpectedly. I'm sure it messed her up pretty bad." Incredulous, she adds, "And yet you still left?"

"It's not like that," I sputter. "She made some poor life choices that spiraled her out of control. A nervous breakdown compounded by everything that happened. Then we got in a big fight because she wouldn't help me out with college even after she got all this money from my dad's life insurance policy."

"Sib, I hate to break it to you, but at what point are you going to deal with your shit?" She narrows her eyes at me, the gold flecks sparking in anger. "This is one of your biggest triggers, and it's only impeding your ability to move on and truly break the cycle."

"So . . . don't go to rehab and deal with my mother instead?" I offer up hopefully.

She says nothing, just glares at the television. The mood has soured, and I don't even giggle at one of my favorite parts of my beloved series. It's when Carrie uses her oven to store her shoe collection. It's relatable that ample closet space would be more important than your ability to use kitchen appliances. I feel the same way.

"Seriously," Adrienne asks softly, "when was the last time you saw your mother? What's her name? Deb?"

"Deborah." I cackle. "For some reason, she hates when people call her Deb or Debbie."

"When was the last time?"

"The day after high school graduation."

"You haven't seen her since then?"

My face flushes. "No."

"Okay, um . . . what about the last time you talked on the phone?"

"Years." I swallow. "I don't know, probably three or four years ago."

Adrienne shuts her laptop with a bang, unable to hide her peeved expression, and I know she's struggling with my answer since she lost her mom at a young age.

Quickly, I add, "I did write her a couple of times, but she never responded."

"And what did you say?" she asks. "Was it an angry letter or a nice one?"

I shrug. "Probably a little bit of both."

"Then how do you even know she's okay?"

Remorseful, I shake my head. "I'm sure I would hear something. It's not a big city; it's a small town, nothing like what you're used to. Everyone *knows* everyone and everything. If she didn't call me in an emergency, a neighbor would."

Looking unconvinced, she chews on her lip while I aim for my nail. "What did you mean about your mom making poor life decisions?"

"Forget it." I turn the volume up.

"This is important, Sib." Adrienne watches me like a hawk, ready to swoop down on my twisted emotions and claw through them like a vulture circling a dumpster. I know she doesn't mean it negatively, but I'm immediately uncomfortable with her prying.

"I haven't even told Holden most of this."

"Why not?"

Swirling the water that doesn't belong in the wineglass, I sigh. "His family life was so perfect. He gets along with his siblings; his family is überclose. There are no childhood scars of any kind, minus when he maimed himself from a bicycle accident when he was a kid." I run a hand through my tangled hair. "Seriously, he is the poster child of a stable and thriving upbringing. His parents are still married, and beyond that, they are actually happy."

"Or do they fake it?" Adrienne says. "Maybe to everyone else they are, but behind the scenes, they are miserable."

"If they're acting, they do a damn good job." I frown. "Besides, why would I want them to be unhappy? I'm not trying to bash Holden's idyllic upbringing, nor do I resent him for having loving parents; I'm simply pointing out his reality and mine are at opposite ends of the spectrum."

"Whoa, baby girl, my intent isn't to pick apart their marriage but to convey how many people hide behind a facade." She snaps her fingers. "Take, for example, the people who post relationship goals all over social media, talking up their marriage and partner, while their close friends know one's having an affair or they're miserable together."

Adrienne shrugs. "You can control the narrative when you are the one who owns the rights."

"Absolutely. I see it all the time with my clients." I bite my lip. "But what makes me not want to confide in Holden is he can't relate to my past."

"But he doesn't have to."

"I disagree. If he can't relate, he can't help me."

"It's not Holden's job to help you, Sib." She holds up a hand before I can retort. "Hear me out. I don't mean it's not his duty to support you; I mean it's not his past to reckon with. Only you can do that. Just like you said, it's not his childhood, so therefore he can't fix it or make amends with it." She nudges me gently. "Only you can do that."

I'm thinking about what she just said when she continues.

"Your father didn't die in a car accident like mine did. Yet I told you about him not because you know what it's like or have lost someone close to you that way, but because you're my best friend and I want to confide in you and give you context about my life." She gives me another example. "Race. You're a white girl from the Midwest. I'm a black girl from Alabama. We both ended up in the desert. You can't relate to my struggles. I confide in you because we can see each other for the individuals we are underneath skin color. You aren't happy with who you are underneath your pasty skin."

I tilt my head at her.

"You cover up your insecurities and past experiences with alcohol." She tugs at a strand of my blonde hair. "And only you can break the cycle in letting drinking be the catchall for what you haven't dealt with."

"Adrienne." I pat her shoulder. "You really are a smart cookie."

"You better mean that seriously, Sib." She settles back against the couch, crossing her arms. "Don't play with me."

Adrienne has known me long enough to tell that when I get quiet, it's because the wheels of my mind are spinning down a path I need to explore.

"Oh no," she teases. "What's going on in that head of yours?"

"Before I tell you this," I warn, "I need you to trust me."

"When you say that phrase, it's usually because you are going to do something asinine that is a huge risk." She fixes me with a pointed stare. "Something that's trouble."

"You're a tad dramatic."

"I strongly disagree," she refutes. "You said the same thing before we went off-roading down a canyon."

"It was a bit of a bumpy ride," I admit.

"We ended up in the water."

"It was a creek, and it was shallower than your swimming pool."

She sighs. "Just tell me what you have up your sleeve."

Taking a deep breath, I tell her what I'm thinking, ignoring her wide eyes and puckered lips, focused on delivering my monologue to the unimpressionable painting behind her.

"Ballsy," she hoots.

By the time I wrap up my idea, I think she's sold by the small grin on her face.

"Risky," she says, fist-bumping me. "But you got yourself a deal."

When Holden returns home later that night, before Adrienne leaves, my ears perk at the sound of my name, and even after I lower the volume on the television, their muted voices don't carry from the kitchen. I wonder what they're saying about me. He's probably relieved she kept me company so I wasn't left to my own devices.

When I hear his footsteps creak toward the living room, I turn the volume back up so he doesn't know I attempted to eavesdrop.

"Is everything okay?" I ask when he strides in, a grimace on his face as if he didn't expect me to be sitting on the couch in our home, watching reruns of my favorite show.

"Yeah. It's just, you know, it just looks so normal." He runs a hand over his face, hiding his emotions from me. "We haven't had a sense of normalcy in a long time."

Though I pat the seat next to me, Holden instead takes the armchair to my left. His outward rejection stings. It reminds me of a middle school dance when I was picked last, and only because my friend Kristin threatened to beat a kid up. He was a skinny twig. She totally could have.

"How was class?"

"It was good. The students are eager to learn this semester, which I love." He runs a hand through his hair. "Did you eat?"

"Not yet."

"Sib, I told you guys to order takeout."

"I don't have much of an appetite right now." I rest a throw pillow in my lap. "What did you mean about this being normal?"

"We just live completely separate lives."

"Is that my fault?"

"Not what I said." He scratches at his beard.

"It seems like a slight." I tense. "You never take responsibility for being a shitty husband."

Swiftly, he stands back up. "Sib, not everything is meant to lead to an argument, yet you always go straight for the jugular."

Hunching over so he can't see my face, I murmur, "Okay."

"We both are guilty of it. That's all I'm saying."

I don't bother looking up at him. "What do you want to do about it?"

"I don't know." He rests an arm on the banister of our staircase. "You are selfish, Sibley. You have no regard for anyone else." I start to cut him off, but he silences me with a deep growl. "Wrecking your vehicle, being irresponsible with your job. You didn't consider how a leave of absence without pay would affect our finances." He stares at me sadly. "And don't think I didn't notice our wiped-out savings."

"That's all I am, isn't it?" I screech. "A meal ticket for you."

If Holden hears me, he doesn't answer. His next words are a slap in the face. "Not to mention your commitment to this marriage. I caught you in a lie a couple weeks ago, Sib."

"What're you talking about?"

"You weren't with Tanner on your birthday." He sinks onto the bottom step as if he's too tired to hold himself upright. "You lied to me. This is all . . . it's all too much."

His words and tone would normally cause hostility in me, but I'm also worn out from mental exhaustion. "Do you want to . . . do you want to get a . . ."

As much as we're struggling right now, I can't bring myself to say the *D* word out loud. Our marriage has been tested and broken, and no matter how many times we fight and talk it out and repeat the process, it's another thing entirely to admit it's irretrievably broken.

"I'm going to move into the guest room for now."

"Don't bother." I slowly rise, careful of my now-pounding headache. "Since I'm going away, I can sleep in the spare room."

"Sibley." His hand reaches out to clumsily touch my shoulder. "I want you to get better. Let's take one baby step at a time. We don't need to make any rash decisions about our marriage right now."

I don't trust myself to respond.

"It's close to ten. Let me help you get into bed and get you some medicine. How's the pain?"

"Slowly getting better."

Gently he guides me up the stairs, his hand never leaving my elbow. When we get upstairs to our bedroom, he scans the ginormous closet as if he's misplaced something.

"What're you looking for?"

"Your luggage." He shifts from foot to foot. "I need to get you packed. Anything you need before we leave on Wednesday?"

"Yeah, not to go."

"Sibley." He sighs. "Please."

I point in the direction of the hallway. "It's in the guest room."

"Thanks." He nods.

"By the way," I say casually, "I saw online they ask for all your medical records before checking in. Did you see that?"

"I had them sent, yes."

"Wow! You are really on it!" I sardonically add, "How long have you been planning my vacation?"

"Sib," he groans. "Your firm reached out to me. We discussed an intervention, but a lot of times, that doesn't work. One of the partners had a bad experience with that, so we went this route."

In the awkward silence, we both go into the master bath to brush our teeth and get ready for bed. He helps me out of my lounge clothing, a welcome break from the structured dresses I tend to wear. I wouldn't be able to wear the formfitting material right now with my bruises.

Sliding into a silk camisole and matching shorts, I ask curiously, "Are you packing for me because you're worried I'll try to slip in some illegal contraband or sexy clothing?"

"Why do you say that?"

I tell him about the prohibited clothing, and it breaks the tension between us. "I'm assuming they don't want anyone to feel uncomfortable if someone's wearing revealing clothing. As a dude, I wouldn't want to sit in group therapy with women in skimpy clothing when I'm supposed to be focused on recovery. One less distraction, I guess."

Smoothing the flimsy strap of my camisole down, I whisper, "You mean like this?" As I lean in to give him a kiss, he swiftly moves his head to the side, blocking me, so I catch his cheek instead.

In a gruff voice, he chastises me. "I was serious about what I said earlier."

"Doesn't mean we can't fool around." I wink.

"You're the only person who isn't taking this seriously." Holden helps me to bed before he stomps angrily away. Pausing at the door before he exits, he says, "We can't solve all of our problems with sex, Sib. Not anymore. Good night."

For once, we're in agreement on something.

CHAPTER 11
Sibley

In the morning, Holden rushes around like a madman, dashing up and down the staircase, his heavy thuds adding to my impending headache. I've started to experience withdrawal symptoms, and my lack of sleep grates on my frayed nerves, along with his inability to stay still. Much to my annoyance, Holden paces in the bedroom, asking me a million questions while he's trying to get me packed, triple-checking the items on the "necessities list."

I finally threaten to kick him out of the room, so he finishes in stony silence. He lugs my suitcase down the stairs, and a final crescendo strikes the landing when the bag hits the floor.

It's too much, and I snap at him in annoyance.

His eyes flash at me in anger, then hurt. "I want today to be a nice day for us."

"Preparing me for rehab isn't a 'nice' kind of a day," I say through gritted teeth. All I want right now is a drink in my hand and my husband to stop his incessant chatter.

"I don't want to think of it like that. I want to think of it like you're going to a spa and coming back rested and well." He adds with false excitement, "Did you see all the activities they have? I looked at the facility list: you'll have a yoga studio and a full gym and even a steam room."

"I have to earn those privileges first," I say sharply. "And maybe if you had sent me to a relaxing spa in the first place, I wouldn't be in this predicament."

He recoils like I slapped him, and I ashamedly stare down at my chewed nails.

"Maybe the next one will treat you better," he mutters under his breath.

"I'm sorry," I apologize. "I'm just agitated. It doesn't make me feel comfortable to live with strangers in an unknown place."

"It will be like college." Then he thinks about it. "Without the . . ."

"Fun," I finish.

Exasperated, he throws himself down on the bed. "I know this isn't what we wanted." He finally stammers, "It's not meant to feel like a prison. The website said the property is over seven thousand square feet, built into the mountain."

"I just don't want to be gone for too long. And forced to sit and talk about my feelings with random people." Before he can respond, I murmur, "I know it depends on the person."

He tries to talk to me about it, but half-asleep, I'm not sure if I answer the last question he asked me.

When I wake up, it's early evening, and a sense of dread gnaws at my stomach. There's an edge I need to take off, and it can only be alleviated by one thing.

The house is eerily silent when I tiptoe down the stairs. Maybe because of our tenuous relationship as of late, I feel like a guest in my own home.

When I call out Holden's name, there's no response, but I find a barely legible note on the marble kitchen island. His scribbled handwriting says he went to grab takeout from my favorite restaurant on our last night together. It's a nice gesture, and I hate the fact I'm more excited to be alone, out from beneath his watchful and judgmental gaze, then to have food and his company.

With him gone, I can go on a mission.

In anticipation, I lick my lips, already tasting the smoothness. My hands are shaking, my heart having palpitations at the thrill, sending shivers down my spine.

It's just one last time, I tell myself. *No big deal.*

I'm in the comfort of my own home, and no one will know.

"It's not like you're hurting anyone," I whisper to the mirror. My mouth salivates, not for food but for the sweet friendship of wine tonight.

Except Holden one-upped me. He did a stellar job of finding every last one of my hiding places—starting with the linen closet.

I wander from our dresser in the guest room to the wicker basket filled with toilet paper in the bathroom. He even removed my stash from the shelving unit in the garage.

Slamming shut the heavy-duty lid of his indestructible toolbox, I'm about to self-destruct.

Hell, he even dumped out the vodka I poured into a gallon jug meant to look like distilled water. I'm rummaging in our shared office for the miniature wine bottles I hid behind a row of lawbooks.

Dropping to my knees, I'm surprised to find something else I'm missing. My purse was returned to me, but my phone wasn't in its usual pocket inside the front zipper. Stranger yet, Holden refused to take me or go look through my vehicle at the junkyard to find it. His excuse was that I'm not going to be able to bring it with me to the clinic, so I might as well get used to not having one for the time being.

My supposedly misplaced cell phone is in one of his desk drawers. When I power it on, the red battery light flashes, indicating it's about dead.

After typing in my pass code, I wait for the phone to unlock.

It doesn't.

Fuck.

Holden changed my pass code.

My heart might as well have jumped straight out of my body, it's pounding so fast. I'm debating what to do when Tanner's face flashes on the screen. At least I can answer his call.

"Hey, Tanner," I answer with fake enthusiasm. "Just a heads-up, my phone's about to die."

"That's all you have to say?"

"What do you mean?"

Exasperated, he sighs. "I've been trying to call you for a few days."

I open and shut my mouth, realizing Tanner most likely doesn't know about the car accident, and I'd like to keep it that way.

"Sorry," I apologize. "As you can imagine, I've had a lot going on. Holden's pissed at me. Did you tell him who I was with on my birthday?"

"Of course not," he says smoothly. "You know I have your back." He adds, "When are you leaving for . . ."

I bite my lip. "Tomorrow."

"How did Holden take it?"

"He's convinced I'm having multiple affairs."

"I wonder why."

"No clue." I play dumb. "Before my phone dies, I need your help. I have, or *had*, a client named Nico Marcona. High-profile divorce with a few mil in assets. I've got bank records and offshore accounts to incriminate his wife, Christine. She's a real bitch, a total nightmare. She's been blackmailing him."

Tanner plays straight into my hands. I can hear him practically salivating over the phone. He loves money as much as I love liquor. I almost feel sorry for the weasel. He's only human, and I shouldn't hold his own demons against him.

But I promptly reconsider.

When you try and fuck up my livelihood and marriage, this scrappy midwestern girl will become the Wicked Witch of the West and shove a flying broom handle up your darkest crevice.

"Leslie has all the account information and an overwhelming paper trail."

Tanner goes for lackadaisical. "You find a good PI to do the grunt work?"

"You know I use our guy, Chuck," I say. "Out of curiosity, do you know which attorney is representing Nico now?"

Dead air follows, and I presume my phone has finally died. Fitting it would be in the middle of an important question.

"You there? Tanner?"

"Still here."

"Did anyone tell Nico what happened to me?"

"No, course not. Bad for business." Tanner probes. "You didn't tell him where you were going, did you?"

"No!" I sigh. "I'm not allowed to contact any of my previous clients."

"Then I'd follow that directive, Sib. Go to rehab. Stop squandering your talent on useless men."

Before I can respond, my phone goes black.

Dammit.

After plugging the phone into a charger, I go into the bathroom and take a long, hot shower, steaming up the mirror, bawling my eyes out where no one can hear me.

Holden changed my pass code, and now I can't see my messages or who said what. I'm resentful I'm being punished when he's the one who missed an important milestone a few weeks ago: my thirty-fourth birthday passed without so much as a happy-birthday emoji.

That would be the day Holden didn't check his social media, I think caustically.

It just so happened that Nico was my last appointment of the day, and Leslie stepped inside my office to say goodbye for the evening and to wish me one last happy birthday. "I can't wait until tomorrow to hear what Holden planned as a surprise."

"Thanks." I forced a terse smile out, but Nico's intuitive, and it didn't go unheeded, at least not by him. I dumbly smiled when he asked about my evening plans. I tried unsuccessfully not to show Nico my disappointment or the tears I was holding back.

"Your husband must be planning one hell of a surprise party."

I couldn't keep the disappointment from my voice. "Then I hope you're invited, because he hasn't mentioned my birthday."

"No!"

"Yes," I said sulkily.

"You mean regarding your plans tonight?" He frowned. "You don't mean he *forgot* your actual birthday?"

"No," I stammered. "I mean, yes." I leaned back in my chair as if I couldn't care less. I'm a tough attorney, not a blubbering Barbie. "At least, he hasn't acknowledged it. Who knows—maybe he will later."

"Did he tell you to be home at a certain time?"

"No." I glanced at my watch. "He has a class to teach tonight."

With a grimace, Nico said, "There's no way I'm letting you spend your birthday alone."

"It's fine, Nico," I objected. "I can go out with one of my girl-friends. They assumed I was busy tonight, so we scheduled something this weekend."

But he wouldn't let me off the hook, intent on celebrating with me. I told him it was a bad idea, but he wanted to know why. "We're friends, right? Friends celebrate their birthdays together."

"But it's not appropriate." I tried to dissuade him. "You're a current client."

He narrowed his eyes at me, and I withered under his disapproving glance. "Today is important, and we're going to make it one for the books," he promised.

I didn't ask him to clarify his statement because I didn't want to go down that rabbit hole.

Was I attracted to him?

No doubt.

It took Nico a couple tries to convince me to have a drink with him, which I think thrilled him because he likes an actual chase, not a sure thing.

After he left my office and I spent thirty minutes freshening up my makeup and persuading my reflection I wasn't doing anything wrong or immoral, I met him at a dark speakeasy.

We sat in a dark leather booth, where we started on opposite sides, trading stories of our past and present.

To break the ice, we did a round of shots.

The liquor flowed, and so did the conversation. It's easy to talk to Nico, not stilted like it is with Holden, who never pays attention. He listens but doesn't hear me.

Another round of shots went down smooth.

Somehow, we ended up seated on the same side—I'm uncertain who suggested it first—and, by then, reasonably inebriated.

And then . . .

Lost in a trance, I don't hear the knock on the bathroom door. Suddenly, I'm brought back to the present when another sharp tap interrupts my thoughts.

I'm sitting on the tiled bench in the walk-in shower when Holden walks in. He peers at my barely visible shape in the foggy glass. "Did you even know I was gone?"

"Yes. I saw your note."

Holding my iPhone up, he says, "I see you found this."

"You had no right to tell me it was lost," I say irritably. "Not to mention changing my access code."

"What did we agree on?"

Furiously, I rub at the steam on the glass to stare him down.

"Sibley." He shakes his head angrily. "What did you tell me would be different after your birthday?"

"You mean the birthday you *forgot*?" I step out of the shower and wrap myself in a towel. "That I would give you access to my phone. And I did," I grumble. "Which is why you were able to change it in the first place."

"You reached out to Nico before you crashed your car." He shrugs. "We agreed you wouldn't text him any personal messages, and you did it anyway."

I don't have a recollection of this, so I shrug my shoulders.

"Come on, let's go eat." Holden points downstairs. "The food's going to get cold."

When we go downstairs to eat, he's lit some candles and set the formal dining table, and it only makes me feel more like a piece of shit. Even sitting close, we have a noticeable distance between us. It makes me sad, and I stare at his profile while he unwraps and uncovers our dinner.

He settles a napkin in my lap, and our eyes lock.

Mine are filled with tears.

"Sib?" he asks. "What's wrong?"

"Nothing." I shake my head, forcing the tears to retreat. "This looks delicious."

"I hope so. It's your favorite." He sits down next to me. "Are you okay? You seem off, like a light bulb just turned off in your head."

"I'm just . . . apprehensive."

With wooden expressions, we sit in silence at the table, both lost in our own thoughts. There's so much I want to ask him, but I'm scared to open our collective wounds. My ego's fragile, and deep down, I'm worried my inability to handle an answer I don't want to hear will set me back.

Twirling some pasta on my fork, I finally say, "I know I need to do this. I know it's been difficult. I want to fix this and fix us. I know I have to accept responsibility for my actions."

"I know, Sib. I just hope it isn't too late."

"Me too."

"Are you scared?"

"No." I meet his eyes. "Petrified."

He grabs my hands in his and holds them tightly.

"Will you please sleep with me tonight?" I plead.

Hesitating, he stares down at our interlocked hands. "I don't think that's a good idea."

"I just mean, in the same bed. Please," I beg. "I don't want to sleep alone tonight. It's my last night here."

Holden relents, and after we climb into bed later, he quickly switches off the lamp on the nightstand. Because of my constant headaches and a good chance of a concussion, we've kept the lights low or off.

He clasps my hand in his, and we lie together, side by side, in silence. I feel impending doom, a sign of a panic attack lurking, and my resolve to never drink again lessens.

I whisper, "It's going to be weird to be cut off from society and have no access to technology. This will be the longest we've gone without communication."

"It might be good for us," he offers. "I think we can talk after you finish detox. That might be a good goal. Being able to speak with your husband after you purge the bad stuff."

"Will you miss me?"

Even in the absence of light, I sense indecision.

Instantly, my body tenses, a knee-jerk reaction. I pull my hand from his.

"Sibley, stop," he quietly commands. "I'm not going to lie and say it hasn't been stressful for a while. You put us through the wringer."

"What about what you've done?" I cross my arms over my chest. "You're not innocent in this, Holden. There's two of us in this marriage."

"I know," he concedes.

"So this will be a nice reprieve for both of us."

"Please don't say it that way."

"Why?" I wish I could turn my back to him. "It's true."

"I don't want to fight," he begs quietly.

"Then let's go to sleep." I bring my hand up in the dark, and a fingernail goes to my mouth, a nervous habit of mine. My nails are already a wreck, but I find comfort in ripping away another sliver of skin, as shredded as my dignity.

I yelp as the metallic taste of blood hits my tongue.

"Stop biting your nails," Holden chastises, yanking my hand away from my face.

Neither of us can sleep, and I fumble for him in the dark, hoping Holden will want to close the void between us. He doesn't swat my hand away, instead choosing to entwine his fingers with mine, but it's another glaring spotlight on our tenuous marriage, and I wonder if we'll outlast the next six months or finally grind to a halt.

He wraps his hand around my wrist, and I become anchored to him. When he does this, I sometimes feel claustrophobic, as if caught in an undercurrent, and if something happens, he'll pull me down with him to drown. But tonight, I need his superfluous touch.

Holden tosses and turns beside me, and coupled with my intrusive thoughts, neither of us can sleep comfortably for more than a few hours at a time.

It's as if we've lost the power to tread water. Now we're just floundering.

CHAPTER 12
Sibley

Bleary eyed in the morning, I'm surprised when Holden hasn't loaded his Subaru up with my luggage but instead has breakfast waiting for me downstairs.

When I'm seated, he tells me there's been a change of plans. He seems nervous, his hands fidgeting as he moves the salt and pepper shakers around. "I talked with Adrienne . . . about, uh, about taking you."

"What do you mean?"

"She'll be here in a few to pick you up."

"You don't want to take me?"

"It's not like that." He removes his glasses. "Crap. I can go if you'd like me to. I didn't mean for it to seem like I don't care . . ."

"No. It's okay." I sip my coffee. "I'm just surprised. You haven't let me out of your sight lately."

"I worry about you." He touches my cheek. "I thought you could use some time with Adrienne. I know she's your best friend and probably a better support system than me right now."

"Thank you." I squeeze his hand in mine. "I appreciate you saying that."

"I always hoped you'd be able to confide in me and tell me all your secrets, but there's so much you keep in, Sib." He replaces his glasses with a sigh. "Or maybe I'm not a good enough listener and haven't made you feel safe enough to share. Either way, you deserve to have your best friend with you, and that's not me anymore." He covers his face with his hands. "Maybe it never was."

His words tug at my heartstrings, and I burst into tears. His own are running down his now-wet cheeks. We swipe at each other's faces and clutch each other's shoulders as if we can erase our past mistakes. We've had a long marriage, and we've made many.

Both of us are scared to move, and our arms stay in a half embrace for a long time.

Eventually, we pull away from each other, and I don't know if this is goodbye or good luck. Either way, we are both hurting, a sense of finality behind our emotions.

When Adrienne arrives, she's unusually stoic, and I can tell she's having a hard time with the reality of today.

We exit through the garage, and my eyes stare at the spot where my Tesla used to sit, now nothing more than an empty space with an oil stain from a previous vehicle. Holden drags his feet behind us and loads my suitcase into the back of Adrienne's small SUV. He sends me off with a tight hug and a chaste kiss, and the smell of his cologne and the look of his sad eyes are etched in my memory as we back out of the driveway.

We have a long drive to what's considered a state-of-the-art, luxury rehab facility inspired by the "tranquility of a resort and the secrecy of a mountain hideaway, with expert staff well educated and trained on addictions," or at least that's what the website touts.

"They have yoga, which I read can help with detox," Adrienne mentions. She's a certified yoga instructor and is a massive proponent of reiki and meditation.

I barely nod.

"Are you even paying attention?"

"Not really."

"Nerves?" She taps her fingers on the gearshift. "Okay, I got you. You're afraid, so let's break it down."

"It's more than that," I admit. "I'm worried about my job."

"You mean because you're taking time off to come here? Sib." She sighs. "You can't focus on that. Your recovery is the most important thing right now."

"I know, but I'm also worried about one of my cases." Adrienne waits for me to elaborate. "I have a client that's getting a divorce, and I just found out the client's wife was at the home of one of my colleagues."

"Okay, but what's the big deal?" She broods. "You think the wife wants representation from your firm?"

"Something we like to call ethics. Both my client and his wife would have to sign off to have two attorneys from the same firm representing them in their divorce."

"Since when did attorneys start having scruples?" she teases. "And did your colleague tell you the wife came to them personally?"

"We only do when it benefits us." I elbow her in the ribs. "Except in this case, it's Tanner."

"Isn't he one of your closest work friends?"

"I thought so."

"And you didn't know they knew each other?"

"Nope," I grumble, wishing I had something to dull the battering ram in my head.

"But how does it affect you?" Adrienne asks gently. "I mean, this sounds like soap opera drama, but why would Tanner be out to get you?"

"Because in my absence, another attorney will take over my cases for me."

"Babe, I love you, but I'm not following this train. What does your out-of-control ass have to do with Tanner and your client's wife?"

"If she and Tanner are hooking up and my client's reassigned to him . . ."

"Then his vested interest is in the wife of your client, which makes you a liability?"

"I'd say collateral damage." I shudder. "If Tanner's successful, he'll represent my client and be privy to all his financial records and bungle his case big-time, but in a way that isn't obvious. I can be the 'fall girl' for the case."

"How would that work out?"

"I have my suspicions." I tear at a fingernail. "But it will be hard to prove when he's not easily accessible to me."

"Then someone better keep an eye on dear, sweet Tanner," Adrienne says excitedly. "What about your paralegal? That Leslie chick? Can she watch your back while you're gone?"

"Possibly." I lean my head back against the seat. "Except I'm not sure where she falls into this."

"You think she's doing you dirty?"

"No. But I don't know what lies Tanner's feeding her or what promises he's made."

Adrienne pats my knee. "I don't want to minimize your frustration and hurt with these people, but this is better than all the courtroom nonsense I see on TV."

I give her a wink. "I'm glad I could provide you entertainment, dear friend."

We become tenser and less talkative the farther out of town we drive, as the reality sets in this isn't a girls' trip to somewhere fun but a severe departure from our everyday lives. The rest of the drive we chat about everything but where we're headed, and too quickly, we've reached our destination, which isn't where I'm supposed to be.

"Are you really sure about this?" Adrienne asks one last time as we pull up the long, winding driveway. Instead of being at a resort-like rehabilitation facility, we're on the outskirts of the desert, about two hours outside the city.

"I am." I ask to borrow her phone. "I'm going to call Holden since we're about halfway to the facility. I'll tell him we stopped for gas."

Holden picks up on the second ring, concern in his voice. "Everything okay?"

"Uh-huh," I say. "Google Maps estimates we're about a hundred and twenty miles away. We stopped for gas, so I wanted to call you since reception's getting spotty."

"That's not a surprise. You're heading up into the mountains. I always lose my signal not far from there."

"I'll check in when I can."

"Don't worry about me, Sib." I can tell he's struggling with finding the right words. "Just focus on your recovery, okay?"

"I will."

"Be safe." He adds, "And put Adrienne on the phone, please."

As I hand Adrienne back her phone, the screen feels damp against my fingers. Confused, I realize it's from the tears sliding down my cheek. I hear Holden ask her to call him once she's dropped me off. Adrienne looks at me and squeezes my arm after hanging up. "It's going to be fine."

"I'm risking a lot." I bite my trembling lip. "Holden's never going to forgive me for this."

"And you're never going to forgive yourself if you don't make amends back at home." She tugs on a strand of my hair. "You know I would never agree to cover for you if I didn't think it was important." She stares at the house up ahead. "I'm going to tell myself the end goal is to help save your marriage and your health. Now, here's your replacement phone. Don't get excited," she warns. "It's basic as fuck."

"Wow. You aren't joking." The one time I lost my phone, it was a wake-up call, since I realized I hadn't bothered to memorize anyone's number but Holden's.

This time, I only program in a couple of contacts, bypassing Tanner's with an angry sigh. I'm supposed to be off the grid, so I don't need many.

Grinning, I see Adrienne saved me the trouble of adding her contact info. She's saved as *Wingwoman*. She's definitely my partner in crime; her status is at a whole new level with our covert operation.

"Thank you," I whisper. "I'm lucky to have you as a friend."

"Now go, or you're gonna make me cry." After Adrienne helps unload my suitcase, she gives me a tight hug. "Let me know when you're safe." Pointing to a duffel bag, she nods at it. "I packed what you asked me to in here."

I open the zipper, and there's an envelope filled with cash, a refurbished laptop, a map, and a few other requests I made.

She also hands me another envelope with a money order inside.

"Did you have any problem getting the cash or money order?"

"No," she says. "I withdrew it from my account, just in case."

"You're the best." I wink. "Wingwoman."

CHAPTER 13
Sibley

I walk toward a small house where an elderly man is waiting near a used car. Barely able to contain my excitement, I've never been so thrilled to buy a car, not even when I purchased my Tesla. The man is shocked I don't want to go on a test drive, but in the interest of time, I do my due diligence and inspect the car, not letting on I know the bare minimum. It's had a recent oil change, he's kept impeccable records on any repairs, and even though the outside has seen better days, the interior is clean.

Adrienne doesn't drive off yet, ensuring I'm not about to be swindled by this unknown seller from a vehicle marketplace and then get stuck in the middle of nowhere.

Giving her a thumbs-up, I present the man with a money order. He hands me the keys to my very used and over-a-decade-old white Toyota Corolla, with striped window tint and rock chips that have dented both the windshield and the body of the vehicle.

But I don't care. It's mine, and it's freedom.

With one last fleeting smile and a heavy wave, Adrienne leaves me standing in front of my "new" used car.

Clenching the keys in my hand, I throw my luggage in the back, ready to start my cross-country drive.

Adrienne was right the other night. Before I can rehabilitate myself, I have to confront the demons of my past head on, and that starts with my only living blood relative.

I have to go back to my childhood home, a farm in the middle of the country, square in the center of the state.

It's time to confront my mother about my father's death and what *really* happened on that night sixteen years ago. The details have startling clarity, even after all this time.

This will take patience and understanding, since my mother and I have never had what most would consider a typical mother-daughter relationship. But then again, I can't even say what that is. I grew up as an only child, a tomboy who preferred to be outside, my father's small shadow.

Our relationship became strained in high school, when I found out some unsavory details about her, and it only culminated in an estrangement after my father's death and my move to the desert. It hurt my mother when I left after my high school graduation, but we'd suffered too much tragedy to make it less than a painful goodbye.

I never looked back as my tires squealed out of the drive so fast gravel sputtered.

The problem with time, I contemplate, is that it passes, and you tend to get stuck in the minutia, right or wrong.

I've tried to reach out to her, but she's been unresponsive. She's never visited, not even to attend my wedding. Previously, her minimal interactions included an occasional phone call or card in the mail, and bizarrely, the greeting wouldn't match the holiday. As she was unresponsive to emails, I extended multiple offers for her to visit over the years, but the plane tickets went unused.

Eventually, our communication dried up, and the years became a long gap of estrangement.

When I reached out recently, nothing but crickets.

As I start the long haul back to my humble beginnings, the thought of facing her now terrifies me. With so many lingering questions, it makes sense to go back to where it all started, to the environment that shaped me, for better or worse. But I have to be prepared for the possibility that she doesn't want to see me, especially since I didn't come home when she was hospitalized for a nervous breakdown after my father died. Though she was stoic for his funeral, she buckled a couple weeks later under the immense strain.

I feel tense even with twenty-plus hours on the road between us, and I know I need to give her a heads-up. Deborah hates surprises and isn't the type to appreciate spontaneity or an unplanned visit.

I keep throwing her curveballs, starting with my conception.

An uneasy feeling settles in the pit of my stomach as her house phone rings and rings. I assume my mother has more than a house phone now, but I don't have another number to reach her on.

How do you not have your own mother's contact info? I think ashamedly. *What if something happens to her?*

But you've tried to reach out, my less critical half argues internally. *On your terms. Always on your terms.*

Disgusted, I grip the wheel. I might be a shitty daughter for leaving, but my mother made her own choices, and I suffered the consequences as a result.

Lowering the window for some fresh air, I crank up the music as the landscape changes from cavernous mountains and narrow roadways at high elevations to rolling hills and valleys.

During the long drive, my mind wanders, and I drift aimlessly to a memory from a few weeks ago, the night Nico and I were seated side by side in a booth, our only distractions each other. Did he rest his hand on my thigh?

Absolutely.

Did I let him?

I'm not a saint.

He made me feel sexy, wanted, vulnerable, tempted—all the emotions that wane after multiple years of marriage.

I twist my hair around my finger in contemplation. Nico and Holden are complete opposites. While Holden is tall and willowy, with shaggy blond hair and a matching beard, Nico is shorter than six feet and built solidly, with dark hair and mostly a clean-shaven face, except when he lets it grow out a little, presumably because he's forgotten to shave.

Holden's blue eyes are pools of intellectual depth hidden behind spectacles. Nico's stunning green ones are fringed with dark lashes, and volatile emotions change their colors.

When I compare the two men, I'd have to say if Holden were my professor, I'd flirt with him, enamored with his ability to have intense and lengthy discussions on a variety of topics. His passion for history is a turn-on, his recitation of facts impressive. He's the kind of guy your parents hope you bring home one day—steady and reliable.

Safe, though somewhat predictable.

Nico, on the other hand, oozes confidence and sex appeal. He's a fire you'd want to burn your hand on, just once, because of the intensity. His passion sizzles with power and dominance. He's the epitome of a Tom Ford cologne ad. Spicy and sensual.

And in our small booth that night, Nico's hand brushed my hair . . .

Involuntarily, I mimic him now, my cheeks blushing at the thought of my reaction when his fingers went from my head to my hands.

Maybe I should've, but I didn't protest when his fingers strangled mine.

A loud honk startles me out of my reverie, and I glance over at a van carrying a carload of teenagers. Laughing and carefree, they're speeding toward their destination, and I wonder where that is. I'm somewhat envious; it makes me long for my youth and the limited responsibilities of being a teenager.

But as an adult, you have limited freedoms as well.

I drive for about ten hours before I'm forced to pull into a rest stop and crash. When I wake up a few hours later, my neck's strained from the uncomfortable position in the back seat I was curled up in. Rubbing my tired eyes, I stop for a gas station coffee before continuing on through a rainstorm in New Mexico and a tornado warning in Kansas.

After taking a quick nap at a truck stop, I need to be caffeinated, and my gaze drifts longingly to the large display of alcohol. I sigh, settling on an energy drink that gives me a rush of adrenaline and a headache.

With shaking hands and no more resolve, I stop at a big box store to pick up a cooler and some supplies. I tell myself just having it in the car will help with my cravings.

By the time I reach the welcome sign at the entrance to my hometown, population 1,250, the slogan of *We move slowly as molasses in these parts* couldn't seem more appropriate. Especially for someone who has driven on little sleep, slogging toward a bed and a shower.

Whether an acknowledgment or a humblebrag, it's evocative of a time that moves listlessly, without the pressures of the big city. Even though sixteen years have passed since I drove out the same way I just came in, the two-lane highway remains unchanged.

I promised Adrienne I would call and update her on my progress. She answers on the first ring, and I can hear the trepidation in her voice. "Did you make it there yet?"

"Almost." My yawn interrupts my unfinished thought. "Only a few more miles." I'm curious to know how everything went after she "dropped me off" at the rehab facility. "How did it go when you got to the clinic?" Adrienne drove all the way there, bless her heart.

"Fine. I sent Holden a picture of the outside of the building. I even dropped a pin at the facility so he knew I was there." She gives a nervous giggle. "And I gave them the updated medical records with your recent injuries."

I thank her for getting her friend, a doctor, to write a letter to the rehabilitation clinic regarding my car accident and subsequent course of treatment. I'm off the hook, at least for now. The facility thinks I'm recuperating from my injuries and will be joining them after I'm cleared to by my doctor.

"You're the best," I say.

"And don't you forget it," she teases. "What do you think your mother will say when she sees you after all this time?"

"I'm more worried about what she'll do."

Adrienne starts to ask a question when a news bulletin on the radio interrupts the music.

CHAPTER 14
Sibley

"Breaking news: a manhunt is underway this morning for two inmates who escaped from the local prison around eleven a.m. 'Deputies have established that the inmates had assistance in escaping from at least one individual on the outside,' said Thomas Delaney, the director of the medium-security correctional institute. State troopers said that both inmates are believed to be hiding out in the vicinity of the prison. Deputies are canvassing the area. Updates will be provided as they become available."

"Holy shit," I whisper. "When did they build that?"

"What's wrong?" Adrienne's voice echoes, cutting in and out. "Are you okay?"

"Yeah. There's just such crappy reception out here," I say. "But I made it."

"Phew. That takes a load off my stress. Glad to hear it. Let me know how it goes with your mom." Adrienne's voice lowers. "Just know I want to be here for you."

I'm about to thank her when I hear the unmistakable blare of sirens in the distance.

My lids jolt open, and sneaking a glance in the rearview, I expect the cop car to speed up and maneuver around me, headed for someone or somewhere else on the endless highway, but there's no sign of life out on this open stretch of the road.

Peering at my speedometer, I realize I'm driving faster than the limit. Like, way faster.

Holy shit. I ram my fist on the wheel. *You've got to be kidding me.*

This Toyota isn't new enough to have Bluetooth, and a distracted-driving ticket is the last thing I need, along with a citation for speeding. The police car slows from behind, which means I'm the culprit.

So much for not drawing unnecessary attention to myself.

It would be my luck that less than two miles from the farmhouse I grew up in, I might be put in handcuffs before my mother knows I've arrived, unannounced, of course.

I wonder how far back the cruiser spotted me. Was it lurking in one of the overgrown fields, or has it been following my progress, and I never noticed, even though the scenery is flat and predictable?

With the earsplitting cacophony signaling me to stop, a bottomless pit of apprehension gnaws in my stomach. The day-old coffee I threw back like a shot of tequila sends a warning signal to my intestines. *Sour tummy* is what my father used to call it when I was a child.

Not only are my nerves shot, but my eyes dart anxiously to the rearview mirror. I didn't expect to glimpse the bumper of a squad car, especially on this open and desolate road.

I grew up out here in rural America, and even though there's an endless supply of soybean and hog-confinement lots, the opposite is true of uniforms and crime. The occasional break-in or bar fight is at the top of the news hour and shared via the gossip chain of the phone or your closest neighbor. It's unimportant to those outside the parameters of small-town life who have kidnapping and murders to contend with, not that we're completely immune to those.

If the policeman has run my temporary plates, I'm in trouble. Driving on a suspended license in a vehicle with a title I haven't switched over is frowned upon.

I'll be in *big* trouble.

With white knuckles, I take my foot off the accelerator and put it on the brake, slowing so I can pull off onto the gravel side. I turn on my hazard lights out of habit, not a necessity since there are more people in the city I live in now than in this entire state. Cattle outnumber residents here.

Sucking in a deep breath, I wait for what's next, running through illogical options in my mind. If I speed off, it'll result in a chase, negative publicity, and an imminent arrest.

So as I stare at my fair skin and freckles in the mirror, the lingering cruiser crawls to a stop behind me. When the dust settles, I make out the slightly balding head of a man staring down at something in his hand.

His phone, I assume.

Hopefully, his wife or his captain texted him, and he's in a rush to leave. Maybe he'll peel off toward the scene of something more exciting than a wannabe drifter. Aren't the prison escapees a more pressing concern at the moment?

A fingernail goes to my mouth in nervous anticipation.

He's about six feet tall and stocky, and his bulging biceps are glued in place by an even tighter uniform. His purposeful stride and swinging arms remind me of someone I used to know, but his eyes are protected in the sweltering June heat by his sunglasses.

Quickly, I move my hands back to the steering wheel so they're clearly in the officer's line of sight.

My window's down by the time he appears to my left, yet I'm reluctant to lower my own shades to unveil my apparent signs of distress. I prefer to struggle with my fragility internally. I want to seem amenable when, in reality, a considerable weight hangs over my head. They say eyes are the windows to the soul, and fortunately, my swollen, tearstained ones are shielded.

The cop pauses for a moment, examining my worn tires, the dented hood that looks like someone took a hammer to it, and the peeling window tint.

His stare lingers on my now-reddened cheeks.

"Good morning, ma'am." He rests a hand on his hip, presumably wanting to appear casual, as if we're two people who've stopped to chat for a friendly conversation, not a traffic violation.

"Morning, sir," I sputter.

"Do you know why I pulled you over?"

Should I try for contrition or humor?

Sarcasm and a timid smile win. I fix him with my best grin, albeit a tired one. "I'm guessing I lost track of the speed limit due to the fact I'm really into the new T-Swift record."

He chuckles, and instantly, I recognize who the voice belongs to. Without being able to see his eyes, I peer into the face of my former friend Miles Fletcher. His family grew up in a neighboring town less than ten miles from mine, and because of the size, most kids were bussed into one central high school.

We were platonic except for an awkward kiss at a barn party one night after drinking a brand of off-label vodka that caused residual pain and the threat of puking long after we'd imbibed. You know, the type that tastes like gasoline as it cauterizes your throat and burns down your esophagus to churn uneasily in your stomach. It's cheap and easy to score or steal and sold in liter bottles that cost substantially less than other brands; you pay for it with the repulsiveness of the substance you can barely swallow.

Miles Fletcher has aged since I last saw him at the end of our senior year of high school. I can tell he's rocking a farmer's tan by the sallow skin sticking out from his shirt sleeve that draws a sharp contrast to the rest of his arm. It reminds me of my father's uneven tans from his time in the fields.

"License and registration, please." He says it politely, but I catch a steely undertone.

I fumble for my purse on the passenger seat.

"This a new ride?"

"Oh, you mean because of the temporary plates." I smirk. "Yes. It beats putting miles on my lease."

His eyebrows rise sky high, and I get the impression he's flabbergasted at who would willingly purchase this junker, bald tires and all.

A girl on the run, that's who.

I pull out the flimsy plastic of my license, biding my time. How could I be so stupid and careless, allowing myself to speed across the rolling prairie? I drove over miles and miles of pavement, surrounded by tall cornstalks and blue skies, without exceeding the limit.

I motion to my plugged-in phone. "Let me pull up my insurance information for you." I don't bother to add that my current policy is for a black Tesla I wrecked. Or that I no longer possess a valid license or the accompanying insurance.

"You don't have a paper copy?" As if reading my mind, he says dubiously, "Doubt you'll get reception out here." He points to a pothole straight ahead. "You have to cross that before it works."

"I'm sorry, Officer." I shake my head. "I don't."

"Let me guess—you're saving the environment by not printing it out, just like those damn paper straws that dissolve before I can drink a sip of my pop." The sneer I give him makes him add, "And yes, lady, I have been out west before."

My lip quivers, and I try for a woman in distress. "Do you by any chance have a tire pressure gauge?"

"You don't have one, with tires this shoddy?" He scratches his chin. "I hope you didn't pay much for this clunker."

"It's a Toyota. They run forever." I cross my arms defensively. "Plus, I couldn't afford much." Desperately, I add, "And certainly not a ticket."

"You should've thought of that before speeding like a bat out of hell, uh . . . Mrs. Bradford. Seventy-nine in a fifty-five!" He slaps my license against his palm. "Are you moving here or just passing through?"

"Visiting," is all I give him.

"Tell you what. I'll bring a gauge back when I'm done writing you a ticket. You're going too fast to get off with just a warning."

I decide now's not the right time to joke about a rumor in high school about how he couldn't satisfy his girlfriend and she cheated on him with the quarterback.

Again he scans my license before his eyes drift to my ring finger.

"Sibley, eh?" He taps a finger at the smiling picture of me from three years ago, when hitting my thirties seemed like I'd hit my stride. If only I'd known what was in store for me. "I knew a girl. . ."

Except my last name is no longer Sawyer, and I'm no longer the girl he used to know.

I take a cursory glance at myself in the mirror. How have I aged compared to my classmates, to the general population? I've always thought I've done well, or at least faked it, able to afford some of the pricier creams and skin procedures to keep a youthful glow that lets me pass for my late twenties.

I decide to test him.

"Fletch?"

"Uh-huh." He doesn't notice his nickname, or if he does, he pays it no mind, laser focused on every detail of my out-of-state license.

And just like the thought of discount vodka, it makes my stomach seethe like I'm back in high school, a red plastic Solo cup pressed to my lips, drinking the vile liquid named after our state. It seems to be the only way to generate brand loyalty for liquor that tastes like an oil field.

His phone buzzes in his pocket, and impatient, he says, "We can skip the insurance. Just need that registration, and I can get you on your way."

"Fletch," I plead. I hadn't planned on announcing I was back home, but it looks like I have no choice.

"What?" he says automatically.

"Why're you such a dumb shit?"

With a swipe, his sunglasses land on top of his head. Narrowed slits regard me with disdain. "What did you just call me?"

I lower my glasses, and our eyes meet. Flicking my index finger and thumb against the license in his hand, I bellow, "Miles Andrew Fletcher, since when did you stop answering to your self-appointed nickname?"

His head instantly bows, a knee-jerk reaction to his mother screaming his full name whenever he was in trouble, which was often. My parents did the same with me.

I grin when his face lights up with recognition. A whistle escapes through the pucker of his mouth. "Wait! *Sibby Sawyer?*" His eyes drift again to my bare ring finger.

"Duh. How many Sibleys do you know?"

"None but you, thank the Lord."

"I see you've taken the town slogan to heart." I roll my eyes. "You always this slow on the uptake?"

"Well, we lost the only fast pony we had." His green eyes dance as he chuckles. My face must give something away because he's quick to point out, "I meant your wild streak. It's sorely missed around these parts."

"Oh, I know what you mean, Fletch," I tease. "I grew up beating you at every game we played. Even girls' softball."

"And broke every heart in the process."

"'Cept yours."

"Don't kid yourself, Sibby."

Sibby. My nickname rolls off his tongue just as quickly as it did back then. It's surreal to hear it after all these years.

"And last I knew, you were some kind of fancy doctor now." He pretends to try to remember my occupation. "What do you call it, a juris doctor?"

"That silly title? It's just a fancy piece of paper I hang in my office."

If I still had an office, I don't bother to mention.

My face burns at the memory of being escorted off the premises of my employer, a potted plant in hand, my navy suede Jimmy Choos clomping down the back staircase so I didn't have to take the elevator and risk the curiosity of more inquisitive eyes.

I focus on the holster that contains Fletch's gun and the handcuffs dangling from his waist while he examines my bare finger again.

It's coming.

"I thought you got married."

"I did."

He doesn't mention the noticeably absent jewelry but prods, "Everything okay?"

I don't bother to tell him I'm supposed to be at a rehabilitation clinic, and wearing jewelry isn't allowed. Or that I left my diamond engagement band and matching ring on my husband's dresser at his behest.

"We're taking a break." It's somewhat of a truth, somewhat of a lie. "Trial separation." I'm embarrassed at the thought Fletch is going to mention the plethora of crumpled, mascara-streaked napkins I've soaked from crying at the breakdown of my marriage and the silent rejection from my own mother.

"Marriage is hard," he says, commiserating. Without thinking, he blurts out, "I hope you picked a better guy than your father."

Both of our faces redden.

Ouch.

Refusing to engage with this subject, I stare at the absence of a band on his finger. "You were smart not to bother."

"Who said I didn't?"

"Miles Fletcher, who was the unlucky girl?"

"You know her. You guys used to be tight. Before the drama started."

That's one way to put it, I guess.

I unhinge my jaw, knowing exactly who he's talking about. I try not to throw up in my mouth at the thought of my archnemesis.

Kristin used to be what is now called a "frenemy," and we had our spats, whether it be over boys or other friends. A drama seeker, she loved being the center of attention at all costs, no matter who got hurt. I learned this the hard way.

When Kristin and Fletch started dating our senior year, I figured they deserved each other. It was after an unforgettable Halloween party, when Kristin spread a vicious rumor without regard for anyone involved. And after she dumped her boyfriend, Josh, for the umpteenth time, she and Fletch decided to give it a go. I never paid attention to see if their relationship fizzled or made it down the altar.

"Kristin and I were married for twelve years," he says proudly.

He would marry her, especially since she did everything in her power to destroy my family. *Stop making it about you,* I warn myself.

"You made it longer than most."

"Would've made it longer, but she, um, she, uh . . ."

I can't help myself. "Cheated?"

"Of course not." Crestfallen, he takes a deep breath. "How could you even ask that, with what . . ."

Shit. Foot, enter mouth. I'm royally screwing up my chances of getting out of here without a ticket, not to mention without a beautiful garnish of silver cuffs that can't be ordered from the Home Shopping Network.

"I'm sorry." I sigh. "It's been a long drive, and I'm not thinking clearly. I'm in desperate need of sleep." Sniffing my armpit jokingly, I confess, "And a shower."

I stare into the same wounded-animal eyes he gave me the afternoon of our earth-shattering fight, one that caused a close friendship of ten years to end promptly and, at the time, felt like an amputation of a necessary limb.

I extend an olive branch in the form of a small smile. "What happened with Kristin?"

"She died. I became a widower, not by choice."

I'd rather puke than say this, but I force it out. It's not like I haven't embellished or lied through my teeth for the majority of my career. "That's awful, Fletch. I'm really sorry to hear it." I touch his hand for a fleeting second. "I wish I would've known. Even with all our differences, that's not fair. And so young." I whisper, "Life is so unfair sometimes, isn't it?"

A rush of anger colors his cheeks. "It certainly is."

"I'm really sorry." I chew my lip. "I know you've had a tough go of it over the years."

"How would you know?" he rebukes. "You up and left. We could've leaned on each other."

Once again, I'm not taking the bait. I mustn't run my mouth right now. I might win the argument, but I'll lose the war. I'm thinking about how much more Fletch could do, like arrest me and haul me off to jail. I've already done a piss-poor job of blending in.

I need to keep him talking so he doesn't mention my plates again. If not, I'll be the headline by tomorrow morning, and if you think people don't read their newspapers in these parts, you're wrong. I can hear my mother now, worried about being the town gossip again.

"How's the farm?" His dad uses six acres of land to grow Christmas trees of different pine variations, including Scotch, white, and red tree species. We used to go there as a family tradition for the choose-and-harvest method, where we would cut down our own, in early December.

"Dad's still chugging away at the tree business."

"Seriously?" I screech. "I figured he'd have handed that off to one of you boys by now."

"He says he'll try for next year, but he always has to have multiple irons in the fire."

"Is Bryce taking over, or are you quitting the force?" His brother is two years older than him, and both are in constant competition to be the favorite child. The sour expression on his face tells me that hasn't changed.

"He'll have to, since I'm about to get a promotion." He shrugs like it's no big deal, but his posture straightens in an attempt to puff out his chest. "The police chief's *finally* retiring next year."

"Congratulations!" I joke. "I'll send you both a bottle of room-temperature vodka."

"Hmm . . ." He taps a finger against his chin. "I don't trust your brand preferences. I'd sooner siphon gas from the tank than drink that poison."

With another glance at my driver's license, he motions to the squad car. "Let me go run this, get the tire gauge, and I'll be back."

"You know, you're only prolonging my arrival," I say. "My mother's going to be all over your ass for keeping me."

"I should be over hers. Deborah never told me you were coming for a visit." He shakes his head sadly.

I'm aloof. "It's a bit of a . . . surprise."

"Surprise?" He fixes me with a stern look. He knows my mother hates surprises. Then he softens his gaze. "Though truth be told, I'm glad to see you. You must've come home because you heard the news."

"What news?" I pop my sunglasses back over my eyes to conceal my bewilderment. "Did something happen?"

Narrowing his eyes at me, Fletch asks when we last communicated.

I shrug. "I wrote her a few letters, and I didn't hear back . . ." My voice trails off. "Was this recently?"

He shifts his weight onto his other leg. "I think you'll see that the farm doesn't look quite the same."

"What do you mean?"

He scratches a mosquito bite on his arm. "She's having a hard time."

"When was the last time you saw her?"

"She called into the station a couple weeks ago."

"About what?" My stomach drops. "Is she okay?"

"I took the call." He motions in the opposite direction. "Deborah almost crashed into the ditch a couple miles from the farm."

"Was she avoiding a deer or coon?"

"No. She thought she saw an animal, though." He adds, "She was pretty shaken up. Said she'd been having trouble with her eyesight."

"Hmm . . ." I offer, "Maybe she just needs an appointment with her optometrist. I'll ask her. Speaking of poor judgment, I bet she wishes she could have avoided seeing you." I whistle. "If I remember correctly, you hit the Eisenburgs' award-winning heifer and our mailbox."

"That old cow was blocking the road," he protests, handing me back my license. "I hope you know I've buried the hatchet with Deborah."

As he fixes me with a hard stare, my cheeks redden. My mother always blamed Fletch erroneously for a broken window that wasn't his fault, but I never set the record straight. I'd scored free concert tickets from a radio station during my junior year of high school. Kristin was dating Bryce at the time, and all four of us went together. Our parents found out, and by the time we got home, we had no idea that we were busted. I had left a ladder hidden, the kind you use to escape a fire, but my dad had locked my bedroom window so I couldn't sneak back inside. I know he meant for me to come in the front door and face him, but Kristin threw a rock and shattered the glass so we could crawl back inside. My mother blamed Fletch because he stuttered and choked on his words for years at the mention of that night.

My throat becomes dry when I think about how junior year was the last time life felt normal. Everything went into the gutter in my senior year.

"Yeah. I should've told her the truth."

"There's more . . ." He opens his mouth, but a crackle comes through his radio, his name loud and clear. He speaks into the receiver and tells dispatch he'll be right there. "I gotta take this." Waving a hand, he says, "Just be cognizant of your surroundings. I'm not trying to scare you, but things have changed since your time, when we could just leave the doors unlocked. You probably know this, since you moved to a big city and all. Safety is an illusion. And go to bed." His pointed stare is directed at my bloodshot eyes and limp hair in need of a wash. "You look like you haven't slept in days."

"Good thing I only have two miles to go." I grin. "But okay. And thanks." I wrinkle my nose at him. "That's a nice way of telling me I look like shit."

A smile curls at his lips. "You know you can always count on me to tell the truth."

I try not to show my disgust. His truth isn't always factual; many times it's a matter of opinion. *His* opinion.

As I'm taking the Toyota out of park, he slaps his hand on the open window to get my attention. "And Sibby?"

Pausing with my foot on the accelerator, I wait.

"I'll give you a warm town welcome back to these parts if you slow the hell down." He bites his lip. "Please drive safely. We don't want to lose any more family members." His eyes linger on mine a second too long. "Or have any more *accidents*."

With a withering smile, I tuck the plastic back in my wallet. The word hits me like the sound of a pistol at the start of a race. I'm swiftly transported back in time to a difference of opinion between Miles Fletcher and me. We both have a different view of the turn of events, how they unfolded, and where to lay the blame.

I think my father's death was a tragic accident.

In contrast, Fletch alleges foul play and something sinister at the hands of my mother, Deborah. I do not agree with him, which puts us on opposing sides, with insurmountable obstacles between us.

Now, after Fletch manages one last nod, his footsteps crunch loudly as they retreat. A lump in my throat burgeoning, I forcefully turn off my hazard lights and jerk onto the blacktop.

It seems fitting that my welcome home would be from the person who chased me away to begin with.

PART THREE
SIBLEY & DEBORAH

CHAPTER 15
Sibley

As I reach the stretch of our twenty-seven-acre farm, I turn on my blinker, signaling out of habit.

I snicker. Using it seems silly, since it's obvious where I'm going.

In the rearview, Fletch slows behind me on the empty highway, giving the customary short, neighborly honk as his arm lingers out of the open window, a small wave as he speeds off.

Now that I've seen the wasteland the farm has become, it doesn't take me long to see what Fletch meant about changes.

Time has hit pause on the stark prairie, and it's as if I'm Rip Van Winkle waking from a very long nap to find everything exactly as it was, but not as it should be.

As I pass the ancient windmill, the blades rotate, lazily moving in the sun. I involuntarily shudder at the root cellar in the distance; it's now padlocked, with a heavy chain tethered across it.

At least no one can get stuck down there accidentally, I think grimly.

My gaze drifts to the toolshed, and I slow to a crawl, but I practically miss the edge of the gravel driveway; the distinction between the fragmented pieces of stone and the yard is now one overgrown mess. The infinite expansion of weeds has swallowed the broad stretch, and dandelions seem to proliferate in every square inch unoccupied by crabgrass.

When I hightailed it out of here, I thought of it like a lousy breakup—permanent and with finality.

Gripping the hard plastic of the steering wheel, I'm overcome with raw emotion. This new reality has me unnerved.

What did you expect? I chide myself. *She lives out here alone like a pariah.*

Did you really think folks would get over what happened out here?

They might've forgiven Jonathan's death, but not that of the church-going, volunteer-loving, perfect mother and wife, Cindy.

I shudder again as I settle back against the seat, my hand hesitating on the gearshift.

Despite the summer humidity, my whole body tingles with goose bumps when the red barn comes into my periphery, a visceral reaction I have when I think of that night.

The gambrel roof of the barn has two different slopes on each side, and even though the roof's designed to eliminate both water and snow, its worn-away shingles signal their own fatigue.

It must be hard to sag under the weight of guilt and time, I suppose.

My heart skips a beat.

If my mother isn't keeping the property up, what did she spend all the life insurance money on? She couldn't possibly be squirreling it away.

Part of the reason so many people think she did him dirty is tied to the exorbitant sum of money my mother inherited after my father died.

But looking at this eyesore, you wouldn't know it.

Maybe that's been her brilliant plan all along. Let the town think she's destitute. I guess after my long-term absence, she'd probably tell me it's none of my business.

Souring on the idea of a reunion and feeling guilty for abandoning this life for a new, shinier one, I already want to crawl under a rock.

If my mother was struggling, why didn't her doctor or the hospital call me?

Because you wanted nothing to do with the likes of Deborah Sawyer, I recall.

But why didn't Fletch bother to pick up the phone?

Because of the very same reasons, I lament.

Parched, I realize how thirsty I am.

At one of my pit stops, I picked up a red plastic cooler. Now I fumble for it in the back seat.

Most of the plastic bottles are filled with alcohol, a trick I've been using for years to avoid detection, which was another reason I wasn't keen on running into the police. Sniffing for one that's vodka, I'm dismayed to find this is my last bottle. After I tip my head back to swig it the same way people throw back coffee, it goes down smoothly, no chaser needed.

After the last drop is drunk, I toss the plastic back in the cooler.

One voice inside my head tells me I'm not an alcoholic while its counterproductive companion tells me I sorely need help.

Regardless, it's not enough.

I need more—a lot more—sedatives or liquid courage to calm my shredded nerves.

If I turn around and go back west, she'd never know I was here. I tell myself if my mother needed my help, she'd have responded to my attempts to reconcile.

It's a painful rejection, but it's one I've had to live with.

If I leave now, I could go straight to rehab, and Holden and my firm wouldn't know about the stunt I pulled.

I can't change the past, and by the looks of the place, there's nothing to salvage.

Except what good is living if I'm confined to four walls? I muse. *Whether it be a rehab facility or jail or in the form of my addiction?*

I squeeze my hands in my lap. *You're not a real addict, Sibley. That's what weak people admit to.*

By now, my mother has probably taken notice of a strange vehicle in the drive. She might have heard Fletch's neighborly honk before he continued on the highway stretch.

If I look through the small window over the kitchen sink, I bet I'll see her ogling at the disruption.

Taking another deep breath, I force myself out of the driver's seat before traipsing through the budding jungle to the front stoop of the faded box.

My mother always kept a well-tended garden and yard. Even after Daddy died, before falsehoods drowned out facts, neighbors pitched in and helped with chores until we got back on our feet. I'm disgusted the weeds have engulfed the wraparound porch to become a single land-scape without any ending or beginning. If you were a painter, you'd just make a swift stroke across the canvas.

How long has it been like this? I shake my head sadly.

Unfortunately, the house is not a pleasant sight for my tired eyes.

It's squalid, with faded siding from a century of battling four sea-sons and uncompromising weather patterns, and I wince at the disre-pair. In some places, vinyl's missing. One of the blue shutters dangles precariously off the window, like a cigarette hanging off someone's lips, signaling it could fall without warning.

Nailed to the spot, I stare at the ripped mesh in the screen door, drooping like a face with partial paralysis. A wave of nausea consumes me, and struck with an uncanny feeling, I pause.

I ran away from this ugly olive-green entrance, with no plans to return.

The red blinking light catches my attention. It belongs to a security camera hanging underneath the roofline.

Tentatively I knock, at first timidly and then with more force.

After all, she's not expecting me.

Thinking the front door will swing wide at any moment, I hear footsteps and the click of the lock, but it must be my imagination, since no one answers.

Shifting impatiently from foot to foot, I'm eager to see her reaction. But there is none. Because the door doesn't open.

I collapse on the rickety porch swing and rest my groggy head in my hands, considering my options. I could take a nap in the back seat and wait for her to come back, but on second thought, the exertion of standing up seems like more work than it's worth.

I moan. Maybe I can roll over on my side and nap until my mother arrives home. But what if she's not coming home anytime soon? Maybe she went out of town. That could be why the yard looks like a wildlife conservation area, I argue to myself as my eyes under their sagging lids peruse their surroundings.

And go where? I think. *And with whom?*

Suddenly a moment of clarity hits.

The hidden key.

Lethargic, I stumble to the side of the house, hopeful the farm's unchanged appearance means the rest is also untouched. We kept a spare key hidden inside an old metal container by the side of the house. Under the rusted lid, there was a tiny crevice in the top where only a small object like a key would fit.

Of course, it's not here anymore.

I decide to check the detached garage, wishing there were a window I could snoop through for my mother's car, just to confirm or deny her presence.

Frustrated, I run a hand through my unkempt hair. When I kick a loose board, I catch a rusted nail and utter a steady stream of curse words.

Unsatisfied, I follow them with a shrill yell, letting the universe know how I really feel about the kinks it keeps throwing in my master plan. I'm loud enough the visiting birds scatter, annoyed by the sudden interruption.

But my luck changes when I spot the rusted container pressed against the garage, partially hidden by an overgrown brush.

As I hold my breath, the box squeaks open, and . . . it's empty.

CHAPTER 16
Deborah

"Come on in," Dr. Alacoy tells Deborah warmly. "I'm just finishing up with some notes. I'll be right there."

Nodding her head, Deborah settles into the leather couch that's starting to feel like a second home, now that she's had multiple sessions.

Though she wouldn't go so far as to say she's a fan of coming, it doesn't cause her as much discomfort as it did. Deborah tells herself the meds can only help her feel better, and this way, she can show Robert she's willing to work on herself and isn't losing her grip on reality like before.

Flustered when she notices the drapes and windows are wide open, Deborah asks Alice if she can shut them.

"Of course." Alice waves her hand at the window. "Sorry. I was in here by myself and needed some natural light and fresh air."

Standing up, Deborah's caught off guard when she notices a blonde woman getting out of a white car across the street and then tossing something in the trash. She's wearing cutoff shorts and a tank top, and her hair rests on her head in a haphazard bun. Or maybe it's intentional, Deborah supposes, since shaggy ponytails and loose-fitting buns seem to be a popular trend.

The woman crosses the street toward her and stops abruptly on the corner. She takes a few tentative steps in the opposite direction and then, just as suddenly, turns around to pause and stare up at the sky. Her movements seem disoriented, as if she's not fully capable of carrying herself upright.

When Deborah shields her eyes from the sun, she notices the absence of a wedding ring. Alice is speaking to her back, but Deborah doesn't acknowledge her. "I got the records from your last MRI."

"Soren," Deborah whispers out loud.

"Beg your pardon?"

Deborah watches as the woman tightens the strap of her purse on her shoulder. When she twists around, Deborah scans the back of her shoulder for the defining mark. Instead, she sees artwork, some kind of tattoo, but can't make out the image.

Soren.

Tears well up in her eyes. She can't help herself.

Deborah cups her hands by her mouth and hollers, "Soren, is that you?" Startled, the woman glances around for the voice responsible for shouting.

"Right here." Deborah knocks at the open windowpane. "I'm right here."

"Do you know that woman?" Alice stands next to her at the window.

"Yes," Deborah manages to choke out. "Please excuse me. I have to go." Not bothering to grab her purse, Deborah darts out of the office and outside, but the woman is no longer standing on the sidewalk. She's disappeared, almost as if she vanished into thin air.

As she walks into a few different stores, Deborah hurriedly scans the faces of the few people she encounters, but none are the woman. Recognition lights up in Deborah's eyes at a sales clerk she knows from church, but unwilling to make small talk, she abrasively asks if she's seen the blonde woman. The clerk stammers as confusion clouds her face.

Frustrated at her slow reaction, Deborah fumes a goodbye and storms out. The blonde woman couldn't have evaporated.

When Deborah is back on the sidewalk, she glances at the parking space where the white vehicle was parked just a few minutes ago.

It's empty.

I must have the wrong spot. Deborah shakes her head as she paces mindlessly up and down the concrete, scanning for the white car.

Clenching her fists angrily at her sides, she blames herself for not memorizing the license plate. A tightness wells up in her chest, and unable to breathe, Deborah rests a hand on her throat, reassured when Alice joins her on the sidewalk.

"Don't let me suffocate," Deborah manages to whisper.

Gingerly, Alice takes Deborah's elbow and walks her back inside the office, where the window and drapes are now closed.

"I think I have heatstroke," Deborah confesses, sinking into the couch.

"I think it's a panic attack." Alice hands her a glass. "What happened with that woman? Who is she?"

"I guess she left." Deborah gratefully sips the water.

"You seemed alarmed to see her. And now you're having a bout of anxiety," Alice points out gently. "Did something happen between the two of you?"

"She's from my past, is all." Deborah twists uncomfortably on what is usually a comfortable couch.

"Do you want to talk about her?" Alice asks. "Soren, is that what you called her?"

"Not right now." Deborah brings a sweaty palm to her forehead. "I didn't know she was alive."

Alice starts to ask a question, and almost as if she thinks better of it, she pauses with her mouth wide open. Deborah thinks she looks like she's trying to catch flies.

With a resigned glance, Alice shuts her mouth and settles in the chair. Holding up a thick file, she flips through the pages. "I got the record of your MRI back, and I'd like to schedule another CT scan."

Deborah is only half listening. "Is everything okay?"

"I think we just need to complete the puzzle," Alice says thoughtfully. "A couple pieces aren't fitting correctly, and I'd like to make sure we have the most up-to-date information possible."

"I see." Deborah leans her head back against the leather. She wishes she had a couch like this at the house. She'd surely be able to sleep then.

"Let me ask you this," Alice says. "How are you feeling on your meds?"

"I'm still adjusting to them." Deborah closes her eyes. "My brain feels like mush."

"Ah, we call that 'brain fog.'"

"It makes it impossible for me to follow a train of thought." Deborah likens it to driving down a street and having it dead-end every time. Her brain merely screeches to a sudden halt.

"Are you sleeping better?"

"I am, but I feel like I want to stay in bed." Deborah clutches the water glass tightly. "It's as if I can't get my day started. When I do get up, I have no energy."

"Do you feel depressed?"

"No." Deborah's eyes flicker open. "I should be thrilled."

Alice waits for Deborah to express her emotions.

"My boyfriend—oh yes, I told you about him. Robert, he talked about us moving in together."

"That's exciting!" Alice says. "Congratulations."

"It seems weird to say 'boyfriend' at my age . . ."

"Are you ready for this next step?"

"I think so. It's just hard because I've been independent for so long." Deborah bites her lip. "I'd be lying if I said I wasn't nervous. I'm super anxious about it."

"Let's talk about your anxiety." Alice asks her questions, and Deborah tries to answer as truthfully as possible.

"Have you dated or lived with anyone since your husband passed away?"

"No. That's another reason this is such a huge change." She takes a deep inhale. "And my husband, Jonathan, we didn't have the best marriage. It was rocky . . . it was always bad. It wasn't a fit."

"If you knew it wasn't a match, I'm curious to know why you married your husband, then."

"I didn't want to." In a tempestuous voice, Deborah recalls her former love. "I dated a guy named Edward in high school. We were very much in love, but he joined the navy and got his papers to go overseas." Deborah is always surprised at the emotion she conjures up when she thinks of this. Alice must notice her discomfort, because Deborah feels a tissue pressed into her hand.

"My father, being a preacher, didn't like the idea of me moving to different military bases or leaving our hometown and his watchful eye, regardless if it was for a good cause like serving our country."

She dabs at the crease of her eyelid. "Unbeknownst to me, my father forced Edward to break up with me on a visit home."

"How did that make you feel?"

Deborah wonders if Alice has been listening. "I felt like my heart had been yanked out with pliers."

"So when did your husband come into the picture?"

"Not long after. My parents forced me to attend a singles mixer at the church. They said Jonathan was a God-fearing fellow, would make a good husband, and had farming in his blood. Marriage was the furthest thing from my mind at the time. Except . . ."

Deborah inhales a sharp breath. "I found out I was a couple months pregnant after I met Jonathan, except it wasn't his. I thought I was depressed, since I was tired and moody all the time. I blamed it on missing Edward, but my mother made me take a test. When it came back positive, she forbade me from telling Jonathan or my father since I was 'used goods,' and certainly Jonathan wouldn't want to marry me." Deborah chuckles. "And she would've been right. When Jonathan asked my father's permission, my mother told me I didn't have a choice, that we had to act fast to pass the child off as his, and six weeks after we met, we were married in my parents' backyard.

"I was absolutely devastated, and I missed Edward like crazy," she admits. "I cried through the wedding and the awkward lovemaking, but he thought it was from inexperience. It was painful; he just didn't know it was the heartbreak kind."

She recounts with a deep sadness, "I found out later Edward sent letters, but my father ripped them up and burned them. At least that's what my mama told me before she died."

"Is that what you meant when you said"—Alice consults the notepad—"that your father could be 'cunning'?"

"Yes." Deborah crumples the tissue in her hand. "After Jonathan and I sat down with my parents and announced we were having a baby, my father cornered me a couple weeks later." Deborah drops her face into her hands. "He wanted me to . . ."

Alice stares at her intently, intrigue written all over her face, the pen dangling in her hand. Then the beeping of her watch interrupts the high tension in the room.

CHAPTER 17
Sibley

Even though I'm dead tired, I can't seem to get comfortable tilting my seat back for a nap. The back seat isn't any better, my muscles frazzled with tension and nervous energy. Disturbed by the eyesore in front of me and a grumbling stomach, I decide to return to town, grab some food, and stock up on supplies.

I'm craving the local diner and some hometown food. The Freeze was the only hot spot in town when I was growing up, the celebratory place to go after home games and a popular date hangout. A small diner located at the edge of the town square, it's known for its fried food and prizewinning homemade pie and ice cream. Black-and-white tiled floors, a jukebox, and red leather booths take you back to an earlier era.

Before I eat, I decide to go to the gas station and stock up on liquor, then go through the drive-through. We only have two gas stations in town, and I pick the closest to the diner. The cashier is on a personal call and doesn't pay much attention to the few liters of vodka I pick up, along with soda water and orange juice to use as chasers.

As I'm waiting at the drive-through, I do everything to ignore the intense craving that's causing tremors throughout my body.

Humming along to music, I play a word game on my phone, but the incessant voice doesn't refrain from berating me about what a loser I am.

I ignore the internal bully so I can eat my food. After swallowing the last greasy bite of my burger, I decide it can't hurt to have a couple of sips of my new purchase before I head back to the farm. It'll mellow me out and help me sleep. And if the inside of the house is as chaotic as the outside, I might want to get a hotel. *You can't afford to stay in even cheap motels,* I remind myself, opening the bottle.

A large swallow burns down my throat, and I hope it stops the headache building behind my temples.

In the side mirror, I notice a rusted-out Ford hanging a left at the stop sign.

It looks identical to my mother's ancient beater. It was old then, and by now, I'd have thought she'd have upgraded, what with all the money she inherited from my daddy.

Thinking about this, I get heated, and wiping a frustrated hand across my brow, I watch her turn past a cluster of brick buildings on the square, then disappear from sight.

She didn't give me one dime.

Thinking about the farm and my deep-seated hatred toward my mother, I continue to take generous sips. Before I realize it, I've successfully emptied a third of the bottle.

After opening my car door, I carefully climb out and throw my empty paper bags in the trash can. I consider driving back to the farm, but without a way to enter, what's the point? Even if my mother is running errands and isn't ready to go back home, she can give me the key so I can go lie down.

I'm starting to feel unwell, the sun beating down as I make my way across the street.

Glancing up at the striped awnings, I consider where she would've gone. There's a beauty salon on this side of the street. Maybe she's in there getting her hair done.

If that's the case, she could be a while, I think impatiently, the buzzing in my head growing louder, decibel by decibel.

A loud voice drowns out even the pounding, but I don't know where it's coming from. I turn around and don't see anyone else on the pavement yelling or even talking.

Weird.

"I need sleep," I grumble.

Pushing myself forward, I walk into the salon, but the receptionist shakes her head. No one by the name of Deborah has an appointment today.

Perspiration drips down my forehead as I fight to stay upright.

Dizzy, I ask the receptionist to use their bathroom. She gives me a curious glance as I pass the desk, my steps uneven and loud, or maybe I just imagine this when it's really the beating of drums in my head.

After sinking to my knees in the pristine pink bathroom, I watch as the remnants of food and alcohol eject themselves from my stomach, leaving me with the taste of bile and salt.

Shakily, I wet a paper towel to wipe my brow and face. I rinse my mouth out and pop a stick of gum, my eyes bleary and unfocused in the mirror.

I turn right instead of left to a red exit sign next to the bathroom and avoid the judgmental eyes of the clientele. I'm relieved the door opens to a back parking lot, and sure enough, there's my mother's car.

She's not visible through the windows of the flower shop or dry cleaner. The next entrance is not glass, just metal, with no windows, just brick.

Curious, I look for a sign, but only letters are sketched on the outside.

Dr. Alacoy is spelled out in bold black stencils, but there are no hours or even a phone number listed. It doesn't specify the type of doctor.

My interest piqued, I try the handle, expecting it to be locked. Surprisingly, it's open.

Since I can't see inside, I expect to be welcomed into a dark lab or something. Instead, the front room is airy and clean. There's no reception desk, just a couple of chairs. The small area is uncluttered. A couple of paintings hang on the wall, but they aren't drab walls; they are painted a warm blue tone.

I'm wondering what type of office this is since I don't see a buzzer or a security camera.

Then, hearing voices echo from behind the only door in the room, which happens to be closed, I tiptoe toward it.

I feel like a snooping intruder, but I guess I am. I sheepishly lean my head against the door. There's no denying one of the voices belongs to Deborah, my mother.

I'm not expecting her to mention my father, Jonathan, in her next sentence.

My breathing becomes labored.

Is this a therapist's office, I wonder?

Touching the wood paneling of the door, I hear Deborah say, "After the wedding, he started using his fists, and I can't describe the relief I felt that the baby wasn't made up of his genes."

Another female voice, louder than my mother's muted one, asks, "Over the years, did you ever want to tell Jonathan the baby wasn't his?"

"Hell no!" My mother raises her voice, sounding upset. "He would've killed me. And our daughter. That's why I never left."

Wait? *What?* I chew on this news as my brain tries to play catch-up.

My deceased father *isn't* my real father? And she's claiming to some doctor he was abusive?

Covering my mouth with my hand, I force myself to keep my emotions in check so I don't fling open the door and unleash a tirade of anger on a mother who doesn't know I'm here.

"And nothing more from Edward?"

"Not until we bumped into each other a few years later, when he was home visiting friends. His parents had moved away by this point." Her tone softens. "And he asked me to leave Jonathan. I was devastated Edward had moved on with his life and gotten married." Deborah's voice fills with contempt. "To make matters worse, he got married to an awful woman."

"He told you this?"

"Yes. He begged me to leave Jonathan, said he would leave his wife in a heartbeat for me."

"Did he know then he was the father to your daughter?"

"No," Deborah cries. "At least not that I know of."

"If he was the love of your life, I'm curious to know why you didn't leave?"

Deborah sounds like a strangled cat. "Even though he would leave his wife for me, I couldn't leave my husband. I was a coward, worried about what Jonathan would do to him. And to us."

"If not for fear, would you have left Jonathan to be with Edward?"

I almost suffocate myself during the long pause.

"Yes," my mother finally admits. "If our daughter wasn't around, easily. It's a double-edged sword, since I would've loved for us to be a family and for her to know her real father. But I knew Jonathan would never let that happen."

"Were you not concerned about breaking up Edward's marriage?"

"Not really," my mother sniffs. "Not really. At the time, he didn't have kids. I know Edward eventually had children, but they didn't live here."

"When did Edward find out about your daughter and vice versa?"

"I believe when she was in middle school. She and I were walking around the town square, and I could feel someone watching us. When I looked up, Edward stood stock still, staring at his spitting image. I didn't even have to say it."

My jaw clenches. Oddly enough, I remember this moment because it stuck out like a sore thumb. In public, my mother barely acknowledged the opposite sex. I thought it was because she was a timid creature—a pushover. But this time, she ran to the car and crumbled into a tearful mess.

No wonder Jonathan never seemed to trust her or *like* her or this sham marriage. I saw how his eyes bulged with resentment when he thought no one was looking.

Now that I think about it, my supposed father was usually in the barn or the fields . . . avoiding her.

"Were you worried about Edward's wife or children finding out about your daughter, that they had a half sibling?"

My mother's response is too muffled to hear.

Another lapse, this time from the woman. "I don't think you've said. What's your daughter's name?"

"Sibley."

"When did you tell Sibley the identity of her real father?"

There's a long pause, or maybe it feels that way because I'm holding my breath.

It's like an explosion of fireworks in my head when Deborah reveals, "I haven't."

Not only is my mother a cheater, but she's also a liar. I knew my mother had been unfaithful. I just didn't realize it was more than once. Not only did Deborah have an affair, but she got knocked up and passed me off as another man's child.

The once-effervescent room becomes suffocating as it sways in front of me, and beads of sweat form on my upper lip at the earth-shattering news. I'm not Jonathan's real daughter, and my birth father is a man named Edward?

Who is he, and more importantly, *where* is he?

A deep pain jabs me deep in the heart.

There's a rustle of tissue or paper, and I can hear Deborah's pitiful crying as she acts like a tortured soul. Always the victim. Maybe Fletch wasn't far from the truth.

I've heard enough.

Eager to flee from the admission of Deborah's guilt and lies, I start to tiptoe away from the door. Unfortunately, my shoe squeaks, and I don't bother being quiet. I start to sprint out into the sunshine, stumbling over my own two feet, a torrent of tears streaming down my face.

CHAPTER 18
Sibley

In the safety of my car, I drive aimlessly with no direction in mind, passing more storefronts, most empty—a reminder that nothing lasts forever—save for a pharmacy or a gathering spot to have coffee. It's hard to have longevity in this town, and apparently, not even my "father" was meant to be a permanent fixture in my life.

Without a concerted effort, I park in front of a bar fittingly called Bar on Main. The other option down the street is Mickey's. These are the only two bars I know of in town, and though they act like archrivals, it's ludicrous to me since both serve the same watered-down alcohol by the same breed of bored bartender, listening to the same type of music repeatedly on the jukebox.

The permanently tired fortysomething woman behind the bar nods in greeting as I sit down on a squeaky barstool.

"ID."

"Seriously?"

Her short bob nods up and down.

"Aren't you cute, making me feel young?" I chuckle. "I bet you say that to all the girls."

"The ones under fifty-five, at least." She shrugs. "What'll it be for your liquid lunch?"

Sliding my ID out of my wallet, I say, "Vodka cranberry, a splash of lime."

After a quick glance at my driver's license, she sets it down and lowers a glass off a shelf. I know I'm out of my bubble when it's assumed well vodka is my preference. She pours my glass and serves it to me on a paper napkin.

Taking a long sip, I feel her eyes boring into the side of my face.

"This is just what I needed." The circumstances of the morning have weakened my resolve when it comes to drinking even more.

Considering me, she puts her hands on her generous hips. "Say, your name looks familiar. You from around here?"

"I grew up here."

"Sibley." She rattles it off. *"Sibley Bradford."*

I hold out my hand to shake hers.

"Miranda." She gives it a limp shake. "Don't know that last name."

"It was Sibley Sawyer." I shrug. "You might know my mother from around town. Deborah. Deborah Sawyer."

"Wait a minute." She peers at me. "You lose your father?"

I nod.

"He a farmer?"

"Uh-huh."

"Yeah. I remember hearing that." She taps a long talon on the counter. "Long time ago, right?" Without waiting for confirmation, she continues. "But those stories don't die." She pours me another round and slides it across the counter. "Where do you live now?"

"Arizona."

"Your mom in the same house?"

"Yep. Still on the farm."

"Is your farm by any chance close to the Guthries' place, John and Nancy?" She huffs a strand of dirty-blonde hair out of her face.

"Not too far. They used to throw all the holiday parties."

"That's it!" She points her sharp fingernail at me. "That's where I recognize you."

"Did you go to their parties a lot?"

"Not often, but I was at the Halloween party *that* night."

I almost heave the vodka and cranberry with a splash of lime back up, my throat burning like I took shots of Fireball instead. Miranda would remember that night my senior year. She would have been present. Why wouldn't she? Everyone knows everything in this town.

John and Nancy Guthrie have two kids close to my age. They were notorious for their epic parties, and the Halloween one was quite the extravaganza, a yearly gathering with hayrides, a bonfire, and a costume party. Much to the disgruntlement of the youth, parents were also invited. If kids wanted to sneak in liquor, they had to mix it in pop bottles beforehand.

My parents, though asked, rarely went to parties.

This year stood out because of my mother and what she did. My mother didn't go to many places alone, probably because we only had one vehicle, my daddy's truck.

This time, my daddy had to go out of town and pick up a malfunctioning part for his tractor. It wasn't until I got older that it seemed weird we only had one car, but I guess I assumed we were poor growing up. My mother didn't work outside the home, and farming isn't an easy way to make a living. So many uncontrollable factors can come into play—the weather, crop prices, and crop production.

That evening was the catalyst that started the downhill trajectory of my life. It might've been only one night, but like a destructive tornado, it ravaged our family and ruined lives and friendships.

Not to mention it carried a health hazard—death.

I remember that night vividly. I was upstairs in my bathroom, putting the finishing touches on my makeup, when my mother walked in.

"Need any help?" My mother smiled at me.

Setting down the eyeliner I used to draw the thin lines, I returned her gaze. "I don't think so." Twirling around, I showed off my black tights and leotard.

"Your tail," she reminded me. "Don't forget your tail. It's the most prized possession of a cat."

"What about the whiskers?"

"What about them?" She put a hand to my face, almost smearing my not-yet-dry whiskers.

"Mother," I said crossly.

"Let me attach it for you." She used a safety pin to secure the long fabric tail in place. It was nothing more than black pantyhose stuffed with black garbage bags and shaped into a bendable limb.

I slid on the finishing touch to my costume with a flourish, proudly staring at the headband with faux-fur cat ears. Giving my real ear a gentle tug, she asked, "Who's picking you up?"

"Kristin."

"I thought you two weren't speaking?"

I sighed at the thought of our tumultuous friendship. We would fight, go weeks without speaking, and then inevitably find our way back to each other.

"We're friends this week," I murmured, though I was pissed because she had decided to do a group *Wizard of Oz* costume when we hadn't been speaking, and admittedly, I was jealous. It was much cooler than my cat attire.

What my mother said next blew my mind. "Do you mind if I ride with you?"

"You wanna go to the party?"

"Yes, I think so." She nervously touched the cross pendant that never left her neck. "I never get out, and it should be fun."

"Will you have a good time without Daddy?"

Frowning at the question, she stammered, "They invite us every year, and we never go. He's not one for hocus-pocus and costume parties. He thinks it's a holiday for the devil."

"And just think, you grew up with a preacher dad." I smirked. "Did he let you celebrate Halloween?"

"We could dress up. The church had its own fall party every year, so I got to trick-or-treat that way."

"Okay." I shrugged. "Just promise you won't embarrass me."

Most teens would be disgusted if their parents asked to ride with them to a party, but I was curious to see my mother in another setting. I offered to help her pick out a costume, but she was adamant she could find something to wear.

When I barged in her bedroom a little bit later without knocking, she quickly covered up her body with a towel. I thought it was due to modesty. We weren't a household that talked about or displayed nudity or sex.

"You know better than to come in without knocking," she chastised.

"I just wanna help with your costume."

"Maybe I shouldn't go," she sighed. "I have nothing to wear."

"Why can't you be a witch and wear your black velvet dress?"

"It's sleeveless."

"It's not like it's inappropriate."

She shook her head like I wasn't understanding, and at the time, I didn't.

Sitting down on her bed, she put her head in her hands. I heard muffled crying, and I thought she was upset at missing the party.

"I'll find you something to wear," I offered brightly.

And so I did.

While I rummaged through old boxes in our attic, she put her dark hair in waves, the perfect accompaniment to the long-sleeve hippie dress I'd found. We located a leather strap for her to use as a headband, and after we'd selected a couple of pieces of chunky costume jewelry, she embodied a flower child from the seventies. As I applied makeup to her face, I realized how pretty my mother was. She was young, only in her thirties, which was crazy to think about. But she never wore makeup, always went plain faced. Dowdy, even.

Using the same eyeliner as I had for my whiskers, I drew a peace symbol on her right cheek.

"All set." I smiled proudly.

She seemed amazed at the transformation, her grin as wide as her flared sleeves. Even Kristin whistled at my mother's costume and whispered to me how hot she looked.

It was true: neither of us had seen my mother dolled up.

And more than that, I saw a different side of my mother, one I had never seen before. Instead of timid, she was glowing, her posture relaxed instead of rigid. She commanded the room instead of begging to blend into the carpet.

When we arrived at the Halloween party, Miles and Bryce were there, along with their mom, Cindy.

I noticed before I took off with my friends that Cindy didn't seem thrilled to see us. Usually, she treated me like one of her kids, the daughter she never had, but as soon as we walked in, her face turned to stone, an impenetrable gaze fixed in our direction.

We said hello, but Cindy was distant.

I forgot about it, because later Kristin and her boyfriend, Josh, had a fight, prompting her to want to leave. She was hysterically crying, and since she was my ride, I told her I would find my mother so we could go.

But I couldn't find her.

Kristin threw a fit, and I told her to go ahead and ask Miles or Bryce to give us a ride home, but she refused.

I went in search of my mother, checking the firepit, knocking on the doors of the closed rooms in the farmhouse, and asking around.

No one had seen her.

Annoyed, I went for a walk, impatient to find her. The evening was chilly, and I was only wearing a thin leotard. My teeth were chattering without the heat of the bonfire.

I should've brought a coat, I berated myself.

As I headed down a dark path toward the silo, I became terrified when a shadowy figure came running toward me. At first, I didn't know who it was, but the pink sequins of Kristin's Glinda the Good Witch costume sparkled when they caught the moon's bare light.

"You don't want to go that way," she warned.

"Why not?"

"Two people are getting it on."

"So? Stop being such a prude." I rolled my eyes. "Who is it? People in our class?"

Breathlessly, she shook her head. "It's adults."

"Let's go see who it is."

"No! It's gross." She stuck out her tongue. "Plus, I thought we were trying to find your mom."

"We are."

"Then let's go back inside. It's damn cold out here."

"I thought you didn't want to run back into Josh?"

"Screw him." She sniffed. "Now that homecoming is over, I'm done."

Though we walked back toward the loud music and sounds from the party, we didn't go back inside. Kristin lit up a cigarette, and I could tell by the way she was chain-smoking one after the other, just like my daddy did, she was agitated.

Josh found her, and now she wasn't in a rush to leave, so they went inside.

Bored, I sat on the steps of the wooden deck, trying to keep myself warm but not wanting to rejoin the cacophony.

It was a full moon, and I was sitting quietly, the darkness enveloping me, when two shadows appeared from the direction of the silo. I was rubbing my legs for warmth, curious to see who the adults were who had disappeared to make out—or do more, I supposed.

Assuming it was a couple, probably a friend's parents, I waited, wanting to tease a classmate about this in the morning. The pair were close enough their shoulders touched, with one leaning into the other. I could tell by the way one arm was draped over the other that they were holding hands.

They stopped as they got closer to the house, disappearing behind a large tree with branches that shielded them from view.

The wood railing hid most of me, but I crouched down and hid underneath the deck, knowing they would walk right over my head when they reached the house.

I peered between the slats in the railing, and when they entered my field of vision, it was like they'd become a different couple. There were at least three feet of distance between them, the earlier closeness either imagined or gone.

My gaze was level with their knees, and my eyes widened when I spotted the knee-high brown boots the woman was wearing.

They were my brown boots, the ones I'd let my mother borrow for her costume.

And obviously, the man was not my father.

I was frozen in horror. He wasn't a stranger either.

He smelled like spruce and the outdoors when he hugged me.

It was Miles Fletcher's dad.

Horrified, I had no intention of ever crawling out of my hiding spot, preferring to curl up in a ball and die. I stayed concealed for what felt like hours but was probably only minutes.

Numbness settled over my body. Some from the cold, some from the shock. My face, my legs, my hands.

When I returned to the party, my mother was sitting on a barstool, talking to a blonde woman. I approached her. "Where have you been?" Even speaking sounded monotone. "We're ready to go."

"Sorry," she apologized. "I must've lost track of time."

Kristin drove us home, but Josh was with us, and I noticed Kristin was talking too fast and not making eye contact with my mother or me. When she dropped us off, her goodbye was forced. My mother didn't seem to notice, and inside, I watched as she hurriedly washed the makeup off her face, all traces of the party evaporating from her pores as if she were Cinderella getting home from the ball, turning back into a frumpy housewife.

I wanted to ask my mother about what I'd seen. The words were on the tip of my tongue, but I couldn't force them out.

The next day at school, my stomach dropped when Kristin brought it up at my locker.

In a whisper, Kristin told me what she'd seen, how my mom and that man had been kissing and necking, their hands all over each other. But she couldn't keep watching; it had felt wrong, so she'd rushed out when they'd started to undress.

She promised she'd never say a word, and I believed her at that moment. I hoped it would become old news now that she had more Josh problems to talk about.

A couple days later, after a fight over something trivial, half the school heard what a cheating whore my mother was.

My contorted reflection in the mirror behind the bar causes me to glance up. I'm grimacing while Miranda stares at me with wide eyes. "You okay, darling?"

"Yeah. Sorry." I shake my head sadly. "Memory lane."

"Yikes. I shouldn't have mentioned that night." Miranda blushes crimson. "You probably get tired of talking about all this old drama."

"I was just thinking how my former best friend and I had a falling-out then," I muse. "Actually, both of my best friends."

"You know, Kristin wrote Deborah a letter before she died."

"Really?" I'm incredulous. "Saying what?"

"I'm not really sure. Hell, it could be just another rumor." She wipes a rag over the bar even though I'm sure it's unnecessary, since the room is empty except for us.

"You know . . ." Miranda sucks on her lip. "You should ask your mother about it."

I watch as her unreasonably long claws get caught in a strand of hair and she mutters a curse word.

Taking this as my cue to cash out, I bid Miranda adieu.

CHAPTER 19
Sibley

When I stumble out to my car and lock eyes with my reflection in the rearview, my face is drenched with sweat, perspiration clinging to my upper lip.

As I drive, I warn myself to slow down. You'd think I'd be overly cautious because of my earlier encounter, but I'm in a warped mood, my foot pressed on the accelerator as the old beater lurches, struggling to gain speed. My only concern is outrunning the instability of the emotions that threaten to internally combust.

I pass a rare sight on the road of another vehicle, an old tan Buick that's at least a decade old but looks brand new. It most likely belongs to an elderly person who drives a few hundred miles a year and keeps it garaged the rest of the time.

Scanning the driver inside, I realize it's Nora, our elderly neighbor, who must be in her nineties by now.

I debate whether to wave.

She's not going to know who I am, but it's the neighborly thing to do. I can't remember her without white hair and gnarly hands smelling of flour and turpentine. The woman always had keen eyes behind her spectacles and an insatiable taste for gossip.

When I give her a shrill honk, I startle the poor woman, though she attempts a flimsy wave. I careen around her; my reckless driving has her behind me in a matter of seconds as I gain distance.

I need to focus on something other than my jaded emotions, and flicking on the radio, I can't settle on rock or oldies. Talk radio can be so dull, depending on the topic and the host.

I find an alternative channel and drum my fingers on the wheel. It's a song popular from my high school days.

I try for the high notes, hitting my lung capacity, and then burst into laughter at my voice, a high-pitched hyena sound that never can reach quite the right note.

Before I know it, I'm sobbing, my shoulders hunched over the steering column as if embracing it.

When I pull into the derelict yard, I have to swerve to avoid one of the farm cats that seem to be in endless supply. Wiping a hand across my nose, I remember why I wasn't able to stay in the first place. I don't have a key.

Most of the windows on the first floor are solid panes and don't open, and the kitchen window is too small for me to climb through. I walk around the perimeter of the porch, but I'm unable to peer inside because the blinds are closed. Shrouded in darkness, the house has an ominous quality to it, even in the daylight.

My mother's bedroom and bathroom are on the first floor, the addition she begged my assumed father for my junior year of high school. He didn't want to spend the money, but she convinced a couple of neighbors to help, and it ended up being a group project.

In fact, after everyone pitched in on our remodel, my parents returned the favor for a few of the neighbors who were tired of their old farmhouses and wanted more functional rooms.

The window in the master bath on the first floor might work. It's not very wide, but I bet I can cram my frame through it.

It's locked, but I have a solution.

I pick up a rock and toss it at the pane. It takes me a couple of tries since I feel off kilter and woozy. After winding up like a baseball player, I launch another stone through the glass, and it finally shatters.

The sound of breaking glass can't repress the acute feeling that someone's eyes are on me.

I stand in silence for a moment. Paranoid, I sneak glances around, barely able to see through the tall, dense grass in some areas.

Ignoring the chill running down my spine and my pounding head-ache, I decide I'm acting ridiculous. It's because of the news flash about the prison; I'm on edge.

In the toolshed, I find a pair of thick gloves and a broom. After using the wooden handle to brush away the excess shards of glass, I drag the metal tin over to the window to use as a stool.

I'm sweaty and hot, and it's not as easy as it looks on television to climb through a broken window without scraping yourself on shards. After I land with a loud thud on the bathroom floor, I toss the rock back outside.

Staring at the splotchy mirror over the sink, I pry open the medi-cine cabinet. Inside is a miniature pharmacy, white and orange pill bottles lining the shelves to full capacity.

Jesus, Deborah, I think, examining the labels. I wonder how care-fully she keeps inventory or if she'd notice any missing.

After I slam the cabinet shut, I step into her mostly tidy bedroom, relatively similar after all these years. Deborah's habits haven't changed when it comes to making her bed. I roll my eyes at the abundance of decorative pillows that take up a chunk of it.

Her closet is still overflowing with clothes that are either too small or outdated by two decades. The unforgiving rocking chair that belonged to her mother rests in the corner of the room, and a fabric seat cushion is now attached, to make it bearable, I presume.

Making my way through the small downstairs, I scrunch my nose at the smell of cat piss and coffee. Since when did she inherit an indoor cat? Feral ones used to run all over the farm, great for catching barn mice, but Daddy always warned us about feeding strays, how they would never leave. My mother had a bleeding heart and begged unsuccessfully to keep every one of them as a house pet.

Mournfully, I study my father's old chair, his existence made known by the plethora of cigarette burns forging a path down the battered leather. My mother tossed almost everything of his shortly after his death, but oddly, she kept his recliner and dining room chair, as if he still needed a seat at the table.

But he's not your father, I woefully remind myself.

Scanning the rest of the small space, I'm baffled by the messiness. Pots and pans and silverware cover every inch of counter space in the kitchen. Boxes of pantry items are stacked on the scarred table and the Formica countertops. I assume the pantry is overflowing, but I'm amazed to find it scarce. It's as if spring cleaning started and never finished.

Disgusted at the dirtiness, I shake my head in alarm. *I guess you have your first project,* I think, ripping off the shred of newspaper clinging to the bottom of my shoe.

When I reach the front door, I fumble open both locks with trembling hands to pretend I entered the way most would: through the actual door.

The adjoining living room has fared a little better. The furniture is the same, old and shabby, but at least it's reasonably clean. I'm already tired of the house's gloominess, so I open the drapes to let some light in through the picture windows.

Intending to wait up for my mother, I make room to sit by moving a pile of blankets on the couch. Noticing my favorite, a crocheted one made by my grandma, I spread it over my lap.

I promise myself I'll just shut my eyes for a few minutes of rest. However, the bright morning sunlight is warm and inviting, consoling me gently to sleep.

It's as if I never left. The hum of the refrigerator, the chitchat of birds, but mostly the solitude: they welcome me home with open arms, their familiarity beckoning me to remember this is where I once belonged.

CHAPTER 20
Deborah

A white vehicle is parked sideways in the drive when Deborah comes home, blocking her path to the garage.

It looks like the car from earlier, but she can't be too sure.

Standing at the rear bumper, Deborah strokes her chin, staring at the ripped remains of where a temporary plate should be, shaking her head.

Deborah notices bald tires and dark tint missing in places, as if someone took a razor blade to shave off portions in vertical stripes.

Peering through the scratched tint, she's disappointed no one's inside, and all she spots in the back seat is a red cooler and an over-stuffed suitcase.

She tries the handle, but it's locked.

That's not the case with the front door, which is ajar. *Did I accidentally leave it open?* Deborah shoves her knuckles in her mouth. She moved the metal tin after the incident. She doesn't keep a hidden key anymore, just in case someone wants to ransack the house.

What the . . .

Deborah peers up at the security camera, irked she can't rely on it to provide her any basic details before she decides whether it's safe to enter. The recorded images take too long to download because of the spotty reception on the farm and typically appear black and grainy on her phone screen. If anything, it's supposed to be a deterrent, except in this case . . .

As she waffles on what to do, Robert doesn't answer, so she shakily dials the emergency number. After all that's happened, she doesn't want to assume the identity of her uninvited visitor.

Relieved an operator quickly answers, she doesn't offer a greeting, just a mumbled string of words.

"I don't understand," the male voice says. "Who's at your house?"

"I'm not sure," Deborah whispers. "Someone's here on the Sawyer property."

"Okay, do you know who?"

"I might know them."

"Is this the Sawyer farm?" There's an air of exasperation she doesn't miss.

"You have to believe me." She grips the phone in her hand. "I'm not lying. There's a strange vehicle in the drive, some type of foreign car. A Toyota."

"No one said you were. Can you describe them?"

She grits her teeth. "I didn't walk inside yet, but if that's what you want me to do . . ."

"What do you mean?" The voice on the other end fights to stay calm. "An *intruder* is *inside the house*?"

"I haven't gone in."

"Wait, hold on a sec!" the man says. "Have you walked around the premises?"

"No," Deborah says.

"Do you have any spare keys the trespasser could've located?"

"I don't think so." This should be an obvious question, yet she doesn't know. Frustrated, Deborah paces the length of the porch, tempted to collapse onto the porch swing, until she notices the curtains are open. Deborah never leaves them open. It might entice someone to take a peek inside the house.

Licking her lips nervously, she wonders if the man is back.

"Please stay out of the house. An officer will be dispatched shortly." The man on the phone sighs. "There was an escape today at the correctional facility."

"What?" Deborah almost loses her balance. "Another one?" She tries to act reasonable. "But there's a car in the drive, so clearly the owner didn't walk here."

"Well, people do drive getaway cars." A keyboard clicks in the background as the dispatcher says, "Expect a policeman soon, ma'am." And then, "I can stay on the line if you'd like."

"Please. I'd like that." Comforted by this, Deborah rests the phone against her thigh, not hanging up, per se, but keeping it there to shutter the conversation, at least for the moment.

Sneaking closer, she peers inside the picture window, spotting a lumpy figure sprawled out on the couch, their silhouette covered entirely by a blanket.

Soren, she thinks hopefully.

Disregarding the dispatcher's advice and unable to contain her nervous anticipation, she gently pushes the olive-green door the rest of the way open. If it is Soren, she doesn't want to prolong their reunion any longer, and the white car outside gives her a sneaking suspicion it might be.

Deborah's met with the annoying squeak she thought she'd become accustomed to. Now it sounds like a brand-new irritation.

"Hello?" She tiptoes into the house.

Her eyes play catch-up, taking a moment to adjust to the dimness from the contrast of outside. A wheezing sound from the living room brings Deborah face to face with the heap on the sofa.

Stunned, Deborah peers at the straggler sawing logs under her roof.

Slowly, she approaches the form tangled up in her mother's cherished blanket, their back to Deborah.

There's no mistaking the freckled skin and blonde hair, and Deborah hovers over her. Pushing aside the strap of her tank top, Deborah's fingers trace the skin, where a small tattoo of a monarch butterfly rests.

The phone slips out of her other hand as if dipped in Vaseline, and Deborah barely catches it before it hits the woman's chest.

CHAPTER 21
Sibley

Even when I hear a loud gasp, I'm rattled but not fully awake.

The squawking continues, and in my slumber, I assume it's a hummingbird outside on the feeder.

"Oh my God, it *is* you!" The voice resonates from above me. "You came home!"

Bemused, I open my eyes, expecting to see my comforter from home draped around me and not a crocheted heirloom blanket.

Disarmed, I'm face to face with big brown eyes and a heart-shaped face that matches mine. The only other trait we share besides our face shape is our fair skin. I used to think I shared similarities with Jonathan, but my mother blew that out of the water.

Her eyes go wide when they see me, squinting as if I'm a mirage.

As she moves her hand to her heart, her skin turns an even whiter shade. "Is that really you?"

We peer at each other. My mother's hair is now shoulder length, chestnut colored, and tinged with gray. My sudden presence has caused a reaction of sorts. I'm still trying to decipher what kind.

I shift awkwardly on the couch, ready to bolt in case it's not a positive one. We didn't necessarily have the fairest of goodbyes.

"As I live and breathe." Her hand reaches out to touch my cheek. "I thought I'd have to die before I saw you again."

I try not to flinch at her touch or her morbid comment.

"You feel hot, and look at you, using a blanket in this heat!" She scoffs. "You came from sunshine; you should be used to it."

Her gaunt appearance is worrisome, skin sagging down to the bones. She looks a lot older than her fifty-plus years, her wrinkles more pronounced in the sunlight.

She tilts her head, as if her eyesight is faulty and she can't rely on what's in front of her.

"I don't like surprises, but this is . . . wow!" She settles back against the edge of the couch, tears welling up in her eyes. "I just don't believe it. Pinch me, please!"

Dumbfounded, I wish I could feign excitement, but the bitterness soaks my lips like the residue of something pungent.

Uncomfortably, I tighten my hold on the blanket, feeling naked as her eyes examine every square inch of me.

Moving to a seated position, I cross my arms over my chest.

I feel feverish, and my skin's flushed from alcohol, sunshine, or trepidation. Maybe all three. My throat is parched, and breaking the torturous eye contact, I ask if I can have something to drink.

"Of course," she says, but she doesn't stand, so I heave myself up. It feels good to stretch my sore limbs. I follow her into the kitchen, where the unpleasant smell again forces me to pinch my nose. "You get an indoor cat?"

"No, but Esmeralda's about to give birth in the barn."

"Why does the house smell like an outhouse?"

"Hmm . . ." She sniffs the air. "I didn't notice."

If she doesn't detect the noxious odor, she must be used to living in these putrid conditions, which is an unsettling thought.

"You want any breakfast?" My mother shuffles over to the refrigerator, and I notice she's limping on her left side. I'm about to ask what happened when I stop to gawk at the fridge's contents. Usually, it's overflowing with more food than a family, let alone one person, could eat. Now, nothing is inside save for a carton of milk, a pitcher of water, and a few expired-looking yogurts, as if someone has cleaned it out.

"Why aren't you eating?" I ask casually.

"I am."

"Then why does it look like the end of a pandemic?"

"If I keep the fridge stocked, all I do is eat."

I'm confused. "Isn't that what you're supposed to do?"

"When you get to my age, you'll see how your body rebels and the calories go straight to your waistline."

"Believe me, I already know," I groan. "But why's everything removed from the cabinets? I can't say I like what you've done with the place."

"I've had some run-ins with mice. It took me a minute to find the little devils."

"When was this?"

"Week or so ago. My favorite kitty, Esmeralda, and her chums were happy to help."

Rolling my eyes at her fondness for nomadic cats, I offer to help reorganize her cupboards.

Before she can respond, the phone rings in my mother's hand, alarming us both. She doesn't answer, instead setting it on the counter. With the kitchen a mess, I have no choice but to search for the least inhabited chair and scoot aside some old magazines and newspapers, dog eared and worn.

A muffled voice interrupts the quiet, and I assume it's a radio announcer until the voice repeatedly shrieks her name. My mother gives a guilty look at her phone.

"Crap," she murmurs. "I must have hit answer instead of decline."

"Who is it?"

"Give me a second." She holds up a finger, picking her phone up from the counter.

I swallow a sip of my water as my mother chatters into her phone. Tilting my head, I recognize the familiar voice. From her one-sided conversation, realization dawns on me. "Shit, did you call the police on me?"

She doesn't respond, but I see the local police department contact on her phone. Horrified, I clap a hand to my mouth. The rock. Her window. Breaking and entering.

Dammit. This staying under the radar isn't working out for me. How does an unexpected road trip turn into two run-ins with the police?

Ignoring me, she says, "I wasn't wrong. She's here; can you believe it?" I watch her grin into the phone. "Yep, all the way from Florida."

Now it's my turn to be confused. Florida? Did she forget I live in the desert?

I pout. She wouldn't forget what state I live in had she bothered to write a letter back to me or return a call.

I jump up, grabbing the phone out of her hand midsentence. "Hi, Chief, this is Sibley. Sorry to give both of you a scare. I surprised her out of the blue."

My mother gapes at me like I'm speaking a foreign language.

I cradle the phone, mouthing, *What's wrong?*

The voice on the other end falters a greeting. "Ah, hi, Sibley. How are you, stranger?"

"Good," I say. "Great." I don't bother to add that while being home for less than two hours, I've learned my mother's a fraud and my dead father isn't my real one.

"It's pleasant to hear your voice." He sounds relieved. "Your mother scared the living daylights out of me when she called 911 and the station received an alert from her security system. Not to mention a woman named Nora said she was almost run off the road by a woman speeding like a bat out of hell. You wouldn't know anything about that, would you?"

In my stupor, I didn't consider Deborah might have alarms on the doors and windows. I'm relieved he doesn't mention the broken window or my drunken shape entering the small space. Again, I lie to the authorities. "I used the spare to get inside, Chief. Didn't mean to spook her. In fact, I already ran into Miles Fletcher." I smirk. "He gave me a warm reception when he pulled me over."

"Then it definitely wouldn't have been you speeding." I can hear his deep belly laugh through the phone. I forgot how much I missed the police chief's discernible guffaw. "I'll bet Officer Fletcher gave you an earful."

"Oh, he did. Said he's vying for your job."

"I'm sure he did. Problem is, I doubt I'll ever get to quit the force." He grunts. "Well, I order you to enjoy your time with your mama. How long are you in town?"

"I don't know," I stammer. "A couple of weeks, maybe?"

"Sounds good." I hear the background noise of the station, and he speaks louder over the din. "Please stop in and see me before you leave. We sure do miss you around here."

My face feels heated. I know he's not referencing when my squad in high school went TPing and included the police station in our harmless prank. It was good fun until someone got a bright idea to use spray paint on one of the vehicles in the lot.

When I'm about to hang up, the police chief stops me. "And Sibley?"

"Yes, sir?" I gulp.

"Don't know if you knew, but they built a men's prison outside of town, and we've had a string of unfortunate incidents. It's important to be conscientious."

"I heard an announcement on the radio!" Here comes another fib. "And it might be an odd coincidence, but I did notice a broken window in my mother's room."

"What?" my mother and the chief both gasp, one through the phone, one poised over my shoulder.

"In the master bath." My voice vacillates. "Please tell me you've now caught them."

The chief urges me to hand back the phone to my mother.

"This can't be happening . . ." My mother starts to shake like a leaf. She disappears out of the kitchen with the phone, and I hear her mumbled cries as she exits the room.

Ashamed at my behavior, I wait until I hear a shriek from her bathroom before I take tentative steps toward her bedroom. She's seated on the edge of the bed, and even though she's no longer speaking to the chief of police, the phone convulses in her trembling grip.

"I know you don't like surprises," I say, attempting a halfhearted apology. "I'm sorry for showing up this way."

She doesn't acknowledge this, instead staring at her gnarled hands.

"I got worried when you didn't answer," I say lamely. "You haven't wanted to communicate."

Her silence is deafening, and suddenly I'm a little girl again, feeling vulnerable and unwanted. Old insecurities rear their ugly heads. It's time to change tactics before I implode. "Can I help clean up the glass?"

Deborah doesn't answer, just murmurs, "They stole from me."

"Who?"

"Whoever broke in." She sighs. "A bunch of my medication is missing."

"Pills?" I ask innocently. "What kind of pills?"

"This is unbelievable, and after what happened last winter . . ."

"What happened then?" My eyes widen. "Is that why you're limping?" With a pounding heart, I wonder if this is what Fletch was alluding to.

She rests a hand on her forehead. "A man tried to . . . he didn't try; he . . ." Stammering, she covers her mouth with her hand.

"What?"

"He attacked me outside." She nods toward the porch. "Out there. Dragged me to the barn and clubbed me with a gun."

"How could you not call me?" I'm appalled. "This is serious, Mother."

She tilts her head to consider me. "Would that have changed anything?"

"I would have come to the hospital."

"Really? We both know you haven't been back since . . ." She hesitates. "Since you graduated your senior year after the unfortunate accidents."

If one could call them that. I shudder. "I wonder if *my* dad would agree to that sentiment." She doesn't pick up on the insinuation about my father, who, in a flash, has been erased as my biological one.

Her eyes cut to my core, piercing deep inside of me. We both know nothing would've brought me back here unless it was her funeral. An uncomfortable moment passes between us.

I shift from foot to foot. "From the looks of the place, I got worried you had moved or were robbed."

"The man didn't take anything." Motioning around the room, she sighs. "And move where? I've got so much work to do here as it is. Besides, who would want my stuff?"

This time I bite my lip to keep from making a sarcastic comment. She's right about one thing—her furnishings aren't high on a robber's wish list.

Why anyone would choose this place to target is beyond me. Everything is mostly old, not even in the antique sense. The grandfather clock is certainly priceless, but it would take grunt work to lift and carry out the door. The clutter makes it hard to ascertain valuable from invaluable. The junk has been amassed just as eagerly as the more essential items. Most of the things are sentimental to my mother, meant for memories, not for resale.

I wait for the inevitable questions. She asks, "What brings you home? Is everything okay?"

No, it's not, I want to scream, but I force myself to say without much conviction, "Nothing in particular. I just wanted to see you." I sigh. "It's been too long."

Her face goes ashen. "I don't remember agreeing to have company right now . . ." Her voice trails off. "A lot is going on, and it's not the best time."

Her thin gold band is still on her finger after all these years, and it only heightens my resentment. It's a slap in the face that she bothers to wear it after all that happened—along with the cross pendant, a paltry attempt to be pious.

I swallow down my anger as we lock eyes. "I need to ask you about my father. About Jonathan."

"Can you excuse me?" My mother presses her fingers to her forehead. "All of a sudden, I'm not feeling well."

"What's wrong?"

"I'm dizzy. This is too much shock for one day. I need to lie down."

The vodka roils in my stomach as if I'm aboard a cruise ship in turbulent waters, and excusing myself quickly, I run to dislodge the contents for the second time today.

CHAPTER 22
Deborah

Deborah goes to bed spooked and wakes up filled with dread when she hears talking in the other room.

Oh no, she thinks, groaning. *He's back. He's probably seated in front of the television.*

Remembering the broken window, Deborah slides into a pair of slippers, not wanting to risk cutting herself on slivers of glass. He must've crawled in the bathroom window quietly. How could she not hear his footsteps?

Slowly, Deborah walks into her bathroom to consider the damage. Plastic is now taped to the opening, and broken shards are no longer on the floor.

That's right: her daughter is here. The sound is her voice.

Deborah goes in search of her daughter to thank her for cleaning up the mess. Her appreciation turns to bemusement as she watches Sibley balancing on a chair in the kitchen, searching in vain for something. Her hands are sweeping across the cabinets like she's looking for one of those secret bugs that people plant to spy.

"What're you doing?" Deborah's mouth gapes.

Sibley spins around and loses her balance. Grabbing the edge of the cabinet just in time, she manages to avoid a hard fall. "Jeez, Mother, you scared me!"

"I shouldn't have to announce my presence in my own home." Deborah tries for a tight smile, but it comes off as a grimace. "Do I need to put a bell on you so I know what you're up to?"

"Of course not." Sibley wipes her hands on the front of her shorts. Deborah asks coldly, "What're you looking for?"

"Tea." Sibley shrugs. "It sounded good right now." They both know this is bullshit, a flimsy excuse. Deborah thought she'd be more skilled at lying by now.

"I don't remember you liking tea." Deborah points to a glass container filled with various tea bags. "But if you did, it's on the counter in front of you."

"Of course it is. Right in front of my face." Sibley's cheeks turn ruddy. "I was looking up instead of ahead." She yanks a couple of tea bags out. "Would you like some?"

Deborah shrugs. "I usually drink it at night, but why not? It's not every day your daughter shows up unexpectedly."

"Yeah, right?" Sibley raises an eyebrow. "Still like it hot, even in the summer?"

"Yes." Deborah fixes Sibley with one last pointed stare. "I'm going to go sit in the living room and take a load off."

Sibley manages a nod.

Deborah collapses into her chair, rubbing the drowsiness out of her eyes. Her daughter arrives out of nowhere and is already ransacking her cupboards? What could she possibly be looking for?

Considering all the options, mostly unpleasant, Deborah wonders if Sibley is trying to catch her doing something. Was she sent here to spy on her? Maybe she's going to plant one of those miniature recording devices?

In distress, she doesn't notice Sibley standing in front of her, a strange look on her face, tea in hand. Pressing a mug into Deborah's palm, she sits down across from her on the couch.

Stifling a yawn, Deborah notices the dark circles underneath Sibley's eyes. "You look exhausted. That earlier nap wasn't enough."

"I was driving almost nonstop for twenty-three hours."

"You didn't stop?" Her eyes widen in alarm. "You should've told me you were coming. I would've picked you up from the airport instead of you driving all this way." Then Deborah could at least have known when she came and went. She wouldn't have come home to her asleep on her couch.

"It's okay." Sibley stares into her mug, refusing to meet Deborah's eyes. "I didn't want to trouble you."

Deborah lifts her chin. "Where's that husband of yours?"

"He's at home." Sibley chews on a fingernail.

"Still have that nasty habit, I see." Deborah frowns at Sibley's hands. "Where's your wedding ring?" Its absence is puzzling to her. Deborah doesn't mention she noticed the enormous diamond in the engagement pictures she found online after she heard about the wedding announcement, but not from her daughter.

No, she had to find out from a neighbor who'd read it on her social media account.

She was peeved. It was the same with Sibley's graduation from college and law school. She did receive a Hallmark card informing her she'd passed the bar and joined a law firm.

It hurt like hell, but she'd be lying if she said it had been unexpected. Deborah's received sporadic high-level CliffsNotes along the way.

"At the jeweler. I decided to have it cleaned professionally. No need to wear it on the farm."

"It would've been nice to finally meet my son-in-law." Deborah knows his name starts with an *H*, but she can't seem to pluck it from her memory.

"Holden had to work," Sibley mumbles.

"Well, it would've been nice to meet Holden," she says pointedly. "And you managed to make it." Deborah chastens, "That seems dangerous, you coming alone in that metal trap with those tires."

Sibley leans her head back against the couch, closing her eyes.

Getting nowhere, Deborah asks, "Is he still in education? A teacher, right?"

"He teaches poli-sci."

Deborah stares at her blankly.

"Political science. Holden's a professor at the university." Sibley's voice squeaks. "That's why he couldn't come. He got tenure, so he's thrilled."

"How wonderful!" Deborah says politely. "Good for him. And you, are you still a lawyer?"

"I am."

"Was it hard to get time off?"

"I was able to juggle it."

Deborah knows the farm's condition has thrown Sibley for a loop, but she hardly owes her an apology. A lot of pressing matters have consumed her time as of late, and she's so tired and bogged down.

And today, Sibley's blue eyes wear the same guilty cloak Deborah's have worn for the past sixteen years.

Maybe Deborah feels high strung because of the timing, skeptical, even, of her intentions. She hates to chew over the timing of Sibley's visit, but she'd be remiss if she didn't. It's odd Sibley would show up around the same time she's making a radical decision about the farm. Deborah didn't expect her to come knocking at the door, certainly not without a phone call.

Eventually, she would've sent a card with a handwritten letter inside, pouring out the feelings she's kept bottled up because Jonathan used to throttle her for having them. It's a hard conversation to have with your child, even at an adult age.

And now Deborah's moving on, tired of feeling exposed on the farm, a sitting duck, if you will. She's ready to branch out in life. If Deborah didn't have Robert, she'd lose her patience and will to live. Smiling gleefully to herself, she thinks that *moving on with Robert* has a nice ring to it.

Deborah's biggest mistake was not fleeing all those years ago after the string of tragedies happened.

Blow after blow.

But she had a target on her back, and it was easier to grin and bear it. Deborah paid the price in silence with a backbone that was stronger than most.

Leaving would've been an admission of guilt and would've caused more damage than staying did, though she couldn't possibly have known it at the time. She and Robert made a pact to stay silent about what had happened the night Jonathan died. It was in everyone's best interests, hers included.

Sibley has no idea what she's given up for her. She's never appreciated the sacrifices, how unselfish Deborah had to be to do what she did, but it's not all her fault. A mother's job is to protect her children, shield them from pain. She didn't want to let her know the man she put on a pedestal was a cruel monster, even if it meant staying silent.

So both women have suffered and spread the blame around the same way you spread a thin coat of peanut butter on a cracker with a knife, stuff it in your mouth, and wonder why your throat has become dry and cotton-like. If you swallow the lies and half truths, they become toxic.

Deborah realizes Sibley's asking her a question. Meeting her daughter's eyes with a blank stare, she waits for her to repeat herself.

"Is my room the same?"

"Yes. You'll probably want to change the bedding, though. It needs a refresh."

"Why?" Sibley winks mischievously. "You have company lately?"

"Heavens, no."

"Do you see Fletch a lot?" Sibley asks. "Or his family?"

"More than I'd like." Deborah snorts. "Miles Fletcher told you he's the next chief of police, huh? That boy is delusional."

"How come?"

"Everyone in town knows he stole money from the officers' union, but the charges never stuck. The district attorney decided not to prosecute, said the evidence wasn't sufficient. Money and power always talk. All of a sudden, the money was found, and the paper wrote some long bullshit article about responsible journalism and fired the poor reporter who broke the news."

"I bet his dad wasn't thrilled about that." The Fletchers prefer to stay out of the papers as much as possible unless it's for a worthy cause, like a charitable donation or a community service award.

"He got off without so much as a hand slap." She sniffs. "Everyone still feels sorry for him since his wife died. Did you know he married Kristin?"

"I heard." Sibley wears a pained expression on her face. "Could it have been a rush to judgment? Even though Fletch and I have differences of opinion, embezzlement doesn't seem to fit his character. His brother, Bryce, would be more likely."

"Who knows?" Deborah shrugs. "He's always been a wild card." Snapping her fingers, she says, reminiscing, "Oh, don't think I forgot when the four of you snuck out to go to some rock and roll mess. Or how one of the Fletcher boys broke your window to sneak back in the house."

A giggle escapes Sibley's lips.

"What's so funny?"

Sibley gives Deborah a smug smile. "I thought you two buried the hatchet, is all." With another yawn, Sibley languidly rises from the couch. "All right. I'm going to go grab my suitcase and try to sleep. Wake me up if you need me."

Speaking to Sibley's back, Deborah says, "I'm going to cook dinner tonight. This calls for a celebration." Her words fall flat. "Anything particular you're hungry for?"

She pauses with her hand on the doorjamb but doesn't turn around. "Haven't had much of an appetite. I'm more concerned with getting rest. Maybe just a salad." Deborah notices how Sibley's hands tremble at her sides.

"We need to fatten you up. You're much too thin."

Sibley doesn't respond, and Deborah hears the slam of the screen door as her footsteps trudge outside.

"Sleep well, honey!" Deborah hollers a few minutes later, when she hears the stairs clunking as Sibley climbs them. After Sibley's bed creaks upstairs, Deborah steps outside to make a call. Without saying hello, she whispers into the phone, "I'm not sure what to think."

"Wait. I can't hear you. Why can't you speak up?" Robert lowers his voice, which is tinged with worry. "Are you okay?"

"I'm not alone, but I'm not in trouble," she says. "But I think she might be. Maybe financially." She recounts for him the concern about the missing wedding ring and the absentee husband. "She's already looking for something." Deborah huffs. "Maybe she's got ill intentions."

Robert lets out a lengthy exhale, a habit of his when he's processing news. "How well do you know your daughter?" he asks gently. "You haven't seen her since she was a teenager."

Deborah bites her tongue. He has a point. She presumed Sibley had her life together; her list of accomplishments and degrees made her seem untouchable and superior. But she's human. And Deborah's certainly no stranger to making decisions that aren't necessarily legal or respectable to survive.

"There's a lot you don't know," Robert says, brooding. "I guess all you can do right now is keep asking questions."

"But if I find out she's using me or spying on me, she won't be here long," Deborah growls.

"Exactly. I won't let her hurt you again."

There's a brief pause, and Deborah knows what he's going to ask. She tightens her grip on the phone in anticipation.

"When are you—"

"You're breaking up. Having trouble hearing—"

"—going to tell her who her father—"

Abruptly, she disconnects, and Deborah's mind loops back to the farm and Sibley's shocking appearance.

An unsettled pit in her stomach makes Deborah wonder if Sibley is telling the truth.

People don't just reappear after so many years, out of the blue, without wanting something in return. The question is, what is it?

CHAPTER 23
Sibley

Fully awake and stifling a yawn, I readjust my arms above my head for a brief minute as I open and close my burning eyes.

Languidly, I crawl out of bed to stretch, reaching the tips of my fingers to my toes, twisting my body to release some of the stiffness from my cross-country drive.

My headache has waned, content to settle into a dull ache, a reprieve from a pounding one. Before I head downstairs, I splash cold water on my dull skin. I run a hand through my tangled hair and brush my teeth, my mouth bone dry.

Grasping the wooden railing on the wall, I descend the stairs. I'm amazed none of us have broken bones from falling down these unforgiving steps; it seems our ancestors preferred a steep incline to a gradual one. Old farmhouses were built with purpose and durability in mind, not comfort. It's impossible to be quiet, with each thud reverberating through the farmhouse. These steps were the bane of my existence as a teen, rendering it impossible to sneak out.

Hence the window incident.

My mother is standing at the stove, her back turned to me. I expect her to raise her head in acknowledgment, but she's murmuring words I can't make out.

She's stirring the pot with a wooden spoon as if she's lost in a trance, hunched over the stovetop.

"Good afternoon, or maybe night, I should say."

Startled, she whips around so fast the metal pot topples, and she yelps as she catches the sides before it scalds her or crashes to the floor.

Horrified, I watch as she leans back against the stovetop. "Mother, be careful! You're going to burn yourself."

Her hands are raised in warning, gesturing at me to keep my distance. Her terror-laden eyes are what concern me the most. She's acting as if I'm an intruder about to cause bodily harm.

"You need to get away from the burner," I admonish.

A deer-in-the-headlights expression remains on her face, the apprehension palpable as she holds the wooden spoon in her grip like she's going to whack me with it if I get too close.

"Mother, what's wrong?"

"Where did you come from?"

Puzzled, I point upstairs. "I was napping in my bedroom."

"I didn't realize . . ." Her voice trails off.

"What?"

"I didn't know you were upstairs, honey."

"Where else would I be?"

"I just forgot, is all. I didn't hear you come down the stairs." She looks apologetic, her grip loosening on the spoon. "I'm sorry, honey."

I give her a questioning glance. "You didn't remember I was here?"

"It's just . . ." Deborah pauses. "There's been a rash of home invasions, and then the window was broken, not to mention January." Her complexion wan, she whispers, "It's a lot to take in for me."

"Why don't you sit down, and I'll finish this?"

"Sure, honey, but don't burn it," Deborah warns.

Sinking into a chair, my mother covers her face with her hands, and at first, I think she's sobbing into them before I notice the way her hands tremble.

Not wanting to further upset her, I soften my voice. "What else is going on, Mother?"

I don't want to pry and tell her I heard as she confided in a strange woman her secret, but I selfishly want her to confess it to me, her daughter, the *one* person who should be privy to this information.

And then what? I think. *So you can go off on her when she's in this fragile state of mind?*

Speaking of selfish—she's the one who kept it from you all these years, my inner child says. *She should be sorry, not you.*

Her voice is muffled. "I'm just wound up."

"What're they going after? Money? Farm equipment?"

"Anything they can get their hands on." She sighs. "I'm just a little paranoid, since the neighbors also came home to a broken window. This was after church last Sunday, and the house had been ransacked."

"Let me get you a glass of water."

"In that case, I better take my medicine." Squeezing her eyes shut, she adds, "And now I'll have to tell my doctor I'm missing some drugs."

I touch her bony shoulder gently. "Want me to go get them?"

"No, I'll get 'em."

"If you don't mind me asking, what are they for?"

"Oh, the usual things people my age deal with. Arthritis. Creaky neck and back pain. Getting old's a pain in the ass." She's lying. Another fib to add to the ever-growing list.

"You're barely fifty, Mother! Are you still seeing Doc Marshall?"

"Yes."

I want to bring up her noticeable limp, but I decide to wait until she's settled down a bit. She's acting like a frightened mare right now, jumpy and confused.

After removing my hand, I find a box of unopened crackers and pour us both glasses of water. Out here, the tap water comes from a well, and it's unpalatable and murky, so we make do with a filtered pitcher from the fridge.

She takes a sip as I maneuver around the kitchen, ladling the stew she's made into two bowls and setting the silverware and napkins on the table.

"Are you sure you want to get up?"

"Yes, honey, I'm fine." She slowly rises from the table and disappears from the kitchen.

I hear the bathroom door shut and the medicine cabinet open.

She returns momentarily with a handful of pills and swallows them down.

We settle uneasily into our usual places at the table and start to eat.

The empty chair between us belonged to my daddy, and we've never used it since his death, as if it would be sacrilegious. I swear I can taste smoke on my lips from his Marlboro Reds, as if he's still smoking next to me like when I was a child.

The only sound is the scrape of our spoons against our bowls and the devouring of food. Our silence isn't companionable, but I wouldn't go as far as to call it unbearable.

We're two people who, before today, haven't spoken a full sentence to each other in years. We're family, desperate for a connection but unable to find the right words to fuse a conversation.

I can tell by the way she pauses after every spoonful to stare up at the ceiling that she's preoccupied.

Finally, she peers up at me over her soup spoon.

"Awfully quiet," she muses. "I figured you'd have a lot to catch me up on in your life."

"Just enjoying a home-cooked meal."

"You stop cooking?"

I don't bother to point out I never started. A Crock-Pot filled with frozen chicken and vegetables is the extent of my capabilities. "I've been on the road, so it's been crap food."

"You have big circles under your eyes." She fixes me with a concerned-mother look. "I hope I didn't wake you up when I was banging pots around in the kitchen."

"Not at all." I offer a small smile. "I did wake up with my mouth watering for a home-cooked meal, though."

"I'm glad you missed something about home." She eyeballs the oversize sweater hiding my shrinking frame. "Looks like you could stand to gain a few pounds."

I have a good reason for losing weight with the amount of stress I'm under, but I ignore her comment, asking where the missing salt and pepper are, a staple at the center of the table.

"Next to the stove."

I spot them knocked over from the near disaster. I want to ask my own burning questions about the farm and her health, yet both subjects seem incredibly delicate. I decide to tread lightly.

"Do you want me to cut the grass and clean up the yard?" I offer. "Or get someone out here to help with the yard work?"

I'm met with a blank expression.

"It's starting to look like a jungle." I keep my voice monotone, not wanting to come off as accusatory.

"Is that why I saw a tiger the other night in the yard?"

I'm terrified she's serious, but I relax when she cracks a small smile. Humoring her, I add, "I wouldn't be surprised if jungle cats did appear. They'd hide fairly well in the tall grass." Narrowing my eyes, I get to the crux of the matter. "Is this about money?"

"Money?"

"Are you short on cash? Do you need money for repairs?"

Her spoon clanks in her bowl. "What're you doing?"

I frown. "What do you mean?"

"You haven't been home in years. Don't stick your nose where it doesn't belong."

"Mother . . ."

"Don't 'Mother' me," she protests. "I haven't seen you since practically birth."

"Always a flair for the dramatic." I pause, letting the soup spoon sink into the bowl and drown in the thick sauce. "Why does it look like you gave up on life, then?"

"I've been busy."

"Doing what?"

"Church. Volunteering." She shrugs. "The usual."

"Mother, you were always so proud of the farm."

"And I still am." Her voice has an air of finality, signaling an end to the discussion. "But I'm tired and worn out. I told you about the disadvantages of getting old."

"You're not that old." I roll my eyes. "But seriously, do we need to think about selling it?"

Her eyes flash in anger. "You would like that, wouldn't you?"

"Huh?" I wave a hand around the room. "Besides the condition of the property, I'm worried you can't keep up with the housecleaning inside. You mentioned a rodent problem, but there are piles everywhere."

"That's because I want to donate most of it to the church."

"Really?" I raise an eyebrow. "The church?"

"Yes. I have no need for it."

"Fine, then. I bet there're some storage bins or empty boxes around we can use."

I chew on a couple of saltines, watching her shakily grip the handle of her spoon, the patterned handle bobbing up and down.

Abruptly, she abandons the metal, and I'm positive it's because of my steady gaze. Giving me a small smile, she asks, "Did you see the old diner's got a drive-through now?" She dabs her mouth with a napkin.

I'm about to respond when she cocks her head to the side as if listening intently to something only she can hear. Frantically, her eyes dart around the room, as if chasing a mosquito on its flight path.

"What's wrong?"

She motions with her finger for me to be quiet.

I crane my neck impatiently. "Mother?"

"Shh . . ."

"Are you okay?"

She nods her head, but it's as if she doesn't hear me, her body twisting in its chair to face the front door, then the window.

She stands up slowly, and her uneven steps reach the stove. Her hands deftly touch the black knob, checking to make sure the burner is off.

I'm confused; I thought I had moved it to the off position. "Did I forget?"

"Nope. I just wanted to check. You know how OCD I am about leaving the stovetop on."

I don't, so I say nothing. When I was growing up, I was the one worried about leaving the curling iron or my hair straightener on, scared I'd accidentally burn down the house.

"Do you want anything while I'm up?"

"No. I'm good." I study her anxious face and quivering lip. "Did you see something?"

"I thought I heard a noise." She dismisses it with a wave. "Must've been a car driving by on the highway."

"Probably." There's not much noise out here on this stretch of road. It's mainly used for farm equipment or local traffic. "You have every right to be on edge," I offer.

"That must be it." Settling back in her chair, she kneads her hands together. "Does Holden know you made it safely?"

"Yes," I hurriedly reply before she can ask another question.

"You still haven't said the purpose of your visit." Deborah rubs a hand over her face. "Though it's clear you want to move me out of here."

I try to formulate a response, but I'm yanked out of my pensiveness at the earsplitting sound of her chair scraping backward. It happens so fast that I'm confident black marks are stretched across the floor.

Standing up, my mother screams, "Someone's in the window! Someone's watching us!"

CHAPTER 24
Deborah

"Who?" Sibley jumps up in response, her eyes darting toward the kitchen window. After crossing the room in a few strides, she peeks out the smudged glass, holding the curtain to the side. Without turning to face Deborah, she murmurs, "Which direction did they go? I don't see anyone out here."

Deborah's face flames red, and she's suddenly embarrassed, worried her daughter is convinced she's lost her mind. Strained from her session with Dr. Alacoy and the unexpected visit from Sibley, she lets out a long exhale, trying to slow down her breathing and subdue her rapid heart rate.

"Was it a man or a woman?"

"Looked like the build of a man." Deborah thinks out loud: "I hope it's not the man from before."

"Did you catch how they were dressed?"

Deborah musters a shrug but says nothing, a weary look crossing her face.

"Are there any suspects in the robberies?"

"No." She sighs. "Another reason Miles Fletcher is useless. Doubt he knows how to dust for fingerprints. I swear he could learn a lot from watching *Law and Order*. The actors have more experience with a crime scene than that idiot."

A pout tugs at Sibley's mouth. "Look, Mother, if it makes you feel better, I doubt someone's going to try anything when there are clearly people at home and it's not even dark yet."

"Then how do you explain what happened in January?" Deborah says, bristling. "One of the coldest days of the year didn't stop them."

"At least my car is in the drive," Sibley muses. "I'd hope a visitor would scare away someone with bad intentions."

"Doubtful," Deborah counters. "The Clancy family was tied up and left in their shed in broad daylight."

Sibley recoils as if she's been slapped with the serving spoon from earlier. "How about I make us more tea?" she offers gently. "I know you said you liked it at night." Sibley pulls out chamomile and busies herself with boiling the water.

Without a word, Deborah barrels into the living room, her limp more pronounced as she tries to scurry toward the double picture windows that face the highway.

Sibley asks, "Could it be the delivery guy? Or maybe the mailman?"

"You know the mailman only stops at the end of the drive."

"What about packages, though? Are you expecting anything?"

"No." Deborah wrings her hands. "Not until I hear from my lawyer."

She didn't mean to let that slip, and glancing over her shoulder, she's relieved Sibley is removing two mugs from the cupboard. If she heard, she doesn't say anything.

Gingerly, Deborah tugs aside the faded curtains, careful not to pull them too far away from the glass lest she meet someone's prying eyes. She intently scans the overrun yard as the sun fades behind the clouds. The burnt orange fades in and out of sight as if playing a game of peeka-boo. She's uncertain whether to be relieved or annoyed when her eyes don't spot anything out of the ordinary.

In the background, the microwave beeps, signaling the water is ready for their tea.

Sighing loudly, Deborah tucks the blanket from her mother around her shivering frame. When it's wrapped around her shoulders, an immediate sense of calm envelops her like a hug until the antique grandfather clock startles both women with a boom as it chimes eight o'clock.

A loud thud interrupts the final ding, and at first, Deborah thinks Sibley has dropped and broken her mug, but she's got one in each hand as she sets them down on the side table.

Sibley's face registers surprise, and her eyes dart nervously around the living room. They make eye contact as pounding indicates someone's at the front door.

"At least they knocked." Sibley tries to act unbothered, but her jaw is tense. "Unlike me."

"Did you tell any of your old friends to drop by?"

"No. I didn't." She suggests, "Maybe it's just the neighbor."

"Maybe." Now Deborah worries Robert has shown up unexpectedly, but if he did, he would have a good reason. Otherwise, he wouldn't barge in, out of respect for Deborah.

"I'll see who it is." Sibley starts to go to the door, but Deborah holds out a hand to stop her.

Ignoring Sibley's protests, she unlocks the dead bolt. "It's okay. I'll answer the door."

She swings it open with a shaky hand, and her hand flies to her heart.

Standing on the other side of the screen door is Miles Fletcher, with damp hair and no uniform, his mouth in a tight line.

"Miles." She tilts her head. "You scared the living daylights out of us."

"Hi, ma'am." He wrinkles his nose in confusion. "I rang the bell."

Deborah isn't a fan of this particular Fletcher. In her mind, he's a lying crook. Her refusal to address him by any title relevant to his position on the police force doesn't deter him from addressing her respectfully.

If he catches her hateful stare, he ignores it, choosing to remove his ball cap and wave it in her direction. "Sorry, I didn't mean to startle you."

"What're you doing sneaking around on the porch?"

His eyes betray a hint of guilt, and he refuses to meet her penetrating gaze. "Is Sibby here?"

"You could've called first to check, but yes."

"I didn't think she'd split this fast." With a tug on his ear, he says, "I wanted to check up on her. Make sure she's getting settled all right."

"I assure you, she's fine, except for the heart palpitations you caused us."

Sibley appears behind Deborah at the door. "I can speak for myself, Mother." As she leans against the doorjamb, Sibley's voice betrays a hint of unease. "Two times in one day. To what do I owe this honor?"

Miles chuckles, but it's strangled. "The pleasure is not mine, unfortunately." He shifts his weight to the other leg. "You got a minute to talk?"

Sibley hesitates for a beat, then agrees, "Sure."

Deborah doesn't make a move to usher Miles into the house, instead shooing them like she used to when they were teenagers. "Why don't you kids catch up outside on the porch. It's such a nice night, and that way you can have some privacy."

"Fine, Mother." Sibley rolls her eyes, first at Miles, then at Deborah. "Can I put some shoes on first?"

"Actually, as peaceful as sitting outside sounds, this is a conversation I want to have with both of you ladies."

"Is it about the string of robberies?" Deborah asks. "Do you have a suspect?"

"I wish." Miles shakes his head. "But no, this is unrelated."

Deborah huffs. "If this is official police business, why aren't you in your uniform?"

"You're going to be glad I'm not in my uniform." A hint of irritation laces his tone. "Mind if I come in first? I need a drink."

"You know I don't keep alcohol in the house."

"Water. Just a glass of water," Miles clarifies.

Both women peer at the sweat dripping down his forehead. Deborah would bet it's nerves and not the temperature.

Sibley locks eyes with him. "I'll come outside. No need to stress my mother out."

"Stop it, Sibley," Deborah says acerbically. "You act like I'm fragile. If Miles thinks I need to know, then it must be *important*."

"Actually . . ." Miles looks forlorn. "It's about you, Sibby."

"Exactly," Sibley pleads. "So there's no reason to upset my mother."

Miles angrily stomps over to the counter. Neither woman mentions he shouldn't drink out of the tap. Deborah assumes he should know better by now, so she lets him.

He slams down a glass. "I want to know what happened so—"

"So you can puff up your chest and put your police hat on?" Sibley grumbles.

"So I can try and help," he finishes. "I want to help you."

"After all this time, you want to help?" Sibley sounds dubious.

Without waiting for an invitation to sit, Miles slinks into a chair, seemingly aware that both women are eerily fixated on his choice of seating. Apparently supposing he chose right, since neither resists, he settles on the patterned chair cover.

Glancing at her daughter's flushed face, Deborah says, "What's going on?"

"I pulled Sibby over this morning on her way to your house. I didn't run her plates then, but I did this afternoon. It seems our girl doesn't have a valid license or insurance for that Corolla out there."

Before Sibley can hide her expression, Deborah watches her jaw drop in horror. Then she regains her composure.

Even though she's not a fan of Miles, Deborah's grateful he came to both of them, although it might have been out of spite or to gloat.

A whimper escapes Sibley's lips. Fists curled into balls, she takes a menacing step toward Miles.

Openmouthed, Deborah and Miles wait for Sibley to take a swing at him or start hollering.

She does neither.

Instead, she crumples into the closest chair.

CHAPTER 25
Sibley

"Fletch," I shakily demand. "What do you want?"

My question confuses him. "What do I want?"

"You can't ever leave well enough alone. You clearly wanted to prove a point."

Defensively, he crosses his arms. "I thought Deborah should know."

"Oh, really?" I grit my teeth. "Like you care."

"She deserves to know why you really came home."

"And what business is it of yours?" I snort.

"When you drive into my town"—he thumps his chest—"I make it my business."

"Look at you, sounding like a future chief of police." I roll my eyes. "This is nothing more than a misunderstanding."

"No! I want to know why the *fuck*—" He quickly shuts his eyes. "Sorry, ma'am, for the curse word. I'm at my wit's end. Sibby." He speaks softly. "I want to know what you're doing home, traveling like a nomad in that hunk of shit outside, creeping into town. You abandoned us all, and now you just show up after all these years, acting like you have no qualms about making us worry about you."

"I didn't creep," I haughtily point out. "I sped through town, or we wouldn't be having this conversation right now."

"Why are you on the lam?"

"You chased me off before, and you want to do it again." My eyes burn with tears. "Damn you, Miles Fletcher."

"You know that isn't what happened," he says coldly. "You never could accept responsibility for your actions."

"What did you want me to do that night, Fletch?" I snap. "Tell your mother she couldn't leave our house? Beg her to stay and talk to me? I didn't tell the police to barricade our property, and I didn't tell Cindy to drive straight into a telephone pole."

My mother shoots me a deadly glare. "The past has nothing to do with this," she cuts in. "Stop avoiding the question."

"I had a car accident."

"That's serious." My mother goes still. "Did you go to the hospital?" She strides over to me. "You could have a concussion; I would know."

I put my hands up to wave her away. "I was checked out by a doctor."

"Was anyone else with you?" Fletch asks. "What about the other vehicle?"

"Luckily, there were no other passengers, and I didn't hurt anyone but myself. The other victims were concrete and a fire hydrant." Shaking my head, I murmur, "I was upset. My husband, Holden, and me"—I'm doubtful Fletch will know his name—"had a blowout fight, and then I had some work distractions that caused me to be inattentive."

Fletch raises a brow. "So that's why that dump outside isn't registered to you?"

"Yes." I bite my lip hard enough to draw blood. "Since my car was totaled, I bought the Toyota and headed here." I sigh. "It was so recent, and I haven't bothered to switch over the title and insurance."

Neither of them says a word. My mother stares at the floor, Fletch at the wall, as I dart furtive glances around the room.

My mother breaks the silence. "But I don't understand why you would drive cross country on a suspended license."

"How does an attorney just disregard the law?" Miles slaps a hand to his forehead. "Oh, wait, you always think you're above the law; that's how."

"Don't start with this 'public servant versus civic duty' bullshit," I snap.

My mother softens her tone. "Your husband was okay with you doing this?"

Shooting Fletch a warning look before he spouts off about Jonathan being a domineering husband, I shrug. "He understood my reasons."

"Well, what do we do?" Deborah's hands reach for her throat, nervously twisting the gold chain.

Clearing his throat, Fletch directs his answer at Deborah because he knows I'm well versed in the law. "I'm not trying to be an accomplice to her bad behavior. Her license is suspended for ninety days."

"Are you going to have my car towed?"

"Maybe." He retorts, "You ran from your problems before, and things haven't changed much, have they, Sibby? Running from the choices you make seems to be your MO."

"What're you going to do?" my mother asks him nervously.

"That depends on Sib."

"What are my options, Fletch?"

"That's what I want to talk to you about," Fletch says sternly. "Let's go take a drive."

Keeping a stiff upper lip, I rise out of my chair. "Only if it's to the nearest bar."

The two of us drive in strained silence to town. It's as if we have to have a drink before we can continue our conversation.

Mickey's gets our business this time.

Swiping his ball cap off, Fletch motions toward a dark back corner. I watch as he brings back a beer and pushes a vodka tonic with lime across the wobbly table toward me.

The bar is relatively empty for the middle of the week. A couple plays darts in the corner while another group of women wearing scrubs looks like they just finished shifts at the hospital. Their incessant laughter is earsplitting, their conversation even louder.

"Play your hand, Fletch." I drum my fingers on the table. "What's the price for your silence?"

"Depends. I don't buy you came home after sixteen years on a whim after a freakish car accident." He wrinkles his nose. "They always say if something smells like shit, it probably is."

"That a pig joke?"

"Sorry! That's right: I forgot *you* forgot where you came from." Fletch grunts. "I'm just worried there's a deeper fissure somewhere. I can't imagine any sane husband telling his wife to go ahead and drive thirteen hundred miles solo after she wrecked her car and lost her license."

I shrug.

"Give me your phone," Fletch demands.

"What?"

"You heard me." He gives me a mischievous grin. "I want to call this husband and confirm he okayed this."

"What's it to you?"

"I just want to make sure you didn't come back to stir up trouble."

"Fuck off."

"No worries, Sibby." He takes a swig of his beer. "I'll call him tomorrow. It's not like I can't use my talent to find your hubby's phone number or workplace."

I really want to flip the bird at him, but instead, I wave my bare left hand in the air. "Maybe, Officer Dipshit, your investigative skills should home in on why I'm not wearing a ring."

"I noticed it before." He rewards me with a glare. "So what? You left it at home."

"If you must know, I pawned it in New Mexico."

He stays silent.

"Tulsa, to be exact."

"I'm sorry," he says with false brightness.

"Don't be. I needed the money."

"Want to talk about it?"

"Not particularly." I guzzle my drink down.

"Okay."

"I'd appreciate it if we could keep this between us, Fletch. I don't want to tell my mother I'm struggling financially and my own husband kicked me out," I say sharply. "I don't want her to worry about me. I'm just going to get on my feet and then . . ."

"Disappear." He narrows his eyes at me. "Per the usual."

"Why? You prefer I stick around?"

"Not with that stick up your ass," he grumbles. "Anyway, why'd your husband kick you out? That seems unusually cruel."

Blowing a strand of hair off my face, I say, "Because he thinks I had an affair."

I watch his stunned jaw drag on the floor. He resembles a cartoon character, and it'd be comical to watch if it weren't about my life.

"And it wasn't just any old affair. It was with a client."

He leans forward, warily waiting for my next admission.

My eyes unleash a torrent of emotion, the floodgates opening. "So not only do I *not* have a license, Holden kicked me out, and I'm stuck figuring out my life in my thirties."

"Hey, that's not all bad." He unearths a crumpled tissue from his pocket and hands it over. "We all have shit to figure out. There's no age you suddenly become immune to problems."

"Thank you." I dry my eyes and blow my nose. "And you're right."

"This is some heavy shit."

"I know." I sniffle. "I'm confident it will all be sorted out. Or at least most of it." I sigh. "So where does that leave us?"

"Look, if anybody asks, we never had this conversation." He stares at me with his puppy dog eyes. "But you can't hide out here forever, Sibby."

"I know." I wipe a hand over my face. "I know."

He settles his ball cap back on his head when we leave and tips it when he drops me off at home. "Always a pleasure to see you, Sibby Sawyer."

I nod.

"And Sibby?"

I turn to face him. "Yeah?"

"Don't let me catch you driving." He salutes me. "Or I'll have to frisk you like I've always wanted to."

"You wish," I say, rolling my eyes as I head for the unlit porch.

When I knock on the front door, I expect to hear my mother's shuffled movements, but the house is completely dark.

Confused, I shake the door handle.

For some reason, my mother left it unlocked. *Probably for you,* I remind myself. I'm going to have to ask her about a spare key. With all that's been going on, it makes me nervous to think someone could walk right in.

I swallow the lump in my throat.

I'm guilty of breaking a window now covered in flimsy plastic, which isn't any safer. If I had known she'd been attacked, I never would have pulled a stunt like that. Even if she lied to me about Jonathan. I'm not sadistic. I'm going to have to get it replaced ASAP.

Inside, I holler her name again. She doesn't respond, but I notice her bedroom door is shut.

I drag myself upstairs. It's time for me to retire to my room. So much has happened, and I can't believe I've been here less than twenty-four hours.

Restless, I pace the room's length. I need to refocus my energy on something other than the cataclysmic change in my lineage.

Anxiety causes the gnawing pit in my stomach to grow, gripping my insides with its sharp claws.

I need to figure out who this Edward man is and how to find him. If he was so quick to shirk his responsibilities as a father, I might not want to know him, but I still have to apply logic where there isn't any.

And how could he be so callous to my mother?

I never heard Deborah say he was married at the time of my conception, but maybe Edward was in a relationship or had moved on and didn't want to dredge up drama.

It should be easy enough to locate someone, but I don't have his last name. I wonder if my mother has anything in storage that might give his identity away.

She was so young when she had me; I bet he was a classmate. Unless he was from another school district, which is common with so many small towns. But if they went together, maybe there's a picture of them at a dance or prom. First thing tomorrow, I'll do some digging to see if I can locate any old yearbooks or photos.

Fighting exhaustion, I'm a lousy combination of nerves and contemplation.

Now that I've moved the red cooler inside, it's safely tucked underneath a pile of clothes and toiletries. Right now, it contains the perfect solution for my current state of mind.

With quivering hands, I manhandle the bottle out of its hiding spot. After unscrewing the cap, I drink it straight, not bothering to hunt for a chaser. It burns through the lump in my trachea and settles next to the knot in my stomach.

I used to think I'd inherited my father's alcoholism, but it looks like I can't lay blame there anymore. During my college days, I started drinking to battle a combination of depression, loneliness, and isolation. As much as I'd wanted to disappear from here, it was hard being in a new state and not knowing anyone. It also helped numb the pain at losing him.

By the second semester, I had flunked out, choosing to either party with my newfound friends or drink by myself while they were in class. After I got arrested for public intoxication and then, another time, woke up naked in a fraternity with no clothes on and no recollection of the night before, I knew my downward spiral needed to pause. I ended up transferring to community college to get my grades up so I could finish my bachelor's. During law school, I managed to keep my drinking to a minimum, immersing myself in the law's intricacies and studying, my new addiction.

Until about six months ago, I was able to have a glass of wine or a cocktail and stop at one.

But then I fell off the wagon, drowning in my unhappiness.

And one became three, and three became seven . . .

A loud roar snaps me back to reality, and staring down at my hands, I find myself in the darkened room, barefoot and sitting cross-legged, against my childhood bed.

Swiveling my head, I realize it's the sound of my mother's tailpipe, clunky and choking for air. When I glance down, the bottle in my hand is empty, and my tongue wags in the opening for one last drop.

I want more.

I paw through my luggage but can't find another bottle.

In my lethargy, I'm trying to determine if I should ask my mother to take me to the gas station. I could pretend I'm craving something sweet.

I could drink wine. Then it wouldn't be a total lie.

With a frustrated sigh, I search for my car keys with difficulty because I haven't turned the lights in the room on in my impenetrable fog.

After I give up that useless hunt, I hear the front door slam downstairs, signaling her arrival. I'm curious to know where she went tonight. I stare at the digital clock on the nightstand, and the red numbers swim in front of my eyes.

Blearily, I rub them.

Frozen in place, I listen for my mother's usual bedtime routine, consoled on some level it hasn't changed. For some reason, I find it comforting after all these years.

The faucet creaks on. She's washing her face.

Then something drips; the pipes still leak.

Her medicine cabinet squeals. Now she's applying her nighttime moisturizer and lotion.

Then one last flush of the toilet.

Calming, like a bedtime story, it always has the same ending. My mother's gliding into bed and her own dreams. She's not going to leave me behind, only slip away for the evening. She won't ever leave me the way I left her.

I drag myself into bed and slide beneath my covers. I used to be a heavy sleeper, but getting to that stage where I drift off—that's tricky. I'm at a point of physical and mental exhaustion and should be dead tired, which I am, but unable to get out of my own head, I toss and turn, the fitted sheet a straitjacket as it bundles me in its cotton arms.

I've still got to acclimate to my new surroundings. I'm not used to sleeping without the air at a stable sixty-eight degrees, and being upstairs, this room's stifling hot.

This house was built eons before central air-conditioning was a thing, and window units are all we have, and for some reason, there's no longer one in my room.

Even with the window open, the outside air isn't moving, as if it took its last gasp before it reached the entrance. My back's drenched with sweat, my skin sticking uncomfortably to the tiny tank top I'm wearing.

As I'm about to go downstairs and try the couch, the click of the doorknob stops my tossing and turning, and I lie motionless, wondering if I imagined someone at the door.

A creaky hinge signals my imagination hasn't run away from me.

My mother doesn't come upstairs much, and my automatic assumption is that she's checking on me. The pitter-patter of uneven footsteps crosses the room, and when she walks over the rough floorboards, the hardwood gives a distinct creak.

Pressing my eyes shut, I pretend to be asleep, like when I was a child and the tooth fairy would come to trade a few dollars for my tiny teeth.

Her weight settles beside me on the bed, and the mattress sags temporarily underneath us. Heavy breathing makes her sound like she just ran a marathon, or maybe she's overheated, just like me.

I doubt climbing the stairs helped her discomfort.

A hand reaches out to touch the back of my neck.

Suddenly ice cold, I'm now the opposite of feverish. An ominous feeling settles deep in the pit of my stomach.

The fingers creep down my shoulder, past the gift I gave myself shortly after my twenty-first birthday, a small tattoo of a butterfly.

Signifying new beginnings, it's a reminder of how far I've come.

Now the spindly lumps are trailing down my spine.

A voice whispers in my ear. "You aren't who you say you are, are you?"

I try to flip over, but her hand presses down on my throat, cutting off my air.

"What're you doing?" I gasp, my hands clutching at her elbows. Using my nails, I scratch her as hard as I can until she abruptly releases her grip.

"You can't take her place." Her weight shifts off the bed, but when I lurch after her, my hand grabs at the air.

When I flick on the lamp, no one's there.

Dizzy, I run a palm over my face.

Was that a nightmare?

It had to be, yet the bedroom door is ajar. I could've sworn I closed it when I came in here. Yes, I'm positive. It was closed when my mother came home.

Agitated, I take a sip of water from the glass on the nightstand, my heart rate through the roof.

I pound down the stairs, a violent maelstrom with increasingly erratic thoughts. Missing a step, I stumble, and I'd have broken my neck if the wooden railing weren't intact to catch my fall.

When I reach the bottom with a thud, my nails trace the uneven walls to safely guide me in the dark through the rest of the house.

Hell bent on confronting my mother, I don't bother knocking on her door; instead I fling it open hard enough that it hits the wall with a bang. I expect her to be awake, and my mouth is ready with a slew of cusswords, but the vitriol disappears from my lips.

I stare in confusion at her four-poster bed and listen to her heavy snores. There's no way she can fake this deep breathing, and I reach forward to listen closer. Something smooth on the floor next to her bed rolls under my foot. When I lean down to grab it, I realize it's a pill bottle.

It's too dark to make out the prescription name, so I cradle it in my palm.

An object catches my attention at the edge of the hallway, and disturbed, I stare at something out of sight and blurred.

I scream at the billowing figure as it approaches.

Sure I'm witnessing one of the many people who have lived and died in this centuries-old farmhouse, I dart to the living room, running for dear life.

Outstretching my arm to restrain the shadow running across the carpet, I find myself grappling with air instead of the clandestine figure. I manage to get tangled up in the cord to a floor lamp and dive headfirst into an old wooden chest that probably belonged to the same generation as this phantom.

Blinded by the pain, I groan, not caring when the pill bottle is released from my clutch.

CHAPTER 26
Deborah

Deborah's always been an early riser, as she was raised entirely on a farm. The work never ceases, and the days start long before the rest of the world begins to stir from their beds.

She's standing in front of the coffeepot, ready to brew her 5:00 a.m. morning joe, when she feels something soft rubbing against her ankle.

Half-asleep, she assumes she stepped on a dish towel that fell to the floor, but then the object purrs.

Dropping the coffee tin, she stares at her pregnant cat, Esmeralda, one of the permanent fixtures of the farm. She's taken pity on Esmeralda by feeding her extra kitchen scraps, since her swollen belly indicates she's about to give birth any day. Deborah doesn't usually let the cats roam freely inside. She only made an exception when she had a mice infestation.

"You little weasel." She grins. "How'd you get in the house?"

After stroking her fur, Deborah plies her with a treat to go back outside. She frowns when she realizes she walked straight out onto the porch, and the sudden realization dawns that both the front and screen doors are wide open.

As she strides back into the house, an uneasy feeling takes root in her gut.

Her eyes dart to the living room, which is in a state of disarray. The floor lamp is upturned, and the cord has been pulled out from the wall.

Magazines and books from the top of the oak chest are scattered across the carpet. Most of their pages are now ripped and torn, as if someone purposely shredded them in a fit of anger.

She walks through the downstairs, and with a sigh of relief, she sees that nothing besides that room has been disturbed.

She doesn't bother to check the upstairs, her blood pressure skyrocketing.

Deborah fumbles for her cell phone, which is charging on the counter. Her fingers dial 911, but she doesn't hit call quite yet, choosing to walk back outside first.

Dammit, anyhow. She hates that a string of robberies has had no suspects—including her own attack—and with the nearest neighbor a few miles away, she's worried that someone could be hiding in one of the outbuildings.

Usually, she wouldn't be caught dead outside in her old ratty slippers and housecoat, but the house feels stifling, and she needs a breath of fresh air.

The sight of Sibley's old car stops her in her tracks.

It hasn't moved, but the driver's door is wide open, inviting her to seek refuge inside. A scented air freshener in the shape of a pine tree hangs from the mirror, doing little to cover the smell of stale fast food.

Deborah winces as something sharp cracks underneath her flimsy slippers. It's a shard of broken glass, the culprit a fractured vodka bottle that's hiding halfway underneath the chassis.

She screams out of surprise, her fist hitting the faded paint of the doorframe.

She notices the key's in the ignition, hanging innocently, a taunting suggestion that the driver intended to get behind the wheel, whether impaired or not.

Disgusted, Deborah snatches it out of the vehicle.

As Deborah lets her eyes drift to the back seat, she's tempted to rifle through its contents, intent on uncovering who this stranger is: supposedly her daughter, yet all signs point to a different girl than the one she knew.

Sibley never seemed like the type to make rash decisions like running out on her husband, not to mention driving on a suspended license.

But what does Deborah know?

It's been sixteen years.

But still . . . it rubs her the wrong way.

Is the visit simply a matter of bad timing or a sly attempt to garner sympathy? She's ashamed for thinking this way, since Sibley is clearly having a tough go of it.

The middle console is empty except for some spare change and a cheap-looking black cell phone with prepaid minutes.

Why would Sibley have a prepaid phone?

Baffled, Deborah presses the power button.

There's no pass code on this phone, no photos, nothing.

Only three names and numbers are stored as contacts. Deborah doesn't recognize any of the three names. One is Wingwoman, another Nico, and the third Chuck.

Stranger yet, there's no Holden saved.

Sibley's an attorney and has to have more friends and acquaintances, not to mention business contacts.

Tapping a finger on the steering column, Deborah realizes she hasn't seen Sibley on her phone once since she arrived. Not to check messages, not to call anyone.

Most people are glued to their devices, so why would she be any different?

True, she could be using it out of sight, but something doesn't add up.

Maybe this is a secondary phone for work? Deborah hasn't considered the fact that maybe Sibley doesn't like giving her phone number to clients. Perhaps this fits the bill for when she wants to be discreet.

Or is she really who she says she is?

A movement catches Deborah's eye in the upstairs window. The blinds are open, and she's startled to see a figure standing there, watching and waiting.

Just like back then.

The shadow crosses her arms, and a moment of déjà vu throws Deborah back to when Sibley was a child, watching from her upstairs perch.

But is it really her?

That always reminded Deborah of Rapunzel trapped in a tower. When Jonathan would disappear into the night or Deborah would silently creep outside to be alone in the root cellar or the barn, she used to feel guilt at the wounded eyes of her offspring.

The night of Jonathan's death, Sibley witnessed the blood and mayhem and was forced to run to the neighbors for help because the phone cord had been cut. Then, though, her face was pressed against the glass as she watched. Now, there's ample distance between her and the window, as if she's part of a covert operation.

Deborah pictures the guilty look on her face when she caught Sibley going through the cupboards. She's about to call the contacts in the phone, but a prick in her foot causes her to cry out.

Gasping in pain, she stares down at the slipper, once pink but now turning red as blood soaks the cotton.

When Deborah looks back up at the window, the blinds are closed.

Much to her chagrin, a curse word slips out of her mouth, and she limps back into the house to bandage her foot.

CHAPTER 27
Sibley

When I wake up, I'm disoriented, and instead of feeling a soft mattress under my back, I find myself lying on something hard and unforgiving, and I'm curled up in an old horse blanket.

My nose immediately wrinkles at the pungency of old hay and caked-on mud, and I'm rattled to find I'm in the loft of our barn. The heavy material of the blanket now clings to me like I'm in a hot oven as sunlight peers through the tiny crevices. The air is as still and immovable as in my bedroom, a sauna in these summer months.

I haven't been up here since before Jonathan's fall out of the loft.

As I slowly ease up into a seated position, my vision's out of focus, as if I'm in the optometrist's chair, reading the fuzzy screen from a distance.

I move to stretch my arms, and the pain's instantaneous, a searing more excruciating than a migraine. Automatically, my fingers go to my forehead to rub the tension, but they connect instead with a large bump, sore to the touch.

No wonder my head hurts, I think. My splitting headache needs something to dull the pain, and I can't conjure up why, the memories of last night a gaping hole.

I rub my watery eyes and sniff at the burgeoning sweat from my armpits, soaked up by my ripped camisole. I'm surprised to discover I'm barefoot and wearing a pair of cotton athletic shorts that are two sizes too small.

After unraveling myself from the stable blanket, I scoot across the hard floor of the loft. The roof isn't high up here, about four feet, so I don't have enough space to stand. I have to either crawl or inch my way toward the unsteady ladder.

In my childhood, this was my hiding spot when I was in trouble. Funny how I always thought I was outsmarting my parents by choosing to hunker down here, as if they didn't know it existed.

With a shaky grip, I drag the horse blanket down the rickety ladder, my eyes focused on each rung instead of the missing slats. My father built a wooden railing to act as a safety guard after a neighbor boy broke his arm at my seventh birthday party when he was roughhousing with another kid. The irony isn't lost on me that it failed to save him.

But after my father's drunken antics, it was never replaced. Now just a few jagged boards remain. I keep my eyes from glancing down at the asphalt floor, where a concave indentation marks the place he took his last breaths. His toxicology results indicated he was at three times the legal limit when he splintered the railing.

Hanging the heavy blanket back up on the hook in the tack room takes skill, and as I try and throw it awkwardly over the metal hook, my elbow jams into the wall, and I keel over in pain.

An old chest rests against the wall, and when I sink down onto it to cradle my sore arm, a rough board catches the back of my flimsy tank.

Irked, I grudgingly stand up and try to maneuver the heavy old wood away from the wall. I'm only able to manage a couple inches, but what it uncovers has my whole body tingling from shock.

A firearm rests not so innocently on its side.

A wave of dizziness overcomes me, and I'm scared to touch the gun, let alone move it.

226

My mother mentioned a gun was used to strike her. What if this was used in her assault?

I open the chest, figuring that there might be a rag or something I can wrap the gun in so as not to disturb any usable fingerprints. I want the police to catch her attacker. Regardless of our past, I'd never wish harm upon her.

Some might believe in an eye for an eye, but not me.

I find a couple of old ratty towels, and my hands shake as I gently use one to wrap up the gun. I look underneath the fabric and am astonished to see old photo albums and yearbooks from my parents' own respective childhoods.

This is exactly what I was hoping to find.

I sink down onto the dusty floor and flip through pages of my mother's yearbooks, examining each name and picture. A couple of Edwards jump out at me, and I repeat their names aloud as a memorization tactic so I can look them up later.

But at the end of the yearbook are the larger senior photos, and when my eyes fall on one of them, it's not even a question. We share an uncanny resemblance: the same light-colored hair, smidgen of freckles, and bright-blue eyes. This has to be him.

My finger presses on his face. *Edward Pearson.*

I'm about to close it when a gauzelike piece of paper comes loose from the back of the book, where it was tucked between the last page and the binding. The faded handwriting belongs to my mother, so time-worn it seems it could crumble from the slightest mishandling.

Silently reading it, I'm startled when a shriek pierces the dead air.

Realizing it's my mother's voice calling my name, I hesitate. I could go outside and give myself away, but I'm not ready to face her yet. A heaviness weighs on my heart as tears stream down my cheeks from what I've become privy to. This diary entry or letter is unaddressed, so it's unclear if she's writing to someone. Even though my mother only has a high school education, she's able to articulate her grief-stricken feelings.

It's from 1986.

This is the last time I will write.

He pretended to be excited at first and said he made an appointment for me to get checked by a doctor. I was surprised because he's been so cold and distant, but I thought maybe he changed his mind. I should've known better.

The appointment he made was to a clinic a few hundred miles away so no one would know. He told me point-blank I was having a procedure done. He said I'm not fit to be a mother, and it would be Satan's spawn. When he pulled up to the front, he told me to go inside, and he would park and be right in, but he never showed. Instead, he disappeared. I didn't know what to do after he drove off. I went in alone and came out alone.

I wasn't sure if he would come back for me. The nurse took pity and let me sit in the waiting room until he finally showed up a few hours later, drunk and cursing loudly. I had to fight with him to get him to let me drive us home. I want to tell my mother, but I'm scared.

But I just wanted to let you know, it's over now.

Forever yours, Dee

A tear slides from my cheek onto the flimsy paper, and swiping it, I watch as a few of the words run on the page. Smeared, just like my family's reputation.

I'm horrified and wholly confused at the agony of what happened to my mother. So Jonathan didn't want me, whether I was his blood or not?

Or was this Edward the one who pushed her to get rid of me? Maybe he didn't want a child, and it wasn't until later that he had a change of heart. He must've had a good reason for not wanting my mother and me to be part of his life at the beginning. Or maybe it was perspective—there's a big difference between a fetus and a teenager.

If he was married and I was conceived during their affair, it would be understandable, though not admirable, that he would step back from Deborah.

I'm torn between the father I had growing up and the father who abandoned me before birth. It's a lot to accept.

To his credit, Jonathan never acted like he resented me. I spent most of my time outdoors with him, his little helper. I would've felt the tension, the same as the hostility I felt between him and my mother. I rarely heard them fight, but unspoken words were often exchanged between them.

Thinking about his dedication to me, I slap the old chest in disappointment. Why wasn't I reason enough for him to slow down on the bottle and quit? It's brutal to realize your childhood was a lie and the adults might as well have been part of a scripted reality series, since they had their own secret lives and failed to be accountable for their life choices.

Contemplating my disillusionment, I sit in stunned silence until heavy footsteps interrupt, their pace quickening as they get closer.

CHAPTER 28
Deborah

After tending to her wound and making sure she didn't track any glass inside, Deborah pours herself another cup of coffee.

Sibley doesn't answer when Deborah hollers upstairs, so she assumes she went back to bed. She remembers how Jonathan couldn't function after a bender, and judging from the empty, broken bottle of vodka, Sibley's going to need a dose of caffeine when she wakes back up.

Careful not to put weight on her bandaged foot, she uses one hand on the railing to guide herself up the stairs and the other to carry the hot ceramic mug. It takes Deborah longer to ascend between her sore foot and limp.

The door's slightly cracked, and Deborah tentatively peers inside. A motionless lump covered in blankets on the bed doesn't stir, and her sour mood tempts her to wake Sibley up to give her a piece of her mind.

Deborah's about to speak when she notices the area rug has been rolled back haphazardly and a pool of liquid is on the floor.

Not bothering to knock, she tiptoes closer. A spilled water glass is the culprit, but her jaw drops at an upended board that reveals a cutout in the floor.

What on earth? Deborah is awed. When did this happen?

Not as limber as she once was, Deborah struggles to lean down and examine the hole. She doesn't want to wake Sibley up, so she pauses a moment, heart beating in her chest, the mug trembling in her hand.

Not wanting to risk burning herself, she sets the mug carefully on the dresser.

After lowering herself with the aid of the wooden chest, Deborah reaches into the opening, her eyes on the mass in the bed.

Her fingers grasp some type of fabric caught on the edge of the rough-hewn wood. Delicately she removes the material from the small crevice, and realizing the thread of the button is snagged, she deftly untangles the thread from its captor.

Deborah gasps as her eyes widen in horror, her brain slow to comprehend what she's holding in her clutch, only knowing that it shouldn't be there.

Dropping it immediately like she's been burned, she recoils as if it's a snake ready to strike. She scoots across the floor and away from the floral-print fabric covered in bloodstains and charred in various places, but she can't stop staring down at the impossibility of it.

It's a dress, *the* dress she wore that April Sunday evening, over sixteen years ago. She gladly watched it go up in smoke, or so she thought—all evidence of that night destroyed on the burn pile. There should have been nothing left but ashes.

So what the hell is it doing in Sibley's room?

Up until that night, it was her favorite dress, but by the end of the evening, it was unwearable and bloodstained.

She claps a hand to her mouth. That fateful day is burned into her memory, just like she thought the dress had been. It's cotton, an easily flammable material, and is covered in large poppies of various colors, with a modest neckline and a few pearl buttons that adorn the front. Deborah never wore low-cut clothing or high hemlines for two reasons, both to do with Jonathan.

First, because he never allowed it.

But second, and more importantly, because the bruises and cigarette burns etched into her skin would have shown. Jonathan was sly, brilliant, always making sure to cause injury underneath Deborah's clothing so it wouldn't be visible. The smacks and verbal abuse happened behind closed doors or when Sibley wasn't around, which became more frequent once she got to high school.

On this particular Sunday, she and Jonathan attended church service while seventeen-year-old Sibley babysat in the church nursery. Their usual routine after church was that Jonathan would read scriptures at home while Deborah prepared the afternoon meal that served as both lunch and dinner.

Deborah was grateful Sibley and her father shared a mutual adoration, even now that she was a rebellious teenager. She was relieved Sibley still seemed to bask in his glow. As much as Deborah was envious of their relationship, she was relieved Jonathan didn't take his temper out on Sibley any more than most parents. Jonathan still disciplined her, but not with the severity or regularity he aimed at Deborah, as if her very presence aggravated him.

That was why it was out of character when he erupted in anger at Sibley on the way home when she asked him about getting her own car. They only had one vehicle, Jonathan's truck, and he refused to let anyone else drive it unless he was riding shotgun.

Slumped in the back seat, Sibley glumly stared out the window.

Jonathan went quiet, which usually meant he was irritated, and it typically resulted in anger being directed at her. This riddled Deborah with anxiety. She had grown used to the calm before the storm, and her body anticipated it now.

Clutching her small purse on her lap, Deborah's clammy hands left perspiration marks on the fabric as she watched him sneak glances in the rearview mirror at Sibley. His forehead creased as if he was deep in thought, and his dark eyes looked like he was watching a tennis tournament, lobbing stares back and forth.

Her distress only increased when they got home to the farm. Though Jonathan was a heavy smoker, he had made a solemn oath never to smoke when he was dressed in the suit he reserved for church. When they clambered out of the truck, he pulled his carton out of the console and lit up without bothering to change.

Their daughter preferred the outdoors and helped Jonathan around the farm and with the animals when they had them. She often imitated him, becoming his miniature shadow. But today, he wanted nothing to do with her, shooing her into the house with Deborah.

Usually, Deborah would change out of her dress as well, but this afternoon, a premonition filled her with dread.

By this point in her marriage, their daughter was a buffer between her and Jonathan. She had been hopeful that Jonathan's mood would mellow as he grew older or with having a child, but it hadn't helped. Other mothers would have wanted a girlie girl, but Deborah felt freed from his constant scrutiny, since Sibley was a tomboy who preferred to be near her daddy. This gave Deborah time to read and quilt, and even though the household chores never ceased, her husband's prying eyes left their target for a while, preoccupied with teaching their daughter about the farm.

With frazzled nerves, Deborah watched through the window as her husband frantically paced outside. Then, needing a distraction, she busied herself at the stove while Sibley helped cut up vegetables.

As Jonathan stomped toward the house, Deborah told Sibley to go upstairs. Sibley gave her a questioning glance but didn't argue, as if she could sense the strain.

Deborah was hit with a cloud of smoke as soon as the squeak of the door signaled Jonathan's presence.

Her hand trembled around the spoon, but she didn't turn around to face him.

In a conversational tone, he addressed her back. "I heard some interesting news today."

Stirring the pot on the burner, Deborah didn't reply.

As Jonathan's footsteps approached her, her natural reaction was to hunch her shoulders. She never needed to make eye contact to tell what kind of a mood he was in. It was obvious from the heaviness of his footfalls.

This afternoon, they were forceful, a shift from the casual strut this morning. Her husband was a crouched tiger ready to pounce.

As a preview of his temper, he rewarded her with a jab between her shoulder blades.

Wincing, she didn't react.

"Don't you wanna know what I found out today?"

"I don't have an interest in gossip." Irritated at these stupid games he liked to play, Deborah was tired of feeling like a helpless rabbit ensnared in a trap while he dangled a carrot in front of her, hoping she'd try to bite back so he could justify his anger.

"Even if it's about you?" Jonathan sneered. "And *your* daughter?"

The timer on the stove beeped.

Deborah watched a tear evaporate in the gravy pan.

"I talked to Cindy," he said. "You know, Robert's wife."

"Okay." She shrugged noncommittally.

"She and I had the nicest little *chat*." The way he said "chat" made her insides churn, and she knew far worse was coming. "Apparently, Cindy and I are the last to know."

Deborah didn't respond, which evidently wasn't the reaction Jonathan wanted, so he slammed his palm against her lower back, causing her to lurch forward.

Gritting her teeth, she said, "I'm not following."

"Is that so?" Jonathan's body shifted to check that Sibley was out of sight. "Cindy filled me in on secrets you've been sharing with her husband. Since the two of you are sleeping together, she said you've been telling her husband many things you haven't bothered to tell me." He pointed upstairs, hissing under his breath, "Like that girl up there I've been raising ain't really mine." Yanking Deborah away from the stove, he pushed her into a far corner.

Gripping her elbow roughly, he ordered her outside to the barn, his words menacing. When she didn't move, he honored her with a sharp kick to the ankles.

"Come on, Jonathan, I made a nice meal. We're about to sit down to—"

A sudden slap across her cheek caused her to flinch. "Don't you dare say a word, you filthy whore."

She lowered her stinging face, her vision blurring as she stared at the linoleum.

"Hurry up and get out there." Jonathan shoved her toward the door. "I'll tell Sibley to finish the potatoes."

Jonathan hollered for Sibley, but she didn't answer.

His footsteps hurried up the stairs, and Deborah was terrified, sure he was going to lose his temper on her.

The vent to Sibley's room was above the kitchen, and Deborah could hear her murmur something about having headphones on. Jonathan's tone had fortunately returned to normal, the anger boiling underneath the surface. It was his next statement that made her stomach bubble with acid. "Honey, if we're not back in fifteen minutes, come out and check on us. I might need help with the cleanup."

Fleeing for the barn, Deborah didn't wait for Sibley's reply.

She stumbled outside, half running as she reached the imposing structure. She climbed into the loft, where an old sleeping bag was shoved out of sight on a rafter, and unrolled the fabric. Inside, Deborah had ripped an opening she could use as a secret compartment.

She reached in to yank out the bulky cell phone, which weighed as much as a brick, since seventeen years ago, they were still in their infancy. Cell phones hadn't replaced landlines or become a necessity at this point, and it wasn't like Jonathan would let her have one.

Fingers quivering, she powered it on, praying it would work. She was still wary of its reliability, as out here, this relatively new technology and lack of cell towers often proved problematic.

During her earlier drill, Deborah had been instructed to find where she would have the best reception, and unfortunately, it wasn't the barn.

Knowing Jonathan would be looking for her at any minute, she sneaked toward the toolshed next to the house. She didn't want to bring Jonathan's wrath anywhere near Sibley, since her job was to protect her daughter.

The first call rang once and then dropped.

When she spied Jonathan stomping out to the barn on a rampage, she crouched down. His fist was curled around something, but she didn't know what it was. Unable to control her shaking legs, she watched him with wild, unfocused eyes.

The cell rang a second time in her trembling hand. Impatiently she whispered, "Pick up, please pick up."

Tears of joy streamed down her face when the ringing was replaced by heavy breathing. "I'm ready," she choked out. Nothing more needed to be said.

Powering the phone down, she commanded herself, *You can do this. He deserves every bit of what's coming to him. Stay strong, Deborah Lee, stay strong.*

Standing up, she buried the phone in the burn pile, where they got rid of sticks and litter, as it was now a liability to be disposed of.

She exhaled a ragged breath as she watched it disappear under a pile of garbage. Deborah was starting to turn when, out of the corner of her eye, she caught a shadow's outline.

Sibley stood stock still, peering through the window in her bedroom.

How much had she seen?

Deborah went as far as gesturing with her hand for Sibley to get away from the window, but she didn't move. With only a pane of glass between them, Deborah could no longer spare Sibley the wrath of Jonathan. She didn't think her daughter knew what he was capable of. If Jonathan found out what Deborah was planning, all bets would be off. She worried she was never going to see her daughter again. When footsteps approached from behind, Deborah locked eyes with her daughter. She screamed for her to run as Jonathan's sinewy arms reached out to choke her, but Sibley was still standing there, as if comatose.

As he dragged her toward the barn, Deborah was sure this would be the last image her daughter would have of her, which would be worse than the violent death she knew was coming.

A loud moan snaps Deborah out of her recollection, and her eyes dart toward the bed. She realizes she's crying, and the wetness dripping down the collar of her shirt and onto her cross pendant is from tears.

Hurriedly, she hoists herself back up, using the dresser as leverage. Noticing the coffee mug, Deborah removes it, not wanting to disclose she was in Sibley's room.

Bile rises in her throat as she stares at the dress, unsure what to do with the evidence from that night.

Deborah intends to shove it back into the hiding spot. But she can't force herself to put it back there. Instead, she crumples the fabric into a ball. This time, she'll watch it disintegrate on the burn pile until it becomes soot.

CHAPTER 29
Sibley

Carefully, I slide the paper back between the pages of the yearbook as a male voice announces Fletch's presence.

He's not going to leave the barn until he finds me.

"You hiding in that damn loft?" Fletch says it jokingly, but we both know it was our go-to place as kids when we wanted to hide. Our loft privileges were suspended indefinitely after that birthday party.

Not to mention the images the loft conjures up now.

I can tell he's climbing up into the loft by the rustle of the ladder and the thud of his boots.

Tilting my head, I wait for the telltale signs he's above me, his heavy steps crossing the creaky boards. When his stomps are overhead, I replace the yearbook and the snugly wrapped gun in the chest and close the lid.

I hear him call my name again. "Sibby, you in here?"

With a small groan, I shove the chest back against the wall. The last thing I need is Fletch poking around the tack room, using his investigative skills to be a pain in the ass.

Even though we used to be close, I don't feel comfortable giving him the gun. After years of tension and then silence, I know how strongly he dislikes my family. He might pretend to be a good neighbor and a law-abiding citizen, but his actions from the past are front and center in my mind.

I reach down to my lower calf, my fingers tracing the small imprint of the scar from my senior year of high school. It was a couple days after the god-awful Halloween party, after Kristin had started the rumors at school, making it impossible for me to walk down the hall without the other kids shaming me about my mother. Fletch confronted me about the allegations that afternoon in the parking lot, and it turned ugly. I was already having a bad enough day, my face red and puffy from crying.

His beet-red face matched mine, but from anger. After slamming his truck door, he got close to me, his nose practically touching my face. "Why didn't you tell me you saw them together?"

"Because I didn't see them doing anything, you know . . . sexual."

"Doesn't matter." He spat on the ground. "You knew."

"Think about it, Fletch," I begged. "It's only *Kristin's* word." I said it like it was ridiculous to trust her, but he cut me off.

"Why on earth would she lie about your mom and my dad?" He fixed me with a cold stare, and it made me long for his puppy dog eyes. "What possible motive could Kristin have to want to spread that kind of a lie?"

"To hurt me. She's always starting drama."

"But why would she purposefully hurt you?" He rubbed his hand gingerly, and I noticed skin peeling from his knuckle. "You guys were friends."

"Because you and I are close." I cringed. "Whoa! Did you punch something?"

"Yeah, my father." He sighed. "We ain't close no more, Sibley." The lack of my teasing moniker hurt. "You can thank your whore mom for that."

"Why is my mom the one to blame?" I shouted. "Your father probably took advantage of her."

"You can't take advantage of the willing." He kicked a piece of gravel hard, and it hit me in the leg. I flinched, not because it hurt but because he didn't apologize. It became a permanent tattoo on my skin.

"Just because you finally got a girlfriend doesn't mean you have any right to hurt me," I cried.

"You're just jealous because I have a girlfriend, and it isn't you!"

"I can't believe what a horse's ass you're being." I shook my head disgustedly. "You and Kristin deserve each other."

His icy glare penetrated mine, and his next comment made my blood run cold. "I'm gonna have to tell my mom about it."

"About what?" I sighed. "There's nothing to tell."

"She deserves to know." He ran a frustrated hand through his hair. "Hell, maybe she already does."

"Fletch," I pleaded. "This isn't the right thing to do."

"Why not?"

"You're gonna get a lot of people hurt."

"Poor Sibley, always thinking about herself. You're so damn selfish."

"You want to hurt your mama?"

"No. But she's a strong woman; she'll know what to do."

"What about my mother?" I beseeched. "What about my daddy?"

"That's their business." He shrugged. "Who knows, maybe your daddy will shoot mine." With an evil glint in his eye, he winked. "Or hell, maybe I'll kill both your parents."

It was a horrendous thing to say, and now, reflecting back on it, I shudder.

Sticks and stones can break my bones, but words can never hurt me. Whoever coined that phrase didn't understand the power of language. His words still haunt me to this day, especially with what transpired after our parking lot fight.

As I shake my head to rid myself of the memories, Fletch's voice echoes from above. "Sibby, is that you down there?"

After exiting the small, closet-like room, I quickly shove the door shut and brush my dusty and sweaty palms on my thighs. "I'm here." I stand at the foot of the ladder.

His head pops over the loft. "I thought I'd come to check on you. Had no idea I'd find you in the barn."

"I was looking for the pregnant cat," I offer dumbly.

"You coming up, or am I coming down?"

Fletch doesn't know about my terror of climbing into the loft and being so close to tragedy. It's pointless to tell him now.

"Down, because I'm not feeling so great." I wipe a hand across my sweaty, pained forehead. "It's like a hundred degrees in here. Feels like a steam room."

"You're from the desert. This heat shouldn't rattle you."

"It's a dry heat," I murmur. "This is humid *and* hot."

Slinking down the ladder, Fletch says, "You're lucky I came out here."

"I am?"

Before he can respond, his eyes latch on to my injured face. "Shit." He whistles. "What happened to you?"

I feign ignorance with a shrug.

"You look like you got in a catfight."

"That's a real possibility out here."

"Seriously, are you okay?"

"Yeah. I tripped over a lamp last night." Conscious of my bare feet and perspiration, I move toward the outside and sunshine, giving us some distance. "Guess I'm still clumsy."

Fletch passes me a bandana out of his pocket, and I gratefully dab the sweat and tears from my face.

Checking out my reflection in the side mirror of his jacked-up truck, I can see the welt on my forehead, red and angry. I lightly touch the purplish bruising, which highlights my right eye.

I flinch. "Did I get in a bar brawl last night trying to protect you?"

"It certainly looks that way." He prods, "You need to put some ice on that head of yours."

"Speaking of protection, why no police cruiser? Do you usually pounce around like a mischievous cat looking for barn mice on your off time?" I lean against his truck.

"If you must know"—he drags his toe in the dirt—"I came to make sure you were okay."

"You mean *babysit*," I moan.

"We used to be best friends," he offers. "I've never liked to see you upset."

"You ruined that." I push his snot rag back in his hand.

"Two-way street, honey." Tucking the red fabric back in his pocket, he says, "And crazy as this sounds, I wanted to check on Deborah."

"I'm confused." I narrow my eyes at him. "You blame her for everything that happened in the past, and now you're a friendly neighbor? What's the catch?"

"She dialed 911 this morning and hung up. I told the officer on duty I'd check on her."

"About what?" I'm suddenly fearful.

"I don't know." He cocks his head at me. "When I pulled in, I noticed the barn door was open. Thought I'd check it out first just to be on the safe side."

"I'll go in and check on her." I shrug. "She probably forgot I was home."

He shakes his head. "I'm telling you, you need to talk to her. I think living on the farm is becoming a little much in more ways than one. She's losing her grip out here. Maybe a change of scenery would do her some good."

I stare down at my dirty feet. I'll never admit to him I have the same concerns.

"She's stopped taking care of the yard," Fletch continues. "And don't think I didn't notice the mess inside the house."

"What do you expect?" I snap. "She was attacked. I think she's scared to be outside by herself."

"What about inside?" Fletch asks. "The old Deborah never would've let her house become a pigsty."

"She had a mice infestation," I argue. "And she's . . . she's redecorating. I'm helping donate a bunch of shit, and we're cleaning it up."

"She calls the police all the time, paranoid someone is watching her."

"Obviously, with good reason!" I yelp. "She got the shit beat out of her. Besides," I add, glaring, "you've always thought she was crazy."

"And was I wrong?" He stares me down with his green eyes. "We're all worried . . ."

"Let me guess, the folks in town?"

"Yeah, people." He lets out a frustrated sigh. "I heard through the grapevine she told some people she's moving to Florida with her boyfriend, yet no one has seen her with anyone."

"What business is it to you who she dates?" I retort. "Maybe I'm helping her enter the dating pool!"

"Nice try, Sibby. This was before you arrived."

"Fletch, I appreciate the concern," I say pointedly. "But in your position, I'd be worried about the rash of home invasions. It's like you're deflecting because you don't have any suspects."

Snorting, he seems incredulous. "Oh, is that so?" He rests against the hood of his souped-up truck. "I wasn't happy when they built that men's prison a couple miles outside of town, no. But we think the suspect or suspects were seeking money or drug paraphernalia."

"And that makes it any less scary?" I argue. "Having someone that's erratic and high is a relief?" A trickle of cold sweat creeps down the back of my ripped camisole.

"I'm not saying that, Sibby. Just trying to be straight with you."

"Oh, I get it!" I hold up my index finger. "You're still angry about the past."

He crosses his arms defensively, his jaw set.

"Spreading useless gossip already ruined two families." I move closer so I can lean into his face. "Sure you wanna do it again?"

"Dammit, Sibby!" He grasps my shoulders. "Not everything is an attempt to get back at you. Look . . ." He shakes me for a moment, then drops his hands to his sides. "None of that matters anymore. I'm not mad at your recollection, and you shouldn't be upset at mine."

The trembling staccato in my head takes a turn for the worse. I close my eyes for a second, drained and bitter, filled with misdirected hatred toward him.

"Believe me," he says, his voice soothing, "I just want to leave that in the past."

"Not true. You just want to convince everyone Deborah's always had a screw loose."

"I know what I heard, Sibby."

"But I was actually there! I know what I saw!" Sickened by the sliver of doubt piercing through my own deep-seated belief of what I knew at the time, especially since reading the letter, I wonder if I've hung on to the ironclad truth of my own convictions for too long. Refusing to think about what Fletch angrily told me back in high school, I suck on my bottom lip.

All these years, I was convinced Fletch wanted to hurt me because of the damage done to his own family. But how much hatred would you have toward someone who made you get rid of your child? And someone who raised their hand to you?

My own instincts tell me my mother had justification for wanting Jonathan dead, as well as a legitimate motive.

I shake my head—and shake the memory loose. "It was an accident," I say sharply.

"If that's what you want to believe, then so be it."

"You think I wanted to lose my daddy?"

His eyes glower. "You think I wanted to lose my mama?"

"Of course not. I think you relied on someone else's accusations." I don't bother saying Kristin's name out loud.

"Mark my words—there was nothing accidental about it. Your mother made sure your father paid the price." He spits on the ground. "And not that he didn't deserve it, but she didn't care about dragging my family through the mud on her quest to break free of Jonathan."

Sometimes when you take a step too far, there's no way to pull yourself back, and you're forced to fall off the cliff, hoping it won't lead to your demise. This feels like one of those times.

"If it wasn't an accident," I taunt, "then blood's on your hands too. You got your own mother killed."

"Stop," he growls in warning. "Don't you dare, Sibley."

We stand in uncomfortable silence, our bodies stiff with tension. He seems to forget my pain isn't any less real than his. I had to live with a mother constantly scrutinized and under attack, and though some felt sorry for her, many thought she'd gotten what she deserved.

He's gawking at me, and I redden at his intense stare. "You know, your freckles get more pronounced when you're upset," he says. "I forgot how they seem to spread over your face."

My hand moves across the bridge of my nose as I fan my flaming skin. Poking my shoeless foot in the dirt, I fight the urge to jump into my beater and head back west. Maybe I was wrong to think this trip would help assuage my own bottomless pit of grief.

"Everything okay, Sibby? You look like you've just seen a ghost."

I put my hand up. "I'm fine. I think I need to go inside and lie down."

"You better go inside and take care of that face."

I nod, needing to be alone as quickly as possible.

"Oh, and here's Deborah's mail. Thought I'd save her the trip to the mailbox." Handing me a stack, Fletch fixes me with a solemn salute. His eyeballs penetrate my back as I walk away.

I want distance between us and our heated conversation, but inside the house is no better, since I'm equally reluctant to confront my mother. I wish I could slink inside without her knowing I've been out in the barn. I'm not ready to look her in the eye, talk about what I found, or explain my battered face.

I'm also not ready to ask the hard questions about my father. Or *fathers*, in this case.

Everything I believed is now suddenly false, outdated, or irrelevant. Lies stacked upon more lies, a house of cards about to fall.

Inside the house, I sink into a chair to sort through the mail. I should put ice on my face, but my inquisitive nature takes over. If I weren't an attorney, I'd be a private investigator, as I've always found researching and digging deep into people a fascinating endeavor. Everybody has a past, and my mother is making me question her innocence the night Jonathan died.

A freak accident is one thing, murder another.

Reading Deborah's mail isn't exactly on the up and up, but after I've sliced the envelope with the mail opener, I can't believe what I'm reading.

My shoulders tremble, then my whole body, and I envision myself at the epicenter of an earthquake, a seismic shift beneath me.

Biting my tongue, I jump out of my chair for an explanation.

CHAPTER 30
Deborah

With the vile dress in hand, Deborah marches outside, planning to take it straight out to the burn pile. She changes her mind when she spots the lifted truck Miles Fletcher drives, but he's not in sight. He must be out here looking for Sibley, she thinks, groaning. She doesn't want to tell him Sibley's inside sleeping, and she silently prays he won't knock on the door.

It makes her uncomfortable to have him snooping around the farm. Hopefully, he's gotten the hint he's not welcome here. He's a trouble-maker, and he's the reason for so much of Sibley's anger. Deborah is clutching the fabric, but she can't stand the thought of its presence, even for a few minutes. After shoving it in the corner of the pantry, Deborah spends an inordinate time at the sink, furiously scrubbing her hands. The mere thought of them touching the dress causes her to vomit.

Wiping a hand across her mouth, Deborah scurries to her bedroom, light headed and dizzy. After swallowing down a couple of pain pills, Deborah immediately lies down in bed. Even though it's still morning, she's tired and drained, never fully rested after a night's sleep.

When she's barely conscious, a loud banging startles Deborah. She's frozen underneath the covers, then yanks them over her face, cringing beneath them in fear. A high-pitched cry comes from the other side of the wall, and she realizes it's Sibley.

"You're not alone anymore. There's nothing to be afraid of," Deborah says softly to soothe her nerves.

From her hiding spot, she's shocked when she hears the thud of her bedroom door and Sibley's angry voice beside her. "What're you doing, Mother?"

"Resting," she says weakly as the covers are snatched off her.

"Mother!" Sibley shrieks. "What the hell is this?"

"I can't see."

"Open your eyes."

Deborah slowly acquiesces. Sibley's hand is raised in the air, waving something around like it's the starting flag at the beginning of a race.

"I don't know what you have in your hand, honey." Deborah lies there listlessly, the shades drawn. "I can't see it. Hand me my glasses."

Sibley quickly presses the spectacles into Deborah's palm while she struggles to sit up in bed.

"Will you flip on the light, please?"

With the room now bathed in a soft glow, Deborah gasps at Sibley's face. Staring at the harsh bruise and redness, she asks what happened.

"I don't recall." Sibley becomes defensive, crossing her arms across her chest. "But maybe you remember this?" She pushes the unsealed envelope into Deborah's hand.

"First, where do you get off opening my mail?"

"You should be thanking me. You're entitled to much more than what this letter from the county's legal counsel is proposing. They're condemning your land, with the intent of building a roadway for the damn prison." Sibley wrenches a hand through her hair. "Not to mention, this is a ridiculously lowball offer so that they can justify destroying farmland to build roads. This is bullshit."

"I don't need to consult you when it comes to the farm, Sibley," Deborah reminds her. "This farm has been in *my* family for generations."

"Exactly! That's my point." Sibley snaps her fingers. "How could you even think about selling the farm to these imbeciles when it should stay in our family for future generations? At least, that's what Jonathan talked about."

"Jonathan talked about a lot of things," Deborah says sharply. "I don't care what he told you. The farm wasn't his to keep or sell. It belonged to my ancestors. He's not here to make more false promises."

Sibley sulks. "I can't believe you have the audacity to sell *our* farm without even consulting me. I presume you weren't going to tell me until after the fact."

Deborah fingers the lace bedspread. "I would've let you know, eventually."

"How thoughtful!" Sibley retorts sarcastically. "There're ways around this. I can do some research. I can read up on eminent domain laws."

"I don't want you to."

"What do you mean?" Sibley's eyes become slits. "Don't you care about them bulldozing our land and thinking they can use that shady legal maneuver to wrestle it from a poor, feeble woman?"

"I'm hardly helpless," Deborah protests. "And it's their business what they do after I sell it."

Sibley draws her mouth into a tight line but says nothing.

"And after what happened . . ." Deborah's voice trails off.

"But where are you going to go, Mother?" Sibley frowns. "You're not well."

"How dare you!" Deborah narrows her eyes. "I'm not an invalid. I am perfectly capable of taking care of myself."

"It's more than that, Mother," Sibley pleads. "I worry about you. You always used to take such good care of the place. I hate to see it so run down." Sibley sighs. "And you—you seem to be . . . so . . . frazzled."

"It's too much upkeep for me, which is why I feel comfortable selling it," Deborah affirms. "And I told you I'm fine."

"It's more than that, Mother." Sibley balks. "I need closure."

"From what?"

"My past." Sibley sinks onto the edge of the mattress.

Deborah groans. "You have to stop blaming me for Jonathan's death. Just let it go."

"That would be convenient, wouldn't it?"

"I wasn't truthful about a lot of things when it came to him, and it's blown up in my face."

"You do seem to struggle with honesty," Sibley says slowly.

Deborah retorts, "You've gone through life thinking an affair caused all this pain. It didn't."

"The day he died. You fought." Sibley pointedly adds, "I remember."

"We always fought, just not in front of you."

Deborah knows both of them have their versions of events regarding the night in question. The significant difference is she was there in real time, while Sibley was in the house. She couldn't have been aware of what was happening in the barn.

"That afternoon." Sibley chews her lip. "You were arguing in the kitchen."

"How could you know?" Deborah says exasperatedly. "You were upstairs listening to music."

"I can hear everything through the floor vent in my room."

"Then you must've heard Jonathan tell me to get to the barn."

"Yes."

Deborah says accusingly, "I saw you standing at the window later."

"And I saw you run out from the barn and throw something on the burn pile before Daddy spotted you."

"It was a cell phone I threw on the burn pile."

"After my father, uh, Jonathan . . . dragged you to the barn, I watched someone sneak onto the property, headed in the direction of the barn."

"You mean Cindy," Deborah says.

Vehemently, Sibley shakes her head. "No! Not Cindy. This person was wearing dark clothes from head to toe, trying to go undetected. I don't think they noticed me watching from the upstairs window."

"Honey, no one else was at the house until the police arrived. You must have imagined someone."

"Who did you call that night, Mother? I wonder." Sibley puts a finger to her chin.

"What do you mean?" Deborah wrings her hands in her lap. "I called 911."

"No, you didn't!" Sibley protests. "That's impossible. The phone cord was cut, and when I ran to the neighbors to call the police, they hadn't been aware of any problems at the house."

Deborah's face scrunches in disgust.

Sibley continues. "And you came inside to change your clothes. You went from wearing your church dress to jeans and a tee." She sucks in a breath. "It was all very suspect."

"I was covered in blood, Sibley." Deborah sniffs. "It wasn't like it was going to come clean in the washing machine, so I burned it. Or at least, I thought I burned it." Deborah swings her legs off the bed. "Until I found it in your room today."

"I don't know what you mean."

"Why is my dress from that night upstairs in your bedroom?"

"It's not." Sibley raises a brow. "At least not that I'm aware of."

"You had it hidden in some secret hideaway, which I never permitted you to drill into the floor. For Pete's sake, when did you make a cubbyhole in our flooring? You're lucky your father didn't find out. He would've tanned your hide. And mine too."

"I don't know anything about your dress."

"Then let me show you." Deborah motions to the door. "I don't like liars."

"That's funny!" Sibley snaps. "Seems you have a lot of truths to tell me about my childhood. Maybe you can start with what happened the night two people died!" Sibley's voice rises in agitation. "Do you understand why something's not adding up? Who was there that night, Mother? Why won't you tell me what really happened to Jonathan?"

Deborah's petite frame becomes smaller as she hunches over.

Sibley's lip starts to quiver. "It's because you killed him, didn't you?" She rests her head in her hands, defeated. "I'm not mad, but you owe me the truth, just like you owe me the truth about my father."

Deborah sits in stunned silence, her head bowed.

"Robert Fletcher came to help get rid of Jonathan, didn't he?" Sibley whispers. "He was the one who showed up unexpectedly. He just didn't expect his wife to follow him."

"No." Deborah reaches for her hand, but Sibley yanks it away. "That's not what happened. I didn't call 911 because I didn't want everyone to know I was trying to leave Jonathan that night. That's why Robert showed up. To help me."

"The two of you were having an affair. I saw you." Sibley keeps her tone neutral. "So Robert was going to leave Cindy for you, and you were going to leave Jonathan?"

"No." Deborah sighs in frustration. "You have that completely backward. You and the majority of the town. Always spreading lies and rumors."

"You have room to talk." Sibley jumps up, stalking out of the room. Deborah moves more slowly, rising to limp behind her.

"What's that supposed to mean?" Deborah follows as Sibley stomps into the kitchen. "Since we're in here"—Deborah points toward the pantry—"go in there and explain to me why my dress mysteriously appeared in this house."

"Who cares about your damn dress?" Sibley explodes. "Or are you worried it's evidence pointing to your guilt?"

"Now! Show it to me."

Sibley stalks into the pantry and comes right back out, empty handed. "I have no idea what you're talking about. I see nothing but coats." She rolls her eyes. "I watched you burn it, and the cell phone I'd never seen before. And you did it before the cops and ambulance ever arrived, so why would the dress make an appearance now?" With a whisper, Sibley adds, "You're losing it, Mother."

Deborah says nothing, just motions for her to step aside so she can enter the small walk-in. With disbelief, Deborah stares at the corner of the pantry. There's no dress balled up on the floor. Jackets and a scarf hang on their usual hooks, but there's no sign of a floral print.

Slowly crouching down, Deborah even rolls her long sleeves up and gets on her hands and knees to check beneath the bottom shelf. There's nothing but dust mites and a gold stud, no sign of blood or a crumpled dress. When she steps out of the pantry to confront Sibley, she says, "You must've put it back upstairs in your secret stash."

"Oh, really?" Sibley puts her hands on her hips. "What happened to your arm, Mother?"

"What do you mean?"

"You have scratches all over your arm." Sibley points at the jagged red marks. "You got clawed pretty bad. Please tell me it wasn't one of the feral cats."

Stumped, Deborah traces the lines. "It must've been Esmeralda," she says, but she knows she probably doesn't sound convinced.

"You better put some alcohol on it." Sibley raises her brow. "And I hope for your sake the cats don't have rabies. We don't need a *Pet Sematary* situation out here."

Deborah bites her tongue and swallows a response.

"By the way, when you were going through my room," Sibley says, "you didn't have to scare the bejesus out of me when you came upstairs last night."

"I didn't come upstairs last night," Deborah says. "I went to bed and conked out."

"So I dreamed that?"

"You were drunk," Deborah says matter-of-factly. "You made a mess in the living room when you tripped over the lamp. At first, I thought I'd been robbed."

"No, I wasn't. I was disoriented. Different surroundings and all. I forgot where I was."

"I found a smashed, empty bottle outside."

"Well, I don't remember why I went downstairs in the first place, but I woke up with a massive headache and a goose egg on my forehead," Sibley gripes. "Is that why you called the police?"

"I didn't mean to hit call, but I saw Miles Fletcher's truck outside," Deborah states. "You better put some frozen peas on your eye."

"No. It'll be okay." Sibley tiredly rubs her eyes. "I'll survive. I don't really remember much about last night. Can we talk about my father?"

"What about Jonathan?"

Sibley fixes her with a glare. "Who's lying now?"

Deborah stumbles backward, relieved to feel the solid edge of the counter cutting into her back. A dizzy spell washes over her like a tidal wave. Pressing her fingers to her forehead, she murmurs, "I need to lie down."

Ignoring the surprise on Sibley's face, Deborah slinks out of the room and shuts her bedroom door firmly against her daughter and questions she doesn't want to answer.

CHAPTER 31
Sibley

After I hear my mother's door slam, I wearily climb the stairs, tracking bits of grass from being barefoot earlier. Not wanting the showerhead's blast or noise, I settle myself on the tub's side to rinse my muddy feet under the spigot. My bloodshot eyes stare back at me from the mirror with a vulnerable rawness that startles me.

Why would she accuse me of having her dress? I ask my reflection.

After swallowing a handful of pills, I strip the rest of my clothes off and burrow underneath the covers, my exhaustion giving way to an uneasy slumber.

Then, unable to sleep, I boot up my laptop, deciding to search for information on my newfound father. Even though he graduated with my mother, I can't find any recent information on him or any type of social media presence. An obituary for Edward Marvin Pearson pops up, and my hands tremble on the keyboard.

Both of my fathers are dead?

I tell myself this can't be the right Edward M. Pearson, but he's the same age as my mother and grew up around here. It says he served in the navy and lived all over the world during his deployment.

Left to honor Edward are his two children, Edward Jr. and Olivia. He was preceded in death by his parents, Edward and Louisa, and his brother, Preston.

A cause of death isn't listed, and minimal details are included. I search for the two kids and find a million Edward Pearsons and a decent number of Olivias, more than I would've thought possible, but none seem to have ties to our small town.

Filled with sadness, I cry myself to sleep, hating the unfairness of never knowing who my father was until it was too late.

I'm discombobulated when I wake. The light streamed in when I first hobbled to bed, but now the moon's the only flashlight. The digital clock on the nightstand informs me it's after 9:00 p.m.

Before I lug myself out of bed, my thoughts drift to my earlier discovery in the barn, and a wave of nausea overtakes me. My racing mind is screaming with an insatiable need that hasn't been fulfilled. The distinct voice in my head always has a solution to my problems. I need something to curb my craving.

When I emerge downstairs, my mother's seated at the table, her fork digging into a baked potato loaded up with butter and sour cream. I'm surprised to see her eating something, considering the state of her fridge.

"I waited as long as I could," she says apologetically.

"Jeez, Mother, it's after nine." I shove my trembling hands in my pockets. "I would hope you wouldn't wait for me to eat."

"I was about to come and check on you." Her hand twists around her fork. "I just didn't want you to think I was spying on you."

"I'm sure you have a hard time getting up the stairs." I shrug. "If you need anything, you can always holler at me from the bottom."

She puts down her fork.

"Are you feeling any better?" I ask. "Didn't you go and take a nap?"

"I did. I feel much more refreshed." My mother gives me a small smile. "And relaxed."

Since my mother finally seems at ease, I should take this opportunity to settle on the couch with her and catch up on the past sixteen years. Find out about Edward and what happened to him. But I don't have the patience to sit down, my body thrumming with nervous energy. After all the nonsense about the farm and her dress accusations, only one thing is on my mind.

Nonchalant, I slide my flip-flops on. "I'm going to run into town."

"For what? I just got groceries."

"I need to just clear my head with a drive."

"Are you sure that's a good idea?" She frowns. "I worry about you driving at night. You gotta watch out for deer."

"I drove all the way here. I think I can handle it." I grab my wallet. "Want anything?"

"Mind if I go with you? It might be good to get some fresh air. We can stop and get some ice cream, my treat."

"As much as I'd love the company, do you mind if I bring some back for us?" Her crestfallen face causes me to hurriedly add, "I was going to try and call Holden. I'm having trouble with my signal out here."

"It can be spotty," she murmurs. "I wondered why I hadn't seen you on the phone. I figured that husband of yours was getting worried. If it's about privacy . . . ," she says with an air of concern.

"It's not. I'll just call him on the drive," I offer. "We can have dessert together. Least I can do for making you wait to eat dinner so late."

"It closes at ten, so you better hurry."

With a nod, I search for my keys.

I'm growing increasingly agitated, since there's nothing more I'd like to do than close the gap between me and my next sip.

"If you're looking for your keys, they're in your ignition." My mother studies me intently.

I don't bother to ask how she knows this or why I left them there. Mumbling a simple thank-you, I rush outside to my car and pause a moment. I hurry to the barn, carefully remove the towel from the chest, and place it on my passenger-side floor mat. I did tell the chief of police I would pay him a visit. He's used to having late shifts and is a born night owl. I'll check and see if he's in tonight.

Sweat trickles down to my tailbone as I drive, and I can't decide if I'm anticipating answers about the gun resting on the floor or the taste of my disease. When I reach the station, I'm relieved to see the chief's vehicle in the parking lot. Even though his gait has slowed with time, he still has a bounce in his step, and he barrels toward me to greet me warmly.

"Sibley!" He gives me a hug and a kiss on the cheek. "How're you?"

"I'm okay." I lean into his arms, smelling his pine aftershave, the scent as much a part of him as the mole on his chin.

"Must be pretty heavy to be back home after all these years." He motions toward his cramped office, made smaller by the files and paperwork that take up every square inch of his desk and a folding chair. "Take a seat." At my questioning glance, he adds, "Wherever you can find one."

"I'll just lean against the wall," I offer, suddenly nervous with the towel-wrapped firearm in my handbag.

"You sure?"

"I'm not going to attempt to clean this mess up," I tease. "It's probably the same files from sixteen years ago."

"Might be." He chuckles. "But seriously, it's so good to see you. I'm glad you took my advice and stopped in."

"Yeah, me too." I can feel my face flush as his pensive stare lingers too long on my bruise. I'm waiting for him to ask me what happened, but he's silently giving me a chance to talk. "You wanna know about my face?"

"Nope. I figure you'll tell me in due time. Something else is on your mind. The gears are turning in your head."

"Is it that obvious?"

"Yep."

I shrug, letting my gaze drift to a family picture taken when his children were tiny. I smile at one of his kids running through a sprinkler system as his wife holds a grinning boy bundled up in her arms. "I love that picture."

"I know. It's my favorite." He barely glances at it. "You're deflecting. What's up?"

I say casually, motioning to the floor, "I found something."

"On the farm?" Leaning his elbows on his desk, he watches me reach gingerly into the handbag resting at my feet. I set the rolled-up towel in front of him on the scratched surface. The chief looks at me, then at the faded towel as if it might bite him.

I warn him it could be loaded.

Raising a quizzical brow, he nods at the desk. "There's a gun in here?"

"Uh-huh."

His nostrils flare. "Where did you find it?"

"In the barn." He waits for me to explain the exact location, and I add, "It was stuck behind a wooden chest in the tack room."

His eyes become narrowed slits as he unwraps it slowly. When the ugly metal object is unveiled, he stands to consider it. "Why did you bring this here?"

"I thought it might help in the arrest of my mother's assailant."

He sucks in a ragged breath and exhales slowly. "That was a tragedy."

"I hope it can be analyzed for fingerprints. With the prison being so close, I figure there's a good chance prints are already in the fingerprint system."

The chief strokes his chin. "Did you touch the gun?"

"Absolutely not!"

"That was a trick question." He lets out a loud cackle. "I'm glad you ended up a lawyer. You always were a smart girl, Sibley."

"I just want whoever did this to be caught, you know?" My voice catches. "I can tell my mother is a nervous wreck because of this."

"That would be the best outcome, honey. This could be what we need to arrest someone," he soothes. "How's everything going so far since you came back home?"

"Well . . ." I take a deep breath. "I have a couple of questions about my mother."

"Go ahead. Shoot."

"I found some old correspondence between my mother and a man named Edward Pearson and . . ."

Perspiration beads his forehead before I even finish. Instantly, the chief shrinks into his chair, as if he wishes he could fold his towering form into it. It makes sense that the chief would know him in this small community.

"So you knew him?"

With a shrug, he claims they were acquaintances, but his sunken posture and red face tell me he's lying. Usually, he has an expert poker face, and I'd know because Jonathan used to play poker with him and told me.

Besides the guilt, recognition and pain are visible in his eyes.

"I just thought since you and Deborah are close to the same age, it would make sense," I offer. "I mean, there were only forty-seven students total in my mother's graduating class."

"And that's combining a few towns," he chuckles.

"Can you tell me about him?"

"I can try."

"Did my mother used to date him?"

The chief shifts uncomfortably in his seat, and I decide to put him out of his misery. I'm just as eager to leave the claustrophobic room as he is.

"Did they have a bad breakup?"

"Not that I recall. Eddie enlisted in the navy and went off to war. Hard to have a long-distance relationship, let alone international." He pokes my elbow. "Remember, back then, we didn't have cell phones or email. Everything was snail mail and maybe even a passenger pigeon."

"I have to ask you something, and let me preface it with: I'm not upset." I consider him mournfully. "I just want to know the truth. The other day my mother was having a nightmare, and I heard her yelling two names: Edward's and Jonathan's. When I woke her up, she kept murmuring she was sorry she didn't tell me sooner that Edward was my father, not Jonathan."

Abruptly, the chief stands up and walks to the corner of his office, his back toward me.

"It's true." My voice shakes. "Isn't it?"

"Sibby." I can hear the hurt in his voice. "I didn't want to be the one to tell you."

"You didn't."

He doesn't turn around, speaking to the wall instead of my face. "Yes. Edward was your father."

"Do you know how I can reach him?" I pretend I don't know this will never happen, ignoring the hard tug on my heartstrings.

"You can't." I watch his neck lower as he hangs his head.

"What happened to him?"

The chief's voice has a hard edge to it. "He killed himself. Supposedly PTSD. He saw a lot of shit he shouldn't have had to see. It's a real, serious thing."

"When did he . . . when did he pass?"

"You were in high school." He grimaces. "Shortly before, yeah, shortly before Jonathan died."

"How long have you known I was his daughter?"

"Edward told me when you were younger, probably when you were in seventh or eighth grade." The chief turns to face me, and I see wetness on his cheeks. "One day, he spotted you walking with your mom,

261

going into the diner, and when he noticed you, it was abundantly clear you shared similar features. Said he about dropped of a heart attack right there. He confronted Deborah, and she reluctantly admitted it."

"But when did you know?"

"That same time frame."

"Didn't Edward know about me before?" I'm suddenly confused. "I thought he didn't want me. Didn't he want her to, you know, get rid of me?"

"Sib, he didn't know your mother was pregnant with you. He was overseas."

"But I found unlabeled letters my mother wrote."

He shrugs. "If that's the case and Deborah sent them to Edward, why does she still have them?"

"No idea." I frown. "Did he ever get married?" I pretend I don't know about his life, about the obituary that mentioned his wife and kids.

"Yes."

"Children?"

"Two." But he adds hurriedly, "They live on the East Coast. I think Boston. And his ex-wife moved there too. I'm sorry I lied to you. Eddie and I were good friends. I was a pallbearer at his funeral when he died. It's a sensitive topic. He was one of my best friends. It's reprehensible to me, such a waste of a good life."

I double over, feeling like I just had the wind knocked out of me. He hurries to my side.

"Are you okay, Sibby?" His huge palm swaddles my shoulder.

"I'm okay," I moan as a stabbing pain guts me, bringing me to my knees. He doesn't move his hand away until I'm settled on the cold tile.

"Be right back." He steps out for a minute and returns with a bottled water, then pushes it into my hands.

"I wish I could crawl down there with you," he says with a ragged inhale. "But these bones creak now. I'm not as limber as I once was."

"You and my mother have that in common. You both keep saying you're old."

He chortles. "I feel like it most days."

I look up at him sadly. "Do you talk to Edward's kids or ex-wife?"

"I don't. And Sibley, let me ask a huge favor. You might feel like you want to reach out to them for some kind of closure or to find out about your father. Understandably, you'd want to feel some kind of connection to your dad." He runs a hand through his thinning salt-and-pepper hair. "I want to discourage this because they don't know about you or know that Eddie had a love child."

"Was he also married when my mother got pregnant with me?"

"No." He moves back to his chair, settling with a thump. "But no one else could hold a candle to your mother, and his ex-wife knew that. There's a lot of sadness in that family. I don't want to open old wounds, especially for those kids."

"You don't think after all this time, Edward's family might forgive the situation?"

"Unfortunately, no." He shakes his head glumly. "It would be awful for both his ex and Debbie to have to relive their relationships with Eddie. Neither would appreciate the gesture." He adds, "And your mother's health is, well, frankly, I was relieved when you came home and I heard your voice." The chief yanks at the top button of his shirt. "At first, I thought she was having hallucinations about you being at the house."

"What do you mean?"

"When she started calling into the station, I thought she was lonely, desperate for attention. I don't blame her. She's out there by her lonesome." He sighs. "I told the other guys to go easy on her, just pacify her. I can't tell you how many times we went out to the farm to check the premises. She swore a masked man was living on her property, down in the root cellar or the barn. She'd find items, but we never could locate the stranger or their stuff. One time, she said a drug dealer was living there and left his stash. We couldn't find that either."

"Is that why the root cellar is finally locked?"

"Yes. I didn't want there to even be a question about if someone was using it as their hideaway. I get why she's scared to be on the farm alone," the chief discloses. "It's not like her fears are unfounded. She was attacked, and then the rash of break-ins . . . not to mention, the prison's her close neighbor."

"Speaking of outsiders . . ." My cheeks blush at my impending question. It feels weird to ask an older adult about dating. "Have you seen anyone at the house? Like, is she dating anyone?"

Surprised at the question, he gives me a thoughtful glance. "No. I can't say I have."

"Nobody at church?"

"I haven't been there in a while." He smirks. "This job seems to take up a lot of my free time."

I chew a nail, absorbing this information.

"Between us, this is an unpopular sentiment, but some of the farms are being asked to sell."

"Yes, by eminent domain." My jaw tightens. "I've seen the mail, and we've discussed it."

"I'm no doctor, and I'm no expert, but this might be a blessing in disguise for her." He throws his arms in the air. "But what do I know?"

"I disagree, but that's a conversation for another day. We have a heritage farm, and that's worth more than they could offer."

"I'm not versed in what that is, I'm afraid."

"I've been doing some research, and farms that have over forty acres and are over a hundred fifty years old have different stipulations and rights than your average farm."

"Interesting." He steeples his fingers. "Makes sense, though."

"Speaking of relics," I tease, "are you gonna stay in town after you retire and the young'un Miles Fletcher takes over the force?"

"Hardly. Though he can deal with the uptick in crime."

A knock on the door interrupts us, and it's another police officer, one I don't recognize. The chief nods at him, slapping a hand on the desk. "I guess this means I should go help Officer Dudley."

I brush myself off and stand up, giving him a small smile. We part the same way we greeted, with a tight hug and a chaste kiss on the cheek. I sniff at the lingering scent of him, the familiarity.

"And Sibley," he whispers in my ear, "take it easy on your mom. She's had a hard go of it." I nod as he pushes me gently toward the door, following behind me. He motions me toward the exit, staying behind to talk to Officer Dudley, a baby-faced but serious-looking cop.

After I reach the only open convenience store, I grab a varied supply of drinks and take long swigs on the way to the diner. When I arrive back home, I park my beater in the same spot at the farm and tear into the opened bottle. Even though vodka doesn't have an odor, paranoia sets in, and I pop a breath mint. I chew and swallow the wintergreen tablet before walking into the house.

My mother doesn't cower when I walk in; her eyes are fixated on something on the ceiling. Her empty plate still rests in front of her, and she hasn't changed position, her arms tucked next to her sides.

I wonder what she's staring at, as I don't detect anything usual.

Not wanting to startle her after our earlier altercation, I say her name before setting down the paper sack of ice cream in front of her.

She looks at the bag. "How's Holden doing?"

Having forgotten about what I said earlier, I quickly feign disappointment. "He didn't answer. I left a voice mail telling him to call me."

Mouth drawn in a tense line, she doesn't reply. When she doesn't move to open the sack, I do and hand her a cup of ice cream and a plastic spoon. "Flavor of the day is blueberry streusel."

After removing the plastic lid, she delicately takes a small bite.

"This is delicious." She closes her eyes for a moment as if savoring the taste. "The best cows make the best milk make the best ice cream."

I giggle at the phrase I used to say as a child after my elementary school class toured a dairy farm.

"If you don't mind me asking"—my mother licks her spoon—"what was your blowup fight with Holden before you came home about?"

"How we spend our time. Our money." I shrug. "The usual marital dissatisfaction." This gives me an opening to ask about her love life and disprove Fletch's statement that she was involved with a make-believe man. "So why haven't you ever gotten remarried, Mother?"

"I don't know. I guess it didn't suit me."

"But you never date, or at least"—I fumble with my words—"you didn't at the beginning."

"I had enough to deal with at the time." Her mouth twists into a small smile. "And how would you know, anyway? Maybe recently I have met someone."

"You're dating?" I screech. "Did you meet up with them the other night?"

She rewards me with a shrug and an impish grin.

"I don't want to cramp your style." I laugh. "But I'm curious to meet them."

"Whoa! Slow down, Sibley." She holds a hand up. "Maybe one day soon."

"Where'd you meet this new man?"

"We go way back."

"Can I have any more details?" I wink at her. "You're playing coy."

"A lady doesn't kiss and tell."

My mood immediately sours. Maybe the truth serum effect of the alcohol is rearing its ugly head, but I blurt out, "Is it Edward Pearson?" It's time to test the waters regarding my real father.

My mother looks like I slapped her. "Where did you hear that name?" She glowers at me.

I shrug. "You guys have history together. An affair to remember, I guess you could say."

"Why would you even insinuate that?" She stands up so fast the table rattles. With a disappointed headshake, she limps toward her recliner in the living room.

I know I'm being cruel, but I can't help myself.

I came home to reconcile myself with my past, not find out I have an entirely different one.

CHAPTER 32
Deborah

Later that night, Deborah's sitting in the darkened living room when Sibley stumbles in, reeking of perfume. She doesn't smell drunk, but she acts it.

Sibley almost trips over her foot, and Deborah hears her growl at what she thinks is Esmeralda but is really Deborah's furry slipper.

"Shit." Sibley grasps the sideboard. "Mother," she asks, "why're you sitting in the dark? You scared the shit out of me."

"I was doing some thinking."

"Okay." Sibley slurs her words. "What about?"

"Your father." Deborah's voice is laced with sadness. "Your *biological* father. Edward Pearson. You asked before, so I'll tell you now."

There it is, out on the table, the bomb dropped straight onto a platter and served up so casually. Deborah's surprised when Sibley doesn't bat an eye but instead fumbles onto the couch. "This should be good. But can you just drop the act?" Sibley points to Deborah's ring finger. "How much longer are you going to keep up the charade?"

With a nod, Deborah removes her thin gold band with finality and lets it fall to the carpet. "I don't know why I've kept this on all these years. Guilt, I suppose."

"Why guilt?"

"Because I couldn't change him." Deborah sighs. "Or make him better. Or save him."

"I figured it was for appearances' sake," Sibley says. "Your dedication to his memory."

"I prefer to memorialize your real father, Edward."

"Why didn't he want you to have me?"

"He didn't know about you," Deborah says, leaning forward. "He didn't have a choice. My father made sure of that."

"Grandpa?"

"Uh-huh." Deborah sighs. "He confiscated the letters I wrote telling Edward I was pregnant."

"So it was Jonathan that didn't want me?"

"Where did you get that piece of nonsense?" Deborah shakes her head in exasperation. "No one wanted me to have an abortion, Sibley."

"You're lying again! I found a journal or letter you wrote where you talk about being dropped off at a clinic against your will!"

Deborah's eyes cloud with tears, her tone dismal. "That's not exactly what happened." Sibley waits for her to continue. "Yes, my father wanted me to have an abortion. I didn't end up going through with it, obviously."

"Wait! It's Grandpa that didn't want you to have me?" Sibley's shell shocked. "Do you think he would've changed his opinion if he had seen what Jonathan did?"

"He did know, Sib." Deborah is forlorn. "But it was too late. After he married us, he watched Jonathan slam my head into a wall after church one Sunday when we were alone in the church office."

Sibley's eyes widen in alarm.

"He was terrified Jonathan would find out you didn't belong to him. The reason he was so upset when he found out I was pregnant was he knew it would be an automatic death sentence. In his mind, he thought he was saving my life—father to daughter. As twisted as it sounds"—Deborah gazes stiffly at her—"I understand now. That's why

269

he took me to the clinic. It was never out of anger against Edward like I thought. My mother told me the truth after my father died, and it breaks my heart, especially since I hated him up until the day he died."

Sibley chomps hard on her nail, her eyes never leaving Deborah's.

"He took me to the farthest clinic so none of the neighbors would find out. He was drunk as a skunk when he came to pick me up, which was out of character. His words were all garbled, just like yours are now. Your grandpa only drank communion wine." Deborah shudders at the terrible memory. "I had to drive us back home. Speaking of life-changing events," Deborah asks, "do you remember the night of the Halloween party?"

"How could I forget?" Sibley gnaws on her nail. "I saw you with Fletch's dad that evening. I was outside when you two came strolling up the walk together, holding hands."

Deborah swallows. "We weren't exactly holding hands. I mean, we were, but . . ."

Exasperated, Sibley exhales. "When are you ever going to tell me the truth?"

"I told you I went to him for help," Deborah murmurs. "He was trying to help me leave."

"Were you going to leave just Jonathan or both of us?"

"Why would I leave you?" Deborah huffs. "Only Jonathan."

"Why was it so hard?" Sibley slurs her words. "Is it because you weren't capable of holding down a job?"

"How can you say that?" Deborah retorts. "I wanted to work outside the home. Jonathan forbade it. He wouldn't let me have a vehicle. He wanted me completely dependent on him so I couldn't leave."

Sibley goes eerily silent.

"Since the Fletchers were neighbors, I drunkenly confided in Robert Fletcher one night when Jonathan and Cindy were out of earshot that I wanted to leave Jonathan. When he confronted me about it later on, I denied it at first, but eventually, I told him I had to. And before you ask why I didn't ask Cindy for help"—Deborah puts up a hand, confident what Sibley's next question will be—"Cindy, for all her strengths, was not known for her ability to keep a secret. You know how hard it is to keep one in this town. Cindy was a sweet lady, but she talked a lot and enjoyed gossip. She would have whispered it to someone at church, who would've told someone else, and before you know it, Jonathan would've found out. It was important as few people as possible knew."

Deborah sucks in a ragged breath. "One time, I tried to leave Jonathan when you were six or seven, and I confided in my best friend. Jonathan went to her house, threatened her with a bat, and, needless to say, she never spoke to me again."

"Isolating the victim," Sibley murmurs. "I'm all too familiar with every personality type and disorder, being a divorce attorney."

"Exactly. You know it's not as simple as leaving an abusive spouse. I didn't want you to become a pawn between him and me. Or worse. So Robert tried to help put a plan in place so I could leave Jonathan and squirrel away money for this purpose. I didn't dare meet Robert at his job or their house because no one could know."

"But at the Halloween—" Sibley starts to speak, and Deborah cuts her off.

"Yes, the night of the Halloween party, Robert and I agreed to meet near the shed. When we met, it was a fast encounter. I gave him some money I'd been saving, and we talked about where I could move. He was trying to find a rental that could house us and was working on getting me a job."

"Do you remember seeing Kristin at all on your walk?"

"No. We were never at the silo, but it's obvious she spotted us at some point. She lied and added sordid details like some bored teenager." Deborah adds, "The Guthries have an old one-room structure they use to store firewood. That's where Robert and I talked for a few minutes."

Sibley stammers, "What about what *I* saw?"

"What you saw was probably a gesture of friendship. I was probably leaning on him or standing close to him so I could whisper."

"So you expect me to believe it was all gossip," Sibley says pointedly. "Your affairs. The assumption you pushed Jonathan out of the loft. And the blame you got for Cindy's death. Not to mention: Why should I believe you now, after all the lies?"

"Because I have no reason to lie. Both Jonathan and Cindy are in the ground."

"They've been dead all these years, and you've never bothered to set the record straight," Sibley retorts in an icy tone.

"I didn't have any affairs," Deborah says bluntly. "But I was trying to make decisions that would have the least impact on other people. I thought I was saving everyone from my hurt."

"A lady at the bar, Miranda something or other, said . . ." Sibley waves a hand. "Oh, never mind. I'm sick of all these innuendos."

Haughtily, Deborah holds her head high. "Said what?"

"That Kristin wrote you a letter. She didn't know what it said, so she was little help except to mention it."

Standing slowly, Deborah reaches underneath the sideboard and thumbs through her keepsake box to bring out a metal tin. "In case what I said isn't enough to convince you, Kristin did write me an apology letter."

She hands Sibley a yellowed envelope, and Sibley gingerly unfolds the double-spaced note, written in ballpoint pen.

Incredulous, Sibley asks, "When was this?"

"A couple months before she died. The cancer was stage four, and she wasn't given long to live. She wanted to make things right before her time came, and it was the least I could give her."

Deborah watches as Sibley silently reads the words on the page.

Scowling, Sibley then folds it up. "She doesn't say why she did something so malicious."

"I asked Kristin that when she brought the letter over," Deborah says. "We had a nice enough chat, all things considered."

"And?"

"She was jealous, plain and simple. She had a crush on Miles, and she hated that you two were inseparable. She said it wasn't her intent to start the rumor, that she'd had a fight with that high school boyfriend of hers—"

"Josh," Sibley offers.

"Yeah, Josh. They fought at the party, and she did see us talking, but that was it. She knew if Miles found out about his dad and me, he would automatically blame you, and it did what Kristin intended. It cost you both a friendship."

"But why didn't you deny it?"

"Because," Deborah sputters. "We weren't doing anything wrong, and if the truth came out about why we were talking, I would've been dead before I even had a chance to leave. Except my hand was forced anyway." Deborah tugs at her chain. "Not to mention: Did you want me to go toe to toe with a teenage girl? What good would that have done?"

"Is that what happened at church?" Sibley points her index finger in the air. "I saw Cindy talking to Jonathan, and his entire mood shifted from easygoing to agitated. He snapped at me on the way home, which was unusual for him. Then you two fought; then he supposedly fell out of the loft."

"Yes," Deborah admits. "It didn't help that Miles also told his mother about us. He followed us a couple of times, and though he didn't see anything happen, he saw us climbing into the same vehicle to look at apartments. Cindy was understandably livid, and that's why she confronted Jonathan at church and told him Robert and I were having an affair."

"Is this why you hate Miles Fletcher?"

"Yes," Deborah acknowledges. "The broken window was an excuse I got to hold on to."

Mother and daughter sit and stare at each other for a tenuous moment, until Deborah starts to tremble. First her hands shake in her lap; then her legs follow.

"Do you want me to get your pills?" Sibley leans forward.

"No." Deborah puts a hand up, woodenly rising out of her chair. Her body starts to convulse, but she slowly advances toward her bedroom.

With a hand guiding her lower back for support, Sibley follows on her heels, as if she's afraid Deborah will fall backward.

When Deborah reaches her bed, she collapses onto the mattress.

"Here." Sibley fumbles for a couple of bottles on the side table.

Shakily, Deborah points to what pills she wants, and Sibley hands her a glass of water from the nightstand.

She swallows them swiftly and lies back on the bed.

Sibley is talking above her, but she sounds like she's in a wind tunnel. Deborah doesn't respond, keeping her eyes shut as she waits for the tremors to subside.

CHAPTER 33
Sibley

The turn of events tonight has quickly sobered me up. Humbled, I sit beside my mother on the bed and wait until she's asleep, her breathing loud and irregular. Instead of answering my question about calling an ambulance, she pressed her lids shut.

I'm torn between going to my room and leaving her alone, terrified she's going to leave me orphaned. The irony is not lost on me—we have had a long estrangement, and it's only now we've reconnected. The fact she lied to me about my birth father is painful, but I understand there was a purpose behind it. I no longer believe her actions were reckless or malicious. The thought of being utterly alone in the world, knowing that both of my fathers are dead, is mind numbing. To contemplate losing her makes me inconsolable.

Knowing I'll be unable to sit still, I bring my laptop from upstairs to sit in her rocking chair. This way, I can keep watch over her declining health.

I'm fully aware that typing in symptoms online will come up with a slew of worst-case scenarios and cause the most even-keeled people to become hypochondriacs. Still, I can't ignore them any longer.

Maybe it's the list of potential diseases that pops up when I type in her ailments—memory loss, vision problems, and tremors—but I'm sure something more profound is lurking beneath the surface.

The search results include a plethora of conditions, mostly neurological. A red flashing arrow in my head keeps pointing to the bold text about degenerative diseases.

Horrified, I wonder if my mother has dementia or some form of early-onset Alzheimer's.

Slamming my laptop shut, I sit immobile, unable to relax, wondering what this means. Do I need to take my mother back home with me?

Does Deborah have her will updated? What about her power of attorney?

Biting my nails, I want to call Adrienne or Holden, but I realize it's after two in the morning back home. Besides, what could I possibly say to my husband? *Sorry, honey. I know I'm supposed to be in rehab, but I didn't go. I went back home instead, and even though we're on the brink of a divorce, can I bring my estranged mom, who you've never met and is sick, home to live with us?*

Confident that sleep won't come easy tonight, I rummage through the stash of pill bottles on the nightstand, looking for a sleep aid. I take a few pillows off my mother's bed and brace myself for a rough night in the rocking chair.

When I wake up the next morning, it takes a minute to realize where I am and why I'm sitting up. My neck is sore and stiff, and I'm groggy and hungover.

I stare at my mother's small form snoring in the bed and then at the laptop on the floor. A nagging feeling that something deeper is going on with my mother exacerbates the pit in my stomach. My jumbled thoughts bounce between what my mother says and does and what's going on around us. If all these peculiarities didn't seem to be adding up to something more significant, I wouldn't be concerned.

Before she gets out of bed, I need to do some digging into her personal effects.

After stretching my achy limbs, I tiptoe out of her room.

I search through the sideboard in the living room, as my mother keeps a locked safe-deposit box inside. She doesn't know I know where the key is, but the upstairs vent is not only a conduit for conversations but also a peephole. The other night, I peered through the slats, and though I couldn't see much from my vantage point, I could see her retrieve the key from an opening in the grandfather clock.

After slipping the key from its hiding spot, I sit cross-legged on the floor and sort through the box. There's not much in there, at least not what I expected. I figured she kept important papers and documents, but it's mainly old articles tied to Jonathan's death. The obit for Edward Pearson is also inside.

As I'm about to close the lid, I see a couple letters that have been sent to her, along with a photo that eerily resembles me.

What the hell? I wonder.

Even the handwriting is similar to mine, down to the swoops and slants of my letters. Rubbing a hand over my face, I command myself to think. Did I send her these? Was this a sloppy mistake on my part?

But they threaten her for money, alluding to graphic details of the night Jonathan died, and the envelopes are postmarked from Florida and signed with only an *S*.

Startled by a thud, I quickly shut the box and replace it and the key where they belong. I creep to her bedroom door to listen, wondering if she's awake. I can hear her heavy breathing through the door, so I escape back to the living room.

My mother still has a wall calendar by her old rotary phone, and I flip through it to locate any information on upcoming doctor appointments or clinic names. I might have to stop in that office and speak to that woman my mother was in session with, a therapist or psychiatrist, I presume.

Thumbing through her calendar, I notice a couple dates that are marked with *AA*, but I highly doubt it's an Alcoholics Anonymous or Al-Anon meeting. Those would be suggestions for me, I think as my face flames red.

Unsure what it stands for, I keep it in the back of my mind.

She has the letter *R* marked in red throughout the last few months. I don't see a pattern, and some weeks have more red marks than others.

On the back of her calendar is a crumpled business card taped to the heavy cardstock. The letters are faded, as if someone kept rubbing at the font with their fingertip, trying to smudge it. I can barely make out the letters spelling out some kind of psychiatrist. A name and phone number are listed, but no address.

When I type the name into Google, the website is bare bones. It's just a woman wearing thick horn-rimmed glasses and a white lab coat that says *Dr. Alacoy, Clinical Psychiatrist*. She's standing against a brick building.

I recognize this as the building I was snooping in. Minimal information beyond the bespectacled doctor's education is listed, not even the address where I was. I dial the number from the card and wait for a voice mail to pick up so I can leave a message, but it just rings.

Disappointed, I hang up.

My mother used to go to a Doc Marshall, who was also my primary care doctor growing up. He's the one who gave me all my vaccinations and a never-ending supply of lollipops to console me. Being from a small town involves a lack of privacy, but that can be positive when you need to reach someone directly. Since you know most people on a first-name basis, you have access to them personally. Case in point, Doc Marshall's cell is written on the back of her calendar.

When I call, he's eager to hear from me, though half-alert, and I realize it's barely 6:00 a.m.

After I apologize for the early call, Doc Marshall listens as I list off the medications prescribed to Deborah. There's a long pause before he admits he hasn't prescribed her any pain pills or seen her for at least a year.

Odd.

The prescribing doctor on the label is not the psychiatrist, Dr. Alice Alacoy, but a different name.

I'm perplexed that Doc Marshall is unfamiliar with either doctor, since he's been practicing for more than forty years in this area. Before he hangs up, he tells me he'll do some checking on both doctors.

When I try to reenter my mother's room, I'm shocked to find the doorknob doesn't move. I knock loudly, presuming she doesn't want to be bothered but still worried. "Can you at least let me know you're okay?" I say calmly. "I've got some errands to run in town. Need anything?"

She dismisses me with, "I'm fine, and no."

With a sigh, I let her know I'll be back later, that I have errands to run. After retreating to my car, I mindlessly stare out the windshield as I drive, counting the dead bugs splattered across the glass. My phone shrills, catching me off guard. "Hello," I answer.

"Hi. I had a missed call from this number."

Worried I didn't vet the caller appropriately, I reply with, "Um, who is this?"

"You called me. Alice." The feminine voice has an air of disdain to it. "Wait, is this a telemarketer?"

"No," I hasten to say. "Are you taking new clients?"

There's a brief pause. In an accusatory manner, she says, "This is an out-of-state number."

"I know. I just moved here."

"Well, no. Unfortunately, I'm not. Goodbye." The woman hangs up.

Weird.

CHAPTER 34
Deborah

Sibley gives her a call a bit later, but it feels forced, like she's doing it out of necessity. Deborah wants to ask what Sibley's doing in town but doesn't want to appear nosy, since she's made it clear she doesn't like being ambushed with questions herself.

When Sibley asks her what's on the agenda for today, Deborah makes the mistake of mentioning she should start going through the contents of the house in preparation for her upcoming move.

Sibley doesn't argue with her, just goes quiet, and Deborah wonders if Sibley is toying with her. In fact, she's anxious at the thought of this practical stranger in her house.

When Deborah woke up today, all the reasons she was distrustful of Sibley came flooding back, namely that Sibley has her dress from that night for a reason, which makes Deborah nervous. Blood is on the dress; mostly it's Jonathan's, and some of it belongs to her, but there was a third person in the barn that night. What if having touched her or moved the weapon incriminates them?

Unease travels through her veins, and suddenly she's restless. Deborah needs a purpose at the moment, something mindless to get her thoughts off her daughter's apparent ill intent.

Sitting in her bedroom, rummaging through her disorganized closet, Deborah's amazed at the number of clothes and shoes that overrun it. She has never considered herself a hoarder or a pack rat, but judging by the old sweaters and seasonal jackets, she should've sorted through this mess years ago.

On her knees, she reaches toward the back of the closet, and her hand touches something akin to reptile skin. Assuming it's a purse designed to look like fake alligator leather, she grasps it and sits back on her heels.

It's not a handbag but an old red leather-bound book. The gold stamped lettering tells her what kind: a baby album.

Deborah cradles it in her hands, not unlike the day she held her own daughter in her arms for the first time.

And just like that, Deborah's transported back in time when she opens the first page and sees the photos of the baby shower her mother threw for her at church.

It was a tense afternoon, mainly because Deborah asked if she could leave her husband, Jonathan, permanently and return home, but her mother would hear none of it. She was of the mindset that women had to have a stiff upper lip.

Flipping to the page with the birth announcement, Deborah remembers how the weather was acting psychotic that March, one day snowing, the next hitting the midfifties, an atypical and confusing pattern for midwesterners.

She entered the hospital a bundle of nerves—anxious, terrified, and excited—and left a few days later. It was a harrowing experience that left her crippled by remorse and agony, on the brink of mental exhaustion.

To this day, she can smell the overpowering medicinal antiseptic that lingered in the hallway and rooms. Closing her eyes, she imagines herself in the corner of the room, witnessing the aftermath of birth.

"Can you believe we made these two little angels?" a young man whispers, gently shaking a tiny fist. Deborah can tell her husband is wrapped around the baby girl's little finger; his cooing noises make it obvious he's in heaven. It's surreal to watch him with a living, breathing baby that came out of her womb less than twenty-four hours ago.

Still not of age to consume alcohol and now a mother of twins, she shakes her head in disbelief, looking down at the baby swaddled in her arms.

Even with a seven-minute head start on her sister, the daughter tugging on his heartstrings is a miniature replica of the other. The firstborn is less than six pounds and only slightly larger than her identical twin. The only difference is the small birthmark, a congenital mole, on the back of the baby in her arms.

"They're *absolutely* perfect," Deborah agrees, gazing between the girls' cherubic faces and their lips curled into matching bows. For once, Jonathan's smile seems genuine, a deviation from the scowl usually affixed to his sun-worn face.

But Deborah knows she can't let her guard down. She has to watch him. Intently.

She can't draw attention to herself or let Jonathan pick up on her lingering stare. He'll get suspicious if she scrutinizes him too closely, when she usually prefers to turn her back to him.

The truth is, Deborah doesn't trust Jonathan with a newborn. He's part of the male species, after all. He's never changed a diaper or calmed down a crying baby.

Even after the nurse pointed out two heartbeats during the ultrasound, Deborah thought she'd misheard. He'd hurled her into the wall the previous evening, and the ringing in her ears still hadn't stopped. A single glance at the gaping hole Jonathan's mouth had become was confirmation. The announcement of twins was shocking.

Secretly, she wanted to gloat and stick her tongue out. Served him right for complaining about the size of her ass and stomach, how round they were becoming. He'd blamed it on how much time she spent in bed. He'd been quick to point out how her thighs jiggled when she walked, whereas before they'd been firm and supple. When he would criticize her, she dreamed of spilling her secret, that she'd lied about the timing of conception, that he wasn't the sperm donor. It was tempting but too dangerous.

His only compliment had to do with the size of her boobs, which he admired in his hands, comparing them to ripe watermelons on the vine, which made her want to go outside and hack them up.

Now her breasts are engorged with milk, and her thoughts drift to breastfeeding and how he'll handle two babies latched on to her nipples, given that he's unable to share what he considers his property.

As if on cue, a small cry escapes from the lips of the baby cradled in her embrace. Deborah wants nothing more than to hold both girls to her bosom and away from their father. Keeping a level gaze as she considers them beside her, lest he notice and ruin an enjoyable moment, she gives him a once-over. He has a funny-looking tan line where the brim of his cap cuts across his forehead, dividing his skin between milky white and bronzed. His days as a farmer are spent in the fields, long and arduous. Living off the land is not for the faint of heart.

Nurse Diana, a stout woman she'd guess to be somewhere in her late thirties, marches into the room, authoritative in every action: her walk, her talk, her purpose in life. She's a natural-born nurse meant to deliver babies.

"See, you're getting the hang of it! I told you the nurturing instinct kicks in." A dazzling smile crosses her face as she observes the two young parents. Deborah's unsure if there's a paternal bone in Jonathan's body. "Did we decide on any names?"

Deborah nods her head before Jonathan can speak. "Yeah, I did." Deborah hates how she sounds: defensive, uptight. Or maybe it seems that way because she's being oddly assertive, a far cry from her usual soft-spoken demeanor. Jonathan's eyes are trained on her, waiting to pounce. Typically, she'd defer to him. But pushing not one but two babies out has given her a take-charge attitude, at least while she's in the hospital, safe from his wrath.

Nurse Diana raises her brow in anticipation, holding tight to her clipboard.

Forging ahead, Deborah says, "Sibley." Then, bravely, "And Soren."

"Oh, those are good! I like! Different. New age. Can you spell them for me?" With a chuckle, she adds, "I want to make sure the birth certificate is accurate."

"S-I-B-L-E-Y." Deborah expects Jonathan to cut in at any moment. "S-O-R-E-N."

"Middle names?"

For once, Jonathan doesn't argue; instead he muses, his eyes fixed on the twins, "I think my mother's name goes with Soren."

Deborah gives him this, his dead mother's moniker, beaming at him. "Sibley Eleanor and Soren Annette," she says with finality.

Diana clucks her tongue as she clicks her pen. "Last name Sawyer?"

Jonathan firmly nods his head as Deborah clenches her jaw over the name Pearson. *They should have his last name,* she secretly laments. "Yes," they both say in unison.

Tears start to run down Deborah's cheeks, and mistakenly, Diana assumes they're from happiness.

"Oh, child, aren't you in good spirits!" She tucks a loose strand of Deborah's messy ponytail behind her ear. She probably doesn't realize it was carefully constructed to cover the bald patch Jonathan caused when he dragged her across the room by her hair.

Deborah's tears aren't entirely in celebration of new life. They roll down her face, a reminder of the pain tugging at her heart. The throbbing between her legs isn't a match for the constant ache of knowing her true love will never have a place in her life or the baby girls'.

Jonathan gives her a small smile, a glimmer of hope in his green eyes. He thinks they can be a family, that the twins will stitch together their broken home just like the doctor did with the tear in her skin. In his eyes, any transgression on his part is forgivable. He only has to go to church to pray, because the pastor preaches nothing is more sinful than divorce. Except for adultery, of course.

And that pastor is her father.

She closes her eyes to stop the wetness from turning into a full-on faucet, to interrupt Jonathan's piercing stare, to protect herself. Her pain is visible, and she doesn't want him to know its extent, not because he would comfort her but because he would enthusiastically find pleasure in her grief. Keeping them tightly shut, she imagines a life with her babies, without him.

It's not until she jerks awake to the sound of heavy footsteps that she realizes she must've fallen asleep. Instinctively she stares down at her now-empty arms.

"I have some news about the twins. One of the girls . . ." Jonathan's voice trails off. "We lost her."

Deborah hears the word *lost*, and she clenches her fist, the one not tethered to Jonathan's hand. It's as if he's talking about something inanimate, like a missing sneaker or his car keys. A newborn baby that just entered the world does not belong in the same category as a misplaced object.

She hears herself speak but doesn't remember forming the words. "How did you lose her?" Her voice sounds calm while her hands tremble. You could almost believe she was asking about breastfeeding etiquette or a preferred diaper brand.

Now, a loud crash in the other room abruptly interrupts Deborah's tearful flashback, and she quickly slams the baby book shut. Surprised Sibley's home already and worried she's going to barge in at any moment and discover her crying, Deborah wipes a sleeve across her cheek, drying her eyes.

Deborah's never dared to tell Sibley she had a twin sister.

After shoving the baby book underneath her bed, Deborah struggles to stand upright, using the flimsy ironing board to help her to her feet. Instead, it topples over and takes her down with it. Yelping, she sits on the floor in frustrated silence at her clumsiness until the sound of the television echoes from the living room.

CHAPTER 35
Deborah

The smell of fresh wood clippings and tobacco drifts to her nostrils, and at first, she wonders if Sibley found a box of Jonathan's things that unleashed the powerful, manly spice.

About to ask, she stops dead in her tracks.

A hand automatically crosses her heart in disbelief.

Sibley's not in sight, but a man is. This one is different from before.

He's seated in Jonathan's old recliner in the living room, wearing a plaid shirt and jeans, his unruly salt-and-pepper hair sticking out in tufts, as if he got electrocuted by a light socket.

Worse, he dares to smoke a pipe in the house without permission, one leg draped casually over his other knee, as if he belongs in *her* home, in *his* chair.

A scream dies in Deborah's throat.

Did he climb in through the broken window? Impossible. She's been in her room all day. But he could've sneaked in and hid. She hadn't noticed the plastic tarp moved, though.

She doesn't want to draw attention to herself. Even if she makes a fuss, she doubts Sibley will hear her in time to make it back to the house.

Deborah can't fathom why a man would make himself at home in front of the television in a stranger's house. Surely this isn't what these crooks are doing when they ransack homes: settling in to watch old reruns of black-and-white movies. Though not much would surprise her anymore.

Maybe the man's ploy is to make himself a guest in people's homes so they let their guard down. To her, he looks like an older gentleman in a commercial selling car insurance, harmless and neighborly. The kind who waves when you drive by or brings you a thoughtful gift on holidays. This could be how he's skirted any type of suspicion; he's just so *normal looking.*

Before her presence is noticed, Deborah moves a couple steps back, keeping her body turned toward the room and him. This way, if he stands, she'll see him coming. She can make it to the kitchen and the front door without going through the living room.

That is, if she doesn't make a peep. In the hallway, she removes her tennis shoes to keep the sound down, since her socks will make less noise on the old hardwood floors and linoleum.

Once she reaches the kitchen, the divided entryway is visible to the living room, so she'll have to risk being seen for a few steps.

Taking a deep breath, she's about to make a run for it when a shrill buzzing drowns the television's sound.

Startled, she almost has a heart attack until she realizes it's the phone ringing.

Fear grips her body in its clutch, and for a moment she stands deathly quiet, waiting for a sign.

Deborah wonders if the intruder will answer or yank the phone out of the wall. Holding her breath, lungs filled to maximum capacity, she scurries past, refusing to look in the direction of the man seated in the living room.

After closing the door softly so it doesn't slam, she staggers down the steps.

CHAPTER 36
Sibley

When I pull into the drive, I almost crash into the garage in fright as a figure unexpectedly darts out from behind the structure.

It's Deborah, and her face is peaked, like she just saw a ghost. Her whole body's trembling, even in the eighty-degree heat.

Swallowing the lump in my throat, I edge the vehicle off the drive, trampling the weeds and shrubs that have popped up as I park next to the garage. I'm more confused when she runs through the brush barefoot toward my car.

As I cut the engine, she yanks on the passenger-door handle and throws herself into the seat before the door's even shut.

I'm deathly afraid of snakes, and at first, I think she spotted one in the garage, taking cover in the dimly lit and dusty area. Imagining one slithering over my foot, I involuntarily shudder.

Her hand grips my elbow and shakes my arm. It appears I'm supposed to be clued into how she's feeling.

Examining her striped socks, I ask, "Where are your shoes?"

"I took them off so I could tiptoe."

"What's wrong?"

"It's . . . there's . . ." She launches into a stream of unintelligible words.

"Oh my God." I signal her to stop talking. "Where's the snake?"

"What snake?" Breathless, she shakes her head. "No, no, no. There's a man"—she lowers her voice to a whisper—"in the house."

"Who?"

"I don't know."

Floored, I shriek, "A strange man is in the house?"

Initially, I think she's messing with me, and I wait for her to crack a smile. Instead, she cowers in fear.

Distraught, I yelp, "Is it the man that hurt you?"

"No," she says tersely. "This one is older. Older than me."

"What does he look like?"

"He's wearing regular clothes, no mask. I was going through my closet, and when I walked out, there he was." She groans. "He's sitting in your daddy's old recliner, watching TV." She throws her hands in the air. "Can you believe it? Television!"

"So you don't think it's related to one of the robberies your neighbors had?"

"I don't know." My mother's twisting her cross pendant tight enough I'm worried she's about to choke herself. "He wasn't searching around or anything. Just sitting. I can't imagine I'd have anything they would want."

"It's not the pastor or the man you're dating?" I ask. "Does he have a key?"

"No. But the door wasn't locked." She looks apprehensively toward the house. "We should call someone or the police. Maybe get Miles over here. That'll be faster."

"What about your security camera?" I ask. "I'm sure there will be a recording of him entering the house." Another thought strikes me. "Could he be lost?" I wonder. "Maybe have dementia and have wandered away from a nursing home?"

"I don't know." She dejectedly sighs. "I guess I never thought of that."

"I'll take care of it, Mother. We can try safety in numbers," I say. "Go inside and ask if he needs help."

"Maybe we should call someone first."

"And leave him inside?" I demur. "No. Not a chance. He might be spooked if he's lost."

"I don't want you going inside. I have no idea if he's armed."

"Where's Daddy's rifle?"

"It's missing. My attacker took it," she whispers. "It never showed up."

"Wait—that's the rifle they hit you with, that old Winchester?" My jaw drops. "I took a gun down to the station that I thought might've been used in your attack."

Her face turns ashen. "Where did you find it?"

"In the barn."

"You weren't at the pond?"

"No." Bewildered, I gawk at her. "Why would I have gone to the pond? I said I was in the barn."

She asks me to describe it, and her face blanches at my description. She's acting like I committed a heinous felony, and I'm disturbed at her reaction, but this isn't the time or place to discuss.

"Can we talk about this another time?" I insist. "We have enough to focus on right now."

Handing her my cell, I instruct her to call the emergency number as a backup. I've already made up my mind it's an elderly gentleman who needs assistance, but I want to alleviate her fears. It can take first responders or police a while to get to the farm, and I don't want to wait that long.

"I'm going to check it out."

She doesn't look happy about this, but she dutifully follows me out of the car.

In the daylight, the deterioration of the farmhouse is magnified. The missing chunks of siding and peeling paint can't hide in the smooth brushstrokes of sunlight.

But now that she's selling, the point is moot.

I start walking, and she follows in my footsteps, like one of her outside cats anticipating mealtime. So close that when I abruptly stop, she lurches straight into me.

Turning to face her, I say, "I don't want you to come in behind me. If this isn't a lost senior citizen, I need you to be prepared to go for help. I left the keys in the ignition. Also, in case I'm wrong," I add, "I don't want him to see you if you haven't already been spotted. If he thinks there's only one of us, it might help our chances."

Nodding her head in acknowledgment, she still doesn't make any move to fall back.

Pretending I'm fearless when my insides are mush, or maybe I'm more careless when tipsy, I'm about to chastise her for not staying back when I trip on one of the porch stairs and almost nose-dive into the cement.

She catches my wrist just in time, so I avoid the spill.

Mouthing a thank-you, I decide the best idea is to walk around the porch and face the trespasser through the picture window. That way, I have a vantage point and a pane of glass between us in case it's not some sweet, displaced man.

"I'm going to go around the side," I whisper.

"Then you'll be in his line of vision."

"Yeah, but then we can see him through the window. We stand a better chance out here."

She loosens her grip on my arm, and I take that as acceptance of my idea.

At the side of the house, I look over my shoulder at her. "Okay, I'm going to stand in front of the window." I demonstrate a hand signal. "I'll warn you like this if you need to run."

The sun lights up her somber stare, and I clasp her fingers gently for a second. "Don't worry; we're in this together."

CHAPTER 37
Deborah

Sibley's words have a soothing effect on her, and she hadn't realized how much she's longed to hear her say they're in this together. It comes too late. Deborah needed to hear her say it years ago, when the squad cars and ambulance swarmed their property and carried out the tortured body of Jonathan while she sat on the stoop and cried. They were crocodile tears, but tears nonetheless. Deborah was cried out from when Edward had died a few weeks before Jonathan.

Sibley didn't come down from her room for days after Jonathan's death, leaving Deborah painfully aware she was on her own. Of course, Sibley didn't know the impact of Edward's death or what he'd meant to her, and she has regrets about that.

With one last fleeting glance in Deborah's direction, Sibley heaves forward, placing herself directly in front of the window and the unknown man.

Observing Sibley's face, Deborah's on high alert, waiting for a sign from her on what to do next. She hopes her daughter is right, that he's not a violent criminal, merely a confused, misplaced elder. It's not like Deborah doesn't know what that's like.

Deborah's hands are squeezed tightly together, anticipating the worst. When Sibley angles her head in Deborah's direction, Deborah's confused at her initial reaction.

Her mouth has dropped open in surprise. "Mother, he's not here."

"He's not in the chair?"

"No. No one's in the living room!"

"That means he went to another room in the house." She covers her face with her hand. "Maybe he went to use the bathroom."

"But you said the television was on."

"Yes."

"It's off."

"So"—Deborah shrugs—"he must've turned it off."

"Let me get this straight. A man was sitting in the recliner watching television?" Sibley peers again into the window. "And he bothered to shut the TV off and go to the bathroom?"

Deborah says lamely, "I suppose so."

Rolling her eyes, Sibley says, "I'm going to go inside."

"Sibley, I'm still not sure that's a good idea."

"We can't stay out here all day. It's hot out here." She wipes a hand across her brow. "And you've got my cell."

Deborah watches as Sibley steps around her and leads the way inside. Both of them take reluctant steps over the threshold into the kitchen. Paralyzed with fear, Deborah stands in the corner of the kitchen while Sibley clunkily moves through the downstairs rooms.

On second thought, Deborah doesn't want to be alone in case the man appears, so she scrambles after her. Sibley's in the bathroom, checking to see if the tarp over the small window displays any signs of tampering.

Terrified the man is going to leap out of her closet at them, Deborah flings the door wide open. With a horrified scream, she jumps as she's hit in the face by a hanger holding an article of clothing. But it's not just any item—it's the dress.

The dress.

Tarnished and bloody, it sways like a lifeless body hanging by a noose.

Deborah's hand covers her mouth as she gives a strangled gasp.

Sibley stands stock still, her eyes narrowed at the offending item. Gulping, she motions. "Looks like we found your dress."

Deborah's fingers roughly grasp the front of Sibley's shirt. "What the hell do you think this is?" Deborah commands herself to calm down, but it's useless, her pulse racing like an engine. "This isn't a game."

Sibley's eyes narrow. "You think I put it here?"

"Oh yes, you did! How does it just appear in my closet?"

Sibley untangles herself from her mother's clutch. "I have no idea why you think I'd have this dress. Let's think about this calmly, Mother."

Her patience isn't soothing but irritating to Deborah. "Don't you dare tell me to calm down!" Deborah cries. "Where the hell did you get this? It was supposed to have burned a long time ago. Did you take it with you when you left?"

Sibley protests angrily, "You told me it was in the pantry, yet it never materialized there."

"Then explain to me how it appears out of nowhere in my closet?"

"Are you kidding me right now?" Sibley glares at her indignantly. "You told me there was a stranger in the house!"

"There was! I've never seen him before!" Deborah spits out. "And I originally found the dress in your room."

"I have no clue what you're talking about." Sibley raises her hands and takes a step backward. "But what would you like me to do with it?"

"Nothing," she snaps. "Just get out of my room."

With an exasperated sigh, Sibley slams the bedroom door behind her, and Deborah fumbles to lock it.

After making sure her closet isn't hiding any live skeletons, Deborah closes the closet door with a bang.

She goes into her bathroom and opens the medicine cabinet to uncap a new bottle of pain pills. She takes a few more than the usual dosage, but anyone in her position would understand. Lingering on the toilet seat, she stares at the trembling bottle in her hand. Deborah wonders what it would be like to take all of them—if they would intoxicate her system immediately or slowly eat her intestines up. Would the pain intensify, or would it all go away as she drifted off to sleep?

CHAPTER 38
Sibley

Frightened by my mother's outburst, I need to defuse the situation, but she wants me out of her sight. From the other side of the door, I inform her I'm going to check the upstairs. If she hears me, she doesn't respond.

When I come back down, I gently tap and try the handle. I'm surprised to find it's locked. "Coast is clear. No one is here."

"Did you check the closets?"

"Yes."

"Under the beds?"

"Even the bathtub."

Deborah's response is a ragged sigh. "I'm going to lie down."

Frustrated that my mother's response to any problem is to lock herself in her room, I pace the faded pattern on the floor, feeling trapped and isolated.

I need a drink.

Just one.

Or maybe two.

I grab some vodka from the fridge, disguised as water, since I know how my mother feels about alcohol.

If I'm honest, we both retreat in our own ways—my mother to her bed, me to the bottle.

After the weird turn of events, I feel like a caged animal; an anxiety attack threatens to cripple me. Unable to breathe, I heave open the screen door and gulp the fresh oxygen outside. Even with the faint smell of manure and grass, if someone asked me what scents I identified with clean air, this would be my answer. As I walk outside, I don't have a destination in mind; I just want to feel the sun and forget the image of the bloody dress and my mother's mask of terror.

The liquid burns so good down my throat. Promising myself I'll only take a few sips, I savor each swallow, ignoring how fast the vodka disappears into my stomach.

I don't know if it's the heat or the brisk pace of my drinking, but a dizzy spell hits me as suddenly as a slap across the face. Before I know it, I'm at the entrance to our root cellar.

The root cellar is nothing more than a partially underground pantry used in centuries past to store produce when the farm was an efficient operation and they had to freeze, dry, process, and can their own food. When I was growing up, it doubled as a storm shelter, and there were many times we took cover from tornadoes cycling over the prairie.

The lock that kept it safely shut before has been cut, the chain dangling loosely off the double doors. The chief did say he had put a lock on it to avoid someone using it as their private hideaway.

Fearfully, I hesitate at the double doors. If it weren't for my liquid courage, I wouldn't consider entering the dark abyss. I tell myself it's because I'm scared to find a convict using it as their living quarters. In reality, the dungeon-like quality of the large room has always made me afraid, since my mother accidentally locked me down here as a child when I was playing hide-and-seek with the neighbor kids.

My bare-bones phone doesn't have a flashlight, so I'm forced to settle with my liquor in the dank atmosphere. The wooden steps are uneven, and it's a rough descent, just like the staircase in the house, except this one delves into the sodden earth.

It takes a moment for my eyes to adjust to the dimness. My hands are squeezed at my sides, and I tell myself I can turn and run back up the stairs if I'm confronted with someone seeking shelter.

I scan the rickety wooden shelves, which hold mason jars of various types of fruits and vegetables, now collecting dust. Relieved I'm not face to face with a living, breathing person, I take tentative steps toward the center of the room, focused on staying calm.

A wave of panic consumes me. I'm glancing over my shoulder, double-checking that the door hasn't closed behind me, when I trip over a sleeping bag rolled up on the floor. There's a lighter next to it, as well as a couple tins of food, but nothing else.

I wish this convinced me that my mother isn't off her rocker, but there's a nagging unease that I can't put my finger on. Originally, I questioned my mother's story of a stranger in the house. It's understandable that she'd be paranoid, with the rash of home invasions. There are so many hiding places and outbuildings on these farms; it's no surprise escaped criminals would use the cornfields for cover and skirt the authorities by seeking refuge this way.

But the likelihood of one just mutely hanging out in her living room?

Infinitesimal.

I stumble back up the stairs to the open air, and even though it's sweltering outside, I feel immediate comfort at being out in the open. If I got stuck down there, my chances of being found would be limited.

There's so much, too much, in the way of unwanted surprises and strange incidents, and it unnerves me—all of it. My mother's behavior has gotten increasingly erratic, or I've been so far removed from it that it's evoking old memories. This trip has been a minefield, and explosives keep detonating.

Not ready to go back inside the house and feeling suddenly restless, I start kicking gravel as I head down the driveway toward the highway.

In the middle of the rolling acres of farmland and cornfields, there's peace and quiet.

If only my childhood home felt that way.

This visit back isn't what I expected. I came home for answers and have developed more questions. I deserve to know what happened that night in the barn, why my mother is acting strange about her health and personal problems, and if there's some kind of medical diagnosis to soften the blow. And suddenly, a chill runs down my spine, my stroll no longer relaxing.

I have a decision to make when I reach the open road. Keep walking or turn around. I don't want to go back to my mother, because she's not *her* anymore. It's a painful realization, and it hits me like a ton of bricks.

I'm spooked when a vibration comes from my pocket before I realize it's my cell.

I expect it to be Adrienne, but the number is unknown, and I frown. I don't want to give up my secrecy, and only my best friend has this number.

It continues to buzz, and I'm torn with indecision. I don't have voice mail set up for obvious reasons, so I have to either answer the call or burn with curiosity. I remind myself I can always hang up if it's a crank call.

"Don't hang up," the female voice pleads when I answer. "This is Leslie."

Shit.

My paralegal, or should I say former paralegal, got ahold of this number.

Since I haven't given my identity up, I'm about to disconnect, but Leslie quickly tells me she and Adrienne had a chat, and Adrienne gave her my number to call me.

Why in the hell would she do that? I fume to myself.

For once, I don't know how to act or what to say. I'm ashamed about my exit from work and afraid to learn Leslie's opinion of me now, but I'm also worried I can't trust her. Even though she was one of my closest confidantes, I can't be too careful. Mainly because I used to count Tanner in that category, and he turned out to be a conniving douchebag.

For all I know, Leslie might be helping Tanner to oust me from the firm. She could be gathering information for him, and if she tells the partners I'm not at rehab, I'd be out on my ass in a heartbeat, which would be precisely what he wants.

Leslie must sense my indecisiveness. Without waiting for a greeting, she starts babbling. "I cannot believe what happened to you, and not only that, I can't believe that someone would want to hurt you. He's a master manipulator, and I had to tell you."

"Who?" I play dumb.

"Tanner," she whispers. "They reassigned me to his desk."

"Are you in the office?"

"Not right now," she says. "But did you know they gave him the Marcona case?"

"Really?" I act surprised.

"But when Tanner met with Nico, Nico hated him and wanted to fire him on the spot. Tanner told Nico you botched his case, which is part of the reason you were asked to take a leave of absence. He actually said your drinking problem became severe enough to land you in rehab because you can't display mental acuity with clients."

"And Nico bought it?"

"Not at first. He demanded a meeting with the partners. Obviously, Tanner begged Nico not to breathe a word of his confession, since he wasn't supposed to share such personal information regarding you."

"So much for that NDA," I mumble. Great. Now Nico knows I was forced out and sent with my tail between my legs to rehab. "Thanks for letting me know."

"Another thing, Sib. Tanner thought I was at lunch, and I heard him raking you over the coals to the partners. He said you're a costly liability that needs to be cut loose." Leslie takes a deep breath. "I heard the partners and Tanner discussing a bar complaint being filed against you."

I try not to scream and pull my hair out. "*Nico* filed a complaint?"

"No. Worse." She exhales a long breath. "His wife, Christine, did."

"For what?" I squawk.

"Unprofessional conduct. Sleeping with her husband, who was your client."

I silently instruct myself to take a few deep breaths so I don't scream or burst into sobs, and Leslie patiently waits for me to regain control.

Maybe my mother and I aren't so different when it comes to persistent rumors.

"Thanks for letting me know, Leslie. I really appreciate it." This is the proverbial icing on the cake. Clenching my hands into fists, I'm lost in a whirlwind of emotions—shock, anger, and disappointment. At some point, I need to call Chuck and tell him where I am and what I'm doing, but I fear he'll tell Holden and revoke our agreement regarding my ninety-day license suspension and replace it with a harsher punishment. Not that I don't deserve it, but I'm not ready to face him or further consequences. I still have to figure out what to do with my mother.

"Of course." Leslie sighs. "I want you to know I have your back. This isn't what I wanted."

"Thanks."

"But Sibley?"

"Uh-huh?"

"I love you to pieces," she says, "but I need you to get off your roller coaster and refocus. You're a lush. A brilliant lush. And I know this complaint is bullshit. But please don't come back until I get the old Sibley back, the one who's a fighter."

Overcome with emotion, I trip over my feet. Before I can respond, a loud blare interrupts the silence.

"Thanks, Leslie," I say hurriedly. "I appreciate you calling . . . and what you said. Talk to you soon." Hanging up, I realize the vehicle honking belongs to our old family friends, the Guthries. I raise my hand in greeting as it grinds to a halt, spewing gravel and a cloud of dust.

Grateful for the ride, since a blister's rubbing against my dirty tennis shoes, I happily jump in the front seat to converse with Nancy Guthrie, the woman who threw the infamous Halloween shindigs. Retired, she's on her way to meet some other ladies for bridge.

"I haven't seen you for ages, Sib!" Nancy exclaims. "Oh dear." She puts a hand to her mouth, aghast. "What happened to your face, honey?"

"I fell down those awful stairs." I touch my face gingerly. "It looks worse than it feels."

"You better ice that." She helps me buckle up my seat belt. "Your family sure knows how to fall. I swear, you're all a bunch of klutzes."

I'm peeved at this comment, but I know she doesn't mean any harm. "I know. I'm surprised I learned how to walk."

"What brings you home, honey?"

"I figured I'd check on my mother," I say. "Do you know if she ever has any visitors?"

"You mean, like a male friend?" She winks at me. "Not that I'm aware. I never see anyone parked in her driveway, least not from the highway. Poor thing, she's had a rough go of it." Nancy sighs. "Getting attacked like that in the middle of the night. This prison stuff has me on edge."

"The county offered her money to sell her place," I say. "What about you?"

"They haven't approached us yet, and I hope they don't. We certainly have no intention of selling."

As we drive into town, I decide now is my chance to ask about Edward Pearson. Casually, I bring up his name.

A look of surprise registers across Nancy's face. "Oh yes, Edward. He graduated from high school with my husband. Dropped off the face of the earth when he enlisted. One of the armed forces, I can't remember which."

"Did you know his wife or kids?"

"No. They never lived that close, probably a good half hour from here. It ended in a nasty divorce, and she moved with the kids to another state. Maybe New York? Or Rhode Island?"

"He died, right?"

"Tragically, yes. He had a lot of problems." Nancy points to her head. "Up here, and well, they destroyed him. He killed himself, and he wasn't that old. Maybe late thirties?" She muses, "I remember my husband said his ex-wife was distraught because she got nothing. Zip, zero, nothing."

"From what?"

"His life insurance policy didn't pay out because it was classified as a suicide. They had a nasty breakup, and after they were divorced, he cut her and the children out of his will." Pursing her lips, Nancy says, "There was a rumor it wasn't suicide, that maybe she poisoned him or someone else had it out for him. I guess he had left her at some point for another woman." Nancy whispers, "I heard that he and Cindy Fletcher were an item."

"What!" I say, shocked.

"Someone even told me years ago that Cindy drove into that tree on purpose because she was mortified everyone found out about it." A guilty expression crosses Nancy's face when she realizes who she's speaking to. Quickly, she adds, "But that's probably just a vicious rumor. You know how people talk."

Turning to me, she says delicately, "The night your father died, supposedly Cindy and Jonathan had talked at church. I know a lot of people thought your mother had an affair, but I heard Cindy got a call from her friend Alicia, and she went to the farm to confront

Jonathan because she thought he had something to do with Edward's death. Edward died only a few weeks before Jonathan, and that in itself was suspicious."

"Wow," is all I can muster, my anxiety at an all-time high. My hands fidget nervously, desiring something to take the edge off.

Another car honks at us, and Nancy's relieved by the interruption. She mentions it's one of her friends from bridge club.

I lie when she asks where I want to be dropped off. I am in need of a drink, but I feel weird about asking her to drop me at the Bar on Main, so I choose the corner by the drugstore instead. I leave her after a quick hug, and when I glance over my shoulder, I'm relieved she isn't watching what direction I go.

I walk the short distance to the bar. It's not until I'm seated on a barstool in the dimly lit Bar on Main, finishing my third vodka cranberry, about to cash out, that I realize I don't have any money. My wallet and purse are back at the house.

Murmuring an expletive, I debate who to call, as the options are limited. It's either my mother or Fletch. I choose the latter, not wanting to wake my mother or ask her to pick me up from a bar. I'm sensitive about Jonathan's alcoholism, and I don't want a lecture. She certainly doesn't need added stress from my drinking.

Scanning through my few contacts, I realize I don't have Fletch's number.

Tapping my fingers, I dial the station, praying he's working a shift tonight. The operator says he is, so she patches me through to his phone. But when he answers, he doesn't understand my jumbled words.

"Where are you?" he asks.

"Why do you have such a bad signal?" I whine.

"I don't. It's not that I can't hear you." He sighs. "You're just not making sense."

Now it's my turn to ask where he is.

"The police station. You called me here, didn't you?" He's annoyed. "My shift started a couple hours ago."

A pregnant pause follows, and we're quiet for a moment, both unsure why I bothered to call him. Miranda's the lone bartender tonight, and she pushes a paper tab toward me, a gentle reminder.

Reaching for my credit card, I come up empty handed, and realization dawns again that I have no way to pay for my drinks.

"Oh, that's right." I slap a hand to my forehead. "I need money to pay. I didn't bring a wallet."

"Pay for what?" he asks. "Where are you?"

"A bar."

"Which one?"

"Guess!" I want to turn it into a game, but he's losing patience with me. "Fine," I concede. "I'm at one of the two."

"What do you expect me to do?"

"Pay." I giggle. "And shuttle me home. You know if your job doesn't work out, you should consider being a ride-share driver."

"Hand the phone to Miranda," he instructs.

"Miranda?" I holler at her back.

"Uh-huh." Indifferent, she's focused on wiping down the mirrored wall that stretches across the bar. When I tell her she has a call, she spins around and wants to know who.

"Fletch." My voice slurs. "Miles Fletcher."

She grabs my cell out of my hand, and I watch her lips move in conversation until she swiftly hands the phone back to me. "Your ride will be here soon."

"Who?"

"Miles, your police officer friend."

"Why'd you call the police on me?" Feigning hurt, I press a hand to my heart. "I'm not hurting nobody."

"No one said you were, darling." She chomps her gum in my face. "But you gotta pay your tab." Motioning around the empty bar, she says, "I got three kids to feed, and as you can see, you're it for tonight."

"How 'bout one more?"

She shakes her head in annoyance and goes back to wiping down the bar and cleaning. A loud screech from the front door interrupts the eighties music, loudly suggesting a good rubdown with oil is needed.

Miranda's dirty-blonde head bobs to greet the patron. "Ah, Miles, it's about time you came in here without an agenda."

"Hi, Miranda," Fletch says in greeting. "I can't always be arresting the town drunks." He motions to me. "On second thought, never mind. She's an out-of-towner that don't belong here anymore."

"Fletch!" I half stand, losing my balance. If it weren't for the counter, I'd have face-planted. Settling back down precariously on the edge of the stool, I offer to buy him a round.

"With what?" His voice betrays his frustration. "I didn't come here for a drink. I came here to pay your tab."

"That's sweet," I stutter.

More to Miranda than to me, he mumbles, "Clearly going to need a ride home."

"Yeah," Miranda agrees. "She's tapped out. Say, what happened to her face?"

"Catfight," he jokes.

I snort. "Can Fletch have one drink, pretty please?"

"I'm on the clock, Sibby." He yanks a fifty out of his pocket. "How much I owe you, Miranda?"

"Twenty-four."

"I'm a cheap date. Liquor's cheap here." I clap. "Back home, it would've been three times as much."

"Guess you better keep at it, then," Fletch mutters under his breath. Handing Miranda the fifty, he tells her to keep the change.

I elbow him in the ribs. "Look at you, baller, giving your hard-earned money away. Guess you can when you take advantage of your neighbors in the spirit of kindness."

Miranda thanks him profusely, and both of them ignore me.

Yanking my elbow, he plucks me from my barstool.

"Ready," he asks, except it's not a question.

I cajole him to sit down and relax as he pulls me out to the waiting police cruiser. After he buckles me into the passenger seat, I inform him I hitched a ride into town.

"You did what?"

"It was Nancy Guthrie. Calm down." I grab his arm. "You're such a stiff."

"And you're a pain in the ass."

"You wanna go to the other bar, grab a drink?"

"I'm working, Sibby. I'm gonna take you home."

Rolling my eyes, I ask, "Can we at least stop at a gas station?"

"For what?"

"I need something to eat." I pout. "Something to soak up the alcohol."

Appeased at this response, he agrees to stop at the gas station, but once we pull in, my stomach clenches when I remember I don't have my wallet, and I need to borrow cash from him.

"I don't have any more bills. I gave Miranda the last of it." Fletch grunts. "I'll just come inside and use my debit card, no biggie."

Shit. I wanted my fix for at home.

Inside, I grab a handful of greasy snacks and playfully sneak a liter of vodka onto the counter. The clerk rings it up as Fletch groans. "What's that?"

"Just a little something for the road." Putting my hands up, I say, "Don't worry, I'll share."

"Oh, hell no, you aren't drinking an open container in my cruiser."

"But"—I offer up a sweet smile—"what if I wait until I get home to open it?"

"You don't need any more magic potion tonight."

Fixing me with a stern glare, he tells the cashier to remove the vodka and ring the other items up. After carrying my pretzels out to the car, instead of eating, I settle back against the headrest and close my eyes.

"Your face still looks like shit. You need to put something on it for the swelling." I can feel Fletch's gaze on me, his hot breath close to my face. "What did you mean back there?"

"When?"

"At the bar." He remarks sharply, "When you said I take advantage of people?"

I shrug. "Who knows?"

"But you said it."

"Just words, lots of words," I slur. "I must've pointed out something I was feeling."

"Nothing you ever say is 'just' words. You don't say something without putting meaning into it." He adds, "At least, you never used to."

As I probe my frazzled brain, it's hard to pinpoint exactly what I was trying to say, so I ask him to put my window down for some fresh air.

I keep my lids shut as the slight breeze whips my hair, and my elbow rests across the passenger-side door.

My eyes flicker open, and I slur my words. "I know what I wanted to ask. Why are you on an offer for a property in Florida?"

"What are you talking about?"

"My words aren't that slurred."

"No idea what you're saying." He raises a brow. "Florida?"

"I found a purchase agreement for a property in Florida that has your name listed and my mother as a coborrower."

"Are you losing your mind too?"

"Cut the shit, Fletch," I snap. "I heard about the union coffers. So you're in a tight spot and coerced Deborah into helping you buy a place?"

"Someone must be talking in your ear. I don't think that made the news out west," he growls. "I have no idea what the hell you're talking about."

"What's your vice?" I ask. "Gambling?"

"It's not the same as yours, that's for sure." He slams hard on the brakes, causing me to jerk forward. "You're nothing but a drunk."

"When we had the fight in the parking lot after school that ended our friendship, why did you say my father might kill yours?"

"Because why wouldn't your father go after mine if he's sleeping with your mom?" He slaps his palm on the wheel.

"But what if they weren't?" I ask. "Did you know your wife wrote my mother an apology letter before she passed?"

"No, she did not!"

"Yes, Kristin did."

"You're drunk and trying to start shit." Fletch sticks his arm out the window. "Look, I know it's not an easy time for you. Deborah's struggling to keep it together, but that's a blatant lie, and I'm not gonna tolerate it."

"I read the letter. It's in her handwriting." I add, "And I know Kristin's penmanship."

"She would've told me," he says defensively.

"You got together based on a lie," I say gently. "That might've been a secret she felt she had to carry to the grave, at least from you."

"You didn't know Kristin like I did." His voice quivers.

"Of course not," I say. "But Nancy Guthrie said something about your mother . . ."

Fletch swerves off the road purposely, and we almost hit a ditch.

"What the hell's wrong with you?" I murmur.

"You! You're what's wrong. Everything turns to shit when you're around."

The uncomfortable silence lingers as we turn down the long driveway. I expect him to drop me off without another word, but instead, he lets the engine idle.

"If my mother hadn't followed my father that night to the farm, she'd still be alive." He jabs his finger angrily in the air. "There was no one else, period. Got it? All the police and fire were focused on your goddamn parents. They had the road barricaded, and my mom would be around today if she had just stayed home."

"Wait just a second," I object. "There was someone else there besides your mother."

"Of course! My father."

Slowly I shake my head, the pieces starting to fall into place. "Someone showed up earlier in the night, and I couldn't make out who it was."

A mosquito buzzes through the open window, and I swat at it in disgust. Waiting for him to speak, I peer out at the night sky, the twinkling stars the only road map out on the blacktop.

Hanging his head, Fletch seems troubled as he stares out the window.

"Is there something else?"

"Nah," he says. "Well, maybe."

I tense up, waiting.

"Have you talked to your husband?"

"No," I sigh. "He won't talk to me."

"Is that so?" Miles points a finger at me. "Funny. I didn't have any trouble getting ahold of him. In fact, 'surprised' doesn't seem to accurately describe his reaction to hearing his loving and loyal wife never made it to rehab and she's spent her time getting plastered out on the farm, stirring up trouble, a family trait."

Unbuckling my seat belt, I ask, "How did you know?"

"You know, you shouldn't be so careless. You left the intake papers in your unlocked car—hell, the keys were in the ignition—and his name was listed as an emergency contact. You really are a piece of work, Sibley Sawyer," Fletch says snidely.

"What do you want from me?"

"I want you to go back home and take your mother with you."

"Why?"

"Because your mother is causing trouble again." He points to his head. "She's sick up here, and now she's telling people she and my dad are dating."

"How do you know they aren't?" I say haughtily.

"Because he's engaged to another woman!" he explodes. "Be a good daughter and get Deborah the help she needs, Sibley." He adds, steel in his voice, "But keep her away from my father."

"Your dad's engaged?" I'm flabbergasted. "Since when?"

"It's none of your business, so get out."

I try the door handle, but it's locked.

"Guess this means we have time for one more question, and since dishonesty is a family trait, I'm guessing monogamy isn't your strong suit. Did you really have an affair?"

The pointedness of his question annoys me.

"Why?" I snap. "Does it change your opinion of me?"

He retorts, "I'd just say, like mother, like daughter."

My reaction is sudden and swift: a hard slap across his cheek. I don't know who is more surprised, but we glower at each other, his tanned face turning fire-engine red.

Reaching a hand up, he strokes his whiskers, never diverting his eyes from mine. "That was uncalled for."

"No," I say. "It wasn't. Let me out."

"Apologize," he demands.

"Seriously?"

A sinister look pins me to the seat. "Or you could say you're sorry in another way . . ." A hand reaches between my thighs. "When's it gonna be my turn?"

"Jesus." I slap his hand away. "Don't start with me."

"Don't you think you owe me?"

"Is that the going rate of a ride and a fifty-dollar bill?" I spit out. "I should sleep with you?"

"Your mother never seemed to be picky when it came to men."

"Really?" I raise my hand, and he grabs my wrist. "Your dad didn't complain, and engaged or not, I bet he's still coming back for more."

His eyes bulge out of his head, his hand cutting off my circulation. "You know, I could arrest you for assaulting a cop."

Reaching across his lap, I don't bother answering, focused on hitting the door lock. After I stumble out, I hear Fletch gun his engine. If it were daytime, I'd see a cloud of smoke and a dust cloud as he sped off.

After wobbling up the steps, I wrestle with the front door. Usually the porch light is the only illumination, but it's burned out. It's not until I'm knocking on the door that I realize how badly I'm shaking.

CHAPTER 39
Deborah

Distracted by clunky footsteps on the porch, Deborah timidly creeps to the kitchen window to see who the culprit is, her tea waiting on the table.

It's Sibley stumbling to the door, the laces on her sneakers untied, her face red and puffy.

Deborah's confused—she thought she heard her come in hours ago and go upstairs to bed. When she checked earlier, her car was in the drive. "I thought you were in your room."

"No. I went out for a bit." Sibley winces. "But I am drained."

"You didn't drive, did you?" Deborah says worriedly. "You look like you could use some tea." Deborah volunteers to make her a cup. "It might help you sleep. This is my kind of nightcap."

Her smile is genuine, and Sibley is obliged to return it. "Sure. Are you feeling okay? You still look tired. You need more rest."

"No. I'm fine, really." Deborah waves a hand at her. "Sometimes, I think it's these pills and the effect they have on me." She gives Sibley's arm a gentle pinch. "Now that you're home, I feel safe again."

"That's good to hear." Sibley sinks into a chair. "But all drugs have side effects. Are these even helping?"

"I hope so." Deborah shuffles to the cupboard to get another mug. "I just want to stop feeling like I'm stuck in a nonstop brain fog. It's like I never have a clear picture in my mind."

"Maybe we need to get your meds adjusted," Sibley suggests. "I'm happy to take you to the doctor. You know I'd love to see Doc Marshall."

"That's nice of you, but I'm good."

"Is there someone else you're seeing? I'm happy to tag along to your next appointment."

"No, thank you." Deborah sets the steaming mug down in front of Sibley. "You look upset, honey. Rough night?"

Sibley rubs the edge of the ceramic. "Oh, Fletch and I had a little fight."

"Another one? You two are nothing but sparring partners, I swear." Deborah chuckles. "Hope this tiff doesn't last as long as the last one."

"I thought you hated him." Sibley examines Deborah over the rim, slowly drinking her tea.

Deborah shrugs. "I know his friendship used to mean a lot to you."

Sibley opens her mouth to say something, then abruptly shuts it.

"Oh, honey, would you mind if I borrowed your laptop?" Deborah asks. "I'd like to look something up."

"I think I left it in your bedroom."

"Hmm . . . I checked earlier and couldn't find it." Deborah sips her chamomile.

"I don't remember taking it back upstairs, but I'll look."

Sibley disappears upstairs for a few minutes, and when she returns, she insists, "It's not up there."

Deborah swallows her last drink of tea. "Let me search my bedroom again."

"By the way, were you upstairs in my room?" Sibley leans against the doorjamb. "It smells like Jonathan's old cologne."

"No, honey. Not today."

"Weird. Well, I'm going to bed. Night."

After Sibley disappears back upstairs, Deborah washes out the mugs and sets them on the counter to dry. A wave of nausea settles over her, and unsteady on her feet, she hurries to the bedroom to collapse onto the edge of the bed. Not only is she queasy, but her eyesight also isn't cooperating. Deborah must've taken too many pills earlier, and according to her stomach, she's going to pay for it. Everything is out of focus, as if Deborah can't hold her liquor and is about to pass out. She hasn't felt this way since the first time she accidentally got drunk on communion wine.

Certain she's about to throw up, she stumbles to the bathroom and splashes her face with cold water. Without bothering to turn on the light switch, Deborah sits alone in the dark for a moment, shutting her eyes against the brewing dizzy spell.

When she opens them, she swears she sees a mysterious figure. Something seems off, obscured, like a shadow puppet dancing across the bathroom wall.

Frantic, Deborah turns on the light, but it's only her reflection lit up in the mirror. While she waits for her stomach to either expel or digest the contents, Deborah brings her face close to the chipped medicine cabinet, staring at her lined complexion.

How did this happen? she wonders. *Where did the years go?*

As she's frowning at herself, Deborah hears a feminine voice ask, "Are you upset about the dress?"

When she doesn't respond, a young blonde girl appears behind her in the glass. "Or the intruder?"

Stunned, Deborah whispers, "You're not her, are you?"

"What do you mean?"

"You're not Sibley."

"Then who am I?" The cherubic face smiles at her, but it appears stiff and forced.

"You sent me those letters, didn't you?"

"Of course. But you didn't respond. I was never your favorite."

"What was I supposed to say?" Deborah removes a smudge on the glass with her finger. "You tried to blackmail me, Soren."

The blonde girl starts to fade from sight, her translucent skin and wheat-colored hair disappearing from view first, leaving nothing but two gaping black holes where her eye sockets should be.

Deborah squints her eyes closed, her fingers gripping the edge of the counter. "Just go away," she urges. "Just leave me alone, Soren."

"Soren?" a voice asks.

When Deborah opens her eyes, the girl has morphed into a woman with similar features. "Who's Soren?"

"Don't play dumb with me."

"*Mother*, what are you talking about? And who's Soren?"

"I thought you were dead."

"Dead?" Now it's the woman's turn to vanish, except her voice is loud and clear. "Whatever gave you that impression? I know you tried to have me killed, but I guess my desire to live was stronger."

"No!" Deborah says forcefully. "You died at the hospital. That's what they . . ."

"Mother," a different female voice interrupts, "you're really freaking me out right now."

"Oh, is that so?" Deborah groans. "What about what you're doing to me? You thought you could show up now, when my life was improving."

"I have no idea what you're talking about."

Deborah slaps her hand on the counter. "You want money. You want me committed. You want to ruin me."

A woman who looks like Sibley but must be Soren is blurred in the mirror. "Committed?"

"Just don't." Deborah holds up a hand, speaking to the reflection. "He told me what you were trying to do."

"I don't understand," the voice pleads. "Who?"

"You can't lie your way out of this. Pretending to be my daughter."

"I *am* Sibley. I *am* your daughter."

"No, you just want to take over her life!" Deborah bellows. "Like a fucking imposter."

"You're deranged, *Mother*." The not-so-nice voice releases a hideous cackle. "A crazy person."

"I'm not crazy," Deborah chants. "I'm not! Stop saying I am."

Covering her hands with her ears, Deborah continues talking between hurried gasps. "I saw the paperwork. You told them I was losing my mind, that I couldn't take care of myself anymore. You told them you were here to save me, except you're not who you say you are."

"That's not true!" Then the calm voice whispers, "I'm worried about you."

"You even got rid of my favorite cat." Deborah points an accusing finger at the glass.

The woman's voice retreats, now barely audible. "What're you talking about?"

"I haven't been able to find Esmeralda for days." Screaming and jabbing her finger in fast pokes, Deborah emphasizes, "Days!"

The woman shouts as Deborah steps back from the sink, headed for a collapse. As the room begins to spin, Deborah closes her eyes, terrified she'll be face to face with the evil doppelgänger if she opens them.

Unwilling or unable to open her eyes, Deborah stumbles toward her bed, her elbow yanked by a force greater than herself. Someone is leading her toward the comfort of her mattress. Without vision, she clumsily grabs one landmark after another—first the doorknob, then the dresser, then the bedpost—before sinking into the bed with a final sigh.

She's pushed down, the comforter pulled firmly over her head. Shrouded in darkness, Deborah can't be hurt. Soren can't reach her now; her voice can't penetrate through the blankets.

But sleep only feeds Deborah more nightmares, and she can't stop picturing the blonde girl posing as a woman in her mind. She wakes drenched in sweat, and terrified she's about to become a prisoner in her own house, she slinks into the wooden chair and slowly rocks back and forth.

The threatening letters Deborah received are too much of a coincidence so close to the unexpected visit of the woman claiming to be Sibley. Someone else knows what happened on the night of Jonathan's supposed accident, and they're sleeping under her roof.

The wolf isn't at the door. She's inside.

Deborah clenches her hands into fists at her sides. She knows what she has to do.

CHAPTER 40
Sibley

It took all I had to support myself going up the stairs. I gripped the railing for both physical and emotional stability. I wanted to confront my mother about the property in Florida, but her erratic behavior and mood swings made me too uncomfortable to bring it up. I need to know if she's suffering from some terrible condition.

I'm weary and tired, and tears start to stream down my face. I blow my nose into a tissue on the nightstand.

Even though I hate the grogginess that accompanies sleeping pills, and even though it's unadvisable to take them after drinking, I need to knock myself out.

Tonight is different; tonight is necessary.

Lying on my stomach, I don't know how long it takes for me to slip away into my subconscious, but a fight has broken out between Jonathan and Edward. I'm in the middle, one on either side of me. They tug at my arms until they stretch out like putty. I scream at them to stop, but they don't, their shouts growing louder as they drown my horrified cries. My limbs eventually fall completely off my body, and I stand there in shock, my protracted arms lying on the floor. Neither man apologizes. Instead, they glower at me and say simultaneously, "I hope you're happy."

Though I wish I could recount all the sordid details, I only know that when I wake, I think I'm still in the middle of a nightmare my brain hasn't entirely shut off yet.

I don't hear the door opening or the quick steps coming to my bed. What I do feel is a sharp object being shoved into my shoulder, where my old birthmark used to be, before I had it removed.

Numbing shock impales me, and my body comes alive with a burning sensation, as if I'm on fire. My first thought is that a baby scorpion stung me, since they live in the desert and close to mountains, and their fast-moving and potent stingers release venom straight into your bloodstream.

Half-asleep, I try to lift my head, but it's useless, since someone or something is holding me down. There's a heavy weight pressing down that won't release me, as if someone's sitting on me.

Assuming I'm paralyzed from the neck down, I flail my arms. Whatever went into me severed my ability to move. I can hear my ragged breathing in the charged atmosphere, but I'm not alone. My attacker's exertion is huffed out in quick bursts.

Fearful I'm going to be suffocated underneath my pillow, I kick my legs out behind me in vain. I try to turn over from my stomach or roll off the bed, but the sharp edge of something is being ground into my shoulder.

Screaming before I'm fully aware of what's happening, I reach a hand back to the source of the pain, and my fingers are met with sticky wetness. It takes my brain a moment to catch up and realize the fluid is blood.

My blood.

I can feel the culprit of my pain—a bony wrist connected to a smooth blade. I shove it as hard as I can, and a thud indicates the perpetrator's fallen off the bed. Hurriedly, I turn over, the sheets in a jumbled heap. If it's one of the inmates, I'm going to have to be ready to fight back. I peer over the bed at the figure lying on the floor. Expecting it to be a masked intruder, I'm dumbfounded to see the shape of a barely buck-ten woman, middle aged, holding a sharp kitchen knife.

"What?" I stammer in confusion. "What are you doing?"

Silence looms, and I'm uncertain if the air is suffocating me or if I'm struggling to catch my breath because of the panic rising in my chest.

"You just stabbed me?" It comes out as a question.

My mother lies on her back, panting. Suddenly, she lets out a low moan. "Who are you?"

"What?"

"What have you done with my daughter?"

"What the hell are you talking about?" I shriek. My hands move forward in a defensive gesture, and then I delicately touch my shoulder blade, where the stabbing pinpricks pulse as if I was repeatedly attacked by a bee.

With the knife tightly curled in her hand, my mother jabs the air. "Who are you, and where did you come from?"

I jostle my back against the windowpane, as far back as I can go without falling out the window, careful not to press the wound into the wall. The moon doesn't even shine in the room, as if scared to illuminate the tragedy. Openmouthed, I stare at her, one hand resting gingerly against my shoulder, the other waiting for her to spring up and attack me for a second time.

Her eyes are a malevolent force, but her screams are worse. "What did you do with her?"

"Who?" I screech. "Who are you talking about?"

We both let loose a string of expletives and squeals; it's unclear who is causing more of a commotion, both of us in a contest to outshout the other.

"You know who!" She explodes up as if blasted out of a cannon. "You're not Sibley—you're Soren!"

She keeps chanting this, and I'm confident her mouth is going to open and expel green bile like in *The Exorcist*. Her brown eyes are dilated, but they also have a vacant gleam, like they belong to an other-worldly species. This crazed lunatic doesn't resemble my mother.

"I'm not Soren. Who is Soren?" I beg. "Why do you keep calling me another name?"

She looks daggers at me.

"Mother." I inch sideways off the bed. "You're scaring me." Carefully tiptoeing toward the corner of the room, I refuse to break eye contact. "Are you having a seizure? Did something happen?"

"No," she gasps. "I don't know why you're in her room." She nods toward the bed. "You shouldn't be in her room."

"Whose room?" I'm puzzled. "I'm in *my* room."

"You convinced her to leave me, and now you want her room?" She kicks her legs against the hardwood floor with such force I'm worried she's going to break them. "You can't have everything! You can't have me all to yourself. She's all I had, and you ruined it." Then, launching into a tirade, she says, "This isn't your room. You don't have a room in this house. Stop lying to me. You're not her. Get out, Soren!"

"Mother," I implore, "I could've slept downstairs on the couch if you preferred." *Or have stayed in a hotel,* I think, knowing I'll never feel safe in her presence again. Rubbing my face, I'm traumatized; the full weight of what happened hasn't fully sunk in yet.

I can't believe the next words I utter. "But you didn't have to stab me over it." Even monotone, the weight of her actions is unimaginable.

In my career, I'm used to calming unruly clients and aggressive colleagues. Lately, I've fielded manipulative coworkers with their own agendas, but even that is new territory for me. It's implausible my own mother could and would stab me with a kitchen knife. This has to be a misunderstanding, a foolish mistake.

Yes, she thinks you're someone else.

The fight I had with Fletch that ended our friendship all those years ago floods my brain with warning alarms, dinging loudly.

Jonathan didn't just fall out of a loft and die. He was murdered by your mother.

When Fletch tried to tell me Jonathan hadn't had a freak accident, I was somewhat relieved. The blame and guilt I felt, not to mention the responsibility, were a lot for a seventeen-year-old girl. I'd wondered if I was the cause of his drinking, of his pain. Maybe he'd hated his life so much he had to lessen the pain daily. But then Fletch started throwing around the word *murder*, and that didn't sit well either. Especially when he implied my mother was the direct cause of it.

No one could blame her, Fletch told me. Everyone knew he was abusive, apparently everyone except me. It was a secret the adults shared, and children like Fletch overheard it when their parents whispered about mine.

Call it lack of awareness or childish immaturity, but I never saw Jonathan raise a hand to my mother until the last time I saw him alive. True, my mother tiptoed around him, but she was always soft spoken and timid. She acted like a domestic servant, but most of the wives on the farms had specific gender roles. I can't say the expectations laid out for her were any different from those of the parents of anyone else I knew. Our households mirrored each other.

I shudder. My last memory of him is when he dragged her to the barn by her hair.

I stare back at my mother as a shattering cry racks her body. She speaks softly to the ceiling. "I thought you were dead."

I hesitate, unsure if I should engage. "Why would I be dead?"

"Because you died at the hospital."

"How do you figure?"

Now catatonic, she doesn't move.

Gawking at her, I feel a trickle of blood running down my elbow. It's not a heavy flow, but it's steady enough to coat the wispy blonde hairs on my arm.

Crouching down, I whisper, "Will you please hand me the knife?"

"What knife?" she says as her left hand grips it tighter.

"The knife in your hand." I crawl toward her slowly. "I'm going to come and get the knife, okay?"

Her eyelids flicker, but she doesn't respond.

Trembling, I stay at arm's length, just in case she bolts upright and attacks me. "It's okay to drop it. I'm not going to hurt you."

I hold my breath until she releases her clutch on the knife. Her palm unfurls to rid itself of it as if it's cathartic to let go, and it clatters to the floor. I draw back tensely when she moves her arms, but they fold over her chest, like she's laid out in a burial casket.

In a soothing voice, I say, "Okay. I'm reaching over to pick it up."

In case she opens her eyes, I keep my hands in front of me and in her line of sight. My fingers scrabble to make contact with the edge of the knife. I try not to focus on the fact the metal is wet with my blood, the surface sticky to the touch.

Gingerly, I rise and step around her immobile body to turn on the light. The room's illuminated in an eerie glow that does little to permeate the darkness.

I stare from the doorway at the petite woman who gave birth to me. In some ways, I would've preferred if a masked intruder were breaking into our home. At least then, we wouldn't have a shared history, and this attack wouldn't be so personal. The woman who pushed me out of her womb now wants to kill me. My own mother just tried to injure or murder me, and neither option is a good one. I'm at a loss for what to do because she doesn't seem to know who I am.

"Mother?"

No answer.

"Deborah?"

I repeat her name a few more times before she stirs.

Raising her head an inch from the ground, she calmly replies, "Yes?"

My fingers touch the gaping hole—half an inch deep, judging from the blade's size. "I'm going to go to the bathroom and see if I can take care of this wound." In my head, I'm yelling at the top of my lungs, but in reality, I speak in a soft monotone. "You stay here, okay?"

Facing her from the doorframe, I step back slowly, scared to turn my back lest she tackle me from behind. In the bathroom, I debate whether to lock the door or leave it ajar. I choose to keep it wide open so I can hear her footsteps if she gets up.

When I drop the bloody knife in the sink, I cringe as water erases the bright-red residue.

Leaning against the counter, I tilt to the side so I can see both the hallway and my shoulder in the mirror. The laceration is narrow but deep, and the sight of blood has never sat well with me.

I dab at it tenderly with a wet washcloth and soap as tears stream down my face. Some from the pain, some from exhaustion, but mainly from astonishment. The bleeding is profuse, so I apply pressure to the rough cotton.

Raiding the medicine cabinet, I find hydrogen peroxide and a large bandage. When the blood immediately soaks through the layer of latex, I wonder if I need stitches and contemplate a drive to the nearest hospital.

Maybe I should take Deborah along with me and have her committed, I think bitterly.

After carefully removing the bandage, I rewet the cloth and ignore what's running down the drain, holding the cloth taut against my shoulder.

When Deborah appears behind me in the glass, I immediately freeze, startled, ready to bolt. My hand instinctively clasps the knife in the sink. Her eyes seem overwrought, and her lower lip trembles. "Honey, what's wrong?" Her gaze lingers on the bloodstained washcloth.

Flustered at her reaction, I don't respond.

"My God, is that your blood?" She takes a step toward me in the small bathroom, and I demand she step away. Impatiently, her hand reaches out to touch my arm. "Let me see it."

"No."

I wince as she roughly pulls the cotton away from the wound.

A sharp intake of breath follows, and I loosen my grip on the handle of the knife.

"What happened?" she asks innocently.

Angrily, I sidestep her to face her concerned expression. "What do you mean, 'What happened'?" If the situation weren't dire, I'd laugh at her ridiculous question and serious expression. This woman should win an Academy Award for acting obtusely.

After moving the toilet lid down, she settles onto the fabric cover. Her eyes drift to the sink, where the bloody knife rests in the basin.

"Is that from my kitchen?"

"I'd say so."

"What in the world were you doing messing around with it?" Her voice is sharp. "You could've really hurt yourself."

My eyes widen in fear. I'm being gaslighted by my own mother.

"I know." I'm brusque. "You could've really injured me."

"We need to talk." With a strained voice, Deborah says, "This is serious."

"I know."

"Is this one of those cutting rituals I hear about on TV? An unhealthy way for you to let your pain out?"

My head swivels to face her. "What?"

"Were you trying to kill yourself?"

"Mother . . ."

"I know you have a lot on your plate, and certainly, you're stressed to the max, but honey, I don't want to . . ." She tears up. "I don't want you to end up like your father. I can't bear to lose someone else, someone close to me."

"Are you being serious right now?" I snap. "I don't know about you, but sticking a knife in my shoulder doesn't seem like a suicidal tendency."

I flinch when she tries to pat my elbow. "We have to get you help. Let me call someone. How about Miles Fletcher? Or maybe your husband?"

"No." My voice echoes loudly in the small space. "I don't feel safe," I say to the mirror.

"That makes two of us."

Without a word, I take the knife from the sink and skirt past my mother. Downstairs, I hide it in the pantry behind cleaning supplies, where she won't find it.

Scanning the kitchen, I take the butcher block of knives and stick it in the empty gun cabinet. The key's hanging out of the lock, so I remove it. It's not like these are the only sharp objects Deborah can use to cause bodily harm, but I'm mollified the rifle is missing and the gun is in the police chief's possession.

As I make myself a drink, mostly to act as a painkiller for my shoulder, I'm on high alert when I hear Deborah creak slowly down the steps. I pray she avoids the kitchen and chooses instead to go to her room. At the bottom of the stairs, I wait with a pounding heart for her decision. Will she confront me again or retreat to her bed?

CHAPTER 41
Deborah

Deborah peers into the kitchen, and her stomach lurches when she hears the clink of a glass. She watches with horror as the blonde woman pours straight vodka into a glass.

A sigh escapes her lips.

Soren.

Trying to pass as Sibley.

Soren is not duping anyone with the vodka-filled water bottles or the liters of vodka. It's dangerous how Soren blacks out with no recollection of what happened the night before. Just like Jonathan would. A flicker of unease crosses Deborah's thoughts. If someone isn't in their right mind when sober, the drinking will only magnify their emotions.

Does she think Deborah wouldn't know every nook and cranny in this house to hide bottles? It's a repeat of history, how Deborah would uncover Jonathan's secrets, wrapped in towels in the hall closet, hidden underneath cushions on the sofa. Poor, innocent Sibley would have a tea party with her dolls and not think twice about the shot glass she used as a cup. It's lucky Sibley isn't stuck with Jonathan's genes. She's a successful attorney with a husband and a career and a life out west. Unlike Soren, who's set on destroying her life.

Deborah must plead with Soren to go.

"Deborah," the woman in front of her sneers. "It's me. Your daughter."

"I know," Deborah says uncomfortably.

"I'm going to go outside and grab a breath of fresh air."

Deborah waits for Soren's footsteps to exit the house and the door to slam shut behind her.

After sinking into her reclining chair in the living room, Deborah rests her head in her hands.

Should she call someone? 911? Miles Fletcher? Robert?

She tries Robert, but his cell goes straight to voice mail. Now that she thinks of it, he's been awfully silent lately. Deborah's been more preoccupied than normal, and she doesn't expect him to come around, but he's been less attentive than usual. Unable to examine this at the moment, she decides on Miles. She doesn't realize how late it is until a muffled voice echoes through the phone line.

"Hello?" his sleepy voice answers.

"Hi, this is Deborah." Realizing he could know a million Debs or Debbies, she quickly adds, "Deborah Sawyer."

"Uh . . . hi," he says. "I know it's you."

"Hi, Miles."

"Is everything okay?"

"Why do you ask?" she says timidly.

"The time. It's after three a.m." He moans. "Did Sibby ask you to call me?"

"Oh. Silly me. You're right; it's late. I'm sorry. And no," Deborah whispers into the phone. "She doesn't know that I'm calling."

"Did something happen?"

"I think my daughter's trying to kill me." With a click, Deborah hangs up the phone at the same time that she hears the thud of the front door. Deborah leans forward, craning her neck to spot the intruder. Her hands grip the faded leather of the chair, and relieved, she exhales a ragged sigh.

It's not a stranger; it's her daughter.

Frantic, she asks, "Sibley, what're you doing outside? It's late."

"I needed to clear my head."

Deborah argues, "Nothing good happens this late at night."

"It's not nighttime; it's after three in the morning!" she shouts. "And you know why I needed air."

Baffled at her outburst, Deborah eyes her with curiosity. "Why are you up this late? Are you having trouble sleeping? My tea is the cure-all for that."

"Your chamomile isn't going to change the fact my own mother stabbed me!" Sibley throws her hands in the air. "You're the reason I can't sleep. You crept into my room like some bad dream."

"Nonsense." Deborah shakes her head in disgust. "What're you saying?"

"I'm saying you tried to hurt me."

"How could you accuse me of something like that?" Deborah's awed.

"Let me guess," Sibley says. "I just stabbed myself in my own shoulder?"

"What're you talking about?" Deborah doesn't know what to say to keep Sibley's temper from rising. She's unclear why she's so angry with her right now. After her own assault, the episode with the stranger in the house, and the robberies, Deborah wasn't surprised when she watched Sibley take a knife upstairs.

But how could she be so careless with it and bring it to bed with her, without covering it properly or keeping it out of arm's reach? When Deborah saw her sleeping with it under her pillow the other night, she almost took it away. With the talk of home invasions, she wanted her to feel safe in her bed, especially since she couldn't give that to her as a child.

"I've been stressed because of my failing marriage and career and imploding relationships, and now my own mother's trying to make me her pincushion."

Deborah feels crestfallen.

"There's something evil in you." Her voice quivers. "I just never wanted to believe it before."

Deborah tries to grab Sibley's arm, but she's purposefully standing out of arm's reach. "Let me see what happened."

"You need help."

"Do you want me to drive you to the hospital?" Deborah offers. "Maybe you need stitches."

"No," she protests. "I just want to fall asleep knowing I'm not going to be attacked."

"Goodness gracious!" Deborah remarks. "Then stop sleeping with a sharp object in bed!"

"How can you accuse me of doing this to myself?"

"Stop yelling!" Deborah admonishes. "I'm sitting right here."

"What is wrong with you, Mother?" Sibley's lashes are wet with tears. "You kept calling me another name."

"Go to bed." Deborah relents. "We can talk about this after you get some sleep."

"That's what I was trying to do before you ruined my night." Beginning to cry hysterically, Sibley stomps back out of the house, slamming the door behind her.

CHAPTER 42
Sibley

I slam the vehicle in reverse before I stomp down on the gas. Chunks of gravel spit as I back up and seesaw out of the driveway, a whir of dust clouding my path.

Speculating about what might be going on with my mother, I wonder if she has dementia or some form of early-onset Alzheimer's. Deborah has moments of clarity, and then she becomes a whole other person. I've read cases and seen movies with these tragic storylines. The patient typically forgets a face or name and gradually loses their cognitive ability to remember people.

This seems, I don't know, drastic on another level.

And *Soren*. I tap my fingers on the wheel.

I need to figure out who this person is to my mother. She kept referring to Soren as "not her daughter," and I'm beyond confused.

Is she seeing double, or is there something going on with her cognitive functions? Maybe she thinks I'm a double, one part Jekyll, one half Hyde.

I remind myself it doesn't have to be rational, because my mother's actions aren't at the present time.

Wasn't Einstein the one who said the definition of insanity is doing the same thing over and over and expecting a different result?

Clearly, I can't get through to Deborah in her psychosis, or whatever she's experiencing behind the vacuous expression in her eyes.

I park my car in an empty parking lot, knowing I can't go back and face Deborah again this evening. For once, I have no desire to ply my nerves with more alcohol. The events of tonight have sobered me up.

I need answers. If Dr. Alacoy won't speak to me on the phone, I'll go to her.

I recline the seat in the car, though it's impractical to think I'll sleep—first because of the pain radiating from my shoulder, and second, because I keep imagining her coming at me with a kitchen knife. I'm tempted to find a twenty-four-hour drugstore, but I remember everything closes relatively early here.

With a couple hours of restless sleep to my name, I rub my eyes at the intruding sunlight and yank down the visor. I manage to fold up in the back seat for a few more hours, a jacket from the trunk slung over my face to block out the brightness.

When the pharmacy opens, I kill some over-the-counter pain pills for my sore shoulder and rebandage it. I wonder if I should call Doc Marshall to check if I need stitches.

Since no office hours are listed on Dr. Alacoy's door, and it's still locked after 9:00 a.m., I wait impatiently at the local coffee shop near the window.

I'm about to call Dr. Alacoy's cell again when a window shade goes up across the street. When I walk in, the door that was closed before is now open, and I'm surprised to find it's a small, cozy office, no bigger than my living room back home. The wall divides the office into two adjoining sections, one waiting area and one patient-treatment room.

"Hello?" I knock on the wood doorframe, startling the woman on her hands and knees.

"Holy shit!" she exclaims, half rising. "You scared me!"

When she stands up, she's a few inches taller than me, even in her sensible flats. She's dressed in a shapeless dress, and her bleached-blonde hair is knotted in a bun on top of her head.

"I lost an earring," she groans, pointing to her earlobe.

"That sucks." Frazzled, I run a hand through my hair. "I don't mean to bother you; I just thought we could chat for a moment."

"Is this about scheduling an upcoming appointment?" she asks. "Unfortunately, I'm leaving on vacation this afternoon."

"No, it's, uh, it's about my mother."

"Oh." She looks confused. "Your mother?"

"Deborah Sawyer. And I'm Sibley."

"Patient confidentiality is my first priority," she explains. "I'm entrusted with safeguarding my clients and acting as their confidante."

"Understandable." I nod in agreement. "We all have fiduciary duties to clients or patients."

"Exactly." She fervently nods too. "You get it. Are you in the medical field?"

"Absolutely not. I can't stand the sight of my own blood." I shrug. "And I have enough problems I can't fix on my own. How could anyone trust my advice, right?"

Dr. Alacoy stares at me with curiosity. I'm blabbering, and I need to stop.

"I just need access to her medical records," I finish.

"There should be a form you can download on my website," Dr. Alacoy says. "If Deborah's willing to sign the HIPAA waiver, it would cover everything but the psychotherapy notes. If you need those, the documentation is more rigorous in terms of consent."

"Actually," I say, trying another tactic, "Dr. Marshall sent me over here. He wanted me to catch you before you left on your trip." I grimace. "He's a longtime family friend and our doctor. He's worried she's in grave danger."

Her brow furrows. "Is that so?"

"Yes. It's an emergency," I say. "Do you know Dr. Marshall?"

"I do. He works out of the hospital, but I still need the paper signed unless he can scan it from his office. We can schedule a time when I get back, if you'd like."

"How about this?" I offer. "I'll go get this signed now. My mother's next door at the salon, and I'll be right back."

"Then why didn't she come with—"

I interrupt. "I'll pay you cash for a full session, whatever the going rate is."

She hesitates.

"Please," I beg. "It's important. If not, I'll have to call Doc Marshall, and he'll probably want to speak with you directly."

Looking flustered, Dr. Alacoy hands me a typewritten form, and I try not to run out to my car. After forging my mother's signature, I wait a respectable amount of time to bring it back in. My sweaty palm perspires on the release as I hand it to her. Trying not to be visible, I wipe my hands on a tissue from my purse.

She peers down her glasses at me. "Does Deborah not want to come in today as well?"

"No. Her hair's going to take a long time," I say lamely. "I think she can wait until you're back from vacation."

Her intense stare is magnified behind the glasses, and I'm worried at the amount of time she regards the signature line on the form. "Just a minute, please."

She disappears into the other room. I assume she's getting Deborah's file out of a locked cabinet, and I impatiently tap my foot. My eyes glance at the impressive array of diplomas on the wall. She went to a top-tier university in the Midwest for her undergraduate studies and a prestigious university for her doctoral degree. There are some additional certificates she's obtained for psychotherapy and hypnotherapy techniques. This puts me a little more at ease, but I'm still distraught at what's transpired with my mother.

Dr. Alacoy returns with a color-coded file open to compare the form I've given her with what must be a signature in her file. "Did you want copies? I will have to charge you for those."

"Yes, please."

"I don't have a receptionist, so it's going to take a minute. Let me do that first." She points to a chair in front of her desk. "Go ahead and take a seat."

Anxiously chewing my nails, I wait for her to return.

Taking a seat behind her desk, she motions to the other room. "I'll put the records in an envelope when we're done." She crosses her legs. "Is there anything else I can help you with?"

"I'm worried about my mother, Dr. Alacoy."

"I must insist you call me Alice."

"Okay," I agree. "My mother . . . she isn't stable."

Alice starts to open her mouth, then shuts it. "I'll let you ask the questions."

"I'm worried about the medication she's on. The pain pills she's taking." I bite my lip. "I've done my research, and these antipsychotic drugs seem to make her worse, or so I presume because of the side effects."

Alice laces her hands together, the quintessential listener.

"She's losing touch with reality, or that's how it seems to me."

"Please elaborate on what you mean."

"She imagines things that aren't there. People." I wait for a reaction but get none. I give another example. "Even the other day, she thought I was somebody else."

"Wait! Let's discuss this further." She leans forward. "You mean she called you by the wrong name?"

"Yes. Not only that, but she accused me of being someone else. Like I was inhabiting another person's body. I'm not sure if this is a result of her meds or why she would act like I was a stranger."

"Hmm . . . not likely."

"Could that vicious attack she had when she was hit with a gun or previous head injuries have caused some type of brain damage?"

"Yes to both. I'm glad you're here because maybe you can check some boxes for me." She pushes her glasses up on her nose. "Do you know much about your mother's background, her history?"

"Some, not all."

"Any drinking or heavy drug use?"

"If you mean pain meds, then yes." I cross my arms. "Is there a reason she's on so many potent medications?"

She raises her brow. "Why, yes, there is." Alice reaches a hand out to gently touch mine. "Permission to be frank?"

"Please," I beg. "Of course."

"I have a suspicion, unproven at this point, of course, that she's starting to show signs of Lewy body disease."

I lean back in my chair. "I'm not really sure what that is."

"It's rare."

"I think I've heard of it . . ."

"A famous actor had it. It's not an agreeable disease, not that there is one." She sighs heavily. "But it's devastating for the patient . . . and their family."

"I don't know what to say." I feel the prick of tears signaling I'm about to lose my shit.

"The problem is, a diagnosis can take a year or longer to determine. Other neurodegenerative diseases mimic the same symptoms, so it's not a quick discovery, rather a slow process. We don't want to rush to a conclusion, since it could hinder her progress if we're wrong."

"Please tell me you're wrong." My voice quivers.

"There's another thing. I don't want to go down a rabbit hole, but there's something else, even rarer, with parallels to your mother's symptoms."

Now I'm on the edge of my seat, sweating bullets as pit stains soak through my short-sleeve shirt.

"It's called Capgras syndrome, also known as the imposter syndrome."

My gaping mouth must give away my skepticism.

"It's a real thing," Alice promises. "Named after the French psychiatrist who discovered it."

"I've never heard of it."

"That's because it's very uncommon. It usually occurs as a result of something else. In this case"—she ticks off all the scary ones on her fingers—"Alzheimer's, paranoid schizophrenia, and Lewy body."

"And what does this Capgras syndrome do?"

"It's a neurological disorder that causes damage to the . . ." She starts to spout some long medical words outside my vocabulary.

Noticing my blank expression, she swiftly stops. "Sorry, I tend to get all scientific. Basically, it's damage to the brain that causes impairment. In this case, it can range from the inability to recognize faces to something more malignant."

"Like how much more harmful?"

She's thoughtful in her answer. "Let's say a person is infuriated with someone. In this case, it's a rage that causes them to use 'splitting' as their defense mechanism."

"Splitting?"

"The person believes their anger is toward an imposter, someone imitating the actual individual. This thought process allows them to still consider their family or friend separate from their rage, as if a different identity. In a way, the person 'splits' into two different individuals. This belief allows them to proceed."

My jaw drops. "So you're saying my mother might be seeing double?"

"Yes, but it's extraordinarily uncommon, Sibley."

Flabbergasted, I rest my hands on my knees.

"I should add, she doesn't necessarily see double in the sense that there's two of you but that you're replacing someone else."

"She did call me another name," I confess.

"What was it?"

"Another *S* name. Sore-in."

"Wait!" A shadow of recognition crosses her face. "Did you say Soren?"

"Yeah." I jump out of my chair. "Do you know who that is?"

"Deborah saw a woman outside during one of our last sessions. In fact"—she scans me up and down—"she looked an awful lot like you. Said she used to know her. Interesting." Alice leans back in her chair, studying me intensely. "This is all good to know. Very insightful. It'll help make the diagnosis easier."

Staring at my bewildered face, she hurriedly adds, "Not easier to handle but more straightforward to diagnose." Perusing her notes, she murmurs, "Deborah hasn't yet mentioned that name in our sessions. Let me ask you . . ." She swipes a misbehaving piece of hair that's loosened from her knot. "When she accuses you of being a fraud, what do you do or say?"

"You mean, how do I defend myself?"

"Yes."

"I got upset and argued with her. Tried to convince her she's wrong."

"Don't."

Dubious, I say, "Don't tell Deborah she's not in her right mind and I'm not lying about who I say I am?"

"Exactly." Alice nods. "I know it sounds counterintuitive, but arguing with her over her reality will only heighten the severity of her reaction to you. In cases like these, it's best to either redirect their focus to another activity or acknowledge her emotion."

"Won't she think I'm lying, then?"

"Not necessarily. It's like playing pretend as a child. You go along with it. In this case, it's for your safety, which raises another question: Has she been violent toward you?"

I hesitate, not wanting to admit the truth. Sidestepping the question, I ask, "Does this disease make someone prone to violence?"

"It depends," Alice discloses, "on what's going on in someone's brain. Have you had any altercations with her that made you feel unsafe?"

"Last night. She, uh, she tried to stab me," I say ashamedly. "Actually, she did."

"I need to take some notes, Sibley. If you don't mind." Her furrowed brow is worrisome. "That's troubling. Violence isn't always a factor, but when it is, it can mean . . ."

A shiver goes down my spine. "She won't stop until I'm dead?"

The automatic flush on her pale cheeks tells me I'm right. Her watch signals a call coming through, and I notice the initials *RF* flashing on the diminutive screen.

I reach down to grab my wallet out of my purse. "What do I owe you?"

She furiously shakes her head. "I don't want payment. Consider this a favor to your mother."

Shakily, I stand, my limbs as rubbery as overcooked pasta. "Even for the copies?"

"No." She stands. "Let me go grab the envelope."

When her ballet flats shuffle back across the room, I snap my fingers, remembering another question I had. "Oh, Dr. Alacoy—I mean Alice." I cradle the envelope underneath my arm.

"Yes?"

"So you're basically telling me to kill or be killed?"

"Well, I don't condone murder." Tilting her head, she murmurs, "I'm telling you to be careful." Sliding her card across the desk, she says, "Even though I'm going out of town, if you need me, here's my cell. If anything changes with Deborah's moods, call me. And Sibley," she cautions, "if you're digging in the past or asking her to conjure up old memories, it doesn't necessarily mean it's for the greater good." She pats my arm. "Sometimes, what we forget is more important than what we remember."

CHAPTER 43
Sibley

After I reach my car, I contemplate the jumble of words Dr. Alacoy mentioned. They spin through my head like it's a turbulent washing machine.

Capgras syndrome.

The imposter syndrome.

Lewy body disease, possibly.

Inside my vehicle, I don't even get the key in the ignition before the sobs overcome me. The idea of my mother losing her mind, piece by piece, is enough to drive me straight to the farm. I can't leave her alone. If she's a prisoner in her mind, descending into madness, she needs me now more than ever. In folklore, there are mythical shape-shifters who, through superhuman abilities, can transform and emulate other beings, whether by divine intervention or manipulation. And though I'm a believer of science and not sorcery, it's as if another person has inhabited her.

I came home to sort out my own past, provide myself some clarity, and now I'm amid a Hitchcockian thriller.

I sadly wonder if it would be different if I hadn't left all those years ago. Deborah has had a rough life, and I've only exacerbated it, whether

I was in proximity or not. And I can't take all the blame; so much was out of my control and without my knowledge.

An unknown number shows up on my caller ID, but I don't answer. I'm not in the mood to talk. It rings again, so I shut the sound off.

When I pull into the driveway, my stomach is in knots and thunderclouds are moving in, signaling a shift in weather. I'm apprehensive about a shift in moods. I guess I will have to wait and see which Deborah I get today.

Will I be an intrusive stranger or a welcomed daughter?

I don't have to wonder for long, because she's barricaded herself inside her bedroom. I guess I have my answer. I sigh.

I search for my laptop and become frustrated when I can't find it. Tempted to knock, I listen at Deborah's door for signs she's awake, but I don't hear any noise from her television or sense any movement inside.

Exhausted, I lie down in bed and stare at the ceiling. The room's now filled with weird energy since my last night sleeping here, when Deborah decided I was an imposter.

Thinking about what the psychiatrist said, I pull out the envelope I have tucked into my tote bag. As I read through the sheaf of papers in Dr. Alacoy's handwriting, I'm struck at the similarity between her writing and someone else's, but I can't place it. It looks oddly familiar.

I hear a loud rumble, and thinking it's Deborah, I sit straight up in bed.

It's not, but it is a sign a storm is on the way.

Unable to sleep, I decide to take a shower, and after locking the bathroom door, I shiver as the water runs down my back. Carefully, I wash the wound on my shoulder. I remind myself to call Doc Marshall and have him examine it. It might actually heal on its own, though I'm sure I'll have a scar.

When I pad across the hallway to my room, there's a mug of tea on the nightstand, piping hot, along with some toast.

Deborah must've limped up the stairs to put them there.

343

My stomach grumbles, and I can't remember my last meal. I quickly dry off and put some comfortable sweats on.

Even though the shower helped, I feel drained, and sitting back on my bed, I devour the tea and toast, almost burnt, just the way I like it. It alleviates one of my needs, and after my hunger is satiated, my need for sleep overcomes me.

Jumpy about leaving my bedroom door unguarded, I gently close the door and turn the flimsy lock before bed.

Later that night, I'm awakened by the sound of thunder booming outside my window—sheets of rain pound at the glass, hell bent on making their way into my room.

I'm groggy and disoriented; my head hurts worse than it would from a typical hangover. It's like I've been drugged.

My purse and phone are gone, along with Deborah's medical records. I wonder if they were missing after my shower.

And what about my laptop?

Perturbed Deborah would take my stuff without asking, I shuffle down the stairs. Narrowing my eyes at the clock on the microwave, I'm stunned it's 8:00 p.m. already. That was quite the nap, though desperately needed after not getting any rest the night before. I feel bad for people who sleep in their vehicles and are confined to the cramped quarters.

I hear light steps, and Deborah walks into the kitchen. In a perfectly normal voice, as if nothing untoward happened last night, she asks, "When did you get home?"

In horror, I realize she might not remember . . . but maybe that's not a bad thing right now.

"Late morning," I offer, trying to discern her temperament. I scrunch my face. "But you brought me tea, and I never left again."

She bites her lip but says nothing.

"By the way, what did you do with my purse?"

"What're you talking about?"

"My purse and phone are gone," I say irritably, "not to mention I still can't find my laptop."

Deborah fingers her necklace chain. "Why would I have your purse and phone?"

"They disappeared out of my room, and you were the only one in there." I sigh. "Look, if this is payback because you blame me for the dress . . ."

Taking a deep breath, I focus on Dr. Alacoy's words. The last thing I want to do is stir the pot and cause Deborah to become unhinged. I'll look through the house myself. My laptop, phone, and purse have to be somewhere.

"I have no idea why you think I'd go upstairs today. My hip's killing me."

"But you brought me tea. And toast."

"I did no such thing. We're out of bread." She looks at me like I'm crazed. "Remind me to get a loaf next time I go to the store."

"I must've dreamed it." I shrug.

"You're probably hungry. Let me see what I can scrounge up." She claps her hands together. "I swear, it's like I go grocery shopping and then the food just disappears."

"With one extra mouth to feed, I guess it must seem that way."

"Uh-huh!" she hollers from the walk-in pantry. "This is quite the storm, isn't it?"

"Sure is." I stare out the kitchen window at the darkened sky.

"I found something," she says triumphantly, appearing beside me with a protein bar.

"Is there anything I can do to help you?" I stare at the expired label on the wrapper. "Maybe go get you groceries?"

"Oh, that reminds me." She waves a hand in the air. "Honey, can you do me a favor?"

Still staring outside at the inclement weather, I half listen.

"Would you mind feeding Esmeralda?" my mother asks. "I don't want to go outside in this storm." She groans as a flicker of lightning dances across the clouds. A couple seconds later, the rumble of thunder follows. The last thing I want to do is go outside right now, but I love a good rainstorm, and we get so few in the desert.

"Yeah, sure. Stay inside," I say. "Mind if I borrow a raincoat?"

"Should be one in the pantry."

Shrugging into a tan jacket, I shove my feet into a pair of bright-red rain boots that are directly underneath the coat.

She hands me a bowl of wet cat food and offers me a flashlight. "I know it's dark out there. You'll probably need this."

"Thanks."

"Make sure you find her. She needs her strength. I know she's gonna give birth any day now."

CHAPTER 44
Sibley

As soon as I open the screen door, a blast of wind hits me straight on. The rain lessens visibility, and I'm forced to step into puddles that go ankle deep.

When I reach the barn, the lightning streaks the sky in a bolt of bright-white illumination. Inside, I smell mildew, since the roof and walls aren't as secure as they once were; the floor is already damp.

I search for Esmeralda, but she's either hiding or on the prowl.

Yelling, "Kitty, kitty," I set the obnoxious-smelling fish-flavored cat food down, then pause to see if she will come running. She's big and bloated, carrying a litter of kittens, and I doubt she moves at the same speed she once did. When she doesn't appear after a couple of minutes, I grab the bowl.

Maybe she's hiding in the toolshed.

When I can't find her burrowed there, I head to the root cellar.

I managed to wrap the chain back around the door handles yesterday, but for some reason, the two doors are wide open, the dirt steps and sod walls naked to the elements. I don't want the cellar to flood, primarily because of the number of canned jars of food that still need to be moved from below.

Hesitating as another flash crosses above my head in a zigzag pattern, I yank the hood over my drenched hair.

The metal handle is slippery as I grasp it for balance and climb inside. The loud crack of a snapping branch on a tree tells me to abandon my plan of searching for the cat and seek shelter back at the house. About to crawl out, I hear a high-pitched whine.

Pausing, I wait to see if I hear it again, but a boom overtakes any noise.

After the next round of explosions occurs, there's another sound, similar to a yelp.

Then soft mewling.

Esmeralda must be hiding out inside the root cellar, but how did the lock get undone?

It was closed last time I came out. The chief said he put a padlock on it. Unless Deborah came down here for some reason . . .

I shake my head, and a resounding clamor causes me to jump.

"Get it together," I hiss. But I recall the chief's words about transients using it as their shelter. If someone is taking cover in the cellar again, do I really want to get stuck with a potential convict who isn't going to care about my survival?

It's an eerie thought, and involuntarily, I shudder.

The mewling now becomes more of a caterwaul, and I wonder if she's about to give birth. I've tried to keep the cat food somewhat hidden under the bottom hem of the coat, but it's a watery mess.

I sigh and take a deep breath. *Just walk down, give Esmeralda her food, and go back. Just leave both doors open.*

I give myself a quick pep talk. *There's nothing to be afraid of; the weather is just making you paranoid. You forget what you do half the time, and most likely, you got drunk and forgot to close the doors.*

This won't take long, and you can worry about trying to clean the cellar out when there've been a couple days of sunshine.

I remember the flashlight, and it quiets my nerves for a moment as I descend the muddy steps, the dim glow providing a thin stream of light.

My hand grips the hard plastic as I reach the landing, confident I'm walking right into a trap. A stranger will be waiting for me, an evil grin on his face as he gleefully hollers that he tricked me.

My heart thuds in my chest as I bob the light around the room. I spot the outline of my mother's beloved cat. She's lying in a sheath of blankets in a bin, and I'm relieved there's no one else.

As she yelps at me, I timidly set the food down, careful not to touch her. She's still a feral cat in my mind, so I don't try to pet her, since it's not like she's had her shots. Worried she'll think I'm trying to invade her territory, I soothingly tell her it'll be all right.

I can grab the bowl in the morning. As I turn to go, loud slamming echoes above me. I don't think much of it at first, assuming it's storm related. As soon as I hit the bottom step, I realize I can't see up into the blackened sky. Both of the doors are shut above me.

A scraping sound is followed by a click and a thud.

"It must be the damn wind," I mutter, hurriedly making my way back to the top. Pressing my hands against the wood, I expect to push straight up without a problem. The doors are heavy, but not unreasonably so. I've never had trouble moving them before.

Neither door moves against my weight.

Grunting, I try again.

They are rock solid, as if held in place by something.

Recognition flickers across my mind in an aha moment, and the sudden onset of panic propels me forward. Shoving my fists against the double doors, I scream bloody murder, hollering for someone to help me, but it's no use.

I start to hyperventilate, sinking to my knees on the wet ground, my ragged breath coming out in puffs.

After I count to fifty, I tell myself it'll be no problem to get out, that I didn't push hard enough a moment ago. The wind must've held the doors in place, like a vacuum that sucks in the air; something must've happened with the atmospheric pressure. I'm not sure if this is a feasible theory, but it calms me for a fleeting second.

Trying again, I casually shove the doors.

Then I lean against the wall and try kicking them.

It's no use. The doors must be chained in place, the padlock secure.

I curse myself for not bringing my phone, then remind myself it wouldn't have worked anyway, especially in this weather.

My mood changes in waves. I'm on the brink of hysteria and then exhaustion as I rattle and thump and pound the doors, my screams drowning out the scared cat, who must think I'm a madwoman.

Covered in mud, I sink to the floor, tears mixing with the residual water stuck to the rain jacket.

With a snot-filled nose, I wipe a hand across my mouth, trying to get a grip on my emotions. Warning bells in my head signal a panic attack is about to happen, the rapid heart rate and struggle to breathe apparent indicators.

"You can't die from a panic attack," I whisper.

I convince myself Deborah will get worried when I don't return promptly. She'll wonder why it's taking this long to drop food off to the cat.

She'll be concerned and come outside, even in this weather, and look for me.

But the most atrocious thought weaves its way through my thought process.

She asked me to feed the cat.

The cat wasn't in the barn, where she said to go.

The doors to the cellar were open, and now they're closed.

How did the doors get shut?

"But Deborah didn't know you would go to the cellar," I babble out loud. "She told you the barn. It's not like she directed you over here."

But she knew you wouldn't give up until you found the cat.

No, she didn't, I argue in my head.

The war continues in my brain until I must concede. The truth hits me like a ton of bricks, doubling me over in pain.

Deborah's madness is taking over.

The doors were purposely shut behind me, locking me down here. Someone wanted me down here, and that person is my mother.

CHAPTER 45
Deborah

After she's left for the barn, Deborah locks the front door behind her and then leans against it. She breathes heavily, and her eyelids flutter uncontrollably, as if she's in a contest to see who can blink the most.

She gives herself a moment to stand unmoving, using the dense wood for support. A pummeling on the opposite side of the door causes her to jump. It sounds as if someone is throwing punches.

Deborah's hand moves to her throat.

She realizes it's someone knocking.

Warily, she turns around.

Swallowing hard, she whispers, "Who is it?"

"Deborah?" a male voice hollers, and she doesn't know whether to be relieved or terrified.

"Uh, yes." She wipes her hands on her pants. "What can I help you with?"

"It's me, Holden."

"Holden?"

"Holden. Holden Bradford." His voice sounds strained. "I know we've never met, but I'm Sibley's husband."

Flabbergasted, Deborah smooths her frizzy hair, matted from the earlier rain. This is not how she pictured the first meeting with her son-in-law.

"It's raining pretty hard!" Holden shouts. "Mind if I come inside?"

Deborah stares out the small kitchen window at the yard, now upset she's let it get so overgrown and wild. What's Holden going to think of the three-foot-tall weeds and the thick grass?

Not to mention her own appearance.

She stares at her reflection, and devoid of makeup, her eyes look sunken in her face. As she glares at the messy kitchen, her heart sinks. He's going to be disappointed at the family he married into.

With a defeated sigh, she flicks the porch light on and fumbles with the lock.

She's face to face with someone who shouldn't be a stranger but nevertheless is.

"Hi," Deborah says.

"Hi." Holden reminds her of a drowned animal. His tawny hair is sticking to his forehead, and his tortoiseshell glasses are fogged. The light cotton jacket he's wearing isn't meant for rain; it's soaked.

"Come on in." She ushers him inside, where he stands dripping in her kitchen. Mud and grass stains cover the front of his denim jeans. His tennis shoes squish on the linoleum.

They stare at each other in awkward silence until Deborah remembers her manners. "Let me take your jacket," she offers. "And get you a towel."

"Thanks. I'd appreciate it." He removes his waterlogged jacket and hands it to her. Underneath his coat he's wearing a T-shirt, and he uses the hem to clean his glasses.

Deborah hangs his jacket up and grabs him a dish towel out of a kitchen drawer to wipe his hands and face. His beard, trimmed, not bushy, has water droplets stuck to it. Giving a quick swipe to it, he asks if he should remove his shoes.

"That's all right," Deborah says, motioning to a chair. "We can sit in the kitchen."

"I don't want to ruin the fabric. I'm pretty dirty."

"Don't worry about it." She ignores his protests. "Sit down. Make yourself at home. Would you like something to drink?"

He runs a hand through his wet hair. "A water would be good, even though I got a mouthful outside."

Deborah points to a single mug sitting on the counter. "How about tea?"

"Tea?" He shrugs. "Uh, sure. That's fine too."

"I made a third, but there's only two of us. Let me just pop it in the microwave for a couple seconds."

"Speaking of, where is my wife?"

"She left."

His jaw drops. "She left to go where?"

"Back home."

"Are you sure?"

"That's what she told me."

Holden rubs a hand over his tired face. "I just drove all the way here on a wild-goose chase. I've been trying her cell for a couple days, and it goes straight to voice mail, which would make sense because she's not where she's supposed to be." He murmurs, "I should never have trusted she'd go of her own volition." Holden yanks his phone out of his back pocket. "Do you mind trying her phone? She's not going to answer if I call."

"Sure." Deborah picks up her cell.

There's a lull as Deborah listens to the phone ring, but no one picks up. After disconnecting, she sets her phone on the table and shrugs. "I'm no luckier. She confided in me about the . . . about the indiscretion, and I'm sorry."

Holden considers her strangely. "She told you what happened at the firm?"

"She just said she needed a vacation."

"That's one way to put it." He uses the steaming mug to warm his hands.

"What do you mean?"

He swallows. "Rehab was a mandatory request from the partners at her firm. They wanted her to complete an inpatient program. It's a requirement for her to come back to work."

"Rehab?" Deborah quivers. "For drugs?"

"No. It's not a drug addiction," Holden says. "Or rather, I should say, it's a different type of drug. Alcohol's classified that way, I guess."

"I'm all too familiar with that one." Deborah feels sorry for Holden. She knows firsthand what it's like to live with an alcoholic: the mood swings, the outbursts, and the instability.

"I knew Sibley's father liked to drink. She said he wasn't violent, just quiet, sometimes moody. 'He liked to ruminate,' I think were her exact words. Runs in the family, I guess. Must've got that gene."

"She's not herself. Far from it." Deborah scratches at her neck. "We've been estranged, but there have been telltale signs. She can't remember what she does or details. She blacks out and forgets. There have been a couple of times I've felt unsafe that she could and would harm me. One night, I went to her room, I don't know, just to stare at her. It's been so long since she's been home, slept in her bed. It was a sense of normalcy for me, I guess. The covers had slipped from her back, and I was going to tuck them back up around her shoulders. She was always like me—no matter how hot or humid it was outside, she still had to have a blanket. I'm the same. She's not who she says she is, Holden. She's someone else."

"I hear what you're saying, Deborah. She's acting completely out of character."

"No," she says impatiently. "I don't think you understand. The woman who showed up here isn't Sibley; she's just pretending to be her. Her name is Soren." Deborah exhales a breath. "Soren came back after all this time."

"Soren?" Holden scrunches his nose. "Who's Soren?"

"Sibley's sister."

Holden's eyebrows shoot up in confusion. "Sibley has a sister?"

"Had."

Alarm registers on Holden's face.

"Hand me the tissues, will you?" Deborah points at a box on the counter next to him. Fisting a bunch in her hand, Deborah coughs a few times, her voice husky. "She had a baby sister. A twin, as a matter of fact."

"Whoa!" Holden twists the mug in his hand. "I had no idea."

Thinking back to that afternoon, Deborah sobs into the tissue. "They were born seven minutes apart, and Soren supposedly only lived for a little over twenty-four hours before the doctor told me she was gone. Then, about six months ago, I started getting letters from a woman who claimed to be Soren. She said she lived in Florida but wanted to get to know me."

"What made you think Soren was still alive if she died as an infant?"

"Jonathan, my husband," she says simply. "I figured he had some-one kidnap her or sold her to a baby snatcher."

Midsip, Holden spits out his tea. "Are you serious?"

"I wouldn't have put it past Jonathan's twisted mind to sell off one of our babies, pretending she was dead."

"That's . . . wow." Holden looks baffled. "That's insane."

"I wish I could say it was far fetched, but people would walk into hospitals and take babies, especially back then. When I got the recent letters, I figured this was the case." She stammers, "And the woman mentioned facts no one else knew. She sent letters from a PO box in Florida. I wondered if it was a hoax, but again, she knew so many tiny details."

"Did she ever send you anything to confirm her identity?" Holden asks. "With the internet and Photoshop, you can fake so much these days."

"Yes. She sent a recent picture, and though I haven't seen her in thirty-four years, there was one identifying mark distinguishing the two twins at childbirth."

Holden tilts his head with curiosity. "What was it?"

"The nurse called it a congenital mole, and it was on Sibley's back, her left shoulder." She drops her head in her hands. "The woman in my house doesn't have a birthmark on her left shoulder."

"Oh, that?" Holden's jaw drops. "Sib had it removed, Mrs. Sawyer. Shortly after I met her. Then she got the tattoo of her butterfly. I'm not a fan of tattoos, but it had personal significance for her."

Deborah is astounded at this news, and she lets her hands drift with uncertainty to her neck.

"It's more than that," she insists. "I've noticed my pills have gone missing. I've counted them, and they aren't all there. I used to keep them in my medicine cabinet, but they keep disappearing. It took me a moment to catch on. First, I excused it as a break-in, but now . . ."

"Jesus." Holden runs a hand through his hair. "This is serious. What types of pills?"

"Strong pain pills and sedatives."

"She did get in a car accident before she got here. She might be having some residual pain." He removes his glasses to rub his eyes.

"I've been trying to convince myself it's because she's sick and not because she wants to hurt me." Deborah sniffs. "I'm worried the combination is making her violent. Holden . . ." Deborah closes her eyes as she says the awful words. "She attacked me. With a kitchen knife."

His jaw drops. "Seriously? I've never known her to be violent."

"She had me pinned on the ground, and I don't know, it was like I was staring up at the devil." Deborah shudders. "Her eyes were soulless and black, as if her body had been taken over. I've never been so scared in my life, and well . . ." Deborah bites her lip. "I've had some pretty terrifying moments."

Stunned, Holden looks ready to burst into tears. "What happened?"

"I had to talk to her. In a soothing voice, I tried to calm her down until she released me."

"Did you get hurt?"

"Just scratches." Deborah shows him her arm. "But nothing serious, thank God."

Holden shakes his head in amazement. "This is unbelievable. I'm . . . I'm in shock."

Deborah toys with the used tea bag next to Holden's empty mug. "She has a lot to work through right now."

Holden taps his fingers on the table. "I need to go find her."

"I'm sorry these are the circumstances we had to meet under." Deborah plays with her cross pendant. "But you got to finally meet your mother-in-law."

"Yes." Holden nods.

"And now it's too late."

"Why would it be too late?"

"Because she's never coming back."

"Why do you say that?" Holden frowns. "Is she . . . do you think she's going to hurt herself?"

Deborah's eyes widen, then start to droop.

"You look tired. I better continue my search and let you sleep. Do you mind if I use the restroom before I go?"

"Not at all," she murmurs, pointing in the direction of the bathroom. "It's that way."

Holden disappears, and when he returns, he hurriedly collects his damp jacket. "Thanks for the hospitality, Mrs. Sawyer," he says politely. "And for the tea. I'm going to take a drive and see if I can locate Sib."

"But I told you, she's gone," Deborah says sullenly. "And what about the rain?"

"The rain's not a biggie." Holden shrugs. "I can handle the weather. I just hope something hasn't happened to her. By the way"—Holden slips his jacket back on—"what kind of vehicle is she driving?"

"It's an old Toyota, white."

His jaw tenses. "You mean the white one outside that looks like it's seen better days?"

Deborah grips the table as she rises. She's unclear what he means. Why would her car be outside if she's left?

Confused, she stares at him like he's mad. "It's not here."

Holden flicks on the light switch he probably assumes will be a porch light, but it doesn't turn on. Peering out the kitchen window, he squints at the car in the driveway, barely visible but parked as heavy rain continues to descend on it.

"It's right here, Mrs. Sawyer," he says politely.

She shuffles over beside him. "What is, dear?"

Pointing at the car, he says, "The car. It's right here."

Deborah swallows hard. "Oh dear. I need to go get my glasses."

Laying a hand on her forehead, she watches Holden nod and hurriedly run out into the rain. *Why is everyone acting strange?* she wonders.

As soon as he leaves, she forgets what he even wanted.

Shrugging her shoulders, she fumbles her way to her bedroom.

CHAPTER 46
Sibley

Teeth chattering, I sit on the muddy step of the root cellar, soggy and cold. Listening to the downpour, I strain to hear what sounds like a yell. It doesn't get any louder or closer, and glumly, I decide it must be hissing from the wind.

Prepared to scream again, I've opened my mouth to holler when I hear a crackle that is sharp and brisk. It sounds like a stick being snapped underfoot.

I beat on the door again, my knuckles bruised and sore, along with my shoulder. "Help me!" I screech, my voice hoarse. "Please help me. Get me out of here! I'm stuck."

I yell this repeatedly as if I'm on autopilot, and then, as abruptly, I stop.

My nostrils flare when I catch the whiff of lighter fluid and charcoal interspersed with the woodsy scent of trees.

It wraps me up in memories of sitting around a bonfire and roasting s'mores. I used to love watching the roaring branches explode into smithereens.

Even though it's one of my favorite memories from growing up, it's out of place right here and now.

As I crane my neck to hear, a knot forms in my stomach.

Did Deborah set some brush on fire?

Horrified, I wonder whether her intent is to suffocate me by smoke inhalation.

I stand and pace back and forth.

No. I shake my head.

No, she couldn't be that sadistic.

She's just getting rid of the burn pile, but I swallow uneasily as I remind myself of what tragic events unfolded after the last time I watched her use the burn pile.

A comforting thought replaces my earlier terror. There's no way she could light a match in this weather; it's impossible to start a fire in this wetness.

But still . . . the smell of smoke is overpowering me.

It's not like Deborah couldn't use a dry piece of tinder or wood to ignite it. It won't spread in the wet grass, but she doesn't need it to.

Trembling, I realize she could also use the barn or shed as a starting point, and before long, the outbuildings would be ablaze.

Peering at Esmeralda in the dim light, I wonder miserably if she and her kittens can claw their way out for us.

I search the empty shelves in desperation, hoping to see a hatchet or saw magically appear just in the nick of time.

I start to wheeze, inhaling the stuffy air and what tastes like a pack of cigarettes.

A wave of sadness washes over me. I'm all alone down here, and no one knows it but Deborah and me.

And when they find my body, my husband will think the worst of me. Holden will continue to believe I had an affair with Nico. He'll never get to hear the truth from me when I'm sober. Or regretful.

I squeeze into the farthest corner and pull my knees up, resting my arms on them. I've made a lot of mistakes, and I can't deny who or what I am. I'm an alcoholic. A functioning one—and as of late, a barely functioning one—but I'm ready to say the words.

I whisper them out loud for the very first time.

To be completely honest, when you're an alcoholic, you miss entire chunks, as you're often either barely cognizant or blacked out.

The night Nico and I went out, my birthday evening, has missing bits and pieces.

But there's no ambiguity in what happened.

Yes, Nico touched my hair and my arm and my knee. But that's where it ended. He paid the tab and, like a perfect gentleman, sent me home in a ride share.

Except when I got there, I returned to a dark house and no Holden.

I was suddenly angry again.

I stomped around, slamming cupboards and doors, and the only party I attended was my own pity party.

Upset, I passed out in the guest room upstairs instead of the master, not bothering to undress.

In the morning, I called Tanner for a ride to the bar to retrieve my vehicle. He had an early meeting and was already in the office, so I took another ride share.

I didn't bother asking Holden because I was still fuming he'd forgotten my birthday. The master bedroom door was shut when I left, and I didn't bother to go in.

I decided to get ready in the office and thought nothing of it.

But when Holden woke up and I still hadn't come to bed, he called Tanner to ask if he'd heard from me. Tanner assumed my husband had taken me out for my birthday, which led to the conversation about how he'd forgotten my birthday and what type of celebration I'd had since I supposedly hadn't come home.

Tanner told Holden I'd called him for a ride to the speakeasy to get my car, and just as I was about to head to my office to shower, Holden showed up in the parking lot of the bar, apologetic.

He promised to make it up to me, but tired and cranky, I dismissed him. "Whatever, Holden. I gotta get to work."

"It's barely six."

I shrugged my shoulders, bleary eyed. Being hungover and lacking caffeine did not bring out morning cheeriness.

"So." He rested his hand on the side mirror. "What did you do last night?"

"Not celebrate with my husband."

"Yeah, I got that. That's on me." He held his hands up. "I'm a shitty husband. Sorry, babe. We can try again next year."

"What exactly are we trying for anymore?" I asked miserably. "It's clear I'm not a priority. Why bother with another year of this?"

"What's that supposed to mean?"

"Forget it." I shook my head. "Never mind."

"Why won't you tell me what you did last night?"

"Does it matter?" I groaned. "You were busy doing your own thing."

Holden's stare didn't waver, his fingers tapping on the open window. "Still waiting."

"Tanner and I grabbed drinks."

The lie was effortless, and at the moment, I didn't feel bad. It seemed, I don't know, minimal. Avoidance of a fight, maybe, when I was the wronged one. My husband had forgotten about me on my important day. I didn't want this to become about my choice of plans instead of his failure as my husband.

"Hmm . . . that's not what he said." Disappointment was etched in the worry lines of his forehead.

My face flushed. "Then whatever he said I did, I did."

"Why would you lie to me?" His blue eyes pierced mine with sadness. "Is that where we're at now? The 'lying and blame game' stage?" He leaned closer to sniff my neck. "You smell like cologne."

"I do not."

"You wore that dress yesterday."

I looked down. "So what?"

"What do you mean, so what?" He punched the door. "You didn't come home last night. You smell like another man. You haven't changed out of your clothes." He peered at the gym bag lying on the seat next to me. "I hope it was a fun sleepover," he huffed.

"If you don't believe me, check the cameras," I snipped.

But I was a drunk, and I hadn't gone in the front or garage door, where the cameras were. I forgot I'd left my house keys in my car.

And I didn't have an excuse for why I hadn't gone through the garage entrance, because there was a keypad. Instead, I'd climbed through our unlocked window in the laundry room.

As an attorney, I understand reasonable doubt.

And Holden didn't believe I was truthful.

It didn't help he snooped through my phone and found a text from Nico checking to see if I'd gotten home okay.

After that, I became more than a booze queen. I became a cheater.

CHAPTER 47
Deborah

After Holden leaves, Deborah is exhausted but restless. Her footsteps pace the worn carpet in the bedroom. She misses the carefree times as a child when she would catch water on the tip of her tongue, so she goes outside to stand in the rain. Even though she gets absolutely soaked, it's utterly freeing at the moment.

Shaking off inside like a wet dog, Deborah wipes her feet on the floor mat, not wanting to track mud through the house. She rubs her face with a hand towel in the kitchen, carefully drying around her eyes.

As she locks the front door behind her, chills run down her spine.

The house is deathly quiet except for the steady thump of the rain hitting the siding. It reminds her of patting someone on the back for doing a good job, except it's uninterrupted.

Suddenly Deborah doesn't like the noise. It's annoying and constant.

She flicks on the television, but the chatter doesn't help. She mutes the sound.

Music. That's what she needs—some good old-fashioned music.

An old radio sits on the counter, and ancient and dusty as it is, it never fails to work. Moving the dial through static, she finds a station that fits her mood. As she hums along to an old tune, a jazz medley by Nat King Cole, she hears the unmistakable roar of an engine.

Tilting her head to listen, she turns down the volume.

There's another clap of thunder, and guessing she's wrong, Deborah cranks the music back up, louder this time, her hips jiving to the instruments.

Moving seductively through the kitchen to the living room, she looks out the window as another sliver of lightning splits open the clouds.

Mesmerized, she intently watches the storm. Deborah's glad she's safe and warm, tucked away inside, as her mother used to say during the bad weather. Her eyes seek out the barely visible barn in the distance.

Her daughter hasn't returned. Eyes darting to the clock, she wonders if she should be worried. Even though the television is muted, she catches the red scrolling bar at the bottom of the screen, warning of possible flooding and a severe thunderstorm watch for the entire county.

The light flickers in the antique lamp, and her eyes move to the ceiling bulb, which taunts her by giving a final burst of energy before fading.

Out like a light, she thinks, giggling to herself.

She's going to need candles, she suspects. The flashing screen announces power outages across the neighboring towns.

Combing through the disorganized junk drawer, Deborah is searching for matches when a pounding interrupts her concentration.

She ignores it, thinking it's the rain.

As she sighs, she hears another thud.

Deborah spins around and, terrified of the noise, claps her hands over her ears. Why won't it just stop?

The ding-dong of the doorbell slices through the downstairs. Licking her lips apprehensively, she tiptoes back to the kitchen.

A muffled voice outside commands her to open the door. "Deborah, open up; it's me." She's relieved it's a male voice and not a female one and obeys. Surprised to see Miles Fletcher dripping water, she hesitates before letting him in.

Faking a smile, Deborah makes room for him to come inside, but only because it's pouring out. "What're you doing out and about?"

"I came to check on you two," he says. "You weren't making sense last night. I figured you ladies were having a fight when you said Sibby was trying to hurt you." He shrugs. "She's not picking up her phone, so I wanted to stop by."

"How sweet but unnecessary." Deborah smiles at him like he's a leper. "You shouldn't be concerned. She left. It's going to be okay now."

"Sibley left?"

"Yes."

His eyebrow arches. "Her car's outside."

Deborah shrugs. "Her husband came to get her."

"I shouldn't have called him." Fletcher sighs. "That was wrong of me."

"You called him?"

"I told him she was here." He runs a hand through his thinning hair. "I let my emotions get the best of me. She told me you cosigned on a piece of property in another state. It was total BS."

"Another state?" Deborah rubs a hand over her face. "Oh dear, I know your father talked about moving away. I don't remember finalizing anything."

"See, that's what I mean!" Fletcher looks pained. "This has got to stop, Deborah. My father is engaged to another woman. This isn't healthy."

Deborah's jaw drops, and she stands in uncomfortable silence.

"That's actually what I wanted to talk to you about." He shifts his weight to the other leg. "I know he's not going to man up and confront you, but I will."

"Is that right? He's engaged?" Deborah clutches at her chest. "I wonder why he never mentioned it."

"Deborah," he says gently, "maybe we could chat for a minute?"

"I don't know if that's such a good idea."

"I'd really like a cup of tea."

Miles settles himself in a chair, and seeing as she doesn't have a choice, Deborah busies herself with the teakettle, waiting for him to talk. He's crossing and uncrossing his legs, and Deborah can tell he's riddled with anxiety. She recognizes it because she sometimes does the same thing.

She puts her hands on her hips. "Why didn't your father come with you?"

"Because he doesn't know I'm here."

Deborah says softly, "I didn't know he was dating anyone else. And he asked me to move with him . . . I just don't understand." Her jaw quivers. "Why didn't he break up with me himself? He hasn't returned any of my calls lately, and I could sense something was wrong." The kettle whistles, and Deborah pours the hot water into three mugs, just in case she has another visitor.

Dropping the tea bags in to steep, she realizes Miles is waiting for her to continue.

"How long has he been . . ."

"Engaged?" Miles wrinkles his nose. "A few months. But he's been seriously involved with her for a long time, over a year."

"Why didn't he tell me," she whispers. "I feel so stupid. And like what we had was a sham."

"Did you think you were in a committed relationship?"

"Uh-huh."

"But a relationship means you hang out and talk and see each other, Deborah."

"I realize this." Handing him a mug, she fixes him with a bewildered stare. "But we did those things."

Miles seems puzzled by this admission. "When did you hang out and talk? You mean, when you would call for help with your security system or a break-in?"

"No." Deborah ticks examples off on her fingers, naming a couple of their dates and what they did. Now that she's reflecting on their time together, she realizes it was never in public, minus the one time he stopped at the grocery store to meet her . . . in a different town.

Shakily, Deborah sinks down into a chair, not caring it's Jonathan's old one. "Look, Miles, I know we've had some issues because of the past. With Kristin—"

"Don't bring her up to me," Miles says in warning. "I don't want to talk about Kristin."

"Okay, then, about your mom . . ."

"Can we please"—Miles's hand goes to his collared shirt, as if he's choking—"stop talking about that night and what happened sixteen years ago. Can we please move on? It can't keep defining our small community and our lives."

Deborah slumps in her chair.

"I forgive you, Deborah. Dad admitted the affair, and we've all moved on."

Fidgeting with her pendant, she murmurs, "What affair?"

Miles clenches his hands around the mug. "The one that cost my mother her life."

Deborah stares at him glumly. "You never did talk to your father, did you?"

He rewards her with a death glare. "What're you insinuating?"

"That if you had an honest talk with your father, you wouldn't be accusing me of sleeping with him when he was married to your mother." She sighs. "Maybe it's you that needs to move on from old rumors and lies."

Blood rushes to his face. "I'm tired of your bullshit, Deborah. You were trying to get my dad to leave my mom for you. He wasn't stupid enough to fall for it, so you got jealous."

"Listen to me." She peers at him closely. "I didn't want this to come from my mouth—I hoped your father would fill you in—but here it is. You remember Edward, one of your father's best friends?"

"Of course." He scowls. "I was at the funeral, but I didn't see you there."

"Edward was my first boyfriend, my first love. We started dating when we were in high school. Edward was Sibley's father."

"What're you talking about?" Miles grips his throat again, as if her words are strangling him. "I know Edward had a wife—or ex-wife, because my dad . . . well . . . never mind." He asks, "When was this?"

"Well, Miles, I don't need to break down conception for you. It happened thirty-four years ago. We dated and got pregnant. He left for the military, and I married Jonathan. We both moved on with our lives."

"But he never said anything . . ."

Deborah swallows hard. "I know."

"So my mother died for nothing, all based on pointless rumors . . . when you were really sleeping with Edward?"

"I wasn't sleeping with Edward then." Deborah shakes her head sadly. "I was trying to leave Jonathan. Your father was helping me."

Miles pounds his fist on the table.

Using a soft voice, Deborah tries to diffuse the situation. "Miles, I had no idea your mother was going to follow Robert to our house that evening. He was the mastermind helping me to leave Jonathan." Her hands tremble. "After Cindy told Jonathan at church that Sibley wasn't his, it was a ticking time bomb."

Deborah doesn't want to dive deep into more old history with Miles, because she doesn't care for him, and it's none of his business. His presence is annoying to her. He has no right to sit down and demand her time.

"My mother told Jonathan no such thing!" Miles clenches his fists at his sides. "You're lying, Deborah. It's pathetic. After all this time, you're still trying to pin the blame on my poor, innocent mother. You're going to hell for—"

He's interrupted by a thud and then the pitter-patter of footsteps. Miles and Deborah look at each other in shock.

CHAPTER 48
Deborah

"No, Miles." A soft, gravelly voice speaks from the hallway. "Deborah's right. Well, partially right."

The footsteps arrive in the kitchen, belonging to a woman wearing black combat boots. Her blonde hair is tightly wound into a chignon, and she's wearing glasses with thick black frames.

"Alice!" Miles screeches. "What're you doing here?"

"Oh, Dr. Alacoy, you scared me!" Deborah half rises out of her chair in surprise. "That's quite the entrance. You could've knocked at the front." She murmurs to Miles, "Did we not hear someone knocking?" To Alice, she says, "We were caught up in a deep discussion. Sorry about that."

Holding up a key, Alice smiles. "Not to worry, I let myself in."

The corners of Deborah's face crease in confusion, and Alice shrugs. "I got the key from your purse during our sessions. When you passed out, I was able to make a copy." Nodding at Miles, she giggles. "Hello, future stepson." The woman reintroduces herself to Deborah. "You know me as Dr. Alacoy. But before Edward divorced me, I was formerly known as Mrs. Alicia Pearson, or Alice. Alacoy is my maiden name. But soon"—she beams—"I'll be a Fletcher. Robert and I are engaged. Woo-hoo! And I'd show you the ring if I weren't wearing gloves. Maybe later?"

Deborah's eyes flicker between Alice and Miles in stunned silence.

"And hello, Debbie." She greets her with a wicked grin. "My current patient—and soon-to-be committed patient."

After first patting Deborah's knee, Alice settles against the kitchen counter. "Go on with your chat, you two. That was rude of me to interrupt in the middle of an intense conversation. Please forgive my impatience. I just want to make sure the story is accurate." She rolls her eyes. "I'm so sick of hearing it told wrong. As much as I wish I could correct everyone, it'd be a dead giveaway I was hiding in the loft the night that Jonathan went splat"—she smacks her hands together—"and Cindy bled to death."

"So you're the woman Sibley saw sneak onto the property . . . ," Deborah murmurs. "I thought she got it wrong. Or she lied."

"Shame on you, Deb. You should've believed your own flesh and blood." Alice lets out a maniacal laugh. "Sibley did come to see me this morning, and we had a nice little chat. She's very, very worried about you. Says you've become unstable . . ." Alice throws her gloved hands up. "But don't worry; we talked it through. I didn't tell her the reason you've been experiencing all the brain fog and confusion and mental anguish is a result of your medication. Before I started treating you, I made sure I had the right diagnosis. Some people wait for the patient to come to them before they treat it, which is so reactive, don't you think?"

She brushes a strand of hair off Deborah's cheek. "But with you, I wanted to be proactive. I owe you that. Especially because you are harmful to society, a real crazy person who belongs in a mental institution. Cuckoo. I gave Sibley your records to show her exactly how batshit you are." Alice grins. "But don't worry—they were in her room, and I got them all back. Plus her laptop and phone. A word of advice: she might want to think of a stronger password in the future."

"Leave her out of this." Deborah's lip trembles.

"She looks just like Edward." Alice sneers. "I wanted to smack the freckles off her face." She leans down so she's level with Deborah, her eyes boring into her skull. "Cindy told me back then she thought you were having an affair with Robert, back in early September. It brought all these suppressed memories back, how Edward was obsessed with you. He never wanted me; he *only* wanted you." Jabbing her finger at Deborah's throat, she cries, "I figured if he was so obsessed with you, I should be too.

"I told poor Cindy you were a shrew, a terrible human being, a whore, a home-wrecker, every word I could think of." Alice lets out a loud sigh. "And she ate it up. I mean, you gave her all the proof she needed." Alice stares at Miles. "Both you and your dumb, dead girlfriend—I mean wife. Kristin." She looks at the ceiling. "Rest in peace, Kristin."

"So it *is* true." Miles leans back in his chair, deflated. "Kristin never did see you and my father doing anything at the Halloween party."

"You're smarter than I gave you credit for!" Alice pats his shoulder. "I had been following Deborah and knew it was totally believable. She'd been meeting up with Robert to plan her escape from her deadbeat husband. You know how small towns are—everybody knows everybody. Kristin coached a sports team my little girl was on at the time, and I gave her five hundred bucks to lie. She had a real mean streak, the perfect mean girl to spread that rumor. Another instance of a poor kid needing a dad in her life."

"But why?" Deborah runs a tired hand over her face. "Why would you do that to my family?"

"Because you ruined *mine*," Alice hisses. "After Eddie divorced me, my poor kids went the same route. Their father abandoned them. Fucking Edward just relinquished his parental rights. Gave up his two children so he could be with you and your shithead kid. We went from having a decent life to being practically homeless. We had to move back to the East Coast so we could live with my parents."

Deborah wrings her hands in her lap. "But Edward didn't leave you for me and Sibley."

"Yes, he did. He moved back into town and started attending all of Sibley's events, watching her grow up, instead of his precious kids that weren't part of some short-lived, puppy love relationship, born out of wedlock and passed off as another man's. And the nail in the coffin"— Alice points a crooked finger at Deborah—"he left everything to your daughter. Everything!" she shrieks. "All in a blind trust when Sibley turns thirty-five."

Miles pops out of his chair, shaking his fist. "I've heard enough! How could my father let this happen?"

"Sit down, you pathetic man-child. You're the weakest link of the Fletcher family." Alice pats his shoulder. "Besides your mom. Cindy was so easy to manipulate." Alice fixes Miles with an icy gaze. "You want to know why your mother died? *You* got your mother killed. You've blamed the poor Sawyer family for everything, and it's your fault she's dead."

"How do you figure?" he whispers.

"Because you convinced her Robert was screwing Deborah. You got her all riled up about it. You wanted Cindy to go over there and confront the Sawyers and your dad that evening.

"I called your mother that Sunday afternoon, right after church, in fact. I'd already put the bug in Cindy's ear, but I told her if and when Robert left, she should follow him. I knew it was go time for Deborah—her fate was sealed as soon as Jonathan found out he'd been playing daddy to a kid that wasn't his for almost eighteen years."

Alice rubs her hands in glee. "Powerful stuff, these rumors. But it wasn't a rumor, was it, since it was true. Edward was the father of Sibley, not Jonathan. And lucky for me, I found an old letter you wrote in that old chest in your barn and gave that to Cindy to show Jonathan."

Alice says in a singsong voice, "I have a confession . . ."

Both pairs of eyes are glued to her face.

"I was the one who pushed Jonathan, but it wasn't intentional. I mean, I intended to push someone, but it wasn't him. I didn't mean to hurt him. I was waiting for you, Deborah."

She puckers her lips. "I snuck into the barn when Jonathan was dragging you by your hair. Frankly, I was hoping he would put you out of your misery so I wouldn't have to. I was hoping he would kill you and then just rot in prison. He was worthless too."

Alice puts her hands emphatically on her hips. "But you were like a feral farm cat, the way you struggled to break free of him. I hid in the loft, staring over the broken railing at the two of you on the barn floor, rolling and caterwauling. It was like a feature film. So, so good. Unfortunately"—Alice feigns sadness—"you got away from him, and you ran like hell. He chased you, but he was wasted, bobbing and weaving all over the place. I could tell it was not going to end well . . . for him. And that made me hella mad. I kicked my foot out and accidentally kicked a metal tin. Unfortunately for him, it clunked over the ladder and down below.

"When he saw the rattling tin spinning like a top, he must've thought you'd climbed up into the loft instead of running back to the house. When he got up the ladder, he didn't realize until it was too late it wasn't you, when he attacked me." Alice murmurs, "In his defense, it was dark, and why else would anyone be up there? He had me pinned down and was walloping me with his fist, bless his heart, before he took a good look at me. In self-defense, I had no choice but to reach for a glass bottle I found and break it over his head. When he stumbled forward, I took the opportunity to push his rancid ass out of the loft." She sighs loudly. "But it was supposed to be you, dearest Debbie. I wasted a solid effort on him instead of you."

"Unbelievable." Miles slaps the table hard, causing both women to flinch.

Alice glances at the digital clock, murmuring, "I wonder how long it'll take Sibley to go mad down there in the root cellar with her crippling anxiety. I wasn't the best hostess. I should've put a couple of bottles down there to quench her alcoholic thirst."

Miles cocks his head to the side. "Excuse me?"

Alice holds up her gloved hand, exposing a tiny gold stud. "And I'm so glad you found my missing earring. I must've dropped it when I was messing with that raggedy dress."

Looking at her watch, Alice says, "It's about time for your next dose, Deborah."

Unexpectedly, Deborah yawns, covering her mouth with her hand.

"I want to commend you," Alice says as she pushes up her glasses. "You've been such a good girl taking your meds. Becoming just the person I knew you could be. And your patience with my mind games. You were so sure you had spirits and ghosts when I pushed you down the stairs. It was brilliant, if I do say so myself, how I could just come and go as I pleased, scaring the shit out of your drug-addled mind. In fact, I bet you feel really tired now. Why don't you go lie down on the couch?"

Too tired to protest, Deborah slowly obliges, limping to the sofa. Her mind should be on high alert, but she feels like she's being pulled underwater, and everything is shifting and hazy, as if waves are crashing over her. She's drowning, yet the pain in her body and mind subsides. There's a clarity she hasn't felt in a long while. On the couch, she curls into a fetal position with her mother's old blanket draped over her. She isn't scared any longer, and numb, she wiggles her toes, her limbs tingling, as if they are detaching from her body.

Even though Alice and Miles are in the kitchen talking, they sound far away, and Deborah hears the chatter as if it's coming through speakers and the volume keeps going down another decibel.

Deborah doesn't have the energy to listen anymore, and drowsy, she presses her eyes shut. The last words are muted, and she yanks the blanket tightly around her tiny frame.

"Are you ready to play nice and help me, Miles?" Alice is saying. "Help me drag her body to the barn. I should've finished this last time, but your father wouldn't let me."

CHAPTER 49
Sibley

The stench of smoke is filling my lungs, but the sound of rain has quieted; it's now a light pitter-patter.

I hear a loud yell, and before I jump up, I wait to find out if it's my imagination or the wind.

My name is called, and I rapidly abandon my corner for the steps. As I bang again on my side of the door, a man hollers from above. "Sibley!" the man's voice screams.

I've never been so relieved to hear my name called in my life.

"I got a call!" the male voice yells. "Sibley."

"Help," I scream weakly. "Please help me."

I can't make out what the man says next, his muffled words too soft for me to hear, but he sounds familiar.

I bang my battered fists against the doors.

The voice is closer now. "Sibley." The man's voice is garbled above me. "Can you hear me?"

"Yes. Yes, I can. Help. Please help."

"I don't have a key for the padlock. I'm going to use the bolt cutters. Can you tell me where they are?"

"Uh, I don't know, the toolshed, maybe?" I holler. I was blitzed the other day and can't remember seeing them there, but it seems like an obvious location.

"I already checked there—that's a negative."

My next guess is the barn.

He doesn't say anything.

"Are you still there?" I shriek.

"I'm here, honey. Just stay calm."

"Don't leave me," I cry. "Please. I'm not going to make it."

"I'm going to get you out of there." He tries to soothe me. "I've gotta go to the barn, so it's going to be a couple minutes. I need you to trust I'm gonna come back."

"Deborah's trying to kill me," I yelp. "My own mother's trying to kill me. I don't wanna burn to death."

"This is the chief, Sibley. I'll be right back."

"Help me, okay? I don't wanna die." My fingers claw at the wood. I hear footsteps crunch above me, and the smoke causes my eyes to water. I sit mournfully on the step, my jacket pulled up over my mouth and nose as I force myself to breathe under the fabric. My ears are perked for any sound of life.

It feels like hours but in reality is probably a matter of minutes before I hear his voice again. I've been forcing myself to run through the alphabet, assigning each animal a letter, and then I moved on to listing the state capitals.

His footfalls are solid and heavy, announcing his presence before he shouts out again, to signal he's above me.

I hear the clank of the chain first before the chief tells me to go to the bottom of the cellar. "We're gonna splinter the rest of this damn thing, so get back. Don't wanna get you in the crosshairs."

"Okay!" I holler. "Okay, moving down now." I lower myself down the steps to the muddy bottom.

"I'll count to ten, starting with one. Count with me."

My voice is shaky against his loud baritone, and when we reach ten, I'm interrupted by the ferocious grunt of the chief as the padlock splits off the chain. If I were in a different kind of horror movie, the person standing outside the cellar with an ax would be the murderous killer instead of the petite, demented mother.

Staring up at the chief of police, Robert Fletcher, I'm reminded of Paul Bunyan, except he's in his black police uniform, the tip of the blade resting safely on the ground, the well-grooved handle cradled in his hands.

He rests the ax carefully on the soiled ground, and wiping the sweat from his forehead, he envelops me in a hug. "Scared me for a minute," he whispers. "Let's get you to an EMT. You need to be checked out and treated for smoke inhalation."

"I'm fine," I sob. "I'm okay."

Trembling, I'm aghast to see a massive cloud of smoke rising from the direction of the barn, the structure nothing more than a burnt-out frame, the partially dilapidated building nothing more than firewood feeding the underbelly of the flames.

"The firefighters are on their way," the chief says.

I nod. I know it takes a lot longer to get emergency services out here on the farm. We rely on well water, which also poses a problem.

"Where's Deborah?" I whisper.

"She's in the back of the squad car," the chief says.

"Where she belongs." Squeezing my eyes shut, I weep. "How did you find me?"

"You can thank your husband."

"My husband?"

"Holden, that's his name, right?" He touches my shoulder gently. "Your mother didn't know where you were. Said you ran off."

"She's a liar. I went to feed her cat for her," I moan. "The fucking cat. Where is he? Where's my husband?"

"Holden's inside the house. He alerted the authorities. I happened to be on call, and luckily I wasn't too far from here."

Shakily, I walk by the police cruiser to get to the house, leaning heavily on the chief, and as much as I wish I could stare straight ahead and ignore her, I can't.

I have to take a peek at her.

With her face pressed against the glass, she's screaming something at me. Her fingers claw to get out; her palms leave smudge marks.

I can't understand her, and truthfully, I don't even stop to listen.

Disgusted, I turn away, the chief shielding me from a confrontation separated by glass.

Holden is in the house when I walk in, as if he has always belonged here, but his nervous energy keeps him from standing still, his tall form fidgeting as he leans over the table.

His blue eyes shift from troubled to stunned when he realizes I've walked in the house. Suddenly he becomes deathly silent, as if the air has escaped his lungs and he can't breathe. After crossing the small space between us, he picks me straight off the ground and swings me around, his arms tight around my back, sturdy. Tears flow freely between us, and I nestle my face into his neck, soaking up his cologne instead of the stench of fire embedded in the strands of my hair.

"Sibley! *Oh my God!* Oh my God, Sibley," he keeps murmuring into my ear.

"I'm so sorry I didn't tell you where I was going," I moan. "I never thought my own mother would try to . . ."

"It's okay, baby, it's okay." He presses his cheek to my face, both wet with tears. "I just need you safe with me. That's all that matters."

CHAPTER 50
Deborah

Sibley walks by, nose in the air, chin up, and Deborah's compelled to get her attention.

The glare she shoots her is worrisome, and for a moment they lock eyes, and then . . . nothing. She turns on her heel and goes back to the house and her waiting husband.

Deborah's not quite sure what she did wrong.

When she came to, she was lying outside near the barn, her clothes covered in soot and gasoline. She stared at her blackened fingertips, which looked as if she'd tried to char them on a grill.

Distraught, she realized the smell of smoke and burning rubble was coming from directly inside the barn.

Gasping for air, she crawled on her hands and knees toward the house. She felt like she was in some type of war zone. Not only was the barn on fire, but so was the toolshed.

The detached garage was nothing more than scorched earth. The fire was spreading quickly toward the root cellar.

A wave of dizziness hit her, and Deborah was slow to stand. She'd been on the couch, underneath her quilt, and that was the last thing she remembered.

Suddenly, she was outside, drenched in mud, with no recollection of coming out there.

And what about Sibley?

Her confusion only increased as her dazed eyes searched the yard. There were no other cars in the drive.

Had she imagined Sibley was there?

Or was it Soren?

Deborah shook her head, blinking rapidly.

Soren's dead, she gently reminded herself.

When Deborah stumbled toward the house, she barreled into a tall, gangly man. Pushing his chest away from her, she backed up. "Who are you? What did you do to my property? Where's Sibley?" she screamed. "Where's Soren?"

The man stepped toward her. "There you are, Deborah."

She looked over his shoulder. Robert Fletcher was behind him, sadly bobbing his head.

The strange man, dressed in jeans and a tee, scratched his beard. He glared at the root cellar as if he'd lost something in there.

What was Robert doing standing outside with an ax?

Oh no, had Esmeralda gotten stuck down there?

She fumbled in her pockets and clutched the small key to the padlock. As Deborah walked toward Robert, she held it in the air, but for whatever reason, he didn't acknowledge her.

Each step ignited a stab in her chest and was increasingly painful. Her hand flew to her bosom, and the key dropped to the ground, already forgotten.

Before she could steady herself, Miles Fletcher appeared, grinning like it was the best day of his life, and placed handcuffs on her. "I finally get the pleasure of snapping these on, Mrs. Sawyer."

CHAPTER 51
Deborah

"I didn't do anything wrong," Deborah protests weakly to the detective. "This is all a huge misunderstanding. I would never harm my daughter."

"How many daughters do you have?"

"Two." Deborah shakes her head. "I mean, one. I lost one."

"How did you lose one?"

Deborah doesn't like his flippant tone. "Childbirth. Identical twins."

"And your name? Ah, yes, I recognize it. Sawyer." His clipped mustache catches spittle when he talks. "Your husband died under suspicious circumstances years ago, didn't he?"

"He was drunk and fell from the loft above. Out in the barn."

"Where were you?"

"In the house."

"That's not what the record shows, ma'am."

"It was a long time ago," Deborah says bitterly. "I want to sleep. I have a pounding headache. I'm exhausted."

His eyes peer at her with disgust.

"In fact, can I get some water?"

"Just admit you did it, and I'll get you an entire watercooler you can drink."

Deborah runs a tired hand through her hair. "Admit to what?"

"That you were after insurance money, for starters."

"I did not set the barn on fire."

"Thanks for providing details on where the fire started."

"I'm not sharing anything. I want to go home. Where's Robert Fletcher?" she mumbles. "He's my boyfriend. He can tell you what happened."

The detective's whole body shakes in laughter. "Oh, really? He's engaged to another woman."

"It's true," Deborah insists. "We're moving to Florida when he retires."

He thumps his hand on his thigh. "That's funny. You're a real firecracker, Debbie, no pun intended."

"What're you talking about?" Deborah lowers her head into her hands. "Can I go home, please? I need to sleep."

"You just tried to murder your daughter, and you want to go home and get some sleep?" He mimics her voice. "Pull someone else's leg, lady. Mine are long enough."

"I killed my daughter?"

"You tried."

"Uh-huh," she groggily moans into her hands.

"So you admit you did attempt to murder your daughter?"

"Uh-huh." Lethargic, Deborah can no longer keep her eyes open. They slam shut, just as her case does in the detective's eyes, and she's once more taken away in cuffs.

CHAPTER 52
Sibley

A few days later, Robert Fletcher, chief of police, sits across from Holden and me at the scarred kitchen table. Deborah claims she has no recollection of what happened, and I believe her, but I know she's sick. Very, very sick. My eyes are red from crying, and a tissue is stuffed into my fist.

"I wanted to update you on the gun you brought in, Sib." The chief speaks softly, without his usual aplomb. "I put a rush into forensics on the gun, not expecting any miracles, since they are one of the most difficult objects to retrieve prints from. Frankly, they're a pain in the ass because of the texture and ridges, and oils from cleaning tend to break down prints." The chief keeps his eyeballs glued to mine, and my palm instantly sweats into the tissue. "Sib, the only prints on the gun are from Deborah."

Nothing in the room moves, not even the air, and no one takes a breath.

Sitting in stunned silence, I finally whisper, "You think Deborah lied about being attacked?"

"No. She was definitely ambushed that night. I saw it for myself," the chief explains. "She lied about the night your father, or should I say Jonathan, died."

"I don't understand." My lips quiver.

"The serial number on this gun isn't recent. We were able to trace it back to Jonathan. He owned it. But there's only one bullet casing missing."

"Okay . . ." I'm not following the chief's declaration. "Jonathan died of injuries he suffered when he fell out of the loft and broke his neck."

"Correct. The coroner listed Jonathan's death as an accidental fall. He was clearly intoxicated, and he died of a cervical fracture. In fact, three out of the seven vertebrae were severed. If he had survived the fall, he'd be paralyzed or a vegetable. His fall couldn't have happened without severe force."

"Yes." I close my eyes at the gritty details.

"But there's more." The chief sighs. "When I went back through the case file, a shell casing was found in the wall of the barn, lodged in one of the pieces of wood. The one bullet discharged from the gun. And reading the report, it doesn't look good . . ."

"What're you saying?" I gawk at him.

"I was only an officer then, and though I was the first to arrive on the scene, I left to fill the other officers and emergency responders in on what happened. There was no bullet hole in Jonathan when I arrived. He was on his back in pain, your mother beside him."

"How is that possible?"

"Because he was shot after we arrived. It looks like the bullet hole entered near his left kidney. This might not sound deadly, but when the intestines spilled into his abdominal area, it caused a deadly infection. By the time he got to the hospital, he was pronounced dead."

"Wouldn't the gun be loud enough to hear, even if you weren't in the barn?"

"Yes. But there's a lot of land, and the driveway is long. I had to go meet the incoming ambulance near the highway to direct them. That left ample time to discharge one bullet."

"Could he have put himself out of his own misery?" Holden asks.

"His prints should be on his gun if that were the case."

"How could this have gotten missed?" Holden is irate. "How did the doctors and police not catch this?"

"I don't know. I was taken off the case immediately," he murmurs. "As Sib knows, my wife, Cindy, was found dead the next morning from injuries she sustained after crashing into a tree. I was beside myself with grief and was off the force for a few months. I had to keep my sons from going off the deep end at the loss of their mother." He sighs heavily. "Not to mention, Edward, Sibley's real father, had died a few weeks before this. It was a rough time. And the awful rumors swirling about your mom and me."

"I know." I put my head in my hands. "I know."

"I'm gonna be really blunt, Sibley." He grimaces. "Because I owe it to you. Your father was a difficult man. Not well liked. A lot of people heard the rumblings about him beating your mother. Because of his fall, he wouldn't have had any quality of life except eating through a feeding tube in a nursing home. In their minds, it was an open-and-shut case."

"So what now?" I ask.

"I'm going to try and protect her . . ." He steeples his fingers as if unsure of what to say. "Dammit, we could almost see the light at the end of the tunnel."

"But she killed him in self-defense," I say pointedly.

"I know, but I can't entirely sweep this under the rug."

"You're going to charge my mother with murder when you know what she went through at the hands of Jonathan?" Incredulous, I practically jump out of my chair. "There's gotta be another way."

"Sibley, you're an attorney. You understand the lay of the land. I can't just unsee this. When I retire soon and this case is brought to light, which it will be, since I'm the one who went to the lab for prints, my entire career will be naught."

I stare at him openmouthed. "She's sick, Chief," I whisper. "You can't do this to her."

He strokes the mole on his chin. "I don't want to dredge up the past, believe me. I'm going to recommend she enter a psychiatric ward for evaluation."

"Just talk to her doctor," I say limply. "They can confirm she's not in her right mind."

"I know," he says mournfully. "Believe me, I know."

CHAPTER 53
Sibley

After the chief leaves, Holden and I sit while he gently holds my hand in his. We both look up at the thud of footsteps on the porch. He motions for me to stay seated, and after rising, he answers the door.

It's the plainclothes detective who I remember was talking to the chief the other day. He has a salt-and-pepper mustache and a shiny bald head, and he gave the chief a run for his money, height wise.

"This can't wait," he says apologetically.

"Understandable." Holden welcomes him in.

"You might notice Chief Fletcher is being arrested outside," he says in far too casual a manner. Holden and I go to the kitchen window and gape as Robert Fletcher is handcuffed and led to the back of a waiting squad car by another police officer. The squad car door closes after his hunched figure.

"What happened?" I ask tensely. "What's going on?"

"Mind if I take a load off?" The man's stubby fingers point to the less cluttered living room. "By the way, I'm Brian Paulson, criminal investigator for the state."

Holden leads me by the arm to the couch while Brian sits across from us in Deborah's recliner. I face him with my puffy, tearstained eyes, waiting impatiently for him to speak. When he doesn't, I break the tense silence.

"Where's Miles?" I ask. "Is he in trouble too?"

He leans so far forward I'm afraid he's going to fall out of the chair. "Can you tell me what you know about Alice Alacoy?"

I retort, "Can you tell me why Robert Fletcher, the chief of police, is being arrested?"

"I promise we'll get there." Brian scratches his bald head. "In a minute. Just bear with me." Brian leans back and stretches his long legs out, which are a contrast to his stubby fingers. "Let's talk. Alice. What do you know about her?"

"Not much." I shrug. "I've only met her once. She was . . . is . . . my mother's psychiatrist. I consulted with her about my mother's health and concerns I had. It seemed she shared them too. There's some obvious medical issues going on with Deborah." I choke back a sob. "And Alice—Dr. Alacoy—provided some good information."

"Like what?" Brian asks. "What type of information?"

"Do we need to discuss my mother's medical history?" I lean back, exasperated. "I don't know you, Mr.—I mean, Detective Paulson."

"Call me Brian." He snaps his fingers at me. "I hear what you're saying. I get it. But all of this is accessible to me anyway, since this is an investigation."

"It's okay, Sib," Holden murmurs in my ear. "You share what you feel comfortable with. The rest he can subpoena."

I take a deep breath. "Dr. Alacoy was watching my mother for signs of degenerative diseases. One in specific—she called it an imposter syndrome."

Brian chomps his gum, blinking rapidly.

"The way she explained it made it seem legitimate. Is it not?" I ask, crestfallen. "My laptop went missing, and I haven't had a chance to research it yet."

"Well, she's not a doctor, so regardless, her opinion is bullshit."

"What do you mean?"

"Alice, the woman you know as Dr. Alacoy, isn't licensed."

"In the field of psychiatry?"

"In any medical field. Period." He points a finger. "She's a scam artist."

I shift in my seat, suddenly feeling feverish.

"The woman you met, Dr. Alice Alacoy, was posing as a psychiatrist."

"Wait, what?" Holden removes his glasses. "How is that even possible?"

"Are you serious? She seemed so knowledgeable . . . how could I not have known?" I bury my head in my hands. "I feel like such an idiot."

"Because she did a terrific job faking her credentials. Alice had business cards printed with the title of doctor, a legitimate website, not to mention the diplomas in her office and her website." He wipes a crumb from his mustache. "Hell, she even purchased a medical liability insurance policy."

He gives me a sad smile. "She will be charged with insurance fraud, filing false health-care claims, larceny by false pretenses, and practicing psychiatry without being licensed to in the state."

"So she made the imposter syndrome up?" I run a hand through my hair. "And I believed her wholeheartedly."

"No, babe." Holden holds up his phone. "This isn't made up. It's a real diagnosis." I scan the article he shows me on his screen, and sure enough, it's a real thing. And like Alice discussed with me, it mirrors my mother's odd behavior.

"I'm lost, Detective Paulson," I say. "If this could truly be what my mother is suffering from, and Alice isn't a real doctor, what does that say about the health-care system?"

"I'm not sure I follow . . ."

"What if she's right? Was Alice just practicing medicine with some type of education background and no credentials, or how could she potentially be accurate with her diagnosis?"

"Wikipedia," Brian says dryly. "And Google. It's not that hard. Everyone self-diagnoses."

"But these are rare diseases. Lewy body and Capgras." I rest my hands on my knees.

"How did Alice manage to prescribe meds without being a licensed doctor?" Holden asks.

"Alice had another doctor, a real one, prescribing your mother copious amounts of medications, including strong doses of heavy tranquilizers. It's amazing your mother is even alive."

"And I guess, why? Why would Alice want to hurt my mother? Or me. We don't even know her."

"Oh, but you do." He drums his fingers on his knee. "Alicia Alacoy is her birth name, but she goes by Alice. Does the name Edward Pearson ring a bell?"

I nod my head slowly. "I just found out he's my biological father."

"Alice is the ex-wife of the deceased Mr. Pearson. They were married for about a decade, according to court records."

"I know Edward held a special place for my mother . . ." I rip a piece of skin off my nail, wincing. "I don't understand how that factors into Alice hurting my mother."

"Alice was convinced Edward had an ongoing affair with your mother, starting from the time they were married. Then she found out about you being his biological child, and well, it's a tale as old as time: she felt the need for revenge.

"When he divorced her, they fought about the usual grievances—money and children. Then she moved to the East Coast to finish raising their young kids. Edward wanted nothing to do with her and, as we say in this day and age, pretty much ghosted her. He didn't communicate with either her or the children. She was understandably livid.

"It went from bad to worse when he didn't support his children, and after he died, Alice was sure she would stand to inherit his life insurance policies, or at least their children would. One didn't pay out because of suspected suicide, and the other went to someone you know."

"I know?"

"Yes. You. Alice found a letter to you shortly after he died, and he had bequeathed everything to you at the age of thirty-five."

Holden mutters, "What in the hell."

"Seriously?" I gasp, staring down at my lap in wide-eyed shock. "My father left me everything?"

The detective nods. "Alice reconnected with Robert Fletcher online about two years ago on social media, since she knew the Fletchers from before. Robert and Edward were best friends growing up. Alice and Robert had an ongoing relationship over the last year and a half. He convinced her to move back to the state and set up a fake practice.

"It quickly went from insurance fraud to a psychological manipulation of your mother. Since Alice knew what happened the night Jonathan died, it didn't take her long to convince Robert to take advantage of Deborah. He's been having severe financial problems for a few years due to his gambling addiction. He has massive gambling debts to pay off. Also, Alice was billing insurance companies, so she was skimming that way." Detective Paulson shakes his head. "They had a lot of irons in the fire."

"Was the intent to kill my mother?" I whisper.

"No. It was a lot more sinister. Robert was trying to scare Deborah off. He had a deal to get a sizable cut from the county if Deborah agreed to sell her farm. And with over fifty acres, he was going to make a pretty penny."

"But why would Robert want to harm my mother?" I shake my head. "She never did anything to him. He was the one helping her leave Jonathan. Why would he want to hurt her now?"

"From everything we've gathered, Robert didn't forgive your mother for the loss of his wife, Cindy. He lost Cindy and Edward around the same time." The detective shrugs. "He never got over losing his wife because he tried to save Deborah, as painful as that sounds.

"The other big reason is as simple and complicated as money." The detective scowls. "Alice blackmailed him and told him if he didn't help with her plan, she'd come forward with information about that night, incriminating him. Plus, she knew he had stolen from the police officers' union and was aware of kickbacks he was getting from the prison."

"So it wasn't Fletch that stole from the union," I groan. "Robert made his son pay the price?"

"Yes." The detective adds, "Robert was about to lose their farm, and as the police chief, he could protect Fletch in some ways. He promised him the chief position after he retired for taking the heat."

"Even with a damaged reputation, Miles thought he could overcome that?"

"With all the politics involved, yes. The chief had enough people in place and connections that the speculation would die down." Detective Paulson adds, "It became old news about the coffers being empty."

"Was the chief behind the push for eminent domain to take over the farm?"

"One hundred percent. He was set to get a 'fee' for the transaction if Deborah agreed to their terms. We found out Robert even forged both Deborah's name and Miles's on a real estate purchase in Florida."

"And the gun I turned in never went to the lab?"

"No. It was shoved in a locked drawer at the chief's home. His prints are on it." Detective Paulson coughs. "We also found the rifle used in your mother's attack. We believe it was Alice, not Robert, who was the perpetrator that night."

I'm curious to know the detective's thoughts on Jonathan. "Do you believe his death was accidental?"

"At this time, yes. By all accounts, Robert had no reason to kill Jonathan. Was he a wife beater who would have been arrested at some point for domestic violence? Most likely, but this is a tragedy, a rare, sad, one-in-a-million tragedy." The detective narrows his eyes. "After Alice pushed Jonathan, it injured him enough he wouldn't have lived through the hospital ride."

"Speaking of the hospital"—I grip Holden's hand in mine—"how did you figure out what happened to my mother?"

"Deborah could barely sit up in the interrogation room. Thank God a nurse noticed puncture marks in her vein." Brian continues, "She'd been heavily sedated and drugged. And you can thank Miles Fletcher for coming forward—he had a bout of guilt that reared its ugly head and said his dad and Alice forced him to help drag her to the barn and start the fire."

"But he didn't try to save me . . ."

I shake my head. At this point, I don't even know the real from the fake.

"Was Fletch," I begin, and Brian narrows his eyes, not recognizing the nickname, "I mean Miles—was he complicit in this?"

"We don't have proof of his involvement with your mother. He did know about his father's debts and the missing funds, but obviously, we'll keep investigating. Apparently, he had shown up at Deborah's house unexpectedly, not planning on Alice showing up."

"So it's true Robert Fletcher never dated my mother?"

"Only to gather information." Brian tilts his head, side to side. "He wanted everyone to think Deborah was losing her mind, so he made sure they were never seen together. Except we got a report they were caught on camera at a grocery store, some twenty-plus miles away. Unfortunately, the camera outside of the house is a dummy one, so we can't check the visitors who have come and gone. The chief was able to pretend it alerted the station because Deborah would always call him when there was a problem. It was there only to further convince Deborah she was losing her grip on reality."

"Are there any ties between Alice and Robert and a man Deborah saw sitting in the house?"

"Look, Sibley, I'll be blunt, and the doctor at the hospital can provide further insight. The types and dosage of pills she was taking—it's . . . a lot. Visual and auditory hallucinations are not abnormal side effects. There's no telling if it was real or imagined." Detective Paulson grimaces. "It's complicated by the fact Alice played a psychological cat-and-mouse game with your mother intentionally. Your mother is a high-functioning woman, and it's impossible to know if the side effects she experienced were part of the medication or psychosis or if they were because someone was actually there. Case in point, Alice pushing her down the stairs. I have no doubt Alice was the 'figment of her imagination' she saw."

"This is all so—there's no other word for it—fucked up." I bite my lip, drawing blood. "I can't believe someone could be so cruel." My lip quivers. "And that I almost fell for it. I thought my own mother would want to harm me."

Holden squeezes my shoulder. "She's in good hands now, Sib, and so are you."

"So when can we see her?"

"I'll let you know as soon as she's well enough for visitors. She's gonna need some recovery time as we try to counter the effects of the drugs." He stands up and shakes our hands. "Just give it some time. You have my word I'm keeping an eye on her."

CHAPTER 54
Sibley

My mother is more present than she's been since I first came home. Her voice is strong and doesn't waver, even with the horrifying details of Jonathan's death. We sit down in the living room, and we have a heart-to-heart that is more of a mother-daughter moment than we've ever had, and even with the morbid details, it's a relief to hear them from her.

"That night, I ran back into the barn because I heard this terrible thud, this horrible, strangled scream, and I knew; I just knew." Her eyes betray a hint of sadness. "Jonathan was on his back, looking up at the ceiling. For once, his eyes had fear in them, like he knew he had broken his body for good. Blood was everywhere, and I knelt beside him and tried to feel his pulse. He wrapped his hand around my wrist, and he whispered he needed to know if you were his." She gives me a watery smile. "I lied and said yes.

"Talk about timing," my mother says sadly. "That's when Robert Fletcher, at the time a police sergeant, ran in. He saw all the blood, and he saw Jonathan had beat up my face, so he assumed the worst—that Jonathan was still in the middle of attacking me, since his hand was wrapped around my wrist. He didn't have time for hesitation. He pulled out his gun and fired at close range."

My mother shrugs. "If you ask me, Jonathan was put out of his misery. He would've been paralyzed if he even survived the ambulance ride to the hospital."

My eyes widen. "What did you and Robert do?"

"We were both in shock. We agreed we would never speak of this again. We both knew what Jonathan was capable of. It was kind of good riddance, as harsh as that sounds. We assumed we had been the only two people in the barn that had seen what happened. Neither of us thought to check the loft. By the time an officer went up there, Alice had snuck off."

My mother rests a hand on my arm. "Then I started getting letters that had details about that night. I thought they were from Soren. Soren was your identical twin."

I'm ill prepared to hear this, but I've already been made aware.

Tears leak down my cheeks, and we both lean into each other. We've lost a lot over the years, our family broken seemingly from its conception. And mine.

We sit with our hands intertwined as she tells me about my twin sister, Soren.

CHAPTER 55
Deborah

Deborah clutches Sibley's hand in hers. Sibley asks, "Did Edward really commit suicide?"

"They're going to exhume his body." Deborah bites her lip. "When he died, I was beside myself. I blamed myself for his death. That I wasn't strong enough to leave Jonathan. That I even married him in the first place. But I had to stop blaming myself because I would've put you in danger and he wouldn't have wanted that either. Even if Jonathan and I had gotten a divorce, he would've used you as a pawn. And when he found out the paternity, well, I shudder to think of the outcome." She hands Sibley a tissue. "Did you know Edward left you his estate, Sibley?"

"I heard something about it. I would've rather known him as my father."

"I didn't know this, but the reason Edward moved back to town was so he could attend your school events. I'm comforted knowing he had at least some idea who you had become." Deborah squeezes her hand. "I know he would be even prouder today."

"And what about the farm?" Sibley sets her coffee mug down on the table. "What did you find out?"

"You were right, honey. There are laws in this state that protect farms that have been in the same family for generations, so that's being taken into consideration, and additional compensation is part of this."

"So what're your next steps?"

"I'm still figuring that out." Deborah winks. "I've got a whole house to move and a daughter that sorely needs"—Deborah doesn't like the word *rehab*—"help. Tell you what, honey: I'll make you a deal."

Sibley clenches her jaw and waits for her to lay out the terms.

"I want you to focus on recovery." Deborah hadn't planned to say this, but it sounds appropriate coming out of her mouth. "I'll come out to visit and stay with you, as long as it doesn't impose on you and Holden. That way, I can help around the house and make sure you are taking care of yourself."

"Promise?" Sibley's mouth relaxes into a grin. "Because if you like the desert, Holden and I talked about building an addition onto the house or, you know, a mother-in-law suite, they call it, or a casita."

"I think you both have a lot on your plate right now without worrying about me." Deborah nudges her. "But I did hear about heritage laws from a sassy attorney, and I'm ready for a change."

"I'm so glad you're alive, Mother." Sibley embraces her tightly.

EPILOGUE
Sibley

Holden receives a call as we're standing in line, about to board the plane. When he holds his phone out to me, I give him a questioning stare.

"It's for you." He shrugs.

"Hello?" I say softly.

"Hi, Sib. It's Chuck." I'm surprised to hear from my old PI friend. "I heard you have a decent reason for not being out west. Some kind of family drama out on a farm?"

"That word doesn't even begin to describe it," I groan. "I thought running from my problems would keep them at bay; instead, I've managed to find myself deep in a whole new pile of shit."

"Well, let me be the first to welcome you back to the desert," he drawls. "If you stop hitting retaining walls and fire hydrants."

"I appreciate the warm welcome," I giggle. The gate agent comes over the loudspeaker with an announcement, drowning out Chuck's next words. I hear something that sounds like "preoccupied" and "exploits."

"Chuck," I murmur into the phone. "As much as I want to talk, I'd like to be able to do it in person and not miss our flight. It's time to board."

"Why didn't you say so?" He snickers. "Then let me be the first to tell you that Tanner Ellis has resigned from the firm."

"What!" I jump up in the air, barely hanging on to Holden's phone. He mouths at me to hurry up and not break his cell.

"Yes. I nailed him for the slick bastard he is." He chuckles. "The partners weren't too happy, to put it lightly. Criminal conduct, conflicts of interest, misconduct involving dishonesty, not to mention the numerous other ethical issues he violated. I don't see how he won't be disbarred."

"And Nico's wife, Christine?" I whisper. "Did you catch her and Tanner hooking up?"

"Yes, and you'll be happy to know the bar complaint against you is being dismissed, so don't you worry about it."

"How did you know about that?"

"I'm offended at your question. You know I keep my ear to the ground. One more thing." He lowers his voice. "Tanner had pictures of you all over his phone, some racy pics, I might add, and a snapshot of a dating profile for you. You got something to tell me, or should I assume this was all him?"

I tighten my grip on the duffel bag over my shoulder. "I won't ask how you got his phone and laptop. We used to be friends, and he no doubt had access to my phone and laptop to get those photos." The exhale I give is loud enough for Holden to peer at me, worry in his blue eyes. "I guess I need to vet my friends more carefully in the future."

"Well, Adrienne and Leslie both check out. I give them glowing recommendations."

"Good to know." I smile into the phone. "And thank you. Seriously. You saved my life. Professionally speaking."

"And now you're going to get your ass to rehab, for real this time, so you can save your personal life and marriage. I kind of like that husband of yours."

"Agreed. And how can you already like Holden more than me?" I grumble sarcastically. "You only met him one time."

"No. We've stayed in touch," Chuck says. "How do you think I know you're coming back home?"

"Because you're a private investigator . . ."

"Good girl." He chortles. "Safe travels, young lady."

The final boarding call blares over the speakers, and after I hand the phone back to Holden, he shoves it in his pocket and curls his fingers around mine.

We are the last two on the plane, and as we settle into our seats, we exchange a knowing look that only two people who have weathered a storm—no, a tornado—can share.

Neither of us knows where we'll go from here, but we're still in this fight together. If there's anything I've learned, it's that I've still got that scrappy midwestern girl tucked away inside me, and I couldn't be happier.

ABOUT THE AUTHOR

Photo © 2018 Diana May

Marin Montgomery grew up in the Midwest but traded cornfields for the desert, and she now calls Arizona home. Originally slated to go to fashion school on the West Coast, Montgomery has always been passionate about writing short stories and poems. After finishing her MBA, she decided to write her first novel at the encouragement of her childhood best friend. When she's not thinking up her next psychological twist, she can be found playing a mean game of Scrabble, binge-watching a variety of television shows, and hanging with her goldendoodle, Dashiell.